Tonight was a dream come true. Tonight was the culmination of two years of watching and wondering. Tonight she wasn't just one of the upstairs maids; she was Lorna Gordon and she was kissing the Duke of Kinross.

Her blood was heating, fire racing along her skin. The wind was blowing the rain on them and she didn't care. The wool of his jacket was beginning to chafe, but she pressed herself closer to him.

Whatever happened, whatever ramifications came from this night, she wouldn't regret it. How could she? However long she lived, she would recall these moments when the Duke of Kinross kissed her. When he pressed his lips against her neck and nibbled on her earlobe. He pulled the mask free from her face, but she didn't care. Let him recognize her now, but it would be too late. She'd already had her kiss. She'd already spoken to him, and he'd talked to her as if she was a woman who intrigued him.

KAREN RANNEY

The Scottish Duke

AVONBOOKS

An Imprint of HarperCollinsPublishers

THE SCOTTISH DUKE. Copyright © 2016 by Karen Ranney LLC. All rights reserved. Printed in the United States of America. No part of this book may be used or reproduced in any manner whatsoever without written permission except in the case of brief quotations embodied in critical articles and reviews. For information, address HarperCollins Publishers, 195 Broadway, New York, NY 10007.

First Avon Books mass market printing: December 2016

ISBN 978-0-06246687-7

Avon Trademark Reg. U.S. Pat. Off. and in Other Countries, Marca Registrada, Hecho en U.S.A.
Avon, Avon Books, and the Avon logo are trademarks of Harper Collins Publishers.
HarperCollins® is a registered trademark of HarperCollins Publishers.

16 17 18 19 20   QGM   10 9 8 7 6 5 4 3 2 1

To the wonderful staff at O'Connor Road Animal Hospital for keeping Flash the Wonder Pooch healthy.

Chapter 1

Blackhall Castle
Scottish Highlands
June, 1861

*I*t would be a waste of my time to tell you this is foolish, wouldn't it? You wouldn't pay any attention."

Nan stepped back and surveyed Lorna, shaking her head all the while.

The room they shared was small and with only a tiny mirror over the common bureau. Nan would have to be her eyes.

Each maid was assigned an oil lamp and a certain amount of oil. If it was used before the end of the month, she had to dress in the dark, a way of ensuring that she rationed the light better the following month,

Lorna hadn't used any of her oil for a week, saving it all for this one night.

"Maybe it is foolish," she said, glancing down at the wide panniers of the gown she wore. "But it is such a magical evening, and when would I have another chance to experience a ball at Blackhall?"

"You're a maid, Lorna," Nan said, sighing heavily. "Not a guest."

"Tonight, though, Nan, no one will know."

Nan made a sign in the air and she obediently turned so that the back of the dress could be inspected.

Things happened for a reason, didn't they? The housekeeper had sent her to find a certain table in the attic and she'd gone, reluctant to climb into the darkened space. She couldn't disobey Mrs. McDermott. The dear lady had taken her on when she hadn't a whit of training or background in service.

To her surprise, the attic wasn't gloomy or dark at all. Porthole windows along the outer wall let in the June sunlight. For an hour she'd pulled up one sheet after another, only discovering the table at the far end of the attic. Between the stairs and the door, however, there'd been dozens and dozens of trunks, each begging to be opened and inspected.

In the third trunk she'd found the carefully wrapped wig and the golden dress with the panniers. A fortuitous find, especially since they'd been preparing for the fancy dress ball at Blackhall for over a month.

She was not one to overlook circumstances, especially when they were calling out to her. Her father had often said that fortune favors the bold—*fortuna audaces iuvat.*

"We could have found a dress for you, too," she said now as she tugged on the wig.

She'd taken the precaution of grabbing some flour from the kitchen. None of her training had given her any insight into fashions from a hundred years ago, but the wig had given off a cloud of finely milled powder and the only thing she could think of to substitute was flour. Nan dipped a powder puff into the bowl and patted it on her temples and the tall crown of hair adorned with gold bows.

"I'm not as brave as you."

"Or as foolish," Lorna said.

"That, too." Nan stepped back and surveyed her handiwork. "Mrs. McDermott will have no choice but to dismiss you if you're found out."

"Then I'll make sure I'm not discovered." She turned and smiled at Nan. "It's a fancy dress ball, Nan. Everyone will be wearing masks. No one will know who I am."

"Oh, Lorna."

"What?" she asked.

Nan shook her head again. "You see what you want to see, Lorna. You have ever since I've known you. You're lucky Mrs. McDermott didn't assign you to serve the guests. What would you have done then? Come up with some sort of sickness?"

"I would have found some way," she said, smiling down at Nan.

She'd been deliberately clumsy this past week, especially in the housekeeper's sight for that very reason. She'd dropped an armload of books she was dusting, fumbled with the jar of spent tea leaves used to clean the carpets, and repeatedly stumbled holding her brushes and pail.

After all that, Mrs. McDermott would have been foolish to select her as one of the servers. Better to dismiss her early, send her to her room, and instruct her to appear at dawn to help clean the ballroom. To her relief the housekeeper had done exactly that.

"Well, how do I look?" Lorna asked, carefully affixing the mask strings behind her ears. That, too, had been another miraculous find, a sign that she *had* to attend the ball.

It was as if Providence, well aware of her barely

contained curiosity and fascination, had provided her with a way to see the Duke of Kinross up close. Granted, it would only be for a few hours on a June night in the Scottish Highlands, but who was she to deny Providence?

"You look beautiful," Nan said, nodding. "The gold makes your brown eyes sparkle. And the white wig accentuates your complexion."

"Could I pass for one of the guests?"

Nan sighed again. "Yes, but I'm not sure that's a good thing."

"My father was Robert Gordon. I'm the equal to most of them there."

"But it isn't because of most of them that you're going, is it? It's to see the duke. We both know how foolish that is."

Lorna reached over and hugged Nan, depositing a fair share of flour onto the other girl's shoulders. Apologizing, she pulled back.

"Don't worry, Nan. I'll go and pretend to be someone else for a few hours. Then I'll return and be a well-disciplined upper maid, I promise."

Nan didn't appear convinced. Nor was Lorna, if she were to tell the truth. It was going to be so difficult to be herself after tonight.

THE LAST THING Alexander Russell, the ninth Duke of Kinross, wanted to do was mingle with his guests. He could put the time to better use. Nor did he have friends among the throng. Acquaintances, perhaps, but few could be called more than that, especially after this afternoon when he'd been subjected to a humiliating rout.

Nevertheless, Alex forced himself to enter the ballroom, pasting a smile on his face that hid his true feelings.

The ballroom had been polished like a seldom worn crown. The three rows of four brass and crystal chandeliers illuminated every inch of the massive room, reflecting light off the windows and making the floor shine.

The jewels in the crown were the women, most of whom had taken to the idea of a fancy dress ball with enthusiasm, choosing costumes ranging from stunning to amusing, with a few ridiculous examples in between. A half-dozen hapless husbands were dressed to complement their wives' choices, but most men were attired in black evening dress.

At least twenty-five of them had witnessed his drubbing this afternoon.

Tonight's entertainment was the last time he'd have to stand here and smile fatuously. He couldn't wait for them all to be driven back to the train station tomorrow morning, en route to their various homes. The Scottish Society for Scientific Achievement could go to hell, and with it their annual medal.

Someone in this room was a traitor. Not to country, even though they might well stoop to that. Someone here, being feted and entertained, had betrayed him. That was the only reason Simons had won the damn medal. Alex's research was nearly word for word with the other man's. His own subjects were more numerous, however, numbering in the thousands to Simons's hundreds. Even Simons's conclusions, enumerated on the last page of his paper, sounded too close to his own words. But his findings had been sub-

mitted to the society a good three months before the
other man's. Three months, yet Simons had been the
one critically acclaimed.

Someone must have leaked the results of his research. Either a member of the society attending this
ball—the last event of a torturous week of hosting at
Blackhall Castle—or someone to whom he'd confided
about his work.

"You must learn to trust people, Alex," his mother
had once said to him.

He couldn't remember why she'd offered up the sen-
timent, but he could remember the occasion. They'd
been standing in Blackhall's chapel and watching as
the bronze plaque had been affixed to his wife's last
resting place.

He could also recall his response. He'd turned to
her and said, "Why?"

She hadn't an answer, which was a pity. Perhaps her
words could have softened his emotion. Ruth, the late
Duchess of Kinross, hadn't been faithful, a fact tear-
fully admitted by her sister Mary.

*You mustn't hate her, Alex. Ruth always wanted admira-
tion. When you were too busy to give it to her, she sought it
elsewhere.*

His wife would have enjoyed this ball. She would
have purchased something ruinously expensive to
wear, and no doubt a little shocking. She would have
flitted among the guests, charming everyone. He could
almost see her golden hair bobbing as she turned to
greet one person then another. The noise level was intense in the ballroom and his memory furnished her
laughter. Those who'd never come to Blackhall would
leave with praises for her on their lips.

She made us feel so welcome.

What a gracious person the duchess is.
How beautiful she is, and that gown!

Ruth had a bright and receptive approach to life. If it was interesting or exciting, she wanted to experience it. Her blond beauty was only enhanced by her trilling laugh, a smile that she used to great advantage, and a skilled, almost manipulative way of making any man feel as if he were the most important person in a room.

Ruth collected people the way other women collected gloves. She had dozens of friends, each one of whom thought she was the most important person in Ruth's life. They never figured out that Ruth didn't care about them individually. She only wanted the adulation such friends brought to her. The more important, titled, or wealthy, the better. He had come to believe it was the same reason she'd married him.

By the second month of his marriage he realized she didn't give a flying farthing for him. He was just a mark on a mental scorecard, an item no more important than a scarf from her dresser or a gown from her armoire.

After her death, he'd been approached by one poor sod who openly wept about her passing. He'd wanted to ask the man if he genuinely believed Ruth had loved him, then realized that the truth wouldn't serve any purpose.

As far as he was concerned, Ruth wasn't capable of loving anyone other than herself.

He had no doubt that, given the passage of years, she would have still charmed people. They would have said things like: *She hasn't changed, has she? She's still one of the most beautiful women in Scotland, isn't she?*

Ruth would have gloried in their comments. She would have draped herself in diamonds whose sparkle matched that in her eyes. *Did you hear that, Alex? They did enjoy themselves, didn't they? We should entertain again soon, I think.*

Even perched in the middle of the Highlands, Blackhall Castle had once been known for its hospitality, its entertainments, and its beauty.

The beauty had never faded, even though it took a fortune to maintain. The entertainments were fewer lately; he hadn't the inclination to invite hordes of people to his home. And the hospitality? At the moment, he wished them all to perdition, including the men from the society in their evening attire, clustered in small groups around the ballroom.

Who would Ruth have dressed as tonight? He suspected she would prefer to come as herself, the Duchess of Kinross. Or perhaps she would have stolen her sister's costume. Mary was Cleopatra, her long, white tunnel-like dress adorned with an intricate gold necklace. His mother was Queen Elizabeth, if he didn't miss his guess, complete with a bright curly red wig.

Why was Ruth at the forefront of his mind tonight? Because he felt betrayed again? Because this was the first ball they'd held since her death three years ago? Because he'd been made raw with this feeling that he'd been a fool?

The orchestra his mother had hired was excellent. They were playing a waltz and a great many people were dancing. He should be a good host and greet his guests, but he had neither the will nor the ability to mask his emotions that well. He was furious, the rage building with each moment he stood there.

He waited until a footman was near, then gave him an order in a low voice. In moments the young man returned with a tumbler filled with whiskey.

"Watch me," he said. "When it's empty, I want you to bring me another one."

"Yes, Your Grace."

He didn't drink often but he would tonight, with the single-minded pursuit of drunkenness. He could only remember two times he'd done something similar in recent memory: the day he'd learned his wife had been unfaithful, and the day she'd died in childbirth, taking his heir with her. Or perhaps the child hadn't been his after all, a question he'd never have answered.

Tonight seemed an excellent occasion as well. He was facing the destruction of a dream, one brought about by someone he'd trusted.

You must learn to trust people, Alex.

The echo of his mother's voice intruded into his thoughts.

Why seemed as good a word as any in response. Or perhaps a resounding *No* would suffice.

Chapter 2

*J*une was a wet month, storms always chasing across the horizon. Tonight another one was coming, but the people crowded into Blackhall's ballroom didn't seem to notice.

Lorna stood at the doorway, mesmerized by the sight. Every woman was dressed in a costume of some sort, and more than a few men were wearing kilts topped with a black evening jacket. One man stood in the corner, a red sash across his chest, evidently accepting the well-wishes of the people clustered around him.

The doors to the terrace had been shut against the rising wind of the storm, making the air even thicker with scents: various French perfumes, men's pomade, heavily spiced punch, and the musty smell of her hundred-year-old dress.

One did not disturb the Duke of Kinross.

One did not make oneself known to the family.

One did not evince any curiosity whatsoever about the comings and goings of the Russell family, especially not the Duke of Kinross or the Earl of Montrassey.

As she had been told, countless times, not only were they her employers, but the Russell clan was vastly influential in Scotland and the entire empire.

She was not to inquire about the meeting in the duke's library this afternoon. The staff had speculated that it had to be a secret society of some sort, due to only footmen being allowed inside the room.

Everyone was careful not to talk around certain people at the castle. Mrs. McDermott, for one. The housekeeper was strict about gossip and would take away your half day off for a week if she found you were engaging in it. The second was Matthews, the duke's valet. He not only gossiped but did so to members of the family.

Lorna knew that because she'd overheard him one night. Every day, after dinner, she escaped to the conservatory, retrieved her father's journal from its hiding place inside the large pot in the corner, and worked on a sketch from memory. Being in the conservatory served a dual purpose. Not only could she sketch in private, but she might see the duke, who had a habit of walking outside every evening. Sometimes he came inside the conservatory, but not often.

She never spoke. Nor did she ever betray her presence. It was enough to simply remain motionless and silent for those minutes, sharing the space with him.

"You're going to get in trouble, you are, disappearing like that," Nan said one night. "If Mrs. McDermott finds out you're not in bed, she won't be happy."

If Mrs. McDermott knew about the times she went to the conservatory, Lorna knew that the housekeeper might well send her packing. And if the housekeeper knew about tonight, there would be no doubt about the repercussions.

Still, she had to take the chance. She might have the opportunity to actually speak to the duke.

The storm was closer. The guests didn't seem to

notice the thunder or the flashes of lightning illuminating the clouds scurrying before it.

She moved toward the terrace doors, taking her time because the dress demanded it. She almost had to walk sideways in order to navigate. How was a woman supposed to tolerate such fashion? With the corset, the wig, and the wire hoops to the sides, not to mention the gold lace at the bodice, she was miserable. At least there was no chance that Mrs. McDermott, or any of the other servants, would recognize her.

She knew, from the earlier briefings, that the housekeeper would be peering through the curtains at the end of the ballroom, just to ensure that everything was going perfectly and that none of the maids or footmen selected to serve tonight were making mistakes. Lorna avoided their eyes, turning away when a maid bore down on her with a tray for the buffet table.

She met the gaze of several gentlemen, more than one interested in the revealing nature of her bodice. She wanted to pull the material up, but it was so tight around her breasts that tugging on it wouldn't have accomplished anything. No, she was definitely not a fan of these fashions, but she wasn't all that fond of hoops and crinolines, either.

The two dresses she'd been given on coming to work at Blackhall Castle were comfortable and only necessitated one petticoat. After all, one didn't expect a maid to be the height of fashion.

After her father's book was published and she no longer needed to be employed, she was not going to worry about what she wore. She'd wear something both comfortable and pretty.

Turning her head to her right, she watched as lightning illuminated the lawn and the encroaching trees. The woods were so dark and so ominous that she sometimes had the thought that the trees pulled up their roots and made a slight step toward Blackhall each night. All the other plants, plus the undergrowth and saplings, obediently followed their elders. If the gardeners weren't industrious enough, perhaps one day the forest would be right outside the window when she awoke. Instead of the turrets and the fireplaces of Blackhall, she would see only branches and leaves waving good morning.

A man leered at her. She looked away, only to find herself the object of another man's stare.

Did they know she was an imposter? A woman in fancy dress who didn't belong with all these dignitaries and important invited guests?

The women with their bright smiles didn't seem all that different from the maids with whom she served. Perhaps their accents were better. They had servants to help them dress, to inspect them before they left their rooms, and to arrange their belongings. They were fortunate in that they weren't dependent on only themselves for sustenance and survival. They had families with wealth or they'd inherited fortunes and homes.

Some of the girls who worked at Blackhall had been educated far above their stations. One girl had a penchant for numbers and helped Mrs. McDermott with sums. Another spoke three languages and amused the others by translating several sayings they could use when a footman or Lord Thomas Russell was too "handsy," a word one of the maids had devised to describe the Earl of Montrassey's habit of trying to feel up the staff.

She hadn't been around the peerage growing up. Her father's friends were learned men who preferred either traipsing through woods, bogs, and marshes, or conversing in smoky, dark pubs. One or two had a title, but they always went by first names and didn't make a point of flaunting their positions.

In her lessons before she'd been allowed to take up her duties, Lorna was informed by Mrs. McDermott that the Earl of Montrassey was the Duke of Kinross's incumbent heir.

"Isn't the duke married?" That had been the last personal question she'd been permitted to ask.

"No, poor man. He's a widower. Her Grace died some three years ago. In childbirth." The housekeeper shook her head. "The wee one didn't make it, either."

She didn't even want to think about how terrible that had been.

Was that why the duke walked every night? Why he stared up at the sky as though seeking answers from the stars?

She couldn't imagine such pain. Losing her father had been torture enough, but your wife and your child?

The terrace door was to her right. If it hadn't been raining, she would have escaped the ballroom with its heavy air and warmth for the clean, bracing air of a storm. No one came up to her to converse. Nor did they question her presence.

But she hadn't come to the ball to dance or to mingle with the guests.

Straightening her shoulders, she scanned the crowd again.

Where was he? Where was the duke?

ALEX NOTICED HER first because of her stillness. The woman in the gold brocade dress was the only person in the ballroom who wasn't animated by laughter or speech or movement. She stood straight as a reed, her hands resting, palms down, on the enormous skirts of her dress. She wasn't smiling, but she was observing. Her gaze behind the gold and black mask darted to the left and right. She reminded him of a gosling hawk, smaller than the others but as fierce when provoked or when hunting.

Who was she hunting?

The footman was standing to his left, waiting patiently for him to trade glasses. Good lad, he was both obedient and diligent. This was Alex's third whiskey, and it was finally beginning to numb some of the anger. With any luck he could get through the rest of the night without accusing anyone or making a scene.

He was the bloody Duke of Kinross. What he said was deemed important, so he damn well better have his facts right before he opened his mouth. He was so damnably important that the tides would swell and the planets realign if he were wrong.

Perhaps he should wave the footman away when the lad appeared again. If he could leave this place, he would retreat to where there were no people, no curious gazes, and no women with their tentative smiles.

The woman in gold wasn't batting her eyelashes at him.

He took another sip, watching her.

"You should have won the damn medal, especially since it means so much to you."

He turned his head to see Thomas standing there. "That's not a criterion, Uncle."

"Well, maybe you shouldn't have anything to do with those idiots at all. You should take up hunting. Your father was a great hunter."

"I have no intention of taking up hunting, either."

Maybe he'd have a few more of those whiskeys after all.

"Why are you wasting time talking to me?" Alex asked. "Aren't there any available wives around you could seduce?"

His uncle had the same black hair as his father's. Thomas's eyes, a crystal blue similar to the eighth Duke of Kinross, were often red, the only indication that the night before had been spent in debauchery. Lately, over the past few years, his face had begun showing signs of dissolution, the clean-cut jaw sagging with the first sign of jowls. His cheeks and nose were often pink. But the charm was still there, evident in the twinkling of bloodshot eyes and the smile that so effortlessly graced his mouth.

"People are watching you, Alex."

"People are always watching me, Uncle."

"You're not acting yourself," Thomas said.

"Just how the hell am I supposed to be acting?"

"Like a host, not a petulant child."

He smiled at his uncle. He knew that Thomas didn't give a flying farthing how he acted. His mother had probably sent his uncle over to lecture him.

Alex allowed his gaze to travel over the crowd, noticing that more than a few of the women were looking in their direction. Even the woman with the pompadour had turned to glance at him, her gaze finally still.

He got a jolt from that look, as if she'd somehow absorbed the power of lightning and was transmitting it to him. Moments passed and he held her gaze. The whiskey in his glass was forgotten. His annoying uncle became invisible, the cautionary words he was speaking inaudible.

He knew her. Or maybe he just wished to know her.

"Are you listening to me, Alex?"

"No," he said. "I'm not."

With some difficulty, he turned his attention back to his father's brother. Thomas had been a surprise to his grandmother, the story went. Born some twenty years after his older brother, Thomas had been only ten years old when Alex arrived and altered his future.

Had Thomas resented his future being altered?

How strange that he didn't know and, until this moment, hadn't cared to ask. Still, Thomas bore one of the family's lesser titles, the Earl of Montrassey. Because he was also Alex's heir, he was considered a Master by Scottish law, but thank heavens no one had to address him in that manner. The Church of Scotland would have had a fit.

"I was given to understand that I was in contention for the award," Alex said now. "I think someone leaked my findings to Simons."

"What does it matter, Alex?"

"It matters, Uncle, because it's three years of my life. It's work I did. It's my ideas that were stolen, my research."

"You're the Duke of Kinross. You've got better things to do than going around the county coating people's fingers with soot."

"I appreciate your sentiments," he said, pushing the words out with some difficulty. He added another hard-won smile, hoping Thomas would go back to finding a bed partner for tonight.

The woman in gold stared at him, her brown eyes sweeping down his body.

Was it the whiskey warming him or her gaze?

He took another glass from the footman, nodded his thanks and drank half of it in one swallow.

She smiled slightly, a worldly expression, one that told him she had noted his anger. If she couldn't understand it, at least she recognized it. No one else had.

Or maybe they had.

Except for the glances when he'd entered the ballroom, he'd been left alone. No one came up to greet him. No guests complimented him on the decor of the ballroom or the quality of the refreshments. No one said a word about his appearance or glanced toward the dance floor in an unmistakable hint.

He didn't dance and most people knew that. Certainly the women with whom he'd been associated over the years. Some people had the patience for the activity and the prattling conversation that accompanied it. He didn't.

The woman in the golden gown didn't glance toward the dance floor once. Nor did her gaze ever shift from him. She was daring and direct and just what he needed tonight.

"Your Grace."

The footman was at his side with a full glass of whiskey on a silver salver. He shook his head, surrendered his empty glass, and strode toward the woman, giving up spirits for another, suddenly more important, thirst.

Chapter 3

The duke was the most handsome man she had ever seen. She knew she wasn't the only female at the castle who stopped or slowed her duties when he walked past. His blue-green eyes were such an unusual shade that she could have stared at him forever. But it wasn't just his eyes that made him stand out from other men. His face was square and strong. He had a cleft in his chin and twin dimples, one on either side of his mouth. They showed even when he wasn't smiling.

The Duke of Kinross didn't smile often.

Instead, he could turn his eyes on you, making you feel as if you were melting into the floor. She didn't doubt he could command her to do almost anything and she would have done it without a word of protest.

He'd never spoken to her. Not in the two years she'd been at Blackhall Castle.

She'd seen him in his kilt before, attire he wore for formal occasions, but had never seen him appear as fierce as he did tonight. He stood there with his uncle, staring at the inhabitants of the ballroom, his face as immobile as stone, his eyes fixed on a point she couldn't see. Tall and commanding, he was the perfect duke, an imposing descendant of all those stalwart men portrayed in the gallery on the third floor. Not one of those ancestors, however, was as handsome.

He made her think of the Highlanders of hundreds of years ago. Men who fought against themselves or the English. She wondered about the story of the first Duke of Kinross, who'd been rewarded for his courage with a dukedom, and had built this castle that was added onto over the years.

Alexander Russell, the ninth Duke of Kinross, was a devastating man. Yet he was a mystery, too, wasn't he? Aloof and unapproachable, except on those nights when he watched the skies and she watched him.

Suddenly, he turned his head and looked straight at her.

Did he recognize her? Was that why his face suddenly stilled?

She couldn't breathe.

She should have asked Nan to loosen the corset a little, but she wouldn't have fit into the dress otherwise. At the time, she'd reasoned that fashion dictated the dress be tight around her chest. Now she felt as if she were going to faint. That would be a disaster, wouldn't it? Not only would she call attention to herself, but she'd be found out.

She'd saved most of her wages for the last two years, but it wasn't enough to live on, not permanently. She'd been more than lucky to be introduced to Mrs. McDermott. She couldn't be dismissed, especially without a reference.

A thought she should have had a day earlier.

Lorna pressed her hand against her waist, watched the duke slowly walk toward her. People parted as he passed, curious glances following him. He was Moses and they were the sea. He was a hot knife and they were butter. He was the Duke of Kinross and they were only observers to this tableau of disaster.

The door was to her right. She could escape the ballroom, go down the terrace steps and around to the conservatory. There, she could hide until she was certain no one would see her gaining access to the servants' stairs. She would retreat to her room, remove this damnable dress, and lecture herself sternly. No doubt Nan would think that she had finally regained her senses.

He was coming closer. His gaze hadn't moved from her face. Was he going to shame her in front of everyone? Would he pull the mask off? Would he banish her in the storm? Or would he simply demand to know why she was here?

She would tell him anything but the truth, that she'd wanted to see him and be seen. For once, she didn't want to be invisible. This one time, let the Duke of Kinross see her, Lorna Gordon. Not a maid, not one of the silent army that served him. Let him see her as a woman. Let them exchange a few words, even if it was polite banter.

Not once had she considered that he might impale her with his gaze, or that he would march on her like a Highlander intent on capturing an English city.

What did she do now? Terror rooted her to the spot. Her hand reached out and grabbed the handle of the door.

She suddenly wanted to be outside, to experience the wind, to tilt her head up to see the fast-moving clouds. But if she opened the door, people would turn to look at her. A few of the women with their elaborate hairstyles would frown in her direction.

"Go ahead and do it," a voice said at her elbow.

He was here. He was here.

At least he wasn't going to shame her in front of everyone.

"Go ahead and open the door," he said. "I'll join you on the terrace. Let them fuss at us both."

If anyone looked at her, it wasn't so much in condemnation as it was curiosity. Who was this oddly dressed woman and why was she with the Duke of Kinross?

Her heart was beating fast. Her mouth was dry. She had imagined being this close to him before, but she'd seen herself being witty or flirtatious or so intelligent that her comments impressed him. She hadn't envisioned being struck dumb.

"Who are you?" he asked.

Relief surged through her, making her knees weak. He didn't know who she was.

"I don't recognize you."

For an eternity of seconds, words simply failed her. Did she tell him she was a neighbor? A guest of a guest? What did she say?

"Marie Antoinette?"

Thank God. He was talking about her costume dress.

She opened the door and walked onto the terrace. He followed her, closing the door behind them. The wind pushed against the impossible towering wig until she thought it was going to topple. She reached up with one hand to hold it in place, startled by his laughter.

"I'm surprised your dress hasn't sailed you over the railing," he said. "Perhaps it would be better if we went back inside."

No, not that. People would listen to their conversation.

The rain began, coming down in a curtain. He

pulled her off to the side, where the roof overhang protected them. It didn't prevent the wind from dampening her face, however, or no doubt ruining the fabric of her borrowed dress.

She should move, should protest. Any of the other women in the ballroom would have done that. Or would they? Would they have remained silent, too, in favor of spending a few quiet moments with the devastating Duke of Kinross?

The light from the ballroom was pressed back by the storm, leaving them in a curiously shadowed world. Hardly proper, was it, being with him in such a secluded place?

"Can I be Marie Antoinette if I don't speak French?" she asked.

"Why don't you?"

"I've never learned."

"A startling direct answer," he said. "Are you normally direct?"

What a curious question. His smile was crooked and amused. It took her a moment to realize that the Duke of Kinross was well on his way to being in his cups, or as her father would say: soused to the gills.

Now she knew she shouldn't be here with him. If he were any other man, she'd leave. She wouldn't even bother making up an excuse, just grab her unmanageable skirts, find the steps leading down from the terrace, and flee as quickly as she could.

Instead, she stayed where she was, one hand holding onto her wig, the other at her waist.

They might have been two servants who met at the market. Or he might have been a cobbler to whom she was bringing a broken shoe. Not a duke and his maid, pretending to be someone else for a little while.

"I've never been asked that before," she said. "I don't know if I'm direct or not."

His smile made his dimples deepen. What a beautiful face he had. She could stare at him for hours. Was he used to people looking at him? Did he think it was because of his title? Or did he realize it was because he was so handsome that others' eyes just naturally gravitated to him?

"Who do you belong to?"

Another odd question, but she had a response to it. "I don't belong to anyone."

"Who brought you here? Who is your escort? Are you married? Do you have a fiancé?"

She really did have to make up someone now, didn't she? Should she invent a husband?

"Why do you want to know?"

"I want to know if someone's going to pummel me if I kiss you."

The bird that was her heart had escaped from its cage and was now fluttering wildly in her chest. She could barely breathe. The silly wig was being buffeted by the wind, but so were the windows. She could hear them shivering in their panes.

She loved a storm. She loved being out in it, regardless of the danger. She would sometimes tilt her head back to feel the rain baptizing her face. In those moments, she was as elemental as the first woman. Yet she'd never felt like she did right now.

He grabbed her elbow and pulled her farther away from the door to the ballroom.

She went willingly, in an excited, panicked rush of emotion. Was he truly going to kiss her? Was the most handsome man she'd ever seen truly going to kiss her? Did it count if he were soused?

He pressed her up against the wall. If she truly cared about the dress, she would've warned him that the wire cage for the panniers was old and easily bent. But she didn't care about anything but the feel of his body against hers, the wool of his evening jacket gently abrading the exposed flesh above her breasts, and the look in his eyes.

She should have been chilled, but she felt heated from within. Was it his grin, slightly wicked and utterly charming? Or the promise of a kiss? Or was it her own daring, out in a storm with the Duke of Kinross?

He lowered his face slowly, giving her time to move away. Instead, she abandoned her wig and gripped his shoulders, keeping him in place. His lips were as soft as she'd imagined, but there her lack of experience showed. He slanted his head to deepen the kiss and she gasped in wonder.

His mouth tasted of warm whiskey.

She'd never considered that his tongue would sweep in to touch hers, or that he would nibble at her bottom lip as if she were a delectable piece of fruit. Nor did she ever envision that his hand would pull away the tight bodice and cup her bare breast.

Or that she would let him. Yes, and more. Whatever he wished to do, he could. Whisper in her ear, please, what he wanted and she'd allow it. Whatever manner of liberties. Whatever sin for which she'd ask forgiveness tomorrow.

Tonight was a dream come true. Tonight was the culmination of two years of watching and wondering. Tonight she wasn't just one of the upstairs maids; she was Lorna Gordon and she was kissing the Duke of Kinross.

Her blood was heating, fire racing along her skin.

The wind was blowing the rain on them and she didn't care. The wool of his jacket was beginning to chafe, but she pressed herself closer to him.

Whatever happened, whatever ramifications came from this night, she wouldn't regret it. How could she? However long she lived, she would recall these moments when the Duke of Kinross kissed her. When he pressed his lips against her neck and nibbled on her earlobe. He pulled the mask free from her face, but she didn't care. Let him recognize her now, but it would be too late. She'd already had her kiss. She'd already spoken to him, and he'd talked to her as if she was a woman who intrigued him.

Marie Antoinette or Lorna Gordon—did it matter?

In the next instant she was free of the wig. Had the wind pulled it from her or had he done so? Again, it didn't matter.

He thrust his hands through her hair, holding her head still.

"You're beautiful," he said, the words freezing her heart in mid beat. This, too, she would remember forever.

He mustn't think she believed him. She was not so desperate that she was naive. Nor so foolish that she'd completely lost her wits.

"No," she said.

"No?" He smiled against her lips. "I think I prefer yes."

Her body seemed to know what to do in response to his touch and his words, but her mind was adrift in a whirlwind of confusion. Did she push him away? Or draw him closer? Did she protest? Or simply enjoy what was happening?

A warning bell peeled in her mind, but she smothered the sound.

Her lips tingled, her ears were filled with the rhythm of the rain and her own heartbeat. She felt earthy, elemental, alive in a way she'd never before been. Her skin was so sensitive that every place he touched with his lips either trembled or quivered, inciting a moan or a gasp from her.

She'd never once discussed passion with anyone, not even Nan, the only close female friend she'd ever had. The maids teased each other or laughed about a certain male servant and his reputation with women, but none of them had ever talked about desire.

Was that what this was, a feeling making her burn as fiercely as one of the falling stars she saw from the conservatory? She might explode from inside, leaving nothing but ashes where she'd once been.

He jerked on the material of her dress, freeing her other breast. She was nearly naked in the storm now and all she could do was moan when his lips left hers and trailed a rain-slicked path to a nipple. She wanted the taste of whiskey on her tongue at the same time she held his head in place against her breast. When he drew the nipple deep into his mouth, she moaned with pleasure.

She could barely stand for the sensations assaulting her. She was going to fall to her knees on the terrace.

She should break away. She should push him back. Her hands went up to grab his jacket, but her fingers curled around the lapels to pull him closer to her.

"I must have you," he said, his mouth once more against her lips. "Now."

His hands raised her skirts, her legs exposed to the blowing rain.

Where were you when you lost your virginity? Not on her wedding night to a man of good virtue and intent. Not laying there clutching the edge of the sheet with trembling hands, biting her lip with worry and barely disguised fear.

No, nothing so proper or expected. Not as a bride, but as an imposter. A woman dissatisfied by what Fate had brought her, evidently willing to trade the one asset she had for something more important. A memory, not simply of the Duke of Kinross, but of a passion so fiery, unexpected, and shocking, that it decreed what happened in those next moments.

Her legs were bared to the rain until it felt like she was being baptized by nature itself. Perhaps washed and readied, an offering to the duke's ardent nature.

Do you take this virgin to be your sacrifice?

He reached down and with heated fingers found her, cupped her within the slit of her pantaloons. A gasp escaped her when his finger entered her, an invasion she'd never before considered. She wrapped her arms around his neck and moaned into his collar as his palm pressed up against her, teasing and spreading the moisture. Not nature's rain, but her own.

He bent, his hands suddenly on her bottom.

The ballroom door opened.

"Alex?"

They froze.

Chapter 4

*T*he duke grabbed her hand and pulled her with him away from the ballroom, through the storm. She ran to keep up with him, her breasts bared to the rain, forgetting about the wig, uncaring if the gold brocade was ruined.

Mary knew her. She paid attention to the maids at Blackhall, if only to criticize their industry to Mrs. McDermott. Mary would have recognized her in a heartbeat.

Evidently, the duke wanted to escape his sister-in-law's detection as much as Lorna did.

They raced over the terrace and down the stairs. When he led them to the conservatory, she should have been surprised, but it seemed somehow ordained. This was where she'd watched him so often. This was where she'd yearned for him.

Wordlessly, he led her to a crimson velvet upholstered fainting couch tucked among the ferns. She half sat, half reclined, as he bent and kissed the rain from her breasts, paying such close attention to her nipples that she closed her eyes to savor the sensations.

His touch was fire and something more, the ability to weaken her knees and silence any warning. Passion made her a puppet, one without a mind of her own.

When he stood and placed her legs up on the couch, she let him. When he slowly peeled back the layers of her skirt, tucking them at her waist, she didn't say a word.

The lightning illuminated them as he traced a path with both palms from her thighs to her waist, pulling off her pantaloons. He jerked off his jacket, revealing his rain-soaked shirt only seconds before kneeling on the couch above her.

"I'm dreaming this," he said, twirling his finger into her nest of curls. "Either that or this is a reward of some sort. I must have been very, very good at something."

He pulled up his kilt.

Although the maids occasionally joked about a footman's equipment, she'd never before seen a naked man. She reached up with both hands and gripped his penis, marveling at the shape and size of it.

He closed his eyes when she touched him. She squeezed experimentally and his eyes opened, fixed on her.

Now was the time to jump up from the couch, explain that she wasn't a woman of loose morals. That he had completely misunderstood her reaction to his kisses and his touch.

She didn't say a word.

Instead, she rose up on her forearms, thinking that she was a decadent picture indeed. She lay before him with her breasts out of her dress, her dress bunched up at her waist, the skirt falling over the side of the couch.

She should have covered herself.

She would be concerned about her lack of maidenly reserve later. Right now she only wanted the ache to ease, and he was making it worse by delicately trailing his fingers along her intimate folds, teasing with a touch.

"Or maybe you're just a drunken dream. Maybe I've imbibed more whiskey than I've thought."

"Is that an effect of whiskey, then? I've never heard of it."

"In this case, yes," he said. "I wished for a distraction and there you were, standing by the terrace doors, looking as if you'd rather bolt than remain in the ballroom another minute."

"I was feeling lonely," she said in lieu of the truth. She'd been afraid he'd found her out, that he'd known she was just a maid at Blackhall.

He'd never seen her in that role, but he was looking at her now.

She would never forget this night. Would he remember?

"There were too many people and they all seemed happy."

"I doubt one of them is as happy as I am at the moment," he said, rising over her. "Or as happy as I'm going to make you, Marie."

He smiled at her, a smile to forever remember.

The storm outside was equaled by the one she was experiencing. Lightning danced along her skin at his touch. Her ears were filled with the sound of her own thunderous heartbeat. Her body was raining as if preparing itself for him.

He lowered himself and suddenly he was inside her, the invasion shocking.

She bit her lip to keep from crying aloud.

He was swearing, a succession of oaths she'd never before heard. But he didn't withdraw. Nor did he release her.

"You're a virgin? Why the hell didn't you tell me you were a virgin?"

She didn't think she was capable of speech even if she had an answer for him.

He pulled back, and for a second she thought he was going to leave her. But he surged forward, driving her down into the padding of the couch. Again he pulled back before pressing hard against her, so deep she wondered if he meant to punish her for being a virgin.

He was still swearing as he thrust into her, each forward motion accompanied by a new word. When he raised himself up, his eyes pinned her to the couch as ably as his arms or his invasion.

The initial shock of his penetration was being cushioned by the growing moisture. Her hands wound around his neck. Her hips lifted, the discomfort easing slightly with each of his movements.

He seemed determined to brand her with his touch and make sure she never forgot the night she surrendered her virginity. How could she?

Bracing her feet against the velvet, she pushed upward, her assault as single-minded as his.

She never expected this. Nor had she considered that he would seduce her, if this was seduction. She'd never be able to enter the conservatory without envisioning this scene, her nearly naked and him with his kilt up around his waist, buttocks pumping.

They should both be shamed instead of entering wholeheartedly into this act. Not love, surely, but earthy sex, enjoyed for the sheer carnal nature of it.

Her body forgot that it was virginal. The soreness, the strangeness of his invasion, faded beneath more pressing needs. Her breasts ached for his lips, her core for something. He kissed her, his tongue thrusting. His fingers were strumming against her, creating unbelievable sensations. He held himself over her until she lifted her hips, her hands digging into his arms.

Every sensation was centered on his fingers and then his lips as he remained motionless and demanding.

"Damn you," he said, bending to suck on a nipple. He thrust into her as if he had no choice, as if his body were a prisoner to the act.

Lightning revealed the tableau, erotic and wanton. The Duke of Kinross furious and erect. His maid moaning as pleasure sliced her in two.

He thrust into her once more, cursing as he came.

WHAT HAD HAPPENED to them? Was this how love-making normally happened, in a furor of passion? Did you normally lose your mind? Did nothing matter but the taste of a lover's lips or having him as close as physically possible? If Mary hadn't interrupted them, they would probably have continued in the midst of the storm. He would've taken her there, against a wall, and she wouldn't have raised her voice in protest.

The duke stood and walked to the windows, putting his hands against the glass and lowering his head between his arms.

Och, she was going to have to clean that in the morning.

He was still fully dressed. She, on the other hand, didn't see how she could possibly put herself back together again, enough to escape to her room. She'd lost her mask somewhere, and where was the floury wig?

She sat up, pushing her skirt over her bare legs. She still had her shoes on, which was a good thing, since she only owned the one pair. There hadn't been any slippers in the trunk, nothing that would have matched the once lovely gold dress. Perhaps it was best that no one asked her to dance. She would've clomped all over the ballroom floor.

"You picked the wrong fool," he said, turning to glance at her.

She looked over at him as she struggled to tuck her breasts back in the dress.

"I don't understand."

His laughter echoed through the conservatory.

"Come now, of course you do. You and your associate no doubt thought I was ripe for blackmail. I'm a duke. I'm wealthy. Of course I wouldn't want the scandal of tonight made public. Here I took a virgin without even knowing her name." He leaned back against the glass and folded his arms. "What is your name?"

She'd seen him every day for the last two years, sometimes more than once. She'd passed him in the hall carrying piles of linens. She'd brought him more than one meal in the library. She'd taken tins of soap to his bathing chamber. She'd fluffed his mattress.

He'd taken her virginity, but he didn't even know her name. Worse, he was accusing her of blackmail.

What would be more terrible to him, that he'd bedded a maid or that he would be portrayed as a lecher? She doubted either would bother him. His next words verified her thoughts.

"You can go back to your confederate and tell him I don't give a flying farthing about scandal. Feel free to brag about your actions of this night. Only I doubt you'll fare as well as I. Women don't, especially if they're light-skirts."

The storm was finally fading; the bursts of lightning moving toward the horizon. He was only a dark shape against the glass.

She was fiercely glad she couldn't see him; it meant

that she, too, was draped in shadow. She needn't guard her expression or smile falsely.

"Does that statement make any sense?" she asked, grateful her voice sounded so steady. "You admit to bedding a virgin and then, in the next breath, call me a light-skirt. Is your reasoning faulty because of the whiskey, do you think?"

"One is physical. The other is mental or perhaps a moral label. I've no doubt you were saving yourself for an episode like tonight. Nor do I doubt that you'll find your calling soon enough."

When she didn't respond, he spoke again. "What? No outraged response? No tears?"

Slowly, she put on her pantaloons, wishing she were alone to dress.

"Would it make any difference what I said?" she asked. To her surprise, her voice still sounded calm. She was anything but. Her heart was racing and her breath was tight.

"I suppose not," he said. "I wouldn't believe you."

"I don't think you believe anyone, do you? Do you imagine the world is out to take advantage of the mighty Duke of Kinross? How sad a life you must live to think that. How narrow and restricted."

He didn't answer her, but then she hadn't expected a response.

She wished she knew where the towering white wig was, but it had probably been blown halfway to Inverness. She would just have to return the dress without the wig.

Standing, she faced his shadow.

"I always thought you were a prince among men," she said. "Now I know you aren't. You're less than that. I'm not even sure you're what I consider a man.

Perhaps a mouse. A prancing, prattling mouse who's afraid someone is going to step on his tail."

As an insult, it had a lot to be desired. But she wasn't going to stand there until she thought of something better.

He was more adept at wounding than she. She couldn't even think of another thing to say to protect herself. She had acted the part of light-skirt, hadn't she? She'd fallen into his arms without a word of protest. She'd let him kiss her and touch her. She'd not only capitulated, she'd enthusiastically participated.

She wasn't a hypocrite. She hadn't felt anything but pleasure in his arms. Once the deed was over, she wasn't going to claim a maidenly reserve. The guilt she was experiencing was for not taking better care of the costume she'd borrowed, not for bedding the duke.

"I enjoyed it," she said. "Whatever word you call me. I have no confederate. I have no intention of mentioning tonight to anyone. I'll let you feel regret. I have no intention of doing so."

She left before he could say another word.

Chapter 5

y ou did what?"

Lorna stared at her friend, the words Nan had just spoken taking a moment to register.

"You did what?" she repeated.

Nan moved from the straight-back chair where she'd been sitting to stand at Lorna's lone window. The unremarkable view was of the lane to the square in Wittan Village.

"I left a note for the duchess," she said. "I didn't sign it, though."

Yes, that's what she heard. She couldn't believe Nan would do something like that.

"But you told her about me? Why?"

"Why?" Nan asked, turning to stare at her. Her hands flew out to encompass the small room where they sat. "Look where you're living, Lorna."

"This is the only lodging I could afford."

"Your landlady is a horror."

She couldn't argue with that. Mrs. MacDonald was nosy, intrusive, and difficult.

"The duchess needed to know she's going to be a grandmother," Nan said. "If nothing else, she could give you some money. How are you supposed to live?"

"I'm doing fine," Lorna said. She sat on the edge of the bed watching as Nan paced back and forth.

"Fine? I wouldn't call this fine."

"I've saved all my wages and I go to market every week. I've made some good customers, people who will come back."

"When the baby is born, what will you do?"

"The same thing I'm doing now," Lorna said, clutching her cloak to her for warmth.

Nan used her half day off to come and visit her. The time they spent together was one of the bright spots of her week.

The past months, ever since learning she was with child, had been difficult ones. Without Nan's friendship, she didn't know what she would have done. The other woman had helped her hide her condition for months. She'd even given Lorna some of her own wages.

Yet all along Nan had fussed at her about her plans.

"If the villagers find out, you'll be shunned, Lorna. Your child will be known as a bastard and you'll be called a whore. Mothers will cross the street rather than allow you near their children. Men will leer at you. You'll be the face of sin."

Nan might be right, but what choice did she have? She had no family. Nor was she going to go to the duke and tell him she was with child. Not when he thought she was the most vile kind of creature, capable of blackmailing him.

"I didn't expect you to betray me like this," Lorna said.

"Betrayal? I'm doing what you should have done months ago." Nan glanced at the walls that she'd tried to brighten with her own sketches. "No self-respecting rat would live here. It's depressing and you've been freezing for months."

"Mrs. MacDonald charges too much for coal."

Money was probably always going to be a problem. She had to be smart about her funds, which was why the room was so cold. When the baby was born she'd make sure the space was warmer.

"You only see what you want to see, Lorna."

She held herself still and silent.

"Even the night of the ball, you had some idea in your mind what it was going to be like, and nothing I could say would stop you."

Nan extended both hands, palms up, fingers pointed at Lorna's belly.

"Look what happened."

What could she say to that? Nan was only stating the obvious.

"My father always said that I should try to see the best in every situation. That's what I'm trying to do."

"There's a difference, Lorna, between looking for the best and seeing only what you want to see." Nan returned to the straight-back chair. "I did what I thought would help you, Lorna. Not betray you. I can't bear you living here."

"Did you tell the duchess where I was?"

Nan nodded.

"You know what's going to happen," Lorna said. "The duke is going to be involved. He's going to make some outlandish demand because he's the Duke of Kinross."

"Better than hear of his child starving to death."

"There's my father's book," she said.

Nan sat back, folded her arms and regarded her steadily.

"If none of my father's friends respond to my letters, I'll travel to London to see a publisher myself."

"If your father couldn't get his book published in his lifetime, what makes you think that you can?"

"Faith," Lorna said.

"Faith won't feed you and your baby, Lorna. Shouldn't you be thinking of him? Shouldn't you be less selfish?"

She stared at Nan, startled.

"Selfish? Is that what you think of me? Just because I don't want charity?"

"Yes." Nan leaned forward. "It isn't charity, Lorna. It's help, and you desperately need it. The duke could provide for the child."

Lorna focused on the threadbare rug beneath her feet. Everything in the room was worn and well used, from the bureau with its ill-fitting drawers to the iron bed frame with its rust spots. Even the ewer and basin were chipped. Mrs. MacDonald, her landlady, was charging far more than the room was worth, but there hadn't been many lodgings available for a woman six months pregnant.

She should have thought of the consequences at the time. When, though? When the duke was kissing her? Or when he led her to the conservatory and she tumbled onto the couch? Or when they shared a glance that held her rooted to the spot?

She'd been a virgin. Was becoming pregnant right away a normal situation?

She'd only told Nan that she succumbed to the duke's advances, not that passion had stripped every bit of sense from her. How did she tell her that the night had been like a whirlwind, the power of desire confusing and mesmerizing her?

Sometimes she dreamed of him and woke feeling as if he'd seduced her again. She would lay in the bed staring up at the ceiling, feeling drained.

"I know you're angry at me, Lorna."

She wasn't angry. She was terrified. Didn't Nan know what she'd done? She had set into motion actions that she herself couldn't alter.

Unless the duke didn't believe her. Unless he considered that it was some kind of ploy, just as he had that night.

He hadn't recognized her the next day. They passed in the corridor, her with a bucket and a scrub brush, tasked with refreshing the rug in the duchess's sitting room. She would have ducked into one of the maids' closets or the connection of staircases built so that the family never had to come face-to-face with a servant, but she was already there. She'd opened the door to the duchess's suite and slipped inside, half waiting for him to say something.

Marie. Is that you?

But he hadn't. Nor had he seen her on any subsequent encounter. For months she'd worried that he might recognize her, but that would have been difficult since he hadn't once glanced in her direction.

She never returned to the conservatory again after her duties were done. Instead, she sat in their small room and worked on her father's book, at least until she'd expended her oil for the week. Then she retired early, trying to bite back resentment because of the duke. It wasn't enough that he'd seduced her, although if she were fair, she'd admit it was a mutual effort, but he'd taken away the little freedom and daily enjoyment she had.

The duke wouldn't believe Nan's words. The duchess, however, was an entirely different matter. How did she convince the woman that it had been a mistake?

The Dowager Duchess of Kinross was one of the sweetest people she'd ever met. Whenever she did something for the woman, the duchess made a point of thanking her. When she was new, the duchess had asked if she liked working at the castle. How did she feel about Mrs. McDermott? When she answered in the affirmative to both questions, the duchess smiled.

"I'm so glad. It's nice to feel at home wherever one is, don't you think?"

Every time she saw the woman, the duchess remembered something about her. They'd spoken of her father and his work. The duchess had even recalled her birthday, which was a sincere surprise.

"I had to do it," Nan said now. "You know that, don't you?"

"I know you think you had to."

She understood, she really did, but understanding didn't make the situation easier. Either the duchess was going to descend on her, or the duke was going to send someone to threaten her. She could imagine what the man would say. Something along the lines of dissuading her from communicating with the duke in any fashion.

She could go for the rest of her life without communicating with the Duke of Kinross. What a fool she'd been about the man.

She stood and stared down at the floor, the window,

anywhere but at Nan. Slowly, she made her way to the door, wishing some words would come to her.

"You're my friend," she said finally. "You've always been my friend, Nan, from the first day we met. That will never change."

They hugged at the door.

"I'll come next week," Nan said. "I'll bring some more biscuits with me. And maybe some coal."

She was not going to weep in front of Nan. Instead, she bid her friend good-bye and watched as Nan left the house and hurried back to Blackhall.

Dear God, what was she going to do now?

She wasn't going to think about the Duke of Kinross. Why should she? He certainly hadn't spared one thought for her.

THE CHINESE PARLOR, decorated in crimson and black, was filled with objects acquired by a previous duke on his journeys through the Orient. Alex found the room oppressive, himself, but his mother liked it not only because of the unusual furnishings but because the room was bright most of the year.

Of all the people in the world, Alex trusted her the most. He'd never told her that, but he suspected she knew. Just as he thought she was aware of most of his feelings.

They'd never talked about Ruth, for example. He'd never expressed how he'd felt to learn that his wife had been unfaithful. Nor had he ever mentioned his confusion and despair over her death in childbirth. Or whether the child who'd died had been his. His mother never speaking Ruth's name was a tacit admittance that she knew how he felt.

Although she was in her late fifties, Louise Russell, the Dowager Duchess of Kinross, didn't seem to age. Her black hair was without a touch of gray. Her face was unlined and her figure hadn't developed the plumpness often associated with matronly women.

If her eyes, the same shade as his, were sometimes farseeing, that was less due to the effects of time than the experiences she'd endured. His brother and sister both died of the influenza epidemic that had taken his father. In a matter of weeks their immediate family had been decimated, going from five to two.

He'd been sixteen at the time and unprepared for the onslaught of grief. His brother, Douglas, had only been ten, and his sister fourteen. Moira had the promise of being a beauty like their mother. Her hair had been black as well, her eyes a clear blue and almost always sparkling with amusement. She seemed to see the world as a great and grand adventure into which she'd been born.

Despite his mother's caution, he had been at Moira's bedside when she died. He held her hand while the fever burned fiercely through her. He'd wanted, in those hours, to say something reassuring, to let her believe that she could win the battle against this insidious disease. In the end, in her last lucid moment, Moira had turned to him and smiled. Just that, a farewell smile, but in her eyes had been a hint of amusement, as if she saw what lay beyond and thought Heaven to be a marvelous place.

Decades had passed, but there were times when he felt her presence so strongly that he wanted to turn to greet her and ask if she was one of the angels. Did she guard the inhabitants of Blackhall? Or did she just report what sins and transgressions they'd committed to the Almighty?

Strange, but he hadn't realized until he stepped across the threshold just now that they didn't often speak of Moira, either. Was that his mother's conscious decision? Did she push away those thoughts that might bring her pain? If so, perhaps he should ask her how he could do the same.

His mother was seated in her favorite chair before the window, her embroidery frame stand in front of her, her gaze on the approaching night. She was so still she might have been a statue, something carved with realism: Dowager Duchess, Receiving Bad News.

Dread kept him silent as he walked across the room.

He sat on the sofa facing her.

"You've been very busy," she said. "I've hardly seen you lately."

"I'm cataloging the samples we've obtained."

"Why does this work interest you so much, Alex?"

No one had ever asked him that question. Nor did he think she really wanted to know now. He had the feeling she was easing into the conversation, that the topic she really wanted to discuss was difficult for her.

His mother had a generous allowance for her personal needs, plus an inheritance from his father. Had she exceeded that? He'd never known her to squander money, but there was plenty in the Russell coffers if she needed it.

He doubted, however, if issues about money would make her uncomfortable.

She was tapping her fingers together. She still wore her wedding ring despite being a widow for years. He'd asked her about it once, and she only smiled softly.

I'm still married, Alex, even if your father is no longer with me.

He was a widower, but he didn't feel the devotion for his wife that she had for his father.

"Do you know how much I love you?" she asked now.

Surprised, he only nodded.

"Up until today, I respected you as well. I've often thought that God gave you to me to make up for the loss of your brother and sister. No mother could ever have been as proud of you as I was."

His mother didn't sound like herself. There was a catch to her voice as if she fought back tears. He sat up straighter, waiting.

"What's wrong?" he finally asked, when all she did was stare down at something in her lap.

Nothing could have prepared him for the look she gave him then. In her eyes was an emotion he'd rarely seen: disappointment.

"You're going to be a father, Alex. The father of an illegitimate child."

"I beg your pardon?"

She smiled thinly at him.

"I know for a fact, Alex, that your hearing is excellent. Perhaps you are just finding it difficult to come up with a reasonable response?"

There was an edge to his mother's voice that he'd never before heard. But, then, he'd never been accused of fathering an illegitimate child. Her words, however, were right on the mark. Surprise rendered him mute.

"The girl is a former maid. I can't help but wonder if the reason we are losing so many maids has something to do with you. Have you been lascivious with more than one?"

He felt like he was in short pants once again, being chastised because he had taken one of cook's biscuits without permission. The back of his neck was heating.

"I have never bedded one of the maids, Mother, and I'm disappointed that you might think so."

"I'm sure that tone works well with other people, Alex, but I'm not impressed by the ducal frostiness."

She held up a letter. "The girl's name is Lorna Gordon. She is due to give birth shortly. Evidently, she's living in Wittan Village."

"I've never heard the name," he said. "I don't know her."

"At the risk of stating the obvious, son, she evidently knows you."

"Is that what she says?"

He strode to stand in front of her chair and extended his hand. She held up the letter and he read it.

"It isn't signed."

"No. Does that make the accusation invalid?"

"It's an extortion scheme, nothing less. I don't know this Lorna person."

His mother looked away from the needlework frame and stared off into space, her hand suspended in midair, the needle pointing toward the fabric she was embroidering.

"I remember her. She's a beautiful girl and so sweetly natured. I was disappointed when she left Blackhall. Mrs. McDermott thought highly of her, plus she made the most wonderful comfrey balm."

"Balm?"

She nodded. "For my arthritis. She refused to take any payment, saying that she'd gathered the herbs on Blackhall land and used our equipment." She smiled. "I quite liked her."

He felt compelled to say something to defend himself, but how did he prove a negative?

His neck was getting warmer.

"You can't honestly believe such a thing of me?"

"It's been three years since Ruth died. I had hoped you would find someone to love, that you would be able to trust enough to do so. But I certainly understand that you're a man and that men have needs."

"Not enough to swive the maids, Mother."

Her cheeks were pink. Was she as embarrassed about this conversation as he? He'd never thought to discuss his sex life—or lack of one—with his mother.

He'd only been with one woman in the last year, and was so desperate to have her that he'd almost caused a scandal.

He stared down at the letter, not seeing it. Instead, he saw *her* with her hair down around her shoulders, her face wet with rain. He would have taken her there, outside, only feet from the ballroom. He'd never felt what he had that night. Never come close to it, and it wasn't the whiskey.

The woman of the storm had disappeared.

He'd been unable to find anyone by the name of Marie. Nor had his careful questions to various people resulted in the whereabouts or the identity of a ginger-haired enchantress. Hell, he didn't even know if the mole near her eye was real or painted on. Maybe the entire episode had been induced by the amount of whiskey he'd imbibed.

No, she'd been real enough, a fiercely voiced shadow, saying words that he hadn't forgotten in all the months since that stormy night. No one else had been able to imbue as much disgust into her insults as she had. Or pinned his ears so effectively to the wall.

Damn her, whenever a Highland storm passed over the mountains, heading toward Blackhall, he wondered if she'd appear again.

". . . do, Alex?"

He realized he hadn't been paying attention.

"Do?" he asked, handing her back the letter. He hoped to God she burned it. Knowing his mother, however, he knew she wouldn't. If he didn't handle the situation, it would only continue to concern her.

"I'll go and see her," he said, the decision only seconds old. "When I go to Inverness in a few days."

"Do you think that wise? Wouldn't it be better to send Edmonds?" she asked, referring to the Russells' solicitor.

"And have Edmonds give me that superior stare? I think not."

He bent and kissed her on the cheek, and left before she could say anything further.

AFTER NAN LEFT, Lorna retrieved her father's book from beneath the sagging mattress. *A Manual of Botany of Scotland: Being an Introduction to the Study of the Structure, Physiology, and Classification of Scottish Herbal Plants and Related Treatments* was the product of a decade of her father's study.

She'd nearly finished the remaining illustrations and had written to several of her father's friends, men who initially expressed enthusiasm about the idea of the completed manuscript. Unfortunately, of the three men she'd written, only one had responded, and his letter was three pages of complaints about his ill health. Only one sentence referred to her inquiry. All he'd written was, "Due to the nature of my health, my dear, I am unable to assist you in soliciting a publisher."

She supposed she could write the other two men again, but she didn't have as much hope as when she began the project. Had she misinterpreted everything? Had those comments his peers made at her father's funeral only been words of kindness? Had they no faith in his work?

She'd been told that her father was a great botanist. She knew he'd spent most of his life studying the flora of Scotland. He'd trudged through marshes and bogs, over glens and mountain crags. After her mother died, she'd followed him from one desolate outcropping to another, learning at his side. She'd sat, patiently, as he spoke to wise women and old men smoking a pipe in front of crowded shops. He'd written down recipes, learned how to concoct various remedies, and painstakingly reformulated them in the hopes of keeping such traditions alive.

"Once upon a time, Lorna," he told her, "we had no physicians or hospitals. We trusted in those who were attuned to nature and the earth. It's knowledge we're losing each day."

She would faithfully copy down each recipe, watch as he prepared them, and then transcribe his notes beside her pictures of each herb.

If, on his expeditions, he occasionally forgot she was there, she didn't mind. She understood his preoccupation and occupied herself with her drawings.

When he died, suddenly and unexpectedly, one April morning after they'd just arrived in Inverness, she was shocked at how few coins stood between her and poverty. The innkeeper's wife, knowing her predicament and feeling some compassion, had recommended her to Mrs. McDermott, the housekeeper at Blackhall.

If she'd known then what she knew now, she would have gladly entered the poorhouse instead. At least she wouldn't be pregnant and she would never have met the Duke of Kinross.

Chapter 6

$\mathcal{A}$lex entered his suite, heading for the dressing room.

"Don't hover," he said to Matthews when his valet made an appearance at the door. "I've just come to change my shirt before I leave."

"More soot, sir?"

"More soot, Matthews."

"It's devilish hard for the laundress to remove the stains."

He glanced at his valet. Did the man realize they were having this conversation with increasing regularity lately or that Matthews was beginning to sound chiding? His mother didn't even employ that tone. Matthews could take some lessons from the Dowager Duchess.

"Then you'll just have to order some extra shirts for me," he said. "That isn't a problem, is it?"

"Of course not, Your Grace."

He doubted it would be. He'd long suspected that Matthews received a bonus from the tailor based on the number of garments he ordered. He discovered the transactions when reviewing his expenses for the last quarter. What Matthews hadn't figured out was that the tailor tacked the amount he paid the valet onto the cost of the shirts, effectively making Alex pay for the bonus.

He allowed the situation only because he hadn't wanted to interview for a new valet, but he disliked being played for a fool. A thought that brought *her* to the forefront of his mind.

Was Lorna Gordon the same woman he'd encountered at the fancy dress ball? Had she been responsible for the single most erotic interlude of his life?

Was she Marie?

If she was, she was trying to take advantage of the situation.

He didn't believe a word of the note he'd read: that the writer was a friend and that her main concern was for the child he'd fathered.

What pap.

He couldn't have sired a child from that one occasion. Marie had appeared to be a virgin, but that might have been either the whiskey or some sort of ruse.

He wished he hadn't drunk so much. He'd not touched a drop of liquor since, his abstinence a penance for the excesses of that night.

He'd been a fool and he was paying for it now, wasn't he?

It was one thing to attempt to blackmail him, but she'd made her biggest mistake by involving his mother. Because she'd done so, he would see her well and truly ruined.

He glanced over at Matthews, expecting his valet to be performing a dignified pout, but the man surprised him.

"Are you certain you don't wish me to accompany you to Inverness, Your Grace?"

"Not this time. I'll only be gone a few days."

He turned away and finished removing the shirt. He held out his hand and Matthews, with perfect valet timing, placed a crisp white shirt in his grip, standing by in case he lost his mind and could no longer manage buttons.

Once he was ready, he made a mental check of his valise, determined that everything was in readiness for the trip to Inverness, and left the dressing room.

As he passed through the sitting room, Alex hesitated at the window. Here he could see Russell land stretching to the other side of Loch Gerry and to the far glens. For a moment he stood there, letting the sight fill him.

Never a day passed that he failed to see its beauty or to be grateful that it was his to steward and manage.

Sir Walter Scott's words in *The Lay of the Last Minstrel* came to mind:

> *Breathes there the man with soul so dead*
> *Who never to himself has said,*
> *This is my own, my native land!*

This was his land, his home, his heritage, and he felt the bond every day of his life.

He left the suite, leaving Matthews to follow with his bag. Only then did his valet express his annoyance with the travel arrangements by sighing loudly and dramatically.

Alex bit back his impatience, concentrating on the sights around him.

Mrs. McDermott made sure every inch of Blackhall was in pristine condition. He appreciated the housekeeper and made sure she knew it, giving her a Christmas stipend that ensured she couldn't be lured away from the castle.

A genuinely pleasant person, Mrs. McDermott

never failed to give excellent service and to do so without whining. Perhaps he should ask her for a valet recommendation. Matthews had been with him for years, but lately the man's behavior was grating.

His mother was right, they had lost a few maids recently. Sometimes, the lure of factory jobs in the city proved to be detrimental to their staffing requirements.

If they needed to increase their wages to entice new servants, he would have to review the situation. He didn't mind spending the money, but he wanted to ensure that the older staff members didn't feel as if they'd been cheated. He wanted harmony in all his homes and especially at Blackhall, where he spent most of his time.

He descended the staircase designed by Sir William Bruce a hundred fifty years ago when the older part of the castle had been renovated. However many times he saw it, he was always in awe of the engineering that had created the masterpiece. It reminded him of the curve of a shell, the inspiration for the gilded iron of the banister and the carved balusters. The staircase curved tightly onto itself, giving a panoramic view of the floors above and below. From here he could see the full entryway as well as the French doors in the rear of the main building leading to the terraced gardens.

At the bottom of the stairs he turned left, making his way down the wide corridor and to the east wing. Pushing open the door to his office, he entered a room filled with two desks, chairs, and three tables set in front of the windows.

His apprentice sat at one of the tables, hunched on a stool, a magnifying glass in one hand and a small card in the other. Jason was the son of Blackhall's head gardener and possessed of keen eyesight and a disregard of time that matched Alex's. He never caviled about putting in long hours. Nor did he have any outside interests other than his work. He was the perfect apprentice, eager to please, industrious, and intelligent.

If Alex faulted the young man for anything, it was that he was a little too perfect. Such people invariably disappointed.

Jason's hair was the color of straw, some strands lighter, as if the sun had bleached them. Until he'd offered the boy a position as his apprentice, Jason had spent nearly every day with his father, learning the gardening trade.

"It's not that I don't like seeing things grow, Your Grace," he'd said once. "It's that I've got no talent for it. Me da's got the gift. I've got the curse. Me da doesn't want me touching anything for fear I'll kill it before it has a chance to put down roots."

The head gardener had verified Jason's words by looking relieved when Alex informed him that he'd like his son to be his apprentice.

Jason had been with him ever since, appearing in the office when dawn lit the sky and working until Alex dismissed him.

"We're making a side trip before we go on to Inverness," he said, entering the room.

Jason glanced up, blinking at him.

"Your Grace?"

"A small personal errand," he said. "Have you packed the cases?"

"Yes, Your Grace."

Jason had copied all the names, occupations, and other details of his subjects onto lists that he was going to take to his Inverness home for safekeeping.

The original cards, the ones with the fingerprints, would remain at Blackhall. The lists, which included the dates he'd taken each print, would go a long way to proving that his discovery preceded that fool Simons. The Scottish Society had only to study the matter to agree.

Unfortunately, he'd learned that logic didn't often lead to the results he wanted. People were unpredictable. Besides, the society had already given him reason to distrust its decisions.

Still, he would try once more. He had a core of iron, a fact they would soon realize. So would the idiot—Lorna Gordon or Marie—who'd left the anonymous note for his mother.

"YOU GOING OUT walking again, Mrs. Gordon?"

Lorna heard the sneering tone in the landlady's voice and wondered if she talked like that to other people or only to her.

Every time she left her room of late, the woman was standing in the hallway watching her, just as she was now.

Mrs. MacDonald, if she'd been a color, would have been a blackish brown, the same shade as a fouled bog, or the color of marshland roots.

"Yes, Mrs. MacDonald, I am," she said, buttoning the top button of her cloak.

"To collect your herbs?"

She nodded, pulling on her gloves.

"I don't want you stinking up my house with those potions of yours."

"They're not potions, Mrs. MacDonald. They're herbal remedies."

"You have a lot of practice in those, do you?"

"My father was a botanist. I learned everything I know from him."

The other woman didn't respond. Instead, she peered down her long nose at Lorna.

Ever since she'd arrived in Wittan Village with her trunk and her story of being a widow, the landlady had watched her with narrowed eyes.

She hadn't expected her to ask so many questions.

"How did your husband die?" Mrs. MacDonald had asked two months ago.

"A carriage accident," she told her.

"You've no family to take you in?"

"No, my husband and I were both orphans."

"No cousins?"

"No cousins. No uncles. No aunts. No relatives of any kind."

That hadn't been a lie. Neither her mother nor father had large families. She'd been alone in the world and had only duplicated that history for her invented husband.

"I don't run a charity here, Mrs. Gordon," the landlady said now.

There was that tone again, when the woman called her *Missus*. Once more Lorna ignored it.

"Don't think you and your bairn have a place here without paying."

"No, Mrs. MacDonald."

The woman finally stepped aside, but Lorna could feel those cold blue eyes on her as she left the house. She was tired, but it was important that she harvest what she could, regardless of how she felt.

At least she was able to sell her remedies at the market. She'd come up with the idea in those terrible months of worry at Blackhall.

Several of the older women of the village used her comfrey joint balm to ease the arthritis in their hands. The Sunshine Ointment she made, so-called because its ingredients made it bright yellow, was helpful in drawing splinters from the skin and reducing the size of boils.

She blessed her education at her father's side. Hopefully, she would be able to continue to support herself using what she'd learned.

She often found herself wondering what her father would say about her current circumstances. He would probably have warned her against the excesses of passion, had she been brave or foolish enough to ask him about that. What would he have said about what Nan had done?

A week had passed and no one had come, which meant that the duchess didn't care if her son had a by-blow in the village. Or maybe the note had gotten lost. Someone could have torn it up before the duchess read it.

She needed to stop worrying and concern herself with the task at hand.

Still, if she'd had the money, she would have moved farther away. Blackhall Castle was too close, and so was the Duke of Kinross.

"HAS ALEX TRULY left for Inverness, Louise?"

The Dowager Duchess of Kinross hesitated in pouring her special blend of potpourri into one of the ceramic jars. She finished what she was doing before turning and smiling at Mary Taylor. The effort required to produce that smile was not noticed by the younger woman, but then Mary rarely saw anything beyond her own interests.

"Yes, Alex has left."

"In this weather? It's icy and snowing. How could you allow him to do such a thing?"

Louise bit back her impatience with some difficulty, managing to answer in a reasonably calm manner.

"Alex is a grown man, Mary. I do not dictate his movements."

"Someone should, if he's going to take such chances. Do you know how many carriage accidents happen in this kind of weather?"

If she didn't stop the younger woman, she was certain to be lectured with facts, figures, and hideous details. Mary read the newspapers and broadsheets from first page to last and accumulated data about horrors the way other women collected gloves, fans, or love letters. Unfortunately, she also had a good memory, which Louise fervently wished were put to better use.

Mary was Alex's sister-in-law. The woman had been at Blackhall for five years, ever since Ruth married Alex. As daughters of an impecunious earl, they'd lived in the family home for which Mary claimed a particularly dramatic attachment. Thornhill, however, was practically a ruin, with a destroyed tower and a roof like a sieve. Instead of spending a fortune repairing and restoring it, Alex had simply offered Mary a home here.

Louise had wished, on more than one occasion, that her son had spent the money on the Taylor family home.

Mary had a habit of bursting into her apartments with little provocation in order to make breathless announcements of minor events. Yesterday it was that the majordomo and Mrs. McDermott were at odds about the silver polish. The day before that it had been that

Alex hadn't appeared at breakfast and was he wasting away?

In addition to intruding on her privacy, the young woman sought her out everywhere, such as now in the family parlor. Blackhall possessed seventy-two rooms, and there were only a few places in the castle where she could escape from Mary.

Louise disliked traveling, but when the weather was better she was going to Edinburgh to hide in their home there. She would give out that she was going to Paris or staying with friends, anything but have Mary follow her. Not that she would as long as Alex was in residence at Blackhall.

"When is he going to return?" Mary asked.

"I don't know. When he does, I imagine."

"How many days, Louise?"

She really disliked being talked to in such a fashion, but for the sake of accord, she merely turned and went back to the potpourri.

"I don't know, Mary."

The woman had not endeared herself to Louise from the moment she'd met her. In that first encounter, Mary had made it known that she knew Louise's antecedents and, in her opinion, they failed to pass approval. Louise's grandfather was an earl, the same rank as Mary's father. Therefore, in Mary's mind, she was a more noble member of the nobility.

In that first meeting it had been evident that Mary was one of those people who had an opinion on everything and wished to share it with the world. Unfortunately, she never changed her opinion. Incidentals like new facts or information never altered what she believed about anything.

"He didn't tell me he was leaving."

"Do you require that he does so?" Louise asked, as pleasantly as she was able.

She occasionally wanted to put her hands on Mary's shoulders, look deep into her eyes, and tell the young woman that she had failed to grasp the reality of her situation. She was here because of Alex's generosity. She was not truly family. She had no right to question everything that went on at Blackhall. Or to comment endlessly about it. Unfortunately, giving Mary a stern talking to wouldn't change anything, least of all Mary's behavior.

Glancing over her shoulder at the other woman, she said, "You do realize that he has no obligation to report his comings and goings to you."

"Of course I do," Mary said, her cheeks deepening in color. "But he asks for my opinion on certain matters and I share my thoughts with him."

Unfortunately, Mary shared her thoughts with everyone. As to asking her opinion, Alex was a man of great tact when he wanted to be. She didn't doubt that her son had asked Mary's advice on something in order to be kind.

Being pleasant to people was more important than lineage, bloodline, or even a title. That knowledge had come to her from her grandfather, the earl, as well as her husband, the eighth Duke of Kinross, a man beloved for his kindness, not the fact that he was a duke.

How nice it would be if Mary could learn that lesson.

Louise hadn't found many people at Blackhall who liked the young woman, with the exception of her personal maid, Barbara, a woman who was known to carry tales, and the stable master, who praised Mary's seat.

Being a good horsewoman did not equate to possessing a good character, but Louise had never made that comment to Mary.

She wished Mary would take herself off to the stables now and spend some time with the new chestnut mare Alex had given her. She didn't begrudge her son one cent spent on his sister-in-law. She knew exactly why he did so, the same reason she would have gladly given Mary anything in order to be spared her presence. The more one kept Mary entertained, the happier everyone was.

More than once, she'd suggested that Mary travel to Inverness, there to be put under the tutelage of Louise's cousin, who had some reputation of guiding a young woman onto the matrimonial mart. Mary had countered that she was the daughter of an earl. Such a rank should be rewarded with an appropriate union. She wasn't, therefore, interested in marrying just anyone.

Louise wanted to tell the poor girl that she had as much chance of marrying a catch as a toad did of changing into a butterfly. She didn't, of course. Just because Mary was rude didn't mean she had to be.

Although Ruth had been an undisputed beauty, her younger sister hadn't the same appearance. Their hair was the same color, but Ruth's blond color had glorious gold and reddish highlights, while Mary's was rather dull. Ruth's nose had been aquiline and nearly perfect; Mary's had a hump on it and her nostrils were, regrettably, overlarge. Ruth's mouth had been generous but perfectly proportioned. Mary's, on the other hand, seemed abnormally large for her face and was made even more so by the fact that she never seemed to stop talking. Ruth's face had been a perfect oval. Mary preferred to pull her hair back into a bun, which only accentuated her wide, high forehead and pointed chin. But for the exact shade of blue eyes, one would be hard pressed to think the two women related at all.

Ruth had been amenable to change; Mary fought it. Ruth had laughed often, having the most delightful wit. Unfortunately, Mary was already curmudgeonly, although she was still a young woman.

Mary needed someone to take her in hand, smooth out her rough edges—while not revealing to her that she had any rough edges, of course—and present her as a fait accompli to a wealthy man in need of a presentable wife. Her antecedents were, as Mary might say, impeccable, perhaps even enough to counter her flaws. She might be the perfect mate for a wealthy merchant who wanted to brag about his marriage into the nobility.

The only problem with this plan was that Mary stuck to Blackhall like a burr, having adopted the castle and the family as her own, especially Alex.

She had an unhealthy fixation on her son, and it appeared to be growing stronger with each day.

"I'm certain he won't be gone long," Louise said. With any luck, her comment would satisfy Mary and the woman would go away.

What a pity it was a terrible day for riding.

Chapter 7

*W*inter left the Highlands with reluctance, evidenced by the sleet mixed with snow that greeted their arrival in Wittan Village. The interior of the carriage was warm from the brazier on the floor. The weather outside the carriage wouldn't prove as comfortable.

Alex gathered his greatcoat around him and opened the door.

"I'll be back in a few moments," he told Jason.

"Shall I accompany you, Your Grace?"

"No, it's a personal errand," he said, not wanting an audience to the coming confrontation.

The address listed on the note turned out to be a narrow house wedged between two others on a lane in the middle of Wittan Village.

Would the note writer be expecting him? Or would she be anticipating his mother's appearance? No doubt she thought Louise would provide any amount of money simply because she mentioned an infant. His child.

What blether.

He stood in the sleet and knocked on the door. His discomfort only fueled his irritation. He knocked again.

She wasn't going to ignore him. If she wasn't home now, then he'd return after he'd been to Inverness.

If she balked at confessing her effort at blackmail, he'd seek out the magistrate for this county. It would be her word against his. He doubted she'd be believed when he produced the anonymous letter in his pocket.

He put a little more effort into the next knock.

The door swung open.

"Awa ye go!"

He was instantly propelled to his childhood and the tales his nurse had told of the *wirrikow*, the demon who took on many forms.

The woman in front of him could easily be a *wirrikow*, with the three hairy moles dotting her chin. They pointed the way to the deep lines beside her mouth that met the vertical lines extending from the corners of her eyes. It was like her face had been folded a dozen times and then unfolded without any effort to smooth out the creases.

"Aye?" she said. "And what would you be wanting?"

She reeked of whiskey and he took a step back, ignoring the sleet for the ability to breathe.

"I don't know you," he said.

As inane a statement as he'd ever uttered, but he couldn't imagine that she was the author of the anonymous note.

She stared past him to his carriage and the crest on the door.

"I've heard tell of you. You're the Duke of Kinross, are you not? From Blackhall Castle?"

"Yes," he said.

"Come in, Duke," she said, holding the door open so he could enter.

He stayed where he was.

"Do you have someone living here who's expecting a child?"

The woman's grin took him aback. "Aye, but why would you be wanting to know, Duke?"

"I need to speak with her."

"Then come in. I can't heat the whole of the outdoors, even for the likes of you."

He entered the house reluctantly, finding himself in a dim, narrow hallway. The air smelled of onions and fish. The floor was dusty, the walls bare of any decoration other than stains. The ceiling sagged in places, making him wonder if the house was going to tumble down around his head.

"Where is she?" he asked, standing as far from the woman as he could.

She glanced at him almost flirtatiously.

"I run a good house here," she said. "I don't hold with male visitors to my female tenants."

"I can assure you, madam, that I have not come here for nefarious purposes. I need to speak with her about a matter of some urgency. Where is she?"

His greatcoat was sodden and his mood was as cold as the foyer. Pulling a few coins from his pocket, he extended his hand to her.

"I need to ask the woman a few questions, that's all," he said.

Evidently, her values were flexible as long as money was involved, because she took the coins, nodding to the second door.

Grateful to be quit of her, he strode down the hall and knocked once.

"Go ahead in, Duke. There's no lock on the door."

He didn't glance back at the woman, just pushed

down on the latch. When the door swung open, he entered the room.

The light from the tiny window revealed a narrow bed, a chest of drawers, and a series of pegs holding the occupant's clothing. The walls were stained but covered with drawings of flowers, their colors taking his eyes from the sparseness of the furnishings.

He didn't see her at first. She stood to his right, her back pressed up against the wall, staring at him as if she expected him to rob her or do her grievous bodily harm.

"You," he said.

He'd been right. Lorna Gordon was Marie.

He was instantly assaulted by memory. Marie, draping herself around him, her leg at his waist. Marie, kissing him mad. Marie, a virgin, the realization punctuating the whiskey and passion-induced fog.

For weeks, whenever he met anyone new on his trips to Inverness and farther, to Edinburgh, he expected to be given some carefully worded demand. He imagined being confronted by a stranger, someone who would identify himself as Marie's "friend" who only wanted to protect her. He never doubted that the protection would take the form of money, some absurd payment he was expected to produce in order to prevent a smear to his reputation.

To his surprise, no one had ever come forward.

Evidently she'd been waiting for this moment.

Her ginger-colored hair was wind-whipped and damp. Her large brown eyes, curiously tilted at the corners, gave her an almost exotic appearance. If nothing else, they encouraged a study of her face. She possessed something less common than beauty and more arresting. Her cheeks were red, her lips pink. Had she been biting them?

She had mud on her chin and it was also dripping from the hem of her dress. A cloak she held bunched in front of her was in a similar condition.

"Lorna Gordon, I presume," he said.

She moved to sit on the only chair in the small room, clutching her cloak in front of her.

Conscious of the landlady, he closed the door behind him and entered the room.

"The very rude Duke of Kinross."

Her voice was curiously educated, her accent one he couldn't decipher.

"Where are you from?"

"Where am I from?" she asked. "Does that matter?"

"Call it my curiosity. You don't sound like a maid."

"What is a maid supposed to sound like, Your Grace?"

"Inverness?" he asked.

"I lived there until I was twelve," she said. "After that, I traveled with my father. Robert Gordon. He was a well-respected botanist."

He glanced at the sketches on the wall. "Did he do those?"

"Does it matter?"

He was getting tired of her answering his questions with a question.

"Are they yours?"

This time she didn't respond.

"If they are, you're talented."

"I can sleep well tonight, knowing the Duke of Kinross approves."

He took a step toward her, noting when she tensed.

Did she expect him to strike her? He'd never touched a woman in anger, and the idea that she thought him capable of it was an irritant.

"What made you come to the fancy dress ball?"

"Foolishness," she said. "A decision I rue now."

"Did you really enjoy it?" he asked, remembering her parting words to him.

Her eyes widened. "Now, that, I have no intention of discussing."

Without giving her a hint of what he was going to do, he strode to the chair and jerked the cloak from her grasp, letting it fall to the floor.

One of her hands went to press against the mound of her stomach. The other clenched into a fist at her side.

He couldn't speak. What words could he possibly say? She was heavily pregnant. He couldn't lift his eyes, couldn't focus on anything but the size of her belly, the perfect roundness of it beneath the dark blue of her dress.

As he stared, he had the curious notion of movement, as if the baby were greeting him in his own way. He wanted, in a way that was unlike him, to put his hand there on that exact spot.

He dragged his attention back to her face.

"When is the baby due?" he asked.

"In a month or so."

"You were a virgin," he said. "Or was that some type of trick?"

She smiled, startling him again.

"I have no idea how to masquerade as a virgin, Your Grace."

"Are you trying to tell me that it's mine?"

"I'm not trying to tell you anything, except that you're not welcome here. Please leave."

"I don't believe you. It can't be mine."

"I didn't say it was," she said, giving him that look again. As if he'd marched into her spartan room with outrageous demands. "Please leave. Take yourself off. Go back to Blackhall. Forget me. Forget you and I ever met."

"We engaged in intercourse, Miss Gordon, but we never actually met."

She stared at a spot to his left. It took him a moment to realize she was trying to calm herself. The frantic beat of her pulse at her neck was clue enough that she was agitated.

"Then there's no reason for us to do so now," she finally said. "I shall pretend ignorance of your existence and I pray you'll do the same. Please leave. Get out of my life, Your Grace."

The last was said between clenched teeth.

He heard a noise and glanced at the door, certain that the slattern of a landlady was listening to them.

"What do you want? Money?"

Her eyes widened. "Is that all you can think, Your Grace? That people want something from you? I would think that would be a terrible way to live, always expecting someone to treat you abominably."

"That isn't an answer, Miss Gordon."

"What do I want? For you to leave. For you never to return. For you to forget that night as I have. For you to scrub your mind free of my name, my face, and anything else about me."

She'd called him a mouse. He'd never been able to forget the insult. A prancing mouse who'd been afraid someone would step on his tail.

"You wrote my mother."

"I did not."

The words were too emphatic to be a lie.

"Then who did?"

"It was a mistake. Accept that and forget it, Your Grace. Go away."

Even if he was able to forget her, there was the matter of his mother. She was not going to ignore Lorna's presence.

She stood quickly, grabbed the back of the chair and steadied herself.

"Please, leave. I want nothing from you but your absence."

He studied her and had the curious thought that she was telling the truth.

HER HEART WAS thumping loud enough to wake her child, who used his heels to punch at her from the inside. She pressed a hand reassuringly against her stomach and received another kick.

Sitting again, she stared up at the duke.

She'd never seen him anything but perfectly turned out. Never a hint of stubble. A wrinkle wouldn't dare appear on his person. Now he commanded her room in his severe black suit. His black hair was brushed back from a face that had always been clean shaven. His blue-green eyes sparkled with annoyance.

If she'd had watercolors she would have tried to replicate the exact color of his eyes, but all she had were her charcoal pencils. Her imagination always furnished the exact hue, however. Even as an old, old woman she'd be able to remember the Duke of Kinross.

He stood motionless, studying her. Even the curtains on the window stilled, the cold draft subdued by his presence.

Did he expect her to swoon because he was in her

cold, dark room? Well, she wasn't. He hadn't been invited here. She could live for an eon without seeing him again.

Why was he staring at her belly? Hadn't he ever seen a woman carrying a child before today? No doubt the women of his acquaintance hid themselves away in the latter months of their pregnancy.

One thing she did know: why she'd been so fascinated with him. He hadn't lost any of his good looks in the intervening months. If anything, he was more handsome than she remembered.

Instead of leaving, he pulled a letter from inside his jacket.

"Who wrote this?" he asked.

She saw no reason to involve Nan simply to answer the duke's question.

"It doesn't matter, Your Grace. Please leave. There's no need for you to be here."

"Is the child mine?" he asked.

She pressed her hand against the base of her throat, the better to slow her pulse a little.

How did she answer that? If she told him the truth, what would be the ramifications?

"Well?"

"What does it matter? I don't want anything from you."

"How will you support yourself?"

"I don't think that's any of your business. Why do you care?"

"Is the child mine?" he repeated.

"You're as annoying as a magpie," she said. "The same call over and over again. Very well, I can be the same. Go away. Go away. Go away. Go away." She added one more for good measure. "Go away."

Perhaps she should have been more cautious in her speech. After all, he was the Duke of Kinross, capable of changing a person's fortunes on a whim. Yet she'd never heard of him behaving capriciously.

His sister-in-law still lived at Blackhall even years after her sister died. Mary Taylor was an exceedingly annoying woman yet the duke had opened his home to her. Surely that showed a generous nature. There were other tales of his kindness, some of which might simply be rumors. He was supposed to be rebuilding the roof of the Wittan Village church and making other changes there as well. She knew, for a fact—having been delegated to arrange the donations—that Blackhall was generous to the poor. Plus, the duke always gave the staff an annual Christmas present. She'd saved that money, the amount making up most of her savings.

Perhaps the duke only acted in an autocratic manner when it came to women who annoyed him or who didn't bow and scrape enough. She was too big to curtsy at this point. She might fall down if she tried.

"My mother says you make potions."

"I sincerely doubt that Her Grace called them potions," she said.

"Unguents," he said, waving his hand in the air. "Lotions. Something for the stiffness in her hands."

She stood, walked to the end of the bed to the small trunk sitting there. She opened it, pulled out a jar, walked back and handed it to him.

"This is what she used in the past," she said.

"How much do you charge for it?"

"The price for it is your absence," she said. "If you leave now, take it with my blessing."

"And if I don't? How much do you charge?"

How had she ever been attracted to this man? How had she thought he was the most handsome creature she'd ever seen? Why had her heart beat so rapidly when she saw him in his kilt? How did the sound of his voice make her skin tighten?

Evidently, her body was not connected to her mind, because even now she couldn't help but recall how he'd kissed her senseless.

She was the stupidest woman alive.

"For the love of all that's holy, Your Grace, will you leave?"

She could just imagine what tales Mrs. MacDonald would tell. The woman was probably listening now.

"I don't want anything from you. I'm sorry someone left the duchess a note. All I want is to be left alone. Please."

Thankfully, he moved to the door, the jar still in his hand.

She'd expected a last barrage of questions, but all he did was glance at her sketches on the wall and open the door.

Just as she'd suspected, Mrs. MacDonald was on the other side, a sly grin on her face.

Lorna sighed inwardly.

They both watched the duke leave the house. The moment the door closed behind him, Mrs. MacDonald rounded on her.

"You're no widow, miss. You're the worst of the worst. I've seen your type, girls who pretend to be better than you are. You're the duke's mistress. Why else would he come here?"

The frontal attack wasn't completely unexpected.

The duke had set things in motion by his appearance. Did he have any idea of the damage he'd done to her? Did he care?

"The Duke of Kinross came for some medicine for his mother," she said. "The comfrey balm is for her arthritis."

Mrs. MacDonald ignored her.

"I'm going to tell Reverend McGill. We'll pray over you, but women like you only bring down good folk."

What could she possibly say to the woman?

She closed the door before her landlady could say another word. Standing at the tiny window, she watched as the duke's carriage disappeared from sight, feeling a strange confusion. She didn't want to see him. She never wanted to see him again. Yes, she'd once been enamored of his appearance and charmed by his smile. Good looks didn't mean a good heart. Nor could she forget the words he'd said to her that night.

Her father had always told her, *A mistake done once is acceptable, Lorna, but twice is the act of a fool.*

She had no intention of playing the fool around the Duke of Kinross. Not again. One life-changing mistake was enough.

Without his charm, he was a little frightening, the look in his eyes daring her to challenge him. But she had, hadn't she? She asked him to leave and he had. A lesson, that. She was not without power in the face of the almighty Duke of Kinross.

The young girl she'd been, wise in the ways of herbs but not men, had nearly swooned over the sight of him. She'd fixed his image in her mind to recall during boring tasks or sleepless nights. She'd marked each separate minute in his company, how he looked, when he smiled, if he glanced in her direction.

That girl had disappeared in the last few months and she'd never return.

Hopefully, the duke wouldn't, either.

But the damage had already been done.

Chapter 8

"Well? Did you see her?" his mother asked.

Alex took off his greatcoat, handing it to one of the footmen.

He went to his mother and kissed her cheek, unsurprised when she enfolded him in a hug. She never said anything before he left Blackhall, but she was always demonstrably joyful on his return.

She pulled back and slapped her hand against his chest.

"It's been a long week and I've been patient, but you must answer me. Did you see Lorna?"

"Yes, I saw Lorna," he said, taking her arm and walking with her into the family parlor. "Where's Mary?" he asked, surveying the room.

"One of the horses has bloat," his mother said. "She's at the stables."

They glanced at each other, complicit in their enjoyment of time free from Mary's constant prattle.

He waited until she sat, then took the chair opposite her.

His mother was as tenacious as a terrier. He expected her next comment and smiled when she made it.

"The child is yours, of course," she said, skewering him with a look.

"She wouldn't tell me."

She tilted her head slightly and regarded him in that way of hers.

"Do you believe the child is yours?"

He stood and walked to the sideboard, where he poured himself a whiskey, the first since that night. Instead of sitting, he walked to the window.

The view was of the north approach to the castle and beyond to Loch Gerry. Everything he could see belonged to the Russell clan and to him as its laird and the Duke of Kinross.

The ownership and the responsibility had never been a burden. From the moment he was born he'd been groomed and trained to manage Blackhall and its lands. Every lesson he'd learned from his tutors and later at school had been to further his understanding of what it meant to be duke. He was educated in mathematics in order to understand the wealth that was his to use and grow. He'd learned about Highland cattle and sheep, how to farm those properties owned in the south of Scotland. He could recite, by rote, all the various tracts and buildings owned in England and all the accounts under his name. He knew, down to a few decimal points, how much his investments had accumulated, what his working capital was, and how much he'd added to the Russell coffers.

He knew his place in the world, what was expected of him, and how he could best achieve his goals.

Lorna Gordon had shifted all that.

Perhaps it wasn't fair to blame her for his sudden disorientation. He was as responsible. He'd been an idiot that night, ridden by lust.

"Is there a possibility it could be your child, Alex?"

"I've never heard of . . ." He stumbled to a halt. He'd

been about to say something personal and private to his mother, for the love of God.

She grabbed the frame for her embroidery, picked up the needle and began stabbing at the fabric.

He wondered what she would do with this project. More than one had been completed and then carefully slashed.

"I hate needlework," she told him when he'd first seen her do it. "But it's either that or whiskey."

He wondered if she still felt the same. Perhaps he should pour her a glass and urge her away from the bright flowered pattern on a beige background. Would she destroy this one, too, or would it become another cover for a footstool?

"Well?" she asked, glancing up at him. "You never heard of what?"

"I can't say."

"You must." She pursed her lips, an expression of impatience he'd seen since he was a boy. "We must discuss this issue. Now is not the time for you to be reticent."

Reticent? That word was hardly fair. It wasn't being reticent to refrain from talking about intercourse with his mother.

He only shook his head.

"Why can't the baby be yours? Did you not have an affair with the woman?"

"No," he said, glancing at her. "I did not. It was only the once."

Her eyebrows rose. "And? It only takes the once, Alex. Surely you know that."

"She's taking advantage of the situation," he said.

"How so? Did she demand money from you?"

"No, she ordered me out of her lodgings."

She'd sat there, stubborn and proud, his recollection of her gaze not unlike that memory of seven months earlier when she'd called him a mouse.

"Your picture of Lorna is not one that I have," she said. "Does she have a delightful smile? And the loveliest brown eyes?"

"Yes."

"That's most definitely Lorna. She's always had such a sweet disposition."

Sweet? He wouldn't label the woman sweet.

After tucking the needle in the top of the fabric, his mother sat back.

"Why are you uncertain about the baby, Alex?"

"She had never . . ." No, the word wouldn't pass his lips.

"She was a virgin?"

He took a sip of his whiskey. "It was only the one time."

"Oh, Alex, I never thought you could be so naive. Of course the baby could be yours. I would urge you to go look in the mirror if you doubt that."

"What?"

Her smile broadened. "Your father was virile, my son, while I was fertile. Nine months to the day of our wedding, you were born. Like father, like son?"

Bloody hell.

"What are you going to do?"

He didn't have any idea. Normally, when he faced a roadblock, he never stopped looking for a way around it. In this part of the Highlands an occasional landslide would obliterate a track around a mountain. He didn't turn around and return to his starting point. He just cleared the road. He faced any other obstacles in his life the same way.

Unless the obstacle was a woman heavily pregnant.

"What if the child is yours?" she asked. "Can you ignore its existence?" Her gaze didn't move from his face. "I don't know how you could. I would hope that you wouldn't."

She straightened her shoulders, placed one hand over the other and stared up at him, unsmiling.

"You've given no thought to marrying again, Alex. You've expressed no desire to do so."

"Why on earth should I? And have my wife bed half of Edinburgh?"

She shook her head. "One bad experience should not color your reaction to all women, Alex."

"What I've seen hasn't led me to give your sex the benefit of the doubt, Mother."

"You have no children, Alex. Did you never think that this might be your only child?"

"No, I hadn't."

Her smile thinned. "Such things normally happen in the course of events, my son. You should have considered that before you took her to your bed."

That wasn't exactly how it had happened.

"Do you dislike her so much, then, Alex? Why would you bed someone you dislike?"

"I don't dislike her," he said, feeling his way through the words. "She's not what I expected." She'd asked him to leave. No, she'd demanded it. He could still see the antipathy in her glare. "She has a great deal of pride."

"You mean for a maid."

He glanced at her.

"She was forced into service by circumstances, I believe. Most women are."

He'd honestly never thought about why someone would come to work at Blackhall. He'd taken the servants for granted, that they would be there when he needed something done, that his meals would be prepared, that his rooms would be cleaned. He didn't think about it any more than he thought about Blackhall's many roofs.

But the servants were people, not tiles.

"She draws," he said.

"She does?"

"Quite well, too."

"Does she?"

He glanced at her. There was a note in her voice he couldn't identify.

"I found her to be a woman of good character," she said, picking up her embroidery once again.

She didn't speak for a moment and he didn't rush to fill the silence with words.

"Why is a woman considered fallen while the man is exempt from any responsibility?" she finally said. "Women who have children out of wedlock are treated badly, Alex. They're rebuffed and reviled, seen as creatures of sin. They can't work if they have a baby to care for."

She frowned at one offending flower and sent her needle like a sword into the fabric.

"Perhaps that's why there are so many baby farmers."

"Baby farmers?" he asked.

She nodded. "Mary told me about them. An article she read in the newspaper. They're women who advertise that they'll care for the infant for a small fee. Most poor girls in Lorna's situation have no choice. They have to go back to work and they have no one to care for their children. Unfortunately, most of those babies die of starvation or neglect."

She sighed, shook her head at her needlework, then glanced up at him.

"I do hope that Lorna is not forced to do such a thing. Does she have any resources?"

He shook his head.

She lived in a hovel. He didn't like remembering her small dark lodgings. The room was cold, the air stagnant with unpleasant smells.

Why had there been mud on her face?

She was sticking to his mind in a way that most women didn't. A series of vignettes replayed themselves in a loop: Lorna with her dress twisted around her waist, her voluptuous breasts revealed in the dim light. Lorna, held captive by laughter as her wig disappeared into the storm. Lorna, her hand on the door latch, wanting to escape the ball. Lorna, heavily pregnant. And one that he remembered too well: Lorna, glancing up at him with contempt in her gaze, as if he were the most loathsome creature on earth.

He was most assuredly not a prancing mouse.

To the best of his knowledge, he'd never fathered another child. He'd always had his wits about him, not to mention discretion. That night, that infamous night—for which he would pay dearly for the rest of his life—was unlike anything he'd ever experienced. Whiskey was partly to blame, but lust was responsible for the rest of it.

He'd had to have her. If it had been up against a wall, he would've done that, too. If Mary had succeeded in interrupting them, he would have turned his head and growled at her, "Go the hell away." Nothing could have come between him and Lorna. Nothing, and he'd never felt that way about another woman.

He should go to his office and concentrate on the treatise he was about to submit to the society. He'd come up with a way of classifying the fingerprints he'd obtained in Inverness. He was separating each fingerprint into quadrants and labeling them by the predominance of each sworl and curve. That way, he could more easily identify a subject than if he had to scan through hundreds and, hopefully—as time progressed—thousands of cards.

He glanced over at his mother. She was smiling as she stared at the embroidery pattern, but he knew that smile was for him.

"I think the child is mine," he said. "Even though she wouldn't admit it."

His child. The knowledge was like a blow to his chest.

Lorna hadn't tried to convince him. She hadn't charmed him or even smiled at him. All she wanted was his absence.

At his comment, his mother's right eyebrow arched toward her forehead. She had the most expressive brows of anyone he'd ever seen. Without a word spoken, she could castigate, ridicule, or question.

He didn't doubt that she was doing all three right now.

"I'll send for Edmonds," he said, "and provide for her and the child. She won't have to worry. She certainly won't need the services of a baby farmer."

"That's generous of you, Alex."

"We contribute to several good causes," he said. He would simply view Lorna as another one.

Once he was certain she was settled, he wouldn't have to think about her any further. He could go about his life without his conscience whispering to him.

As far as his memory, he would do everything in his power to forget her.

Chapter 9

$\mathcal{L}$orna put on her cloak and gathered up her herbs, all neatly tied with ribbon. She'd carefully penned instructions for their use either as a tea or a soak. A more difficult task than it had seemed at first because her fingers were stiff from the cold.

She'd managed to avoid her landlady for two days, but she wasn't so lucky when she opened the door.

Mrs. MacDonald was standing there waiting for her.

"You make sure you sell enough of those herbal remedies of yours to pay the rent."

Every week when she went to market, the landlady said the same thing. Every Wednesday she gave the woman the same answer.

"I'll do my best, Mrs. MacDonald."

"You see that you do. I'm not a poorhouse."

Short of bodily moving the woman, she had to stand there and listen to her harangue. She was not going to hang her head low. Nor was she going to cry. Doing so would only please Mrs. MacDonald, but it wouldn't soften her heart.

"If I don't get to the market," she said after a moment, "I won't be able to sell anything. The best spots will be taken. Do you want your rent?"

Greed evidently worked when nothing else did.

The woman stepped back, letting her escape.

The day was bitterly cold and stormy, with cold drizzly rain that was mostly ice. Despite the weather, the market was crowded. She found a place near the end of the first row to set up.

Although she saw many of her regulars, she wasn't making as many sales as she had the week earlier, which was a disappointment. She'd promised herself that if she made the same as then, she would splurge and buy some coal to heat her room.

Several villagers passed her table without glancing at her once. Only old Mrs. McGowan stopped by to comment about the cold.

"It's the *faoilteach*," the woman said. "That's why my joints hurt so bad."

She went on to tell Lorna that, according to the Highland superstition, the weather between the eleventh and fifteenth of February predicted the rest of the spring weather. The worse the *faoilteach*, the better the weather to come.

Yet however pleasant Mrs. McGowan was, the woman didn't buy anything.

Lorna didn't have a wide selection of herbs and preparations. The comfrey balm was popular. So, too, the St. John's Wort oil, which could be used in a variety of remedies. In addition, the mint teas were popular throughout the year.

One by one the people she knew passed her by, making her smile feel stiff, and not from just the cold. The market was her only source of income and she couldn't afford to go into her savings yet. That was for when the baby was born and she wouldn't be able to harvest any herbs or come to the market for a few weeks.

She was not going to be despondent. Her sales might pick up before market day was over.

"What have you to say for yourself, woman?"

Startled, she glanced up to find Reverend McGill striding toward her small stall.

She attended services each Sunday, ever since arriving at Wittan Village two months earlier, enduring McGill's earnestly grim sermons. He mourned the old days of publicly shaming a sinner and said so often.

She met with him that first week because to do otherwise would be to elicit the suspicions of the villagers, not to mention Mrs. MacDonald. He'd offered his condolences on the loss of her husband, a falsehood that made her conscience itch. She wanted to confess her ruse yet she realized how important it was to maintain the appearance of a widow, one so desperately poor that she couldn't even afford to dye her dresses black.

The pretense had worked, at least until the Duke of Kinross had shown up at her door. Damn him.

The appearance of the minister at the market wasn't wholly unexpected. Mrs. MacDonald had threatened to speak to him days ago. Evidently, the woman had found the opportunity to do so. Lorna thought she might be addressed after church services, but she never thought Reverend McGill would choose the crowded square to single her out.

The man was dressed in severe black with a white knotted neckpiece. His bushy hair was gray and so were the sideburns and the beard that cupped the lower half of his face. A thin mouth and deep vertical grooves etched into his skin indicated that this was a man who didn't see much humor or good in the world.

"Is it true that you have whored?" he asked.

She knew, only too well, that the man could shout the rafters down. Any moment now he was going to raise his orator's voice so the entire village could hear him.

What could she say to stop him? Not one word or explanation came to mind.

It was the Duke of Kinross's fault. God should not have created such a beautiful creature. I was only human.

Hardly something she would say to a minister, especially Reverend McGill.

Nan had warned her, but she had never envisioned a scene like this. She met the eyes of several of the villagers she had gotten to know over the last months. Mrs. McGivry, who bought her tea to soothe her toothache. Mr. Wilson, who used her comfrey balm to ease the ache in his back. Their eyes were flat and condemning, even as Reverend McGill's voice grew louder.

He pointed a long bony finger at her and asked, "Are you a widow or a whore, Lorna Gordon?"

She was too late. His voice was already loud enough to summon the dead from their graves.

People stopped and turned. The entire village seemed to be on the green, and each inhabitant was now staring at her.

Her cheeks prickled with warmth.

His attention dropped to her stomach. She placed her hand atop it as if to protect her child from his venomous look.

He stepped toward her, reached into his cloak, and pulled out a Bible.

"Swear to your widowhood, woman," he said, stretching out his hand. "And no one will gainsay you. Upon this holy book will you swear to be free of fornication and whoredom?"

He wanted her to swear that she'd been married? That she wasn't an unwed mother?

When she hesitated, he smiled.

"God sees your sin, daughter," he said, the Bible still held out in front of her.

What did he expect her to do, fall to her knees and beg for his forgiveness? Would that work? She'd never heard of the man comforting anyone. But condemnation? He evidently relished that part of his ecclesiastical duties.

He stood in the same stance, arm outstretched, hand holding the Bible, legs widened, almost as if he were going into battle. Did he think that she epitomized the Devil himself? Did the good reverend see himself on the side of the angels?

At first there were only a few people behind Reverend McGill. Then they formed a ring around the reverend and her. Now the circle was three deep, as if the entire village had left their houses on this miserable gray afternoon and were intent on watching this drama play out.

ALEX ENTERED THE carriage after giving his driver instructions to take him to Wittan Village. He was under no illusions that Charles was ignorant of who he was going to see. The man might be the epitome of tact, but he kept his eyes and ears open.

Alex had never thought to be in this situation. He'd behaved in a way that would have outraged his father. No doubt the situation would amuse his uncle no end. If possible, he wanted to make sure Thomas never heard about Lorna.

Outside the village, the carriage slowed, then came to a stop. Alex heard his driver's voice through the metal grate.

"Your Grace, it looks like there's some kind of disturbance in the village square."

"What kind of disturbance?"

"It's a mob, sir, and they're surrounding a woman."

When Charles spoke again, there was a curious note to his voice.

"Your Grace, it appears to be Miss Gordon."

Of course Charles would know her.

Alex opened the carriage door and left the vehicle, striding toward the crowd.

"Your Grace, do you want me to come with you?" Charles called after him.

"No, stay with the carriage," he said.

Rank did have some privileges, one of those being that people listened to him. Yet he'd never faced down such a large mob before, one that was eerily quiet. The only voice he heard was a stentorian one, speaking of hellfire, damnation, and the evils of sin.

LORNA WAS MORE than willing to swear on the Bible if it meant protecting her child, even if the price she paid was being doomed to eternal judgment. But she'd waited too long. When she raised her hand to place it on the book, Reverend McGill withdrew his arm.

"The Session has met, daughter. They wish you gone from this place before you soil others with your presence. These good people have no wish to have a fornicator and a harlot in their midst."

She knew enough about the Presbyterian religion to know that a Session was a meeting of church elders, men who were often influential in village life. Perhaps she was fortunate that the Reverend McGill hadn't appeared with a contingent of angry men.

"Who is the father of your child?"

"Does that matter? Isn't it my sin that's the topic of discussion?"

She shouldn't have said anything. She'd just made the situation worse, if that was possible.

His face grew more florid. His lips thinned to the point they disappeared in his face.

"Not only a fornicator and a harlot but a blasphemer! You will not name him?"

"He's not a villager," she said.

They stared at each other for a moment that lasted as long as a week. He could stand there and huff and puff, but she wasn't going to say anything else. He'd already essentially banished her from the village. If he could, he would have put her in a cage in the village square. Behold, an object lesson.

"The good citizens of Wittan value their immortal souls. Unlike you. The congregants do not want you here."

She and her father had often been looked at strangely during their travels. His, after all, was an odd occupation. As a botanist he was more interested in plants than people. To that end, he would go anywhere to see something that other people rarely saw or wouldn't care about if they did. She'd often heard people jeer or deride him in the places they stayed. They didn't know about his three books or that he had been a widely respected professor. He was just an odd man who climbed hills or traipsed through bogs to find things that grew in weird places.

It doesn't matter what other people think, he'd said when she had the courage to mention the comments.

This was the first time she thought he might have

been wrong. As she watched Reverend McGill, she realized it mattered what other people thought of her.

"Do you think news of your sin hasn't traveled far and wide, daughter? Not only have you transgressed, but you show no signs of remorse. Nor have you asked forgiveness of the congregation." He stepped forward. "And you entered into sin with one of those among us who should be above reproach."

To her surprise, he turned and pointed at someone else.

"Fornicator!"

Shocked, she watched as the Duke of Kinross stepped out of the crowd.

He took in what was happening with one glance, then strode toward the reverend. Whatever he said to McGill silenced the minister.

The duke came to stand in front of her. "Get your things," he said. "I'm taking you out of here."

"I can't leave," she said. "It's market day."

"I don't know if you noticed, Miss Gordon, but it's about to be a market riot. Gather up your things."

He swept up the bundles of herbs on the table, bruising half of them.

"Don't do that," she said, pushing his hand aside to gather them up with more care.

A moment later she glanced at the silent minister. He might not be talking, but he was certainly glaring at her.

"What did you say to him?" she asked the duke.

"I told him that if he wanted the church roof replaced, he'd be better off finding another sinner to expose."

Her eyes widened. "You would do that?"

"Yes, I would do that."

He grabbed her arm, but she shook it off.

"I'm not going with you," she said in a low voice. "Don't you understand? That's the worst thing I could do. I can just imagine what Mrs. MacDonald would say."

"Who?"

"My landlady."

"I don't care about Mrs. MacDonald," he said. "But you're not safe here."

"I would have been fine but for you."

"I beg your pardon?"

"If you hadn't come here," she said, "no one would have known. I was getting by."

"You're living in a hovel."

"I was getting by," she said.

He ignored her. "Don't you have a warmer coat? You're nearly blue with cold. Your cloak is too thin and your gloves are inadequate."

"Fashion criticism from a duke?" She frowned at him. "I don't care what you think about my attire, Your Grace."

"You're coming with me. If you wish to make a scene, that's fine. I don't care. You're still coming with me."

"No one's going to hurt me. I'm perfectly safe here."

He lowered his head almost as if he were going to kiss her. "Look around you, Lorna."

She glanced at the reverend, who was standing there scowling at both of them, then at the crowd milling closer. Nan's words came back to her. *Mothers will cross the street rather than allow you near their children. Men will leer at you. You'll be the face of sin.*

She had never expected to see the condemnation on the faces of some of the sweet ladies who'd purchased balms from her, or the men who'd been so gracious when she first arrived.

"If you'll escort me back to my room, then," she said.

"Only to get your things."

Did he think she had somewhere to go? She wasn't like him, with homes in half a dozen cities.

He pushed through the crowd, still holding onto her hand. To her surprise, the villagers parted, but they didn't do so silently. She had never heard some of the words shouted at her, but she was well aware of others.

She was not a whore and she wanted to plant her feet right there and defend herself. The duke was having none of it.

She nodded to the duke's driver, a man she knew from Blackhall. Charles was a burly figure with a pockmarked face and a nose that had been pummeled a time or two. His hair was a mixture of black and gray, like her father's had been. Charles was known as a peacemaker among the staff. If there was a disagreement, people let him mediate it. If an actual fight occurred, someone always summoned him to break it up.

She suddenly noticed the distance from the ground to the vehicle.

"How am I supposed to get up there?" she asked.

In the first six months her stomach was only a small bump. Since then she'd ballooned up until she was having difficulties seeing her feet. Putting on her shoes was a challenge each morning.

"There are steps," he said, bending down to unfurl them. "If you'll allow me to assist you?"

How was he going to do that? She felt as large as Charles, but all her girth was in the front. Nor had she been particularly graceful of late.

She had to get into the carriage somehow. Better to grit her teeth, chew on her pride, and let him help.

Placing her right hand on his arm, she glanced at him.

"I can't see the step," she said, her cheeks feeling on fire.

She felt his hand on her right foot.

"If you'll just lift it and allow me to guide you," he said.

She did, thinking she was bound to topple backward. He placed his left hand on the small of her back in support. Somehow, he helped her step up, taking her weight on his arm and pushing with his hand on her back.

"Now for the other foot," he said, repeating the effort.

Incredibly, she made it inside the carriage and gratefully sank onto the seat.

"Was your wife as large in the latter days of her pregnancy?" she asked.

"I don't know," he said. "I didn't spend much time at Blackhall."

Shocked, she watched as he sat in front of her.

"You don't know?"

"No."

He had the most annoying habit of reducing her to silence.

Chapter 10

*I*t only took a minute to reach her lodgings. Lorna dreaded seeing Mrs. MacDonald, who had either heard of the meeting in the square or had attended it.

"She's thrown your belongings in the street."

She glanced out the window to find that he was right. Everything she owned, pitiful amount that it was, had been tossed into a heap in front of Mrs. Mac-Donald's house.

Two boys were rifling through her trunk. She doubted they'd find anything of interest unless they were fascinated with bottles and dried herbs. But her father's manuscript was in the bottom of the trunk and they couldn't be allowed to touch that.

Before she could say anything, the duke had opened the carriage door, and while the vehicle was still moving slowly, he was there. The boys ran away, but he didn't try to catch them. All he did was gather up everything and place it in the trunk. Charles dismounted and loaded it atop the vehicle.

She was too stunned to protest, too shocked to make a sound.

What was she going to do? Where was she going to go now? Her meager savings, sewn into her petticoat, would be enough to rent another room, but where?

The next village was miles away, which meant Nan wouldn't be able to visit her again.

While Charles and the duke were talking, the door of the house opened to reveal Mrs. MacDonald standing there, a stained apron tied at her waist, a sneer on her face.

"Aye, you've got a trout in the well, don't ye? I'll not have your like in my house, Miss Gordon. I'd suggest you seek out the parish poorhouse, but they only take women of good character."

Mrs. MacDonald wasn't finished. Her voice rose to a shout. "You'll need someplace to go when the duke tires of you. I hear they need women in Australia. All they care about is that you're warm, a woman, and willing. You could find a home there, you and your cludfawer."

When the duke entered the carriage, he blocked Lorna's view of her former landlady.

"Cludfawer?" he asked.

"An illegitimate child," she said softly.

"Don't pay her any attention," he said, settling in opposite her. As they began to move, he startled her again by taking off his coat and tucking it around her. "You're cold."

Other than Nan, it was the first time anyone had been kind to her for months.

Of course she wanted to weep. The day had been eventful and horrid.

ALEX WAS TRYING to marshal his thoughts into some semblance of order.

He hadn't expected to see Lorna standing there, proud in her thin coat, facing the weight of the village's disapproval. The bulge of her stomach was obvious to a blind man. So, too, her defiance. She'd stood there alone, facing the reverend with more courage than he'd ever seen.

She was beautiful in a way he'd never before considered. In a way that was elemental and spoke to the continuation of the species.

The night of the ball he'd expected her to be experienced, not virginal. And now? Hardly virginal, but delicate, almost innocent, with her red cheeks, her warm brown eyes, and a mouth that smiled slightly while hinting at delicious kisses.

She'd been amply endowed before. He could still recall the shape of her breasts in his hands. But carrying a child had added to them, until they pressed against her bodice. He wanted, in an impulsive way quite unlike him, to reach out and press his hands against them to measure their weight. No doubt she'd slap him if he dared do something like that.

He knew, without asking, that she would nurse her child. Ruth would not have, and had already hired a wet nurse, the woman ready to be summoned after the delivery.

He settled back against the seat, allowing himself to open the door to thoughts of those days three years ago. Nothing beyond the conception of the child had involved him. He'd been informed of what would happen, but he'd never been consulted. Men weren't, he'd been told. His opinion hadn't been sought, either.

It was as if the birth of his heir didn't concern him one whit.

Perhaps it hadn't at that point. His emotional estrangement from Ruth had led to a physical separation. He'd spent more and more time in Edinburgh, until he'd finally come home three weeks before the baby was expected. However, he'd used his own initiative and hired a doctor. A useless precaution, as it turned out.

The birth had been difficult from the beginning. He knew something was wrong when the midwife had requested his mother be in attendance and she, in turn, had sought out the physician he brought with him.

Two people trained in the art of birth attended Ruth, yet they couldn't save her. At first it had seemed the child might survive, but that wasn't to be, either. He'd been a little boy with a perfect porcelain face who appeared to be sleeping. His mother had held his child and rocked him for a few moments, tears falling down her face.

He'd walked out of the room without speaking to anyone.

Now he was faced with the same god-awful situation.

Why hadn't Lorna protected herself? Why hadn't he? Why had he allowed lust to overwhelm him when he'd never done so before?

It was her, of course.

Even now the attraction was evident. He shouldn't be lusting for a woman so far gone with child. But it was his child. That shouldn't have aroused him, either.

What was the word? Gravid? He'd never considered it before, but it meant full, didn't it? She'd been empty and now she was full. He'd done that.

Perhaps it was something merely biological between them. A random act that had been ordained because she was female and he was male. He knew he'd never done anything so precipitous. Nor had he ever wanted another woman the way he'd wanted her. Enough that he hadn't bedded anyone since.

She was going to have his child.

Fate couldn't have picked a more confusing woman than Lorna Gordon. First she was a mystery, then a ghost. She'd been a maid, yet she was filled with pride. He'd expected her to be greedy, but she'd banished him from her room.

They were strangers who'd had an intimate encounter, one resulting in a child.

At Blackhall he would ensure she had whatever she needed. Once she was there, perhaps this fascination she held for him would ease. He would be able to return to his work without images of her appearing before him.

He'd summon a new doctor, someone with more expertise in birth, and keep him at Blackhall until she delivered. He'd install a different, more competent midwife. He'd check in on Lorna every day. He'd know what was happening, unlike before.

There, a plan, and one he would implement immediately.

"What were you doing there? Did Reverend McGill send for you?"

"Send for me? No. I wouldn't have come even if the reverend had dared to summon me."

"Then what were you doing in Wittan?"

"I am willing to concede that the child you are carrying is mine."

"How very kind of you."

He ignored her sarcasm. "In addition, my mother thinks highly of you, as does Mrs. McDermott."

"While I am grateful for such a character reference, I really don't care what you think of me."

"You can't return to Wittan Village."

Her eyes narrowed and her lips thinned. She glared at him as if he were the most loathsome creature she'd ever seen.

"How will you support your child?"

"That is none of your concern."

"Come to Blackhall," he said. "There's a small cottage on the grounds that used to belong to the gamekeeper. I'll have it prepared for you. You can live there with your child. All I ask is to be able to visit from time to time. You'll be given an allowance and the child will be educated as befits his station in life."

"As what, a bastard?"

"No," he said stiffly. "As my child." When she didn't respond, he said, "I'm offering you a home, Miss Gordon."

"Everyone will know."

"Everyone knows now. Or do you think you're immune to gossip? The minute my mother read that letter, word spread."

She turned away, staring out at the view of the icy scenery.

What the hell was she thinking?

"If you go anywhere else, the same thing will happen. Maybe not right away, but eventually. You'll be isolated, cut off from others by condemnation. That won't happen at Blackhall."

She glanced at him. "So you'll command people to be pleasant to me, is that it? You'll dictate how they feel, what they say?"

"No. They'll respect you because you're a family guest."

She turned back to the window.

What else could he say to convince her? Blackhall

was not unlike a village, but at least he could control how she was treated there. He couldn't do anything in another village.

"What would your father want?" he asked, searching for something to say. "What would he want you to do?"

"You don't know my father. He didn't care about what other people said."

"But he'd never been unmarried and pregnant, had he? Don't be stupid and stubborn."

"Don't be ducal and despicable."

He considered her for a moment. He had handled the whole matter clumsily. He needed to be more charming and perhaps more honest.

"I came to Wittan to tell you that I believe the child you carry is mine. I'm willing to provide for you. I've settled an amount of money on you to be administered by my solicitor. However, that does not make your situation any easier. As I said before, even if you go and live in another village, you're bound to be found out eventually and treated exactly the same. Come and live at Blackhall. You won't face that kind of intolerance."

"I won't be your mistress," she said.

One of his eyebrows arched upward. "Not in the condition you are, surely."

"My declaration is hardly amusing," she said.

"Amusing? God forbid," he said. "This is the least amusing situation I've ever found myself in."

"If I return to Blackhall you must let people know."

"Must I?"

She nodded. "I don't want it bandied about that we're lovers. It's one thing to have made a terrible mistake once, but to compound it would be idiotic."

At the time, she'd said she enjoyed herself. Had she changed her mind?

"Promise me," she said, "that you'll make it known that I'm not your mistress."

"How am I to do that? Call a meeting of the staff? Oh, by the way, the enceinte Miss Gordon and I have had no relationship at all."

He focused on her. She didn't look away.

"Do you think they'll believe that?" he asked.

She took a deep breath before answering.

"I can't do anything about the past. It's going forward that I'm concerned about."

He turned his head and stared out the window.

"You're safe from me, Miss Gordon. I shall not sully your person. God forbid."

Chapter 11

*L*orna lay her head back against the seat and closed her eyes. She'd never been hated before. But she'd never before disobeyed the basic tenets of propriety. She'd bent rules. Then, she dared to walk among the righteous people of Wittan Village without hanging her head in shame.

After Reverend McGill's ranting this afternoon, she had the feeling she would be considered immoral regardless of what she did from this point forward.

Harlot. Whore. Fornicator. Those labels might well be affixed to her for life.

She'd been terrified facing the minister and the crowd he was whipping into an angry frenzy. But, then, she'd been equally frightened on first realizing she was pregnant. She knew the minute the housekeeper discovered her condition she'd be released from service. What would she do? Where would she go? How would she survive?

She hadn't had time to feel shame. She'd been too busy making plans. She'd kept her position until it was difficult to hide her pregnancy. She left Blackhall before Mrs. McDermott or the members of staff knew of her condition. She'd chosen Wittan Village in which to live because it was close enough for Nan to visit.

Her plans might have worked, too, if the duke hadn't appeared. Everything fell apart the minute he showed up. It was as if she'd been paddling toward shore all this time. Suddenly she was hit by wave after wave and was now floating alone in deep ocean currents.

She knew she wasn't the first woman to find herself in trouble. Was every village in Scotland filled with only virtuous females? Was that why there was such venom against her? Were they fearful that the village girls and young women would succumb to passion as easily as she had?

Although she didn't want to go back to Blackhall, she couldn't think of another option. He was right. Even if he settled money on her—which she would take for her son's benefit, not her own—the same situation might easily occur in another place.

She was so tired of being afraid.

If nothing else, returning to Blackhall Castle would mean an end to the fear.

What was he thinking? Why didn't he speak? She could almost see the duke sitting there frowning at her. Sometimes she thought the vision of the man was papered to the inside of her eyelids.

Would her son look like him?

She believed, from the beginning, that the child she carried was a boy. She would love him with all her heart and always protect him. She didn't want him to lack for anything. No doubt every mother felt the same.

Mother. She'd said the word over and over to herself for the past eight months and it still had the power to scare her. She was Lorna Gordon, but in one short month she was going to be a mother. Her child was going to stare up at her with innocent eyes and expect her to provide love, safety, food, and warmth. She would. Somehow, she would, even if it meant dealing with the Duke of Kinross.

How would the others see her return? She'd left as a maid with good references. She was going back as the mother of an illegitimate child: the duke's bastard. She could just imagine the talk in the servants' quarters. They wouldn't be any more understanding than the villagers of Wittan.

Putting aside her pride wasn't an easy thing to do even if it was for the best. Yet she couldn't rid herself of the feeling that she might come to bitterly regret this decision.

She opened her eyes to find herself the object of his study. To be stared at so single-mindedly was nerve-racking, but she wouldn't look away. Instead, she held his gaze for as long as she could, anything but think of that night. Anything but marvel at how handsome he was and what an effect he had on her, even heavy with his child.

Her breasts were tender, but the nipples shouldn't harden just because he was sitting close. Her body shouldn't remember each touch of his fingers on her skin, how his cupped hand smoothed from her shoulder down her arm. How he stroked the length of her legs as if he'd never seen such limbs before and marveled at all the curves and hollows.

She had to remember that he hadn't truly seen her, not in the two years she'd worked at Blackhall. She had to recall that he was the Duke of Kinross. She had to call to mind their stations in life, so different that one should never touch the other.

But they had, hadn't they? On a magical night that shouldn't have been but was, and one that extracted a heavy price for both of them.

ALEX WONDERED IF he was wise taking Lorna back to Blackhall. Probably not, but at least he'd be able to protect her there.

Also, he would see her every day.

She would be a constant reminder of his flaws of character, of his failings. She'd be an object lesson of sorts or a human hair shirt. Perhaps he'd simply wonder about his insanity on that far-off night. He'd see her as she was, just another woman. Any fascination that lingered in his mind would be blown away by the winds of rational thought.

She wouldn't be an enigma to him. She wouldn't occupy space in his mind. She would fade away.

He would stop thinking about her and be about his work.

As it was now, each time it stormed, she entered his mind. Every dark cloud summoned her.

What kind of fool was he?

The kind of fool who brings a woman heavy with child into his home. He could just imagine the reaction from the other residents of Blackhall. A damn good thing he was the titular head of the family. Everyone would simply have to accept Lorna's presence there.

"Who wrote the letter to my mother?" he asked. "It wasn't you, was it?"

She looked directly at him.

"No, it wasn't. I would much rather you had been left in ignorance. If you hadn't come to Wittan, I wouldn't have had to go through Reverend McGill's trial by shouting."

He couldn't argue with her. An irritant, that.

"Who was it?"

She closed her eyes. "Does it matter?"

"A friend, then? Someone who disapproved of your decision to live at Wittan?"

She smiled slightly. "Yes, she most definitely disapproved."

The carriage had only gone a short distance before Lorna made a curious sigh, settled into the corner, and fell asleep.

Her bonnet, an ugly blue thing with a single squished fabric rose, looked uncomfortable. So, too, the bow beneath her chin. He wanted to take it off, smooth his knuckles over her flushed cheek and procure a pillow for her.

He watched her for several moments. Her head rocked a little with the movement of the carriage and her eyelids fluttered.

At first he thought it was a trick of the light, but her complexion possessed a radiance it hadn't had before. Her lashes were long, hiding her deep brown eyes, her lips full. Her cheeks were still flushed. She had an attractive neck, and he'd never noticed such a thing on a woman before. His gaze traveled to her bosom before he forced himself to look away.

As they turned into the grounds of Blackhall, she blinked open her eyes.

"I fell asleep," she said softly, her lips curving a little as if she ridiculed herself.

He nodded. "You needed your rest."

She only continued to smile at him, her gaze warm. What was she thinking?

He should have focused on the approach to Blackhall, or come up with the right words to explain his actions to the inhabitants of the castle. Instead, he found himself staring into her eyes, trying to remember if he'd ever seen that color of brown before, lightened with gold but with a dark circle around the cornea. They fascinated him with their curious tilt.

Or maybe it wasn't her eyes that intrigued him as much as her smile.

She wasn't the most beautiful woman he'd ever seen, but there was something about her that drew his eyes to her again and again.

She sat there enduring his stare, only patting her skirt with the tips of her fingers.

What he was feeling now wasn't lust but a curious tenderness. He wanted to keep her safe, ensure she was cared for and protected. Surely those emotions were only because of her condition. Any decent man would feel the same.

"Is the child mine?"

"I thought you said you were willing to accept that it was? Have you changed your mind, Your Grace?"

"No. I'd just like to hear you say it."

He half expected her to demur or refuse to answer.

"Yes," she said, keeping her gaze steadily on his face. "It's yours. I've not lain with anyone but you."

He only nodded, feeling a tightness in his chest he hadn't anticipated.

"We're almost home," he said, unnecessarily as it happened, since they'd already turned into the gates of Blackhall.

The day was an ugly one, the sky filled with gray and lowering clouds the color of a dove's belly. Yet the gray stone, black chimneys, white sills and door frames of Blackhall were beautiful in any weather. The pine forest was a deep emerald backdrop providing touches of color.

Instead of following the road around and climbing the hill to where Blackhall was perched overlooking the loch and the glen, Charles turned left, traveling down a much narrower road. Once past a section of forest, the carriage stopped.

"I think this will be a good place for you to call home," he said.

She didn't say anything as he opened the carriage door and extended his hand to assist her.

He held her cold hand, wishing her gloves were thicker. The faint tremor disturbed him. Was she afraid?

He stared down at their joined hands, wondering what words would ease her mind. Should he tell her that he thought her eyes were fascinating? The up-turned corners made him want to study her face. Her teeth weren't perfect. Two of them in the front over-lapped slightly and she must be sensitive about it. A few times he'd caught her putting her hand over her mouth or glancing away when she smiled.

If he wanted to ease her mind completely, he should tell her how often he remembered that night. Too many times to make him completely comfortable. He'd expected to be able to dismiss her as a drunken esca-pade, but he recalled everything that had happened between them.

Did she remember?

Where had she learned to kiss? For a virgin, she'd been too skilled.

Her lips were pink and full, and as he watched, she bit the bottom one. He kept her hand in his, wanting to warm her, to do something else for her, but he didn't know what.

After opening the cottage door, he let her enter without him, turning to Charles and giving him a set of instructions. Only then did he follow Lorna and set about to make the cottage as comfortable as possible.

The building had only been vacant for a month or two, the gamekeeper having been lured away to another estate. He hadn't yet replaced the man. When he did, he'd either offer him one of the other cottages on the estate or a spacious room in the servants' quarters.

This cottage was the closest to Blackhall. The thatching on the roof had been replaced in the last six months. The walls had been whitewashed recently. The stone floors were strewn with leaves but were otherwise in good condition. The only problems that he could see were dust and the cold.

Kneeling on the hearth in the cottage's parlor, he began to build up the fire.

"You know how to make a fire, Your Grace?" she asked.

He glanced at her, his greatcoat around her shoulders. She was dwarfed in it, but at least she was warm. A good deal warmer than he was at the moment.

"My parents were determined that I wouldn't be helpless. I can also tie my own shoes, obtain my own food, and shave myself."

"I'll bet that doesn't please Matthews," she said.

He glanced at her over his shoulder. "Do you know him?"

Of course she would. Maybe he just wanted to ask her opinion of the valet. It wasn't forthcoming.

"You should take your coat back," she said.

"No. You keep it. At least until you're warmer."

Standing, he went to her. "There's nothing I can do about your hands. We have to buy you better gloves."

"I can't afford a cottage, Your Grace, but I can get my own gloves."

She was stubborn, a trait he'd already noticed, but at least she wasn't foolish. She'd come with him without a fuss. She'd known there was no possibility of remaining in Wittan.

"The reverend is a fool," he said.

"The reverend is Church of Scotland." She smiled. "He was only spouting what he believed. I am the Whore of Babylon to him. I'm the epitome of all things bad and horrible. Children should be spared the sight of me. Men are tempted by me. I'm an example to women of what not to do. The wages of sin and all that."

He guided her to one of the two overstuffed chairs in the cottage's parlor.

"All that?" he said as she removed his greatcoat and sat.

"All that," she said.

He placed his coat on her lap so she wouldn't get cold, letting his knuckles graze the curve of her stomach.

"You should rest," he said.

"I've already taken a nap. I feel like I sleep all the time."

"You were tired."

"I've been tired for the last month," she said, smiling.

His command of the English language often failed him around her. Another irritant to add to the list.

He glanced toward the fire. "A puny effort," he said. "I need more kindling."

"I think it's well done for the first one you've made in years."

How did she know that?

Her smile was teasing rather than mocking, an expression that deserved a response. He smiled back at her. They were, in that moment, in perfect accord.

Naked, they hadn't had any difficulty communicating. Perhaps he should just shut up and kiss her, a thought that had the effect of emptying his mind.

For a long moment he simply stared at her.

"I've sent for Mrs. McDermott," he finally said, sanity coming back to him in short bursts. "Also, a contingent of maids to set the cottage to rights."

She glanced around her. "All I see is a little dust," she said. "I could take care of that."

"You have enough to do."

"What have I to do?" she asked, again with that teasing smile.

"Unpack your trunk. Settle in. Prepare yourself for being a mother."

She looked up at him and there were questions in her eyes. Once more he wanted to say something to her, but the words wouldn't form. He wanted to ease her mind about the future, to apologize for the cruelty she'd endured today. He wanted to offer some explanation for the world in which they lived, a society that held women to account but not men. Most of all, he wanted to do something more than stand there, ducal and authoritarian, maker of an inept fire.

"I've also sent for Peter," he said. "He's one of our footmen."

"I know him," she said. "Very tall, bright blond hair and a contagious smile."

He nodded. "That's Peter. He's going to be assigned to you. Send him to Blackhall if you need anything at all. Plus, I'm having your meals delivered three times a day. That way you won't have to worry about cooking."

She was blinking rapidly. "You've been very kind," she said.

Once again he wanted to say something, but words flew from him like caged birds set free.

"An hour or two more, that's all, and then you can settle into your bed."

She nodded and he moved away to stand in front of the poor excuse for a fire, willing it to burst into flame.

In moments Charles returned with the housekeeper and three maids, all of them wide-eyed and standing in a straight line as Mrs. McDermott marched forward to speak with him.

She was a tall woman on the thin side. Her hands were large and capable; he'd seen her beat a rug one spring morning. Her face was thin, too, her cheekbones prominent as well as the ridges where dark brown eyebrows sat ready to frown at one of the staff. Keeping her face from severity was a head of lustrous brunette hair alive with red and gold highlights and a ready smile that often curved her mouth.

She wasn't smiling at the moment, however.

"Miss Gordon will be staying here," he said. He hadn't figured out a way to adequately explain the situation, but hoped she would be able to read between the lines. "I need the cottage readied for her. Sheets on the bed, dishes in the kitchen, that sort of thing."

She nodded, her face giving nothing away. If she disapproved, he wouldn't hear of it from her.

"We'll do a fast clean, Your Grace, and schedule more for tomorrow. Would that be acceptable?"

"Excellent, thank you."

She turned to give out her orders.

"Abigail, you'll see that the kitchen is tidy. Hortensia, sweep and mop. Nan, you'll ready the bedchamber."

They all nodded and dispersed to handle their duties. He noted that one of the maids—Nan, he thought it was—waved to Lorna with her hand down at her side. Lorna smiled in return.

He followed Nan into the bedroom.

THE WOMAN WHO was turning the mattress was short, barely to his shoulders. Her black hair was arranged in a bun with several tendrils loose around her face. Her cheeks were plump and pink, her mouth small but curved in a pleasant smile when he appeared.

"Are you Lorna's friend?" he asked.

She blinked at him but answered nonetheless. "Yes, Your Grace, I am. Nan Geddes, sir." She bobbed a curtsy.

"What is she like as a friend?"

A curious question, since he'd never once asked a similar question of anyone.

"I'm not certain what you want to know, Your Grace," Nan said, frowning. "I would trust Lorna with my life, even though we sometimes disagree about things."

"What things?" When she didn't answer, he tried to explain. "I want to know who she is," he said. The truth, if she but knew it.

"Wouldn't it be better to ask Lorna?"

"I read something recently that a man is known by his deeds, how he treats animals in his care, and his friends."

"Does that apply to women as well?"

"I would think so," he said.

"She works hard. Sometimes too much."

"On her herbal remedies," he said.

She shook her head. "Not just that. On her father's book."

"Her father's book?"

Nan nodded. "Lorna is determined that it will be published. She's drawn the most beautiful pictures in it."

He tucked that knowledge away to think about later.

"She used to feed the birds here. And a pesky squirrel on the grounds. As for friends, there's me, of course, but she has a great many friends at Blackhall. People like her."

"You live in the servants' quarters?"

She nodded. "Aye, Your Grace."

"Would you like to live here instead? With Lorna?"

"Here, sir?"

"I don't want her to be alone. I've already arranged for Peter to be on duty, but I'd prefer she had a friend with her."

"Oh, sir, I'd be pleased to."

He turned to leave, then stopped himself, glancing back at her.

"Did you disapprove of her living in Wittan?"

For a moment he wondered if she would answer him.

"Yes, Your Grace," she finally said. "I did."

He nodded, one mystery answered. Now if he could only solve the greater enigma of Lorna.

Chapter 12

The duke had protected her from the Reverend McGill, saved her father's book, and given her his coat. Not only that but he'd settled an amount of money on her so she wouldn't have to worry about the future.

The Church of Scotland wouldn't approve, but they didn't have to give birth to a child and rear him.

She didn't want anyone to think she was the duke's mistress, but wouldn't taking his money be the same thing? Probably, but she wasn't going to be foolish when it came to her child. He shouldn't suffer for that night. Nor was she going to compound her stupidity by refusing to take aid after she'd been almost banished from Wittan Village.

When a circumstance changes, you must change with it.

The memory of her father's words eased her mind a little.

She was prepared to face an arrogant duke. She was more than capable of handling him in that guise. But the Duke of Kinross being charming? That was something else entirely.

Seeing him smile thrust her into the past, into a stormy night when she was pressed up against him, her arms wound around his neck. He kissed her senseless and she'd been desperate for more.

It was safer if he'd maintained that persona she'd seen most of the time, preoccupied, distant, almost cold, detached from the world as if it didn't interest him. Only sections of it had, small pieces that he plucked from the main. Until this moment she'd never been one of those fascinating bits.

She pulled his greatcoat up around her neck, breathing deeply of tobacco and something spicy or exotic like sandalwood. "Do you smoke a pipe?" she asked when he came back into the parlor.

He shook his head.

"Why do I always smell tobacco around you?"

"Do you? I occasionally smoke a cigarillo."

She nodded. "That's it, then."

"Is it a displeasing odor?"

"No," she said. "Not at all."

"Good."

"Is that important to you, that you're not displeasing?"

"Not at all," he said.

Then he did something startling. He bowed slightly before moving away.

She closed her eyes, mulling over that odd gesture.

"Would you like some tea?"

She opened her eyes to see Mrs. McDermott standing there, hands folded at her waist, the expression in her eyes carefully neutral.

When Lorna first met the housekeeper in Inverness, the woman was visiting friends. Her squarish face had been transformed by laughter and the humor in her eyes. Now, eyebrows arched like question marks over her dark blue eyes. Her mouth, often smiling, currently bore a polite and false expression.

Mrs. McDermott had always been fair to the staff and approachable. She was the first to defend anyone if she was accused of a misdeed. Although there was a majordomo on staff, most of the footmen preferred to go to the housekeeper if they had a problem or needed an issue addressed.

Mrs. McDermott didn't look the least bit approachable at the moment. Instead, the look in the housekeeper's eyes reminded her of Reverend McGill.

"Yes, please," Lorna said now, attempting to rise. "I would like some tea." It was easier to sit in the overstuffed chair than to get out of it.

"You sit there, Miss Gordon," the housekeeper said, reaching out and placing her hand on Lorna's arm. "I'll fetch it for you."

Miss Gordon? The coolness in the other woman's eyes was a clue, then, to her reception at Blackhall.

"I didn't want to come back, Mrs. McDermott. I didn't have a choice."

The housekeeper didn't say anything, just stood in front of the chair with her hands folded at her waist. Evidently, she didn't approve either of the living arrangements or the situation.

Lorna glanced away, the temptation to cry almost unbearable. If she did, she wasn't altogether sure she would be able to stop for a while. Instead, she leaned her head back against the chair and closed her eyes.

"You'll think whatever you want to think, Mrs. McDermott. I've changed my mind. I don't want any tea, thank you."

She heard the woman move away.

Finally, they were gone, all of them, even Nan, who'd excitedly announced that she was to live with her in the cottage and wasn't that grand? Mrs. McDermott hadn't said another word to her, but her sharp eyes seemed to be everywhere. When the duke had come to stand in front of the chair where she sat, Lorna was conscious of her glance, not to mention the interest of Hortensia and Abigail.

"There are two bedrooms," he said. "I've had your trunk put in the larger one."

"Thank you."

"You might want to make the smaller room a nursery."

"Yes. Thank you."

"Can I get you anything?"

"No," she said. "I'm fine."

She wasn't fine and he seemed to know it. He stood there, making no move to leave.

"You've been very generous. Thank you."

"It's hardly generosity," he said.

She nodded, which she hoped would preclude his explanation. She didn't want him to tell her that anyone would have done the same, or that the duchess had been the instigator, or that the situation called for gentlemanly action on his part. The fact was, silly as it seemed, she wanted him to care for her, to have done all this for her.

She wanted him to *see* her.

Her son chose that moment to roll from one side to the other.

The duke stared down at her stomach, his expression making her smile.

"He likes to somersault sometimes," she said. "Every once in a while I think I can see a foot or a hand poking me."

"Does it hurt?" he asked.

"No. It's just his way of making sure I haven't forgotten he's there. I can't help but wonder if you were the same."

He opened his mouth, shut it again, then opened it once more, as if words wanted to be spoken but he held them back by dint of his will.

What did he want to say?

"He's a large baby," she said.

His frown deepened. "Is that unusual?"

"I don't think so," she said. "Especially since you're very tall." She patted her stomach as she sat back in the chair.

"I should be going," he said.

She nodded, but he made no move toward the door.

"Is there anything I can get you?"

"No," she said, smiling.

"Is there nothing you need?"

"No. I'm used to doing for myself, Your Grace."

She wasn't a cherished guest but a former maid, now hugely pregnant with the duke's by-blow.

Suddenly she was so tired she could barely keep her head up. She didn't have the strength for verbal jousting.

"Thank you, again," she said, hoping he took the hint.

He did. He bowed to her once more. She inclined her head in a gesture she'd seen the duchess make.

Did he know how handsome he was? Had he been told that by countless women? Did he remark on his likeness when he stared into a mirror? Did he give thanks that he was so attractive?

At the ball, women had followed him with their eyes as he crossed the room. He'd seemed impervious to their attention. Had a lifetime of admiration made him immune to women's glances?

Would their son be as handsome? Would that prove to be an asset or a deterrent?

"May I call on you?" he asked, further surprising her. "I'd like to make sure you're all right."

"Of course. It's your cottage."

"Perhaps you can teach me more about herbs you've found at Blackhall," he said.

"I'm afraid any explorations are beyond me at the moment," she said, smiling. "Perhaps another time."

She was imagining things. He did not look disappointed. No, she was simply too tired to make sense of anything at the moment.

He walked to the door, his stride the same as she remembered, the stiffness of his shoulders just as she recalled from all those times she'd watched him. Had he ever known that she sat in the conservatory after her work was done, hoping for a glimpse of him?

What a fool she'd been.

What a fool she still was.

Once she was alone, she laboriously made her way out of the chair and explored the cottage.

Her new home could easily accommodate a family, with its five rooms. In the bedroom the late afternoon sunlight poured in through the white curtained windows, bathing the white and blue counterpane on the bed. A bureau with a white china washstand atop it, plus a wide armoire of the same walnut wood, sat adjacent to each other on the far wall. The third wall was occupied by a desk and a narrow bookcase, currently empty.

Instead of a baby's nursery, she would put her herbs in the smaller bedroom.

There was even a bathing room, and although it didn't possess all the fixtures found in the duke's quarters, it was remarkably modern. The kitchen had a pump for water and an oak table with four chairs. The large parlor possessed two chairs in front of a spacious fireplace—one of the maids had built up the duke's fire—two bookcases, and a small settee upholstered in a rust-colored fabric.

The parlor window boasted a view of one wing of Blackhall through the trees. He was so close.

May I call on you? He might forget she was here or he might come every day. Either would be disconcerting.

She hadn't felt this emotional since that stormy night, but now she could easily return to the overstuffed armchair and cry for an hour or two.

"Isn't it wonderful?" Nan said, entering the cottage followed by a gust of frosty air. Her cheeks were bright pink, but so was her nose. She held a valise with one hand and her coat closed with the other. "I knew it would work out. I did."

Who was seeing things that weren't there now?

Nan dropped her valise on the floor, coming to her side. She took Lorna's hand and led her back to the chair.

"You make yourself comfortable here and I'll unpack."

"I don't want you to do everything," she said, a weak protest she recognized even as she sank back down into the comfortable chair.

"Nonsense," Nan said. "You can talk to me while I work. I can hear you fine."

She disappeared into the bedroom and proved that by barraging Lorna with questions.

"What did the duke say to convince you to leave Wittan?" she asked. "Did he meet that terrible landlady of yours? You won't ever have to go back, will you?"

"I doubt I'll be welcome," she said, and told Nan about Reverend McGill.

Nan emerged from the room wide-eyed.

"Oh, Lorna, I am sorry. How awful for you. I'm so glad we don't have to go to his church, aren't you?"

As a member of the staff, she'd been expected to attend services at Blackhall's chapel. They'd always had a visiting member of the clergy, and on the rare occasions when no one could make it through, because of inclement weather or a scheduling conflict, either the duke or the dowager duchess read the lesson.

If Reverend McGill had ever officiated, she'd missed that service.

"Well, that's done and it's over. You're home now and that's all there is to it."

Home? She supposed, in an odd way, Blackhall was her home. After her mother's death, when she was ten, she'd followed her father all over Scotland on his quest to learn everything there was to know about Scottish herbs. They'd never stayed longer than six months in one place. She'd lived at Blackhall for two years.

Emotion overwhelmed her. She was grateful to Nan for many things, but mostly her friend's loyalty. Nan had helped her do her work when early pregnancy had made her sick, helped her pad her dresses so she looked like she was gaining weight, hiding her pregnancy. Even leaving the note for the duchess might be considered an act of friendship.

When she began to cry, it was a relief.

"It's going to be all right, Lorna," Nan said, coming to her side. "It truly will. Plus, we'll be together. We'll have a grand time of it, the two of us."

"He bowed to me," she said, wiping her tears away. "The duke bowed to me."

"He did?"

She nodded. "Why did he bow to me?"

"Don't dukes do that?"

"I have no idea what dukes do," she said.

"Well, Lorna, you know more than me," Nan said, smiling and staring pointedly at her stomach.

Because she had no answer to that, Lorna retreated to silence.

"HAVE YOU LOST your sanity, Alex?"

Alex glanced up from his desk in his library to find his uncle striding toward him.

When he was five, Alex realized that his aloof older brother wasn't his brother at all, but his father's. Thomas was an uncle, a relationship that took a while for him to understand.

Thomas made a detour to the sideboard and poured himself a brandy.

Alex put aside his work, moving to one of the wing chairs in front of the fire. Thomas joined him there, stretching out his feet toward the hearth and regarding his snifter of brandy the way a jeweler appraises a fine diamond.

In a way, perhaps Thomas was an expert of sorts when it came to spirits. He drank so much and so often that he'd acquired a tolerance for alcohol and the ability to mask when he was drunk. Most people didn't realize that the fascinating conversations they were having with the Earl of Montrassey wouldn't be recalled by the man in the morning. Or that his seduction of a certain female would disappear from his memory with the dawn.

"I think it's a blessing, really," Thomas had once said. "The Almighty evidently doesn't want me to suffer a guilty conscience. Poof! He wipes it all away. Each morning I am as sinless as a babe."

Thomas was a charter member of Beggar's Blessings, a club founded for libertines in Edinburgh in 1750. The club went on to have branches in Inverness and then London, where the membership extended to include working men as well as the nobility. The only requirements of membership were to pass the marathon masturbation initiation and to add to the club's collection of pornography. His uncle had done more than that. Thomas had come up with the idea of having lectures to teach advanced carnal arts and hired various "posing girls" who acted out pornographic material for the enlightenment of the membership.

Nor was Thomas the least discreet about belonging to such a club. Or about his drinking and wenching, either.

"Are you really going to lecture me on my behavior?" Alex asked.

"You're an absolute fool to bring your mistress to Blackhall," Thomas said. "It's as much an admission that the child she carries is yours."

"I believe it is," he said calmly. Unlike his uncle, he had a conscience, and it still reminded him of events of a certain stormy night. Not to mention how Lorna had been living since leaving Blackhall.

"That's no reason to be saddled with its support for the whole of your life. My God, if I had to pay for all the children I've created, I wouldn't have two farthings to rub together."

"How many children do you have, Uncle?"

"Five at last count, I think. Although, there was one girl in Inverness who was rumored to have given birth to twins. I don't know if it's true or not. Perhaps I should check."

His father had been one of the most moral men Alex

had ever known. He often wondered how his uncle was so different. The man served as an object lesson of sorts. On the rare occasions when Thomas offered an opinion about something at Blackhall, Alex chose the opposite solution. That he objected to Lorna's arrival was a point in Alex's favor.

"Bed the girl if you must, Alex, but do it away from Blackhall. You don't want the whole countryside to know you acknowledge the child. You'll have the old biddies wagging their tongues from morning until night. It isn't done. A man's get is his business. It isn't paraded around like you're proud of it. Hide the girl away. If you're determined to support the child, do so, just not at Blackhall."

"You don't disappoint, Uncle," he said. "I thought you would react this way and you have."

"I'm giving you good advice, Alex. This will come back and haunt you. Have you any thought for your mother? What is she going to do when she learns what you've done?"

"Mother knows."

Thomas frowned. "What do you mean, Louise knows?"

"Just that. She's aware of the entire situation."

He'd had a meeting with his mother the minute he left the cottage. He hadn't wanted one of the gossiping servants to tell her the tale.

He wasn't altogether surprised when she didn't look upset. In fact, she appeared pleased with the developments. She'd even kissed him on the cheek when he finished explaining what he'd done.

Thank you for that, Alex. I can't wait to see my grandchild.

Thomas shook his head now. "Don't you think you're taking confession to extremes, Alex?"

"She was the one who originally informed me of the circumstances, actually. Someone wrote her."

Thomas finished off his brandy and placed the empty snifter on the table between them.

"Good God. What did she say?"

"You mean after the weeping and the gnashing of teeth?"

His uncle smiled. "Yes, after that."

"She surprised me," he said. "I think it's because she's given up hope of my ever marrying again and she wanted grandchildren. She's looking forward to the child."

Thomas stood. "Get rid of the girl."

"She's not going anywhere, Thomas," he said, his annoyance spiking.

"I've found that conscience is a damnable task maker. It pokes and prods and reminds me, a good deal, of your mother."

He was the one to smile now. Louise was the only one who dared to lecture Thomas on his drinking. Or when he tried to be overly friendly with the maids. *Thou shalt not bother the staff* was one of her commandments.

He had certainly broken that one, hadn't he?

At least his uncle hadn't made that point. It was only a matter of time until it occurred to him.

When his mother upbraided Thomas, the man's behavior changed, if only for a few weeks. Lately, he'd taken to remaining away from Blackhall more often than not. It was evidently easier than being subjected to Louise's lectures.

"I'll take your words under advisement, Uncle."

"Which means you'll do no such thing, of course,"

Thomas said. "Your father used to say the same thing often enough. Maybe I should use those words to your mother and see if they're successful."

Alex didn't bother hiding his smile. "I doubt it," he said, "but I'd like to see you try."

Chapter 13

$\mathcal{L}$orna was dozing in the overstuffed chair in the cottage's parlor, the sun warming her and making her as indolent as a kitten. She slept better here with her feet on the needlepoint ottoman than she did in the bed in what she considered the Virgin's Room.

The dream she was having was lovely. She was sitting on a knoll of earth on a blanket. Her infant son played beside her, intrigued with each of the delicate toes his father praised.

She drew up her legs, wrapped her arms around them and placed her cheek against her knees, watching the two of them. In the depths of her sleeping mind she knew that what she was seeing wasn't real, just as she sometimes dreamed of her dead father.

Nan said she saw things as she wanted them to be, not as they were. This was most definitely a case of doing exactly that.

This dream could never come true.

The duke would never sit on a blanket and play with a baby. Nor would he ever glance over at her with a look of love in his eyes. She wouldn't reach out and touch his face with her fingers, trailing a path across his bristly cheek. He most certainly wouldn't smile at her exploration, grab her hand and kiss her fingertips.

She felt so much love in those moments that she thought she might burst with it.

"Lorna."

She heard her name, knew she was being called, but she didn't want to leave her delightful dream.

"Lorna."

Someone was gently touching her shoulder. Blinking open her eyes, she saw Peter bending over her. A moment later she realized she'd fallen asleep, again, in the parlor.

"Lorna, the duchess is here."

She blinked up at him, trying to make sense of his words.

"The duchess?"

He nodded, a lock of blond hair falling over his brow.

"Yes, my dear, and I'm so sorry to interrupt you."

They both glanced toward the doorway where the Dowager Duchess of Kinross was standing, removing her gloves. Her face was arranged in a pleasant expression but her eyes didn't miss anything.

"Your Grace."

The duchess removed her heavy black wool coat to reveal an emerald silk dress padded with a simple hoop. The skirt was gathered up in several places and adorned with black braid, as was the corset. The hat was emerald as well, with a black feather sprouting from the rakish brim.

The duchess was fashionable, wealthy, and more than a little frightening. Lorna would have been intimidated by the woman's presence had it not been for memories of the other woman's kindness.

"Your Grace," she said again, feeling inept.

She truly wanted to curtsy to the woman, but there

was no possibility of that. In the last few days, Peter had to assist her in standing. Besides, she didn't want the duchess to see that her blue dress—the only one she could still wear—was much shorter than propriety allowed.

She felt like one of those huge hot air balloons she'd seen in the newspaper.

"My dear," the duchess said, "I've interrupted your nap. I'm so sorry. I remember how hard it was to fall asleep at night. Should I come back at a better time?"

"Of course not, Your Grace," she said.

The duchess sank into the chair next to Lorna, reached out and took Lorna's hand, holding it between hers.

"All three of my children were as large as your child. I was quite ungainly by the time I gave birth."

"I waddle like a duck," Lorna said, smiling. "And I've outgrown all my clothes." She couldn't even fit into her shift, a comment she was not about to make to the duchess.

"As did I, my dear. My husband told me that I was radiant and graceful. I laughed uproariously. But he was like that, a kind and good man even in the most difficult circumstances."

The duchess glanced down at their joined hands, then back up at Lorna. Tears pooled in her eyes. She shook her head as if to negate her momentary grief.

"Look at me, going back into the past. But when I saw you, my dear, it reminded me so much of that time. I'm sure there were petty annoyances and irritations, but thinking back I don't remember any of those. I was filled with such joy."

Her smile was watery and bittersweet before she cleared her throat, sat up straight, and released Lorna's hand. "I've come to welcome you back to Blackhall, not regale you with tales of my past. How are you settling in?"

"I'm very comfortable here," Lorna said. "The duke has done a lot to make me feel pampered and privileged."

"He thinks highly of you, you know."

She didn't respond to that. The duchess was attempting to be polite, and sometimes, in the absence of other compliments, people manufactured some. She was more than certain that the duke thought no such thing. She doubted if her name ever came up in conversation. How did he discuss his soon-to-be illegitimate child with his mother?

Lorna glanced at Peter. The weather was too cold for him to stand outside the cottage. He'd made the kitchen his base of operations, spending the time sitting at the table carving.

"Would you like some tea?" she asked, hoping Peter would jump in and offer to prepare it.

She knew that the duke had installed him there to run errands between the cottage and Blackhall, but he'd been personally helpful as well as kind to her in the past few days.

"That would be nice," the duchess said, standing.

To Lorna's surprise, the duchess insisted on making tea, bustling around the small kitchen as if she were familiar with such tasks. Lorna overheard the conversation she and Peter had about his carvings and his working with wood.

In a matter of minutes the duchess returned to the parlor, followed by Peter carrying a teapot and two cups on a tray. After placing it on the table in front of the chairs, he bowed and retreated into the kitchen again.

"Such a tactful young man," the duchess said, sitting in the adjoining chair once again. "I've always liked him."

"Why don't you employ a lady's maid, Your Grace?"

The duchess glanced over at Lorna. Her smile was genuine and warm, but then the woman had always been gracious to her.

"What an odd question. Is it because I'm no stranger to making tea?"

Lorna shook her head. "No, it's because we always wondered in the servants' quarters. You should have had a lady's maid, but you never employed one."

"Privacy," the duchess said. "I quite like my own company, and I've found that the more servants one has around, the less privacy you have. I did have a lady's maid once, but she developed a *tendre* for my husband's valet. It became a comedy of errors, I'm afraid. Besides, it's not all that difficult to dress yourself if you don't lace yourself too tight or insist on those ludicrous hoops that make it impossible to enter a doorway." She glanced over at Lorna again. "I'm afraid I'm not all that fashionable."

"I wouldn't say that at all, Your Grace. I, on the other hand, haven't been able to contemplate wearing a corset for several weeks. Nor have I been able to see my feet." She looked at the other woman and made another confession. "I've only been able to fit into this one dress," she said, looking down at herself.

"That is as it should be," the duchess said, giving her a smile. "You're going to have a child. No one cares what you wear. Are you feeling well?"

Lorna nodded. "Very well. The first weeks were difficult, but only two things bother me now."

"I'll bet I can guess what they are," the duchess

said. "Sleepiness and a need to use the necessary every quarter hour."

Lorna nodded, smiling.

"While time and nature may blunt the memory of a great many things, you remember those last months quite well." She sipped at her tea. "I understand Miss Geddes lives with you. Is she here?"

"No." Nan went to work every morning, just as if she lived in the servants' quarters.

"Good. That will give us time to talk."

The older woman didn't speak for a few minutes, and when she did, she surprised Lorna again.

"My son says that you're an artist. I didn't know that. Would you be willing to show me some of your work?"

This morning she'd been reading through her father's book, carefully inspecting each drawing to ensure it was what her father would have wanted.

"Over there, on the table," she said, pointing next to the tray.

In seconds the duchess had retrieved the journal.

Directing her gaze out the window, Lorna concentrated on anything but the duchess thumbing through her father's journal. No one else had ever read it.

On one page, following her father's instructions, she'd listed the herb, its common and Latin name, and where it could be found. Below that she explained how the plant was efficacious for which ailment, and then provided a selection of recipes her father had chosen. She drew the plant on the facing page.

In all her editing of the journal, she never changed her father's words, but she had added to the original drawings, making each the best she could.

"I confess that I'm amazed."

She glanced at the duchess.

"I had no idea you were so talented, Lorna."

"It's mostly my father's work."

"Your drawings, though."

She nodded.

"You are truly a gifted artist."

Warmth raced up from the pit of her stomach. Not one person, even her father, had ever said such a thing to her, and she'd fed on the crumbs of his praise.

"Thank you."

"No thanks are necessary, my dear. I should thank you. What a pleasure it would be to read this. You say you've tried to get it published?"

For the next several minutes she explained that she'd written friends of her father's but that none of them had seemed interested.

"I haven't given up, though," she said. "I think my father would have wanted me to keep trying."

"It would be a beautiful book," the duchess said. "Not to mention an important one."

The duchess continued to look through the book while Lorna sat silent.

"I don't know quite how to ask this question," Lorna finally said. "But I've discovered that if I don't give voice to my curiosity, it doesn't go away."

"Ask me anything you like, my dear. I will try to do my best to answer you."

"Why don't you hate me?"

The duchess reared back and stared at her, surprise widening her blue eyes.

"I beg your pardon?"

"I'm a source of scandal, Your Grace. One that involves your son. I've been shamed out of Wittan Village. If people aren't gossiping about him now, they certainly will be."

"Oh, good heavens, we've always been a source of scandal. We're the Russells of Blackhall Castle. Any titled family in Scotland is the source of talk, my dear. Any family with wealth or power or prestige is. It's the price you pay. Besides, this scandal will just take the place of the previous one. These things go in cycles."

Lorna couldn't bite back her curiosity.

"What previous scandal?" she asked.

"You haven't heard about Ruth?"

"She died."

"She did."

The duchess had the same direct look as her son. Or maybe he'd inherited the ability to pin someone with his gaze from her.

"She died in childbirth, my dear, but I will not have you worried or afraid for your health. Alex has hired a renowned doctor and a skilled midwife is already in attendance."

"He has? She is?" It would have been nice if the duke had informed her of those arrangements.

The duchess nodded.

"Ruth was, shall we say, bored with being with only one man. She had numerous lovers, a fact evidently well known in Edinburgh."

"His wife was unfaithful?"

The duchess sighed again. "Ruth acquired lovers like you might collect herbs. She wasn't the least discreet about the practice."

"Was the woman insane?"

The duchess stopped talking and stared at her.

"How could any woman choose another man over the duke?" Lorna asked. "I can't imagine such a thing."

"Oh, I do like you, my dear," the duchess said, reaching over and patting her hand. "If the poor thing hadn't died in childbirth, I'm very much afraid Alex would've caused even a greater scandal and divorced her. That is, if she continued to behave as she had. But he was willing to give it a go and was prepared to be a good husband and father. Unfortunately, Fate stepped in and he didn't get a chance."

They sat silent, the moment spent in contemplation of the tragedy that had befallen the Duke of Kinross.

"I'm so glad you agreed to come and live here," the duchess went on. "We'll have many more talks. Right now, however, I shall not tire you out. You should take another nap." She stood and pulled on her gloves, all the while smiling down at Lorna. "Is there anything I can bring you?"

Lorna hesitated long enough that the duchess tilted her head, studying her.

"What is it, my dear?"

"An imposition," she said.

"Nonsense. What is it you need?"

"A table," she said. "And a stool. Somewhere to arrange my herbs. Some of them are poisonous and I'd prefer not to do any work in the kitchen."

"Then you shall have a table and a stool. May I come again?"

"I would like that very much," Lorna said.

Instead of moving toward the door, the duchess startled her by bending down and kissing her on the cheek.

"I grew up an orphan in my aunt's home, my dear. From an early age I understood life to be exceedingly short. Too short to allow other people to dictate what you do or say, wear or believe. I am grateful for that lesson because it allowed me to appreciate every single moment of joy I was given. I hope you do the same."

Lorna stared after the duchess long after the door closed.

Chapter 14

$\mathcal{T}$he last of winter sat on the shoulders of the mountains, broke its boredom by blowing the remainder of its frigid breath over the glens and into the woods. This morning crystal shards had been draped from the trees, ice changing the grass to a glittering green. This part of the Highlands was inhospitable to strangers in the frozen months. Even the hardiest Scots hunkered close to the fire and blessed their good fortune in having a well-built home.

Spring was like a wave to visitors: come, it's safe now. You're welcome here.

The last weeks in Wittan Village had been cold and miserable. Here in her cozy borrowed cottage, Lorna was perfectly comfortable and waiting the onset of spring. Those two months in Mrs. MacDonald's dark and dank room were in the past, the memory of them almost like a bad dream.

She discovered that the absence of worry was a monumental gift she'd been given. With her immediate needs satisfied, she didn't spend any time being afraid. Her days were more than pleasant; they were perfect in their simplicity and peace.

When she wasn't dozing, she occupied herself with

reading, experimenting with various recipes from her father's book, and daydreaming.

"You used to clean my rooms," a voice said.

Lorna emerged from talking to Peter in the kitchen to find Mary Taylor standing in the parlor.

"I could never find anything after you cleaned," Mary said. "Did you ever steal from me?"

"Do you normally enter someone's home unannounced?" she asked.

"This cottage belongs to Alex."

"Did he give you permission to be rude?"

"Did you ever steal from me?"

"No. I've never stolen anything from anyone."

Mary cocked her head and regarded her, eyes narrowing.

"I'm not certain I believe you. I think I should have addressed the matter at the time, however. Now might be too late, especially since you would've gotten rid of anything you stole."

"Is that why you came, to accuse me of stealing from you?"

Lorna wanted to sit, but she didn't move toward her favorite chair in the parlor. Sitting there was a little like being an overturned turtle. She needed help getting up. The last thing she wanted to be was vulnerable around Mary Taylor.

Instead, she slowly walked to the settee and sat on the end. The horsehair stuffing was hard and uncomfortable, but at least she didn't have a problem standing once she sat.

She folded her hands and pretended a calm she didn't feel. Her emotions hadn't been especially volatile until the last week. Now she wanted to shout at the woman to leave her alone, to leave her house, go away. Anything but be here, with accusations that had no basis in truth, simply because she could make them.

She saw Peter out of the corner of her eye and shook her head. She didn't need rescuing.

"What a pity you've forgotten your place," Mary said. "You think you're special because you're having Alex's child. But you're not, you know. You're nothing but a servant. One who's dropped down a peg or two. No one has any respect for a woman who births a bastard."

How she disliked that word. Even more so people who said it with such glee.

She didn't bother to respond. Mary evidently wanted to insult her. Once she had, perhaps she would simply leave.

"I wouldn't have given you this cottage if I were Alex," Mary continued. "Instead, I'd offer you a lean-to, or a place in the barn with the other bitches until it was time for you to whelp. When you were done, I'd make sure you were gone."

"Luckily for me," Lorna said, "you aren't the duke."

"How proper you sound. Almost as if you had some breeding."

"You're very critical of other people for a poor relation," Lorna said.

She shouldn't have retaliated, but she was not going to be Mary's victim.

She was no longer a maid at Blackhall, her only recourse to bend her head and listen to complaints and comments. A few of the staff had gone to Mrs. McDermott, who, in turn, had taken the matter to the Dowager Duchess. Unfortunately, no one could control Mary's vitriolic tongue. Those mornings when assignments were changed, you could hear the moan when someone was given her rooms to clean. Mrs. McDermott only narrowed her eyes, a quick reprimand without a word spoken. At times Lorna wondered if caring for Mary's rooms was penance for bad behavior.

Like it or not, she was going to bear the duke's child. She was not going to be treated like one of the poor servants who had no other choice but to endure Mary's abuse.

"Why aren't you living in your own establishment?" Lorna asked. "Why are you here at Blackhall? You're living with your brother-in-law. How does that give you a pedestal on which to view others?"

Mary's face was immobile, but Lorna had the impression that her control was hard won. A muscle flexed in her cheek and her chin jutted out as she tilted her head back.

"My father was an earl. My sister married a duke. My family has status. You have nothing."

"No, we both have nothing. At least I have the sense to recognize it."

Mary took a few steps toward her.

"He might have made you his mistress, but he doesn't care anything about you."

"Will you leave?" Lorna stood, clasping her fingers across her belly.

Perhaps she'd been too quick to wave Peter off. She was very much afraid that Mary was going to strike her.

"I'll see you gone from here, you and your bastard. That is, if you survive the birth." Mary stared at her stomach. "My sister died bringing his child into the world. What a pity if that should happen to you."

There was so much hate in Mary's words that Lorna

shivered. What must it be like to wish another person dead?

She remained silent until the woman turned and strode to the door. Only then did Peter come out of the kitchen, staring after Mary.

"You've made an enemy," he said.

Lorna nodded, certain of it. "She loves the duke," she said, the words causing Peter to turn and gape at her. "She sees me as a threat. She always looks at him as if he's steak and she's a starving puppy."

The expression in Mary's eyes promised that her words weren't simply idle boasts. The woman would do anything to banish her from Blackhall.

LOUISE, DOWAGER DUCHESS of Kinross, checked her appearance in the mirror prior to heading for the family dining room for lunch.

Circumstances had developed perfectly. Now all she had to do was institute her plan.

Alex had never made any secret that he had no desire to marry again. Despite his responsibility to the dukedom, he'd been stubbornly adamant about that fact. Thank heavens Lorna had attracted him enough that he'd lost his head. If he hadn't, they wouldn't be in this predicament. Thank heavens, too, that Lorna was the sweetest girl, one she could wholeheartedly see as her daughter-in-law.

All she had to do was expand on that initial attraction while eliminating any obstacles.

One of those was standing in the hallway waiting for her.

Louise bit back her sigh, forced herself to smile, and greeted Mary.

"You have to stop him," Mary said. "You have some

influence over Alex, Louise. You have to do something. Make him send her away."

"You're speaking of Miss Gordon, I presume," Louise said, continuing toward the dining room. Perhaps if she kept walking it would dampen Mary's enthusiasm for this particular conversation.

"Everyone is talking. All the staff. She has to leave Blackhall."

"The only people I know who are talking are you and your maid," Louise said.

Mary stopped in the middle of the corridor. "What are you saying, Louise? That I'm spreading tales?"

She really didn't want to continue this conversation, but she'd already erred by making that comment. She turned to face Mary. If any of the maids were in the corridor, they would certainly have a tale to carry back to the servants' quarters, wouldn't they?

"You're always the first to tell me what's going on, Mary. What someone has said or done. Who has had an affair, what maid has been disciplined, who has dissolved into tears about which slight. I've never known anyone so interested in other people's lives as you are. It's an indication, don't you think, that you need to find more to interest you."

Mary's face was becoming florid, her eyes narrowed. No doubt she was going to launch into a tirade at any moment, insulting Louise's antecedents or her taste in clothing, furnishings, or food. The woman was a canker and a boil in her otherwise pleasant life.

"I never knew you had such disdain for me, Louise. Or for what goes on in your own home."

Truly, must she endure this woman? Why couldn't Mary have an appreciation for Edinburgh like her sister? Or even Inverness? For that matter, why couldn't

Mary be as licentious as Ruth? At least an affair would keep her occupied.

"She's brought scandal to Blackhall," Mary said.

"I'm afraid Ruth already did that, Mary," she said, starting to walk again.

When Ruth was alive, Mary had been eager to bring her tales of her sister's infidelity. Had Mary forgotten that?

She reached the family dining room finally. The presence of the others didn't guarantee Mary's silence, however. The younger woman had been known to talk a subject to death.

She wondered what Mary would say if she learned that Lorna had the same concerns as she did. In Lorna's case, however, she didn't want to bring scandal to the family. Mary was desperate not to be coated with it.

Was Mary's concern about the opinions of other people so strong because of her own penchant for gossip? How odd that she should not want to be tarred by the same brush she wielded with such passion.

"Let me be more direct," she said, turning to the younger woman. "I quite like Miss Gordon. I don't want to hear any words against her. Not from you, Barbara, or any of your confederates. Is that understood?"

She smiled pleasantly, but there was a firmness to her expression.

Life had delivered several lessons to her. She had to remain strong and fight for what she wanted, even as the Duchess of Kinross. She'd taken those lessons to heart and had no intention of being thwarted by the likes of Mary Taylor.

The woman was not going to interfere with her plans.

"WHAT WERE YOU thinking, Alex?"

He turned to find Mary standing in the door to his office. She wasn't allowed in here. No one was unless he specifically invited them, which he'd never done.

She'd broken his rule, which was irritating enough. The look on her face was another annoyance. Mary was angry and he didn't have any doubt why.

He'd managed to avoid her for the last week, but only by being a hermit and having his meals either here or in his sitting room. She was here now and they might as well have this conversation.

Standing, he rounded his desk, glancing at Jason. The young man interpreted his wishes correctly and got up, brushed past Mary with a smile and left the room.

"Yes?" Alex said, stopping in front of her.

He'd address her trespass at another time, when she wasn't about to have a tantrum.

"That woman has lost no time ingratiating herself with your mother. She's a nobody, a maid, Alex. You shouldn't have brought her here. If you wanted to make her your mistress, you should have installed her in Inverness. You go there often enough."

He hadn't hesitated giving Mary a home when Ruth had asked it of him. That didn't give her the right to criticize the choices he made. She didn't seem to realize that, however, since she was still discussing Lorna.

"Does she need her own private footman, Alex?"

"She might need something. I felt it necessary."

Why the hell was he explaining anything to Mary?

"What's your objection to her being here?" he asked.

At least his sister-in-law was capable of embarrassment, if her pink cheeks were any indication.

"She's going to take advantage of your generosity, Alex."

"I've seen no example of that."

In fact, Lorna hadn't wanted anything from him, a comment he didn't make to Mary. He disliked her questions and her interference. He didn't need a second mother.

"She's my guest, Mary."

"She's more than that and we both know it."

"Do we?" he said, returning to his desk.

Jason had finished transcribing the last revision of his treatise, and he was going to deliver it to the Scottish Society in Inverness next week. He couldn't review it for errors, though, as long as Mary was determined to harangue him.

"She's all sweetness and sugar, Alex, but the woman has designs on you, I can tell."

"What are you talking about?"

"She as much as insulted me," Mary said. "She asked me to leave the cottage."

"You visited her?"

"I felt it was my place as a member of the family," she said. "She's so pregnant it's embarrassing. It's worse than embarrassing. It's coarse."

How did she think babies came into the world? Had she said the same thing about Ruth?

"She's my guest, Mary," he repeated. "That means anything she wants, she gets, including her privacy."

He watched as her eyes narrowed, her thin nose flared, and her flush grew a deeper red.

"Leave her alone," he said. "She doesn't deserve your antipathy."

"She's used the situation to better herself," she said.

"She's a maid, Alex, yet you're treating her like an equal."

Mary had been living in what was little more than a ruin when she came to Blackhall. She and Ruth were daughters of an impecunious earl. What would have happened to her if he'd hadn't offered her a home? A thought that evidently had never occurred to her.

"The child will be an embarrassment, Alex. A shameful reminder. A bastard."

"You need to leave," he said, annoyance seeping into his words. "I have work to do."

"Of course," she said, moving to the door. Once there, she turned and studied him. "You will take my words to heart, though, won't you?"

He nodded, intent on getting her out of his office.

When she was gone, he sat once more, staring at the title of the treatise but not seeing Jason's careful penmanship. Instead, he saw Lorna's face, carefully expressionless as Reverend McGill called her a whore.

Evidently, there was more than one narrow-minded bigot in the vicinity.

Chapter 15

*E*very morning, Nan trotted off to Blackhall, enjoying her new popularity. People were curious about Lorna, and since Nan was also living in the gamekeeper's cottage, they went to her for information. Her friend was an expert at saying nothing while seeming to say something.

"They want to know if the duke has visited," Nan said this morning.

"What did you tell them?"

"That if he had, I wouldn't know, working alongside them all day."

"He hasn't," Lorna said.

Each one of her needs had been taken care of, including food. One of the girls from the kitchen brought her noon and evening meal, complete with entrée and a dessert. She was being treated like a valued guest, which meant she didn't have to lift a finger.

She was also being ignored by the Duke of Kinross.

Peter sat in the kitchen carving a header for the front door. After that, he informed her, he was all for making the cradle a little fancier. The duchess had brought that on her last visit.

"It's the Russell cradle," the duchess had said. "Every Russell child has been placed in that cradle."

Neither of them mentioned this child wouldn't officially be a Russell. Instead, he would carry the Gordon name.

"It needs something, Lorna," Peter said when first viewing the plain wooden cradle. "Some flowers, maybe. Thistles or something."

She was in the process of sketching what she'd like him to carve, a task she thoroughly enjoyed and one that kept her from thinking about anything else. She found herself so involved in her drawing that she didn't hear anything until Peter cleared his voice at the door.

"Begging your pardon, Lorna, but the duke is here."

"Ask him to come in," she said, staring down at her journal and trying to compose herself.

In seconds he was standing at the entrance to the parlor, removing his coat.

Today he was dressed simply in a white shirt and black trousers. But no one would mistake him for a servant or worker on the property, regardless of his casual attire. First of all, his shirt was too blinding white, indicating that it was a special item of care in the laundry. Probably the laundress herself worked on it. Secondly, and more important, he had an air about him, one of command, perhaps, or maybe it was simply of belonging.

She told her heart to stop beating so fiercely, but it was no use. One glance at him and she changed from the woman she knew herself to be to the girl who'd watched him from behind the ferns and fronds in the conservatory.

It hardly seemed fair that he was so beautiful and a duke. It was as if all the good fairies had been present at his birth, determined to visit every blessing on this child.

May he be intelligent.

May he possess the ability to charm.

May his smile bestow such magic that people will recall it forever.

May he be the most handsome of men.

Would those magical beings have also granted him a certain enchantment when it came to women? Would they have transported themselves into the future, seeing not the bairn but the man? It seemed as if they had, because he certainly possessed carnal talents.

"I didn't mean to interrupt you," he said, glancing down at the journal on the arm of the chair. "What are you working on?"

She smiled, and although she didn't normally like to show her incomplete drawings to anyone, she held out the book.

"Something to adorn the cradle," she said.

"The family cradle?" he asked, taking the book from her. "It can benefit from some adornment."

"Peter will be doing the work. He's very talented," she added. "Have you seen his carvings?"

"I haven't, but I'll rectify that situation as soon as possible."

He didn't hand her back her journal, but began to look at the other pages. She wanted to ask him to stop but was too late. One page in particular caught his attention. He angled his head and studied it.

Oh dear.

"I didn't realize you drew anything but herbs," he said, showing her the page that interested him.

Eyes and more eyes filled the page. His eyes glancing to the left or right or staring straight ahead. She'd been fascinated with his eyes.

She glanced away, focusing on the view from the parlor window.

"Peter isn't the only one with talent."

She glanced back at him.

"Thank you," she said.

"Your sketches are only in pencil," he said. "Why is that?"

She blinked at him, surprised. Even the duchess hadn't noticed that and she'd studied her father's book for some time.

"I don't have the money to purchase any watercolors," she said. There, the truth, given to him without fanfare.

He stood there silent and unspeaking, making her wonder what he was thinking.

She had this odd and unsettling wish to reach out and touch his face, to stroke the edge of his jaw and brush her knuckles against his skin. She wanted to bury her face in the crook of his neck and breathe in his scent.

The afternoon was advancing, the shadows lengthening. Soon it would be dark and Nan would return.

It was safer to stare out the window again than at him. From here she could see a wing of Blackhall, the sloping lawn leading to the forest and beyond. As a servant, she'd often explored that area, since she had no family to visit on her half days off.

"I've brought you some books," he said. "And a table and two stools. The former was my idea, the latter my mother's."

The duchess hadn't forgotten. Lorna hadn't wanted to remind her, thinking that to do so would be rude.

"Will you show me where you want the table?" he asked.

He held out his hand, and she had no choice but to place hers in it. With a little effort, she was standing, but too close to him. She wanted to take a step back but the chair was there. She could always sidestep but was very much afraid that her belly would come into contact with some part of his body.

He shocked her by placing his hand on her stomach, resting it gently against the fabric of her dress.

Not a word passed between them. He didn't comment on how large the child was or how ungainly she appeared. Nor did she remove his hand.

A minute passed, then another. Finally, he dropped his hand, his head came up, and he regarded her silently.

"You don't have to be solicitous of me," she said. "I don't demand it of you. Nor do I expect it."

"I think, perhaps, you should."

With that surprising comment he stepped back.

She led the way to her bedroom, since Nan was using the smaller chamber, and indicated the back wall. To her surprise, he didn't call for his driver to assist him. Instead, he and Peter moved the furniture themselves. In a few minutes everything was in place.

He smiled as he passed her. She walked to the front door, to find that he hadn't brought the carriage. Instead, he'd come to the cottage in a pony cart.

"She's Old Gretchen," he said, glancing at the pony as he reached for the books in the cart. "She's a sweet little thing, but she's stubborn."

Old Gretchen turned her head and stared at her, the expression in the pony's big brown eyes one of irritated acceptance. Almost as if the animal were saying, *You and I, we are in this together. We have to do as we are told, but we don't have to like it.*

"A pony cart?" she said, stepping back into the

warmth of the doorway. "I didn't know that Blackhall had such a thing."

"It dates from when we were small. A present from my father."

She could instantly see them, the children of Blackhall laughing as they rode over the paths winding around the castle.

"Old Gretchen, does she date from that time, too?"

He glanced over his shoulder at her and smiled with an effortless charm. She was going to do her best to remain unaffected by him.

"No, that was Angus. Poor old boy's been gone for a few years now."

"Yet you still have a pony."

"Mary's to thank for that. She rescued Old Gretchen from someone who was ill-using her. I think she paid twice what the pony was worth."

Mary was, no doubt, nicer to animals than she was to the people who served her. Was it something the peerage were trained to do in the nursery? Along with learning their letters, were they taught to ignore anyone who wasn't their rank? Or if they did notice them, to treat them with derision?

He stopped and looked at her.

"What is it? Have I said something?"

She shook her head and he blessedly dropped the subject.

"I found a few volumes on herbs," he said, glancing down at the books in his hands. "And one on Blackhall, in case you were interested."

"I recognize the books on herbs. They're from the library. I confess that I borrowed a volume or two from time to time," she said. "I didn't think you'd mind."

Books were to be read, and when they weren't, it

seemed almost sad. She knew he used the great library at Blackhall, but she doubted anyone else did. One of her tasks had been to dust the books periodically, and she could always tell which volumes were well-used and which had never been moved from their spot on the shelves.

"I wouldn't have if I'd known," he said. He joined her at the door. "Are you going to tell me what annoyed you?"

She had a choice: to be entirely honest with him or to attempt to be as charming as he was being. She had little hope for the latter and she doubted the wisdom of the former.

"Lorna?"

She glanced up at him. He'd used her name before, but had he ever studied her so intently? The effect was disconcerting; it was as if he could not only see her, but into her.

He entered the cottage, closing the door behind them. She watched as he put the books in the bookcase in the parlor and returned to her side. Slowly, probably to give her time to move away if she wished, he reached out and took one of her hands.

Her fingers curled around his. For just a moment it seemed as if they were in perfect accord, if one could discount their circumstances. She could almost envision the tableau they made: duke and female servant. A girl in trouble because of the lascivious attentions of a peer. A story of ruination that might have appeared in one of the scandalous newspapers she'd been forbidden to read as a young girl.

But it hadn't exactly happened that way, had it? She was as much to blame as he for that night. Perhaps more so since she'd stepped outside her station.

"Are you going to tell me?"

"You really don't want to know, Your Grace," she said.

"And if I said I did?"

"Honesty might be a great virtue," she said. "But it can be overrated. Besides, I'm here on sufferance, although I'm sure you won't admit it. If I make you angry, what's to keep you from snapping your fingers and banishing me from Blackhall?"

Where would she go then?

She pulled her hand free and walked into her bedroom again.

He followed her.

"You think I'm that much of a monster?"

She turned to face the duke.

"You're not a monster at all, Your Grace. I don't know you. Despite what we might have shared and share now," she added, glancing down at her belly, "I have no idea who you are."

"Then why does it annoy you when I try to show you? Or if I want to learn who you are as well? Do you want my word that I won't banish you from Blackhall regardless of what happens between us? Then you have it. I give you the freedom to say anything you wish or do anything you want to do. I shall not retaliate in any way. You have my word, and no one can say that I've ever broken my word."

She studied him for a moment before speaking.

"I'll tell you what annoyed me. I'm going to ensure that my son notices everyone. He's not going to behave like a segment of society is completely invisible. He's not going to be served and waited on and cleaned around without being aware of the people who do that work."

She'd tested his new declaration, hadn't she? A muscle flexed in his cheek, a sure sign that he was irritated. Perhaps her rough edges were rubbing against his. Not that he would admit to having any, but she knew the Duke of Kinross a little better than she'd admitted. He was occasionally brusque, periodically insensitive. She didn't know if he was capable of changing or of even wanting to, but if he meant what he said, she had at least a modicum of freedom to question his behavior.

"I fluster people," he said. When she looked at him in surprise, he continued. "Mrs. McDermott requested that I don't address the maids. She said they giggle when I do. It stops them from their work."

He was right about that. Whenever one of the girls had an encounter with him, it was recalled in rapturous, sighing detail at their meals.

"Because you look like a prince," she said.

Not at the moment, however. He was scowling at her. Did princes frown so forcefully in novels?

"I never considered that Mrs. McDermott had asked you to avoid the staff," she admitted. "I doubt, however, that it's your sister-in-law's problem. Nor can I imagine anyone giggling after an encounter with her."

"I'm sorry about Mary," he said. "She said she visited you. I'm sorry for her rudeness."

"How do you know she was rude?" she asked.

"It's Mary we're talking about, isn't it?"

She bit back her smile.

"Shall I talk to her?"

"Good heavens, no. Please don't do that. It would make the situation worse. At least I no longer have to clean her rooms."

There, she'd mentioned her circumstances. She

could see the situation as it was and not as she wanted it to be, as Nan had always counseled. She was a former maid at Blackhall. She and the duke had a fateful encounter one night, that's all. She was not charmed by him. She felt nothing for him but gratitude.

"She can't be allowed to be rude to you, Lorna."

She only smiled, not setting him straight. Mary could be rude to her, and she would be, in tiny ways that would never be seen by anyone else. She knew people like Mary. The sister of an inn owner where she and her father used to stay was of similar character. Lorna's sheets were scratchy, her soup cold, and any comments or requests were always met with innocent eyes until her father turned his back. Then the woman would mouth some insult and Lorna knew she was being singled out for torment simply because she'd once complained to her father about the woman's treatment.

One of the maids at Blackhall had been as sly, but Mrs. McDermott hadn't been fooled by the girl. An accusation of theft lodged against another maid had been disproved and the sneaky lass sent home.

However, it would be better, if more difficult, if she remembered her father's adage. When she achieved perfection, she could dictate how others behaved.

"What are you going to do here?" he asked, placing his hand on the top of the table.

She sent him a quick smile, grateful for the change of subject. She was not going to let Mary Taylor ruin her mood.

"I'm going to arrange my herbs and perhaps develop new teas."

"Your landlady didn't destroy your supplies?" he asked.

She shook her head. "I was able to save most of them." She bent, and would have retrieved the small casket containing the most valuable herbs from inside the trunk, but he was there before her.

"Let me," he said. "You sit. Tell me what to do."

She folded her hands atop her stomach, biting back the questions that immediately came to mind.

Why was he being so charming? Why, for that matter, did he want to know so much about her? Why did she think it would be better—and safer—if he remained the aloof Duke of Kinross?

Chapter 16

*L*orna perched on one stool while he sat on the other retrieving items from the small trunk.

He was surprised to see that she had a wide arrangement of bottles, from pale green to dark brown, some with stoppered tops. Others had corks carefully carved to fit.

"Were these your father's?" he asked. She nodded, then smiled, the sweetness of the expression causing him to stop and stare at her.

"My father never threw anything away. We went from city to city carrying items we didn't need. But he could never part with the perfect bottle or the ideal funnel. Or even mixing spoons. I'm a little more ruthless."

Or she couldn't afford to transport more than she could carry. He could almost see her, regretfully discarding something her father had treasured, tucking away the memories it evoked, but ridding herself of the physical object.

He thought of Blackhall and the possessions of generations of people still occupying the attic and spare rooms. Without trying he could find a snuffbox with his grandfather's initials or a hand mirror his great-great-grandmother had used.

He disliked the twinge he felt at the paucity of Lorna's belongings and found himself changing the subject yet again.

"Do you have a favorite city in Scotland?"

"I like Edinburgh," she said. "And Inverness, although it's completely different. Every city has a flavor to it, don't you think?"

"Have you ever been to Paris?"

"No," she said. "I've never been outside Scotland."

"Cities in other countries have a certain flavor, too. I think it's more pronounced in France. London seems to be the capital of the world. It's frenetic with its activity, but it can drain you after a while. Paris has a certain calmness to it. Maybe it's because I don't speak French well and if you don't understand the language you're on an island."

"I don't speak French, either."

"Well that's a blessing," he said. "I needn't try to impress you with how fluent I am." He glanced at her, smiling. "I'm not."

"Oh, but I bet you know all of the best words in French. Men normally do, don't they?"

One of his eyebrows rose. "And from whom have you gleaned this knowledge of masculine traits?"

"The footmen," she said, smiling. "I believe it was Peter, as a matter of fact, who told me that they exchanged the best words in about five or six different languages, the better to impress their lady loves."

"I think it was for another purpose entirely," he said. "There's a certain latitude of swearing in polite company when no one knows what you're saying."

"Have you ever done that?"

"I think I've done everything impolite, rude, foolish, and borderline stupid when I was a young man. I was aided in my debauchery by my uncle. My mother called it my yearning-to-be-free phase. I called it my growing-up phase. Either one is correct."

They didn't speak for a few moments as he carefully withdrew bunches of herbs from the bottom of the trunk.

"I didn't realize you could dry so many different types of herbs," he said.

She had wrapped them in burlap, and once she peeled back the fabric, he could see that they were additionally covered in newspaper.

"Some of them can only be used after they've been dried," she said. "Others are more efficacious when they're fresh."

"How did you learn about working with herbs? Was it something your father always did?"

She shook her head. "Originally, he concentrated on wildflowers. His first book was on them." She recited the title and he made a mental note to procure it for his library.

"My mother fell ill," she said. "She was in a great deal of pain toward the end. Father was furious with the doctor because he couldn't help her. The only thing was laudanum, and that kept my mother asleep except for nightmares when she'd wake screaming. Father sought out treatments everywhere and met a woman who gave him a tea that helped with the pain. After Mother died, he began his research into herbs and herbal remedies."

"And took you with him?"

She nodded. "Sometimes, we would spend months at one location. But more often it was only weeks. My father had been a professor and believed that education was the greatest gift he could give to me, but that it wasn't always found in books."

Perhaps that's why she was who she was, a woman with many layers of complexity. Just when he thought he was able to put her in a certain category, she said something that made him realize she wouldn't fit there at all.

"It was the best kind of education," she said. "He spoke with people all over Scotland: elderly men and women, young girls who'd learned everything at their grandmother's knee. He found old books and writings. Once he even copied some pictures in a cave.

"He was fond of saying that he'd not devised any of the cures himself. He had simply collected them from the people of Scotland."

"Not unlike how I collect fingerprints," he said.

"You took my fingerprints once," she said, staring down at her hands.

"I did?"

She nodded. "Mrs. McDermott rounded us up one morning and gave us instructions. We were to go to your office. We weren't to speak or ask questions, and if you addressed us, we were to be polite and respectful. Either you or your assistant put soot on our fingers and then made us press them against a card."

He didn't remember. Oh, he remembered the parade of maids, all right, but not her. Why not? Had he been blind that day?

"Did I speak to you?"

She smiled in response. "You held my hand gently and told me I had interesting fingers."

How many times had he made that particular

remark? A hundred? Five hundred? Women who were uncomfortable in his presence seemed reassured by it.

"What else did I say?" he asked, wishing he'd at least been original.

"You repeated my name as you wrote it on the card."

If he'd followed his usual routine, he would have retrieved the jar of finely sieved soot, a clean card, and a feather brush he'd had made for him in Austria. Dipping the brush into the jar, he would sprinkle soot on the relevant finger, blow off the excess, and place the person's finger against the card. As he'd gotten better at the process, he'd rarely had to repeat it. His earlier cards were not so pristine, however, and showed his inexperience.

"But why fingerprints? Why do they interest you? I would think that Blackhall takes all of your time."

"Two reasons," he said. "The first is that I can hire people with more practical experience than I have. My solicitor, for example, is from a firm that's handled the family business for decades. The steward hires people to maintain the property. The housekeeper and majordomo handle the day-to-day affairs of Blackhall. My interference only compounds any problems that might exist."

She didn't say anything. She wasn't, as many women he knew, eager to fill the air with words. But her silence sometimes felt like a measurement, almost as if she were gauging his words for hidden truths or falsities.

He never felt that way with anyone and it both intrigued and irritated him. He found himself wanting her praise, not her condemnation. That, too, was unusual. He'd never deliberately sought anyone's approval.

"The second reason is that I need something that's mine. I love my home but it's more a responsibility than a possession. It doesn't actually belong to me. I'm only the steward for Blackhall. I hold it in trust for future generations. I've been taught that from the moment I knew I was going to inherit all of this."

"But why fingerprints?" She studied her own fingertips again.

He wondered if he should continue and tell her the truth of why he studied fingerprints. If he did so, it would be the first time he ever shared the knowledge with anyone else. Would she ridicule him for it, or would she understand? He'd only know after he told her the story.

"As to why," he said, "it all started with a broken jar. One day, not long after my father died, I found my mother crying. She was holding pieces of this broken jar that he'd given her. I'd always thought it was ugly. It was blue and white with holes in it."

"A potpourri jar," she said.

He nodded.

"It had been a gift from my father and she was brokenhearted to find the pieces in the rubbish. No one came forward to admit that they'd broken it. I examined the pieces and noticed that while the outside of the jar was heavily glazed, the inside wasn't. There in the middle of one of the shards was a fingerprint."

"Your first fingerprint," she said.

He nodded. "I wouldn't have noticed, except that whoever picked up the pieces had something on their hands. Then I realized that it was the potpourri from the jar. Something cinnamon I think. I don't remember. But it made a perfect impression of the fingerprint."

"What did you do?"

"I began with my own fingerprints," he said. "Once I realized they were different, I started making impressions of other people's fingerprints, comparing them to the original."

"Do you still have the shard?"

He glanced at her. "I do," he said, smiling.

"You figured out who did it, haven't you?"

He nodded. "I matched the print a long time ago. I even confronted the perpetrator, who didn't remember breaking the jar. When he did, he apologized to my mother."

"It was your uncle," she said.

He nodded again.

"Why is it important to take people's prints?" she asked. "Are there that many broken jars at Blackhall?"

"There are other thefts," he said. "Other crimes. What about if one man kills another?"

"Could you really find a murderer?"

"If the cataloging system is good enough," he said. "That's what I'm working on now. I've listed people by location and occupation for future reference. I want to come up with a way to categorize their prints, too."

She smiled in approval, or at least that's what it felt like to him.

"Are they truly all different?"

He nodded. "Not only among people," he said, reaching out for her hand. "But even on your own hand. That's why we take prints of all ten fingers."

Spreading out her fingers, he tapped the forefinger. "This one is different from your thumb, for example."

"Truly?"

Her eyes widened and a smile curved her lips. He suddenly wanted to thank her for that, for not being bored, and for allowing him to explain. If she were indulging in pretense, she did it well enough that he was fooled. Or maybe he wanted to be.

In a very real sense, despite the number of people at Blackhall, he was isolated. He'd created a moat around himself and he was beginning to be aware of it. When he was younger, he had counted quite a few men as friends. As time went on, however, he found he had less and less in common with them. He didn't particularly care for horse racing, gambling, or the company of women who were bored in their marriage and wanted a liaison. He was interested in more than what he saw or experienced, ideas that frankly bored others when he expounded on them. Consequently, his friends had dropped away or become acquaintances only.

He'd admired those men he met at the Scottish Society meetings. They'd seen him as more than his title. Nor were they a bunch of fawning sycophants. Instead, they challenged his ideas and made him work for recognition. Perhaps that's why he felt their rebuff of him so keenly.

What had she said? Something about not knowing him. He didn't know her, either, except physically. He knew that she had a mole near her shoulder blade, that when he kissed the side of her breast near her underarm, she was ticklish. He knew, in a way that surprised him to realize it, more about her reactions to passion than he had his own wife. His couplings with Ruth had been done in polite silence, with deference to her innocence and genteel nature.

She'd obviously not retained any innocence or gentility.

Lorna had kissed him without reservation, had been as carnal as he. Even as a virgin she'd been open and willing and passionate and courageous in revealing everything she felt.

She'd sketched him. He recognized his own eyes, his face turned away, his profile, and his frown. In one caricatured sketch, she had drawn him with a crown on his head and an ermine robe. Had he acted regal in some way, enough that she saw him as a king?

Perhaps he didn't know her, but he wanted to. The interest was a dangerous sign. He'd find himself confiding even more in her. Beyond that, he might tell her about his days, share his thoughts with her.

She already occupied too much of his thoughts.

If he wasn't careful, she would come to mean too much. She would become important to him. That shouldn't happen.

He'd avoided personal entanglements for years, enough that his mother had lectured him about his duty to the dukedom. Lorna was an entanglement he'd brought on himself, and if he didn't keep her at arm's length she might prove to be a complication.

He didn't want her that close. Emotions lurked just beyond the horizon, emotions he didn't want to have, feelings that would be difficult.

No, she mustn't be allowed to get that close. He would be pleasant, but nothing more. He'd allow himself a cursory interest in her, but that was all. He would be a polite stranger and only that.

"Why?" he asked, turning the tables on her. When she glanced at him, he continued. "I can understand how you would draw your father's herbs, but how did you go from that to making teas and balms and lotions?"

"At first it was a way of testing the recipes he'd been given. Then I realized it was something I enjoyed, something of my own," she added, using his own words. "I modified some recipes because the herbs weren't available year round, or they were too hard to find."

She fell silent for a moment, and when she spoke, she once again surprised him.

"Thank you for giving me a home here," she said. She fiddled with the fabric of her skirt before glancing up. "Thank you for allowing me the freedom to say what I feel."

"I apologize for not seeing you," he said. "I tried to find you. I just didn't think that you would be at Blackhall."

She looked taken aback. Did she think that he never regretted what he said or did?

"Your apology is accepted, Your Grace," she said, giving him a bright smile.

He sat and watched her for a moment, unwillingly captivated. He'd never considered the matter, but perhaps a woman with child was naturally beautiful. He didn't know. All he knew for certain was that Lorna was. The sun bathed her face, giving her a radiance. Her brown eyes sparkled at him as her lips curved into an enchanting smile.

"No," he said. "Alex."

Her eyes widened. She didn't say anything for a moment.

"I believe we've gone past the need for formalities, don't you?"

To her credit, she didn't glance away. She never had, being one of the few people he'd met who didn't wilt in the face of his determination.

He had to remember to keep her at arm's length.

"Or Kinross, if you prefer."

"Alex," she said.

He nodded, feeling a need to acknowledge her capitulation.

"Lorna."

It wasn't the first time he felt as if they were attuned to each other, but it was the first time that he also felt the moment was dangerous, one that he recognized.

He should leave now, before he became even further ensnared. Now, before he wanted to stay, engage her in conversation, ask about her thoughts. Too late, that moment had passed a while ago. But it wasn't too late to leave to protect himself.

"I've picked out a name for the baby," she said, startling him.

"Have you?"

His voice was carefully neutral, not revealing how he felt about her announcement.

"Robert," she said.

"What if it's a girl?"

"It isn't."

"How can you be so sure?"

"I just am," she said.

"Robert isn't a Russell name."

"He won't be a Russell," she said softly. "He'll be a Gordon." When he didn't speak, she added, "It's my father's name."

He nodded, wondering why what she'd said had so shocked him. He'd known his child was going to be a bastard. What he hadn't realized was how much the idea revolted him.

When he finally left Lorna, he felt a reluctance to do so. That, too, was a warning, one he'd be a fool to ignore.

Once back at Blackhall, Alex headed to his office,

where he dismissed Jason for the day. When the door closed behind his assistant, he went to the long row of card files containing the hundreds of fingerprints they'd taken. It was an easy enough task to locate those for the servants at Blackhall.

The card was in his handwriting, but he couldn't remember the occasion or even the day. Lorna must have sat in front of him, but he'd been interested in her fingers, not her appearance. Still, he'd written that her hair was ginger, but he hadn't indicated that there were red and gold highlights in it.

He'd noted that she had brown eyes, but he hadn't said that they were filled with intelligence, that she sometimes held a spear in those eyes, and that she was not the least bit cowed by him. Had they talked? Or had he been curt with her, as he'd been told he was by others in similar situations?

He'd only indicated that she was on the staff at Blackhall, one of the upper maids. Not that one night she'd masquerade as someone else and he'd be completely convinced she was enchanting and fascinating, only to realize that she'd vanished.

He'd written nothing about her ability to scorn him with a glance.

He hadn't the Sight. How could he have known that one day he would stand here, clutching her card and wondering about her?

She was talented, something he hadn't expected. She was also occasionally defiant, another character trait he hadn't anticipated.

He knew that she wasn't going to change the name of her child. He could offer her any number of inducements, promise her anything, but he knew he'd come up against the wall of her determination.

The idea of his child being named Gordon was irritating. No, perhaps more than that. His son shouldn't be named anything but Russell. He would be a Russell. He should carry the name.

Did Lorna's thoughts ever return to that night? How many times had he wondered where she was? She'd simply disappeared, a storm sprite who'd vanished as ably as a drunken thought.

Not anymore. He knew exactly where she was and what a danger she posed for him.

Chapter 17

The duchess came often to visit her and was turning out to be a fascinating woman, quite different from anyone Lorna knew. In her own way the Dowager Duchess of Kinross was an iconoclast, not unlike her father.

Yesterday, she'd arrived attired in a dark blue dress not unlike the servants' uniforms. In her arms were a selection of garments.

"These will fit, my dear." She held up one of the dresses. "It's called a contouche or a robe à la française. It slips over your head and will be so much more comfortable for you."

She was overwhelmed by the woman's generosity and her concern. The duchess was correct, the French garments were blessedly comfortable, tying in the back and not requiring a corset, petticoat, or shift.

"Alex says you're adamant the child is a boy," the duchess said after Lorna had changed into one of the French dresses.

"I am."

"I felt the same about him," his mother said, smiling at her. "I quite like the name Robert. I understand it was your father's name?"

Had Alex repeated every bit of their conversation to his mother? She nodded.

"It won't be long now," the duchess said. "Only a matter of days, I think."

She'd felt the same, a sense of expectation that she'd never experienced.

"You have everything you need?"

Once more Lorna nodded.

"We have a wet nurse in readiness as well, my dear."

"That won't be necessary," she said.

"You are quite a determined young woman."

"I know that it's probably not proper, Your Grace, but I have every intention of nursing my child."

The duchess surprised her by smiling.

"I did the same, my dear, much to the horror of my mother-in-law. She was under the impression that I would do irreparable harm to myself, the family's reputation, and to my children if I continued as I was doing. She never did recover from my rebellion, poor thing, or that Craig was always on my side."

"I'm sorry about his death," Lorna said. "And about your children."

"Thank you, my dear." The duchess fell silent for a moment. "I learned a lesson that I would impart to you. I expected years of happiness with Craig. Instead, I experienced one unimaginable, horrible week of death. My beloved Craig was gone, never to draw breath again, no matter how much I pleaded with him not to leave me. My darling Donald, a bright chubby cheeked boy, was gone, impatient to be running through the fields of Heaven. My precious daughter left me with a smile."

She placed her hand in the middle of her chest and

pressed her other hand atop it as if to keep her heart inside.

"I feel that smile every day. Sometimes I wonder if Moira isn't with me still, an angel who brings thoughts of joy whenever she appears."

Lorna blinked back her tears. What strength it must have taken the duchess to live through that terrible time.

"Alex wanted to return to school, too soon, I think. I worried that he never truly allowed himself to mourn."

"How did you let him go? How could you bear it with the loss of your other children?"

"How smart you are. You're the only person to have asked me that question, Lorna. Everyone else saw it as natural, the progression of life after death. It was the hardest thing I've ever had to do, other than attend the funeral of my two children and my husband on the same day. But to stand there and watch as his carriage took him away was nearly as difficult."

"What did you do at the castle all alone?"

"I found myself wandering from room to room. I almost asked one of the maids for a feather duster, so that I could keep myself occupied as I went. I made notes about collections that we had that no one paid any attention to anymore. I read. I wrote letters to people I hadn't written to in years. I was probably a pest in my correspondence."

"I'm sure you weren't," Lorna said.

They smiled at each other. Although they had little in common, they were becoming friends. To have the Dowager Duchess of Kinross as a companion and champion was a heady thing.

"As to the lesson, my dear, it's to live fully each day.

Tomorrow everything may change. You're not guaranteed happiness, after all."

She thought about the duchess's words for a long time. Because of Alex, she could enjoy each day and not simply endure it. And happiness? It was there in the small things, the ease of drawing water from the kitchen pump, waking in the morning in the sunny bedroom, sharing memories with Peter over tea.

She began to count the passing days, wondering when her child would be born.

Walking was more laborious, but so was sitting, sleeping, and even dressing. Thank heavens for Nan or she would have had to call Peter to help her on with her shoes as well as assisting her to stand once she'd sat.

She kept herself as busy as she could, working on her sketches and testing more herbal recipes.

A few days earlier she'd crumbled some of the dried herbs into empty bottles and made labels for them. Now she went to her table and picked up the jar of meadowsweet, considering the contents. Fresh meadowsweet flowers were fluffy and white. Once dried, they took on a golden color and a fine-grained appearance.

She had enough to prepare a tincture for the duchess, a small way of thanking the older woman for her kindness. The mixture would help the arthritis in her hands along with comfrey balm.

From her tools, she selected a large spoon and her ivory funnel. She used the spoon to measure out a portion of meadowsweet and the funnel to place it in a clean bottle. To this she added bogbean, a three-leafed plant that grew near lochs. A measure of whiskey, often used in her remedies, was poured into the bottle before it was sealed and placed out of the sun. Ideally, the meadowsweet mixture should steep for six weeks, but she'd still had good results using it in less time. She duplicated the process until she had half a dozen bottles resting on the table.

"Did you know that the flower of the foxglove is called witches' thimbles in this area of Scotland?"

Startled, Lorna glanced up to find the Earl of Montrassey leaning against the door frame.

"A bit of lore I never get to impart. My visit to you has given me the perfect opportunity."

The duke's uncle, according to words she heard the majordomo use, had the randiness of a young buck. The earl was well-known for his attempts to get a girl alone. Even Mrs. McDermott had issued her own kind of warning about the man, couched as it was with half sentences and a distinctively pink face.

It's best if you're not alone around his lordship, Lorna. That's why staff is assigned two to a room on the family floor. If you find yourself in a difficult position, leave immediately and seek me out.

She'd only encountered the earl once when she was alone. He hadn't been interested in dalliance as much as venting his temper. He'd been in the duke's library on the ground floor. When she walked in with her dust rags and brushes, he'd pointed to the ruins of a darling statue of a Greek goddess. He'd evidently just thrown it against the wall.

Clean that up, she recalled him saying as he passed her in the doorway.

"I don't use foxglove often," she said now. "It's dangerous in some applications."

As he entered the room, she turned back to the table.

He reached past her for one of the bottles containing crumbled herbs. She slapped his wrist when he grabbed it, then pulled it from his grip.

"Leave that alone," she said. "It's toxic."

He withdrew his hand, looking down at her with a thin smile.

"Yet you use it in your potions," he said.

"I don't make potions. Only tinctures, teas, poultices, and balms. I use that one in a poultice. With pork fat. It's helpful for gout and rheumatism."

"You're quite the healer."

She frowned over at him. "I'm not a healer," she said. "Nor have I ever called myself one. I use herbs in ways that have been used for hundreds of years. Nothing more."

"Yet you still sell your cures, I understand. And have given them to my sister-in-law."

"For her arthritis," she said.

"What would you prescribe for me?" he asked, sitting on the stool next to her. "What ailments would you treat?"

"I think it would be best for you to consult your physician," she said.

"Then you believe in modern medicine."

"Of course I do."

He reached out and fingered several of the closest bottles. Since none of them were potential poisons, she allowed him to examine the labels.

"Are there herbs of a singular nature here? Something along the line to prevent a woman from having a child, for example?"

He glanced over at her and smiled that wolfish grin.

"No," she said.

"Pity," he said, reaching out with a forefinger to push a bottle back in line. "You might have used it for yourself."

"Is that what you've come to say, your lordship? That I might have been more careful? What an insightful comment. I would never have considered such a thing if you hadn't mentioned it."

"Mouthy little piece, aren't you? I hope you put that mouth to good use with Alex. That's why you're here, isn't it? As a reward for your, shall we say, talents?"

She was too warm, the waves of heat rushing over her also spawning nausea. She rose from the stool and moved to the door, avoided looking at the earl.

He was, in his way, as frightening as Reverend McGill. But the reverend had only accused her of being a harlot. He hadn't treated her like one.

At the door she folded her arms and stared at him.

"I'd recommend St. John's Wort," she said. "It helps reduce the craving for spirits. It also aids in brightening the mood."

"Do you think I need to be treated for my craving for spirits?"

She wanted the earl gone, out of the cottage. Whether he liked it or not, this was her home, and he had no right to insult her in it.

"I've never seen you sober, your lordship. I would venture to say you begin your day with whiskey. Or brandy. Or wine. So, yes, I think you have a great *craving* for spirits."

His face lost its leer. She wasn't certain, but she thought she might have surprised the man.

Did he expect her to sit there and cry because he was being mean to her?

"Thank you for coming to welcome me back to

Blackhall," she said, making her way to the front door. As she passed the kitchen she motioned to Peter, then turned to the earl. "I'm sorry you have to leave so soon, but perhaps next time you can let me know you're coming. I'll brew you a tea."

"Something to give me the trots, no doubt," he said, surprising her with an amused smile.

"No doubt."

"I like you, Lorna, the maid. Perhaps if the circumstances were different, you would have chosen me over my nephew."

She kept her smile fixed by sheer will.

"I think we could have had a most interesting relationship," he added, nodding to Peter and leaving the cottage.

As the door shut, she said, "Tak the door wi' ye."

Peter grinned at her.

"Are there any other Russells at Blackhall?" she asked Peter.

He shook his head, smiling. "There's a second cousin somewhere, but he lives in London. And I've heard tell there was a great aunt or something that emigrated to Australia."

"No one else like Mary or the earl?"

"That's the lot of them."

She shouldn't have allowed the earl to disturb her so much.

"Well, if any more of them turn up, tell them I'm asleep and can't be bothered."

Peter's smile broadened. "That I will, Lorna. That I will."

Chapter 18

She really didn't feel well, but Lorna hid it enough that Nan went off to work without knowing. Instead of sitting in the comfortable overstuffed chair and occupying herself with reading, she kept herself busy by sweeping the whole of the cottage. When that was done, she washed her undergarments, placing them on the windowsill to dry in the sun. After cleaning up Peter's shavings from the kitchen table, she swept the floor again.

A vague back pain made her wonder if she'd done too much. But when it strengthened until it felt like two strong arms trying to crush her in a vise, she realized what was happening.

It was time.

Her son was making his way into the world.

She bit her lip, closed her eyes, and tried to breathe deeply through the pain. Minutes passed, but they were the longest of her life. She was panting when the cramping finally eased.

She opened the cottage door, and when she didn't see Peter, she panicked. Holding onto the door frame with both hands, she tried to calm herself. He'd probably just gone to Blackhall and would return soon. First babies didn't come fast. In fact, they often took hours to arrive. She probably had time to walk to Blackhall a dozen times and back.

She started to walk toward her bedroom when a sudden burst of nausea had her leaning against the wall.

"Lorna?"

Peter, thank heavens.

Without opening her eyes, she said, "Would you let them know, Peter? The baby's coming."

"Now?"

She opened her eyes, turning to face him.

"Soon enough," she said, forcing a smile to her face.

He nodded and left the cottage without a word. She could hear his running footsteps on the road.

She wished her mother were alive, wished she could be with her now. She'd confide in her mother that while she wasn't afraid, she didn't anticipate the pain to come. She wanted to be with someone who had gone through it. She wanted someone to hold her hand through the worst and tell her that it was going to be all right.

She glanced around the cottage, her gaze lighting on the pink and purple hyacinths the duke—Alex— had sent from the conservatory. Spring was here and the bouquet seemed to herald the season. He'd brought her another book on herbs, one that had absorbed her nearly as much as the novel she'd chosen from the bookshelf.

Of course he was on her mind; his son was about to be born.

The cottage was spotless, everything put away, and not a speck of dust to be seen. There was nothing more to do than make it to her bedroom.

Walking was difficult because it felt as if she'd

gained a hundred pounds in the last five minutes. Should she go to bed now? If so, she'd have to prepare it. She had an old blanket to put over the mattress and a set of darned sheeting she'd held back for just this occasion.

Peter had finished augmenting the cradle delivered from the castle. The plain headboard now boasted a carved frontispiece with thistles and acorns. He was working on the footboard now, carving a picture of a stag surrounded by Blackhall's forest.

She would be rocking her child soon enough. She could almost see him there with his shock of black hair and his blue eyes.

Instead of removing her clothes, she began to walk, finding some comfort in the movement. The next pain didn't come until she heard the door open and her name being called.

She smiled at the sound of the duchess's voice. How like her to be first to the cottage.

"I'm in here," she called out, just as the arms encircled her again, squeezing from the back. She held onto the dresser with both hands, bowing her head in subjugation to the pain.

"Oh, my dear, is it time? I had hoped to be farther along in convincing you."

She sincerely hoped that the duchess didn't require an answer because she was incapable of speaking at the moment. She was dripping with sweat and couldn't concentrate on anything but the pain.

The duchess stood with her, one hand on her back as she began to sway back and forth. Blessedly, the older woman didn't ask any questions or say anything else. Then again, perhaps conversation would be better than focusing on the constriction wrapping from her back around to her front.

Her son was making no secret of his impatience.

"Convincing me of what?" she finally asked, biting out the words as the band of pain began to ease.

"To marry my son."

That comment certainly took her mind from labor.

She turned to look at the duchess, who blotted her face with a lace handkerchief. "Your Grace, have you forgotten? I was in service here."

"Of course I haven't forgotten."

Her stomach tightened, a sign another contraction was about to begin. Were they supposed to come so close together? She took a deep breath, steeling herself.

"You must relax into it," the duchess said. "Let the pain win. Pretend it's the ocean and you're a boat riding a wave."

The analogy helped a little. The duchess's presence helped even more. When she didn't mention marriage again, Lorna concentrated on her labor.

In between contractions, the older woman assisted her in stripping the linen from her bed. She placed one hand on the wall and the other on her stomach as she watched the duchess pad the mattress with the blanket, then tuck in the darned sheets.

"I'm going to use this," Louise said, tearing up a pillowcase and making two ropes that she attached to the corners of the headboard. "I'll send you another from the castle."

"Are you going to tie me to the bed?"

The duchess chuckled. "No, it's for you to grab when you'd rather pull off Alex's head. I felt the same about my darling Craig."

Since the duchess was sitting there, obviously expecting Lorna to disrobe in front of her, she removed the robe à la française she was wearing.

Lorna grabbed the nightgown from the drawer and removed her undergarments. When she got to her shoes, she glanced at the duchess, who only laughed.

"Sit down and I'll take them off," she said, smiling. "This reminds me so much of myself. Craig used to have to do the same, as well as massage my feet."

Lorna wasn't the least surprised to see tears in the older woman's eyes.

"Your child will be my grandchild. I never thought to have another chance at one. I realize it's terribly selfish of me, but I would prefer if he wasn't ostracized from the moment he drew breath. I want him to be a Russell."

She only stared at the duchess. Evidently, the woman hadn't given up the idea.

The pain chose that moment to strike. Long moments passed during which she could hardly breathe, let alone speak. When the cramping eased, creeping back behind the dark curtain where it lived, she opened her eyes again.

"It would cause a scandal," she said. "A duke can't marry a maid."

"The world will be petty and brutal in their assessment of the situation. Do not delude yourself that society is anything but rapacious." The duchess smiled. "But also remember this. Even kings married commoners. Elizabeth Woodville was married to Edward IV. Henry VIII married four women without a royal pedigree."

"I doubt they'd been maids," Lorna said.

"How many years were you in service, Lorna?"

"Nearly two, Your Grace."

"And how many years were you your father's daughter?"

"For the whole of my life," she said, understanding.

"Which is longer and more important?"

"The world will not think that."

"No, they shan't, but they will be even crueler to your child if you don't marry Alex. Would you have him labeled a bastard?"

The calm and loving Dowager Duchess of Kinross uttering that word was a shock.

"What would you do for your child, Lorna?"

"Anything," she said, the answer coming so quickly there was no need to think about it.

"Then you know how I feel about Alex and, in turn, for this child. I would do anything for them. And for you, Lorna."

"A friend of mine says I see what I want to see," she said. "That I ignore what's real." She glanced away, then back at the duchess. "I'm trying not to do that, Your Grace. Your son doesn't care anything for me. He's been cordial and charming, but I don't pretend it's anything more than that."

"You've always struck me as a proud young woman," the duchess said. "You didn't go to the poorhouse when you were desperate and alone. You sought out work on your own. You refused to wallow in self-pity. Why are you doing so now?"

"I'm not." The response came immediately to her lips. "How can you say I am? A marriage between us would be ridiculous, not to mention scandalous. People would never stop talking about it."

"No, they wouldn't," the duchess said. "But, then, they will talk regardless. If it wasn't this marriage, it would be something else. People will find things to discuss. Alex is a wonderful topic for them. He's brooding and a loner. He has a sorrowful past, and he's handsome. What better target for their gossip?"

She blinked at the duchess. What on earth could she say to such an attitude? Something, anything, to make the other woman understand. But before she could interject, the duchess continued.

"You are going to find that people will criticize you regardless of who you are or who your family is or what your station is in life. Almost no one measures up. Your grandfather was an earl? My father was one." She smiled. "The faster you realize that it doesn't matter, the happier you will be. That is one thing I've never had to teach Alex. He doesn't give a fig what anyone else thinks."

"That's because he's a duke."

"Oh my dear," she said, "Alex has been that way all his life." She held up a hand. "Before you say that it's because he was the heir to a dukedom, I assure you that he was as self-possessed in the nursery before he truly understood who or what he was. You could do worse than to emulate him, and that's said with a mother's usual pride."

"Has he agreed?"

"Yes," the duchess said. "Now it's your turn. I won't have my grandchild born a bastard. Say yes."

What choice did she have?

"Yes," she said, the word uttered on a tidal wave of pain.

PERHAPS THERE WAS a place in Heaven where mothers go to be lectured. The admonitions would only last an hour or two, Louise was certain. After a respectable amount of time, and a genuine, soul-wrenching confession, the mother would be led away to the main part of Heaven and fitted with a pair of angel wings.

At least that's the way she thought it should be.

She'd lied to Lorna. In addition, she had every intention of lying to her son. The result was worth any amount of chicanery. The child soon to be born must be a Russell.

She sent Peter for the midwife, and when the woman arrived she motioned her into the bedroom.

"Dr. McElwee will be here soon. If he needs to examine her, I'd like you to remain in the room with Lorna."

"Aye, Your Grace."

Louise turned and studied Lorna's face. The poor dear was dozing. Lorna had some rough hours ahead of her. Russell babies were always large and birthing them wasn't easy.

"I'll return in a little while," she said, leaving the bedroom.

To her surprise, both Dr. McElwee and Alex were in the parlor. Nan was making tea, while Peter was standing at attention as if ready to take orders from Alex at any moment.

"Would you see to her, Dr. McElwee?"

After exchanging a few words with the doctor, she motioned to Alex, grabbed her shawl, and left the cottage, walking some distance down the road toward Blackhall.

"If you wanted to go home," he said, striding toward her, "why didn't you take the carriage?"

"I wanted to talk to you. Alone. With no one to overhear."

She turned to face him and took a deep breath,

praying for the wisdom to say the perfect words to convince him.

Alex speared his fingers through his hair.

"Is she going to be all right?" he asked. "This won't be like Ruth, will it?"

She frowned at him. "Of course not."

"How do you know?"

"I just know."

"Did you feel that way about Ruth?" he asked.

"Alex, Lorna's going to be fine."

He nodded but didn't look reassured. "Is she afraid? She never mentioned that she was to me. I know you two have grown close in the last weeks. Did she say anything to you?"

"No, she didn't, and I think she would have if she were. Alex, it's all right." She placed her hand on his arm. "Truly, it will be. In the meantime, we need to make plans."

"Plans?"

"You have to marry her, Alex. We haven't much time. Lorna's labor is well-advanced." When he didn't comment, she said, "Do you want your child born illegitimate?"

"Of course not," he said. "I had this idea that I could petition the court after the fact, but that's not practical, is it?"

"No, it isn't."

He nodded again. "It would necessitate the world knowing his status, of course. I'd be dragging his name and his reputation through the mud. Yes, he might be legitimized, but at what cost? He'd be known as the Bastard Duke. That's unacceptable."

Folding his arms, he stared off down the road to Blackhall.

"Even the word is ugly, Mother. I was at school with more than one boy whose birth was questioned. Life was miserable for them. I don't want that to happen to my child. She must agree to marry me."

She blinked at him. This was much easier than she'd thought it would be.

"She already has. She wants the best for her child, of course. This wouldn't be the first marriage to be performed on the birthing bed. Besides, I think you and Lorna suit quite well."

He glanced at her. "Do you? Well, we don't have any other choice, do we?"

"Oh, my dear darling Alex," she said. "The time to choose was approximately nine months ago. Now's the time to pay the piper."

EVERYONE WAS TOO damn calm. They didn't seem the least bit anxious, as if the sounds from the other room were normal.

Alex had never been on the battlefield, but he could well imagine a wounded man making the same noises, especially as he tried to stifle his cries of pain from being heard by his fellow soldiers.

What had possessed him to think that he needed to be here? He wanted to be a hundred miles away. Far enough that he couldn't hear Lorna's agony.

What if history and tragedy repeated themselves? Was that why his mother had hugged him earlier, given him a bracing smile, then insisted on being in the room with Lorna?

The cottage was too damn small. He knew that now. He'd paced off the exact distance from the front door to the farthest wall at least fifty times. Why didn't he just go back to the castle with instructions for someone to send him news on the hour? How long was this supposed to go on?

He halted at the far wall, but instead of turning and retracing his steps, he placed both hands flat on the window frame, wishing it weren't night, that he could see beyond the glass.

Taking a deep breath, he let it out slowly, pretending a calm he didn't feel.

He turned his head to see Peter standing there. He should say something to the young man, especially since the footman's face was a peculiar shade of gray. Dear God, did he look the same?

"It's all right," he said, hearing the faint tremor in his own voice and making an effort to steady it. "Women do this every day." So much for platitudes.

Peter nodded. "My sister went three days, Your Grace."

Three days? He couldn't last a few more hours. If he couldn't, what the hell was Lorna going through?

How did women survive this? If his mother was in the room with him then, he would've pulled her aside and asked her the question. She would probably have patted him on the shoulder and smiled a Madonna-like smile, a combination of maternal wisdom and pity.

He couldn't leave. They were waiting for the odious minister. The idiot Reverend McGill was the closest clergy.

Another scream, this one longer than the last, made the hair on the back of his neck stand on end.

Men were supposed to be the stronger sex, weren't they? They went off to battle. They were seen as conquerors. They built things. They discovered continents. They manipulated science to create what would have been inconceivable a hundred years earlier.

Yet women continued the species. They labored to bring children into the world and did so without asking for recognition.

Fear was an icy fist in his stomach. It harnessed his breath and made his heart race. He would stay where he was, staring through a window at a world he couldn't see.

Another scream had him walking to the closed door. It was as much a barrier as if it had been a brick wall. He wasn't wanted or needed in that room. He was superfluous and unnecessary in the business of giving birth. All he could do was pray, an activity at which he was woefully inept.

Hopefully, God would not judge him on the infrequency of his prayers, or if He did, not apply his sins to Lorna or their child.

The front door abruptly opened, revealing Reverend McGill.

Their gazes met in recognition of the last time they'd encountered each other. McGill had called him a fornicator and he'd threatened to withhold any funds for the church roof if the man didn't shut up.

"Thank you for coming," he said, striding to the door. As if the man had any choice. He'd given Charles instructions to take someone with him to convince Reverend McGill that it would be advisable to agree to officiate.

He didn't get a chance to explain anything because the bedroom door opened and his mother stood there. At the sight of the minister, she smiled.

"Just in time," she said, motioning them forward.

Grabbing McGill by the sleeve, Alex made for the bedroom.

Chapter 19

*T*he marriage of Alexander Brian Russell, ninth Duke of Kinross, to Lorna Anne Gordon, spinster, occurred only three minutes before the birth of their child.

Reverend McGill couldn't help himself and launched into a speech about how women were duty bound to experience pain in childbirth. He was stopped in the middle of his tirade by the Dowager Duchess of Kinross who eyed him with disfavor and said, "A little less original sin, Reverend, and more wedding vows."

A scant three minutes later, Robert Russell arrived accompanied by a gusty sigh of relief from the midwife, who knew only too well what had happened to the previous duchess. Alex, somewhat stunned by the events of the past hour, heard the news that he had an heir with calm acceptance. The Dowager Duchess beamed, her tear-dampened smile one of the first things the mother saw as she was given her large and demanding son.

The newly born Robert Russell—Robbie—was already voicing his displeasure with the proceedings, thereby echoing the Reverend George McGill's mutterings as he affixed his signature to the necessary documents.

Lorna crooned to her child as he was placed on her

chest. He immediately curled up and thrust his fist in his mouth.

He was going to be a duke. She'd given birth to a duke. How astonishing.

She was a duchess. It didn't seem possible, especially when she glanced up and found herself pinned by her husband's gorgeous eyes. *Husband*. The word didn't seem the least bit plausible. She couldn't be married to the Duke of Kinross. She'd watched him from afar, marveled at his handsomeness, dreamed of speaking to him one day.

Now they were married.

Now they were parents.

The whole thing was too improbable. Perhaps she was dreaming and memories of the hastily performed ceremony would disappear the minute she awakened.

No, the Reverend McGill was standing in the corner. She would never have dreamed about him.

If this wasn't a dream or a figment of her imagination, then she was certain that the rest of the world wasn't going to be so pleased. Take the Earl of Montrassey, for example. Or Mary Taylor.

Nan, bless her, had attended the hurried ceremony as they clustered around her bed. Toward the end Lorna had been hard-pressed to repeat the words of her vow because her son—their son—was demanding to be born. Thankfully, only the midwife and the duchess were in the room when that event occurred. After she and the baby had been cleaned up and the linen replaced, everyone returned to greet the heir.

Now she wished they'd all leave so she could sleep.

Robbie, however, didn't appear sleepy. He was squinting up at her and pummeling her with his tiny fists.

She glanced at the duchess, and bless the woman, Louise understood what was needed immediately. In moments she'd shooed everyone from the room except Alex.

Today, Lorna reflected, she'd been naked in front of the duchess and the midwife, and now, in order to breast-feed her child, was revealing herself to Alex. It was the first time since that night nearly a year ago. She would have preferred to be alone, but how did she banish the duchess and her husband?

Husband. One again that word didn't make any sense. How could that gloriously handsome man be her husband?

The duchess helped Lorna sit up a little, unfasten her nightgown, and put Robbie to her breast. Only then did he stop waving his arms around and settle down.

Glancing up, she saw the duchess's face contorted with the effort of balancing emotions. The older woman was weeping at the same time her mouth was curving into a smile. Robbie's birth must have brought back memories of the children she'd lost.

Somehow, she wanted to ease the pain of this moment for the duchess.

"Thank you," she said softly. "I haven't missed my mother as much as I thought because you were here."

To her surprise, the older woman bent over the bed and kissed her cheek. Then she left the room, but not before Lorna saw the tears on her cheeks.

"Was I wrong to say what I did?" she asked, glancing at Alex.

"No," he said. "It was the best thing you could have said."

He wasn't looking at her, but at their son, rooting at

her breast. Was he going to argue about her decision to nurse her own child?

She would not change her mind. Although he could turn that brilliant blue green gaze on her and make her thoughts fly away as if they were frightened starlings, she wasn't going to agree to a wet nurse.

"He's big," he said.

She kept her attention on their son. "Your mother said that her babies were all large."

"He has my hair."

She nodded. Her imagination had conjured up a shock of black hair, and that's exactly how Robbie looked.

"And my nose," Alex said.

She tilted her head slightly and studied her son. He was an infant image of the duke.

"And your chin," she added. "Plus, I don't doubt he has a ducal temperament."

"Exactly what is a ducal temperament?" he asked.

She would have smiled if she weren't so tired. The effort seemed suddenly beyond her.

Robbie was asleep, and she wanted, very much, to join him.

"Could you put him in the cradle, please?"

She always wanted to remember the expression on Alex's face: startled bemusement followed by sheer terror. His hands flailed in the air as if she'd asked him to hold a pot of boiling water without a cloth between him and burning hot metal.

"He's your son," she pointed out. "Did you never think to hold him?"

He didn't answer her. To his credit, he stepped closer to the bed. He might look like a condemned prisoner, but he manfully held out his arms.

"Sit there," she said, gesturing toward the side of the mattress with her chin.

He did so, angling his body so that he was half turned toward her.

"Now, cup your arms," she said. When he did as she asked, she realized she wasn't too tired to smile after all.

She made the transfer easily. As he balanced their child in his arms, she buttoned up her nightgown.

Words weren't necessary at that moment. They would have been an interference as son met father. Robbie squinted up at Alex, waved his fists a few times, then made a soft snuffling sound.

"He's asleep," Alex said a few minutes later.

She nodded, almost asleep herself.

"What if he wakes up when I put him in the cradle?"

"Then you'll have to rock him," she said.

She lay her head back on the pillow, the last image before sleep claimed her the sweet picture of Alex smiling down at his son.

THOSE MOMENTS OF sitting there, Robbie's head cradled in his elbow, the baby's bottom in his palm, were silent and almost prayerful.

Nothing mattered but Robbie. The child's parentage was unmistakable. It was like looking in a mirror, albeit a younger one.

The sight of that tiny chest rising and falling, his feet kicking the blanket, the mouth pursing and relaxing, was enough to render Alex silent and awed.

For the first time in three years he allowed himself to think of that poor infant who hadn't survived his birth. He would have been like Robbie, each small breath he took the promise of another. Whether the child had been his or not didn't matter. He should have felt the loss regardless.

In the silence, he faced Ruth's ghost, bowing his head in the face of that death as well. He'd been numb and angry, feeling lost and stunned. Had he ever felt the grief? He'd been a young man when he fell in love with her. He'd never believed that she would betray him, but she had. Yet the young man who'd loved Ruth had never had a chance to feel pain at her death. He hadn't just created a moat around himself. He'd built a wall.

In the last three years he'd thought himself complete. Oh, there were niches and hollows in his life. Until now, until this moment, with Lorna asleep and his child in his arms, he hadn't known how empty the hollows or how cavernous the niches.

He had a wife. He had a son.

He carefully placed Robbie in his cradle and sat watching as the two of them, mother and son, slept.

Alex had been reared to understand that he was steward of Blackhall and his other estates. He comprehended that it was up to him to make wise decisions to increase the family coffers.

Until now, he'd never felt the weight of responsibility so keenly.

He had a wife. He had a son.

He reached out a hand and covered Lorna's where it lay on the bed. Somehow, it was necessary to make a connection with her, to let her know he was still there.

His wife.

Her long eyelashes lay atop the shadows beneath her eyes. Her cheeks were pink, her mouth the same color. Someone had brushed her hair and it lay against the pillow, almost summoning his touch. One finger did just that before he returned his hand to cover hers.

He had a wife.

He'd never thought to marry again. Never believed that it would be important to do so. He'd already had his heir in his uncle, if anything happened to him. Now he had a son.

Thomas probably wouldn't be happy. Or it could be that he'd be relieved.

He had a wife.

Lorna sighed in her sleep, and he wanted to hold her, comfort her, tell her that he was there, watching over her.

In the last hours, he'd been too terrified to draw a deep breath. When he first heard his son's newborn cry, it wasn't for him that he was concerned. His first question had been about Lorna.

His wife.

He would have to arrange for her transport to the castle. Tomorrow, perhaps. Or should they wait a week or so? He didn't know, but it was somehow important that she take her rightful place at Blackhall.

She hadn't seemed all that pleased during the ceremony. Of course, she'd been in labor at the time. Was she unhappy that he was her husband? Surely other unions were built on flimsier ground.

He had a wife.

Of course she was his wife. It had almost been destined the moment he'd taken her from the Wittan Village square and brought her to this cottage. The moment he'd kissed her in the rain. The moment he'd seen her standing there with her towering white wig and gold mask.

They were destined to be together, a thought as sharp as a blow to his chest.

THE STRANGE CONVOY he'd arranged made it by degrees to Blackhall. The first carriage held Lorna, the baby, and his mother. The second held Peter, all of Lorna's belongings except for her herbs, and Nan.

Alex sat beside Lorna, watchful for anything that could cause her discomfort. His mother was giving him what he considered her "Russell look," something she'd borrowed from his father. Comprised of a frown, watchful stare, and thinned lips, it as much as shouted: *I'm disappointed in you. You have not lived up to the expectations I had.*

Other than insisting on transporting Lorna to Blackhall, he hadn't done anything but accede to her wishes. How was he to know that he'd violated all the tenets of new motherhood?

"She isn't supposed to move for two weeks, Alex. Nor get out of bed. You try giving birth and you'll understand."

Lorna didn't appear worse for the disruption. In fact, her eyes were sparkling when she did glance at him. Most of her attention was devoted to Robbie, and the ease with which she handled the baby amazed him.

They weren't going to take the formal entrance. Instead, they would enter the back way, normally used by tradesmen. He didn't want Lorna subjected to the intense scrutiny of the curious staff. Nor was she dressed for her first appearance as a duchess. In fact, she wasn't dressed at all. His mother had brought one of her French nightgowns, laboriously embroidered by some nuns in a convent in France. He'd wrapped his greatcoat around her to keep her warm. The thick white cotton was too virginal for his taste, especially since his wife didn't appear the least virginal with her hair around her shoulders, her pink cheeks, and the pink mouth that reminded him too much of her kisses.

He'd been intoxicated by Lorna's kisses.

His wife. He should repeat the words a few hundred times and maybe he wouldn't be feeling so . . . not out of sorts as much as confused. No, confused wasn't the right word, either. He was befuddled, perhaps. Bemused. Beneath it all, whether befuddlement or bemusement, he was strangely happy. He hadn't expected to be happy at this moment. Nor had he anticipated feeling this odd buoyancy accompanied by an unfamiliar peace.

Was it being a new father? Or was it being Lorna's husband?

She glanced at him again as if hearing his thoughts. Her smile lit up something inside him. He liked her. An odd realization to have at this moment. He admired her, and he didn't think he'd ever used that word about another woman.

He'd spent hours thinking about her, trying to understand the former maid with her artistic talent and her determination.

When his father died, along with Moira and Donald, it had been a dark and terrible time. But he'd had his mother to give him emotional sustenance and never had to worry about his next meal. Lorna had, but she hadn't appealed to the parish poorhouse. Nor did she live off the charity of others. Instead, she'd come to Blackhall and worked as a maid.

He'd visited Mrs. McDermott last week and asked her a question that had concerned him for a long time.

"Why did you employ her, when she had no references or experiences?"

When she hesitated, he moved to assure her that he wasn't criticizing her decision.

"It's my curiosity," he said, trying to explain. "You maintain an admirable staff, Mrs. McDermott. In fact, I'd say that no one could do a better job at Blackhall."

Once she was appeased, she told him what he wanted to know.

"I felt sorry for her, Your Grace. She was so brave, but it was evident that getting the job was important to her. Even a matter of life or death. Poor lass, it was obvious she hadn't eaten well for some time. But she had a way about her, you know?"

Yes, he knew.

He wondered what Mrs. McDermott would think to learn that he'd married the young maid, the courageous lass with the sparkling brown eyes and the enchanting smile. She certainly hadn't approved of him moving Lorna into the cottage.

When they arrived at the castle, he sent Peter to fetch three other young men along with a chair. All four men could be trusted to keep their counsel and not talk about this ignominious arrival.

In the interim, he assisted his mother and then Lorna from the carriage, carefully transferring his well-bundled son from his mother's arms to his grandmother's.

"You might not get him back," he said to Lorna after watching his mother's face. In her eyes was a joy he hadn't seen for many years. She cooed to Robbie and he stared up at her, transfixed.

Lorna only smiled at him, placed her hands on his

shoulders and allowed him to half lift, half carry her to the ground.

When the chair arrived, she looked at him quizzically.

"If you'll sit," he said, having been informed that stairs were a difficult feat for a new mother, "the footmen will carry you to the second floor."

His mother nodded approvingly, then ignored them all as she carried Robbie into Blackhall.

They climbed the steps slowly in deference to Lorna's condition. The baby gave out a wail, summoning all their attention. Alex had not yet gotten used to his son's cry. It tore the skin off his back and alerted all his senses. He immediately wanted it to stop. Either Robbie was hungry or wet or was frightened. Someone had to fix the situation now.

His mother began to bounce the baby in her arms, a curious rocking motion that evidently soothed Robbie. The baby still wanted his mother, since he turned his head and began beating on his grandmother's chest.

"Look here, son," Alex said, going to his mother's side. "There's time enough for petulance, but this isn't it."

Before his mother could stop him, he scooped Robbie up in his arms and resumed his journey up the grand staircase, all the while addressing his son.

"When we get your mother settled, there will be time enough to make your needs known. Only ten minutes, that's all I ask."

Robbie stared up at him, one fist inserted firmly in his mouth.

It was strange seeing his features melded in this perfect little boy. Something creaked open inside

Alex, a gate he hadn't known was closed, a door that had never been unstuck. Something new and novel flooded through him. Gratitude, perhaps, or something else. Joy, pure, sweet, and elemental, nearly swamped him.

They watched each other, father and son, as he entered his suite. Robbie was reclaimed by his grandmother and Alex was banished as Lorna was settled into the bed.

He stood in the sitting room glancing around at the chamber he'd occupied since he was sixteen. Everything was the same, from the oil painting of Blackhall above the fireplace to the escritoire crafted in Edinburgh on the far wall. The scarlet curtains were exactly as they had been for a dozen years, hemmed with gold fringe and held back with braided gold ties.

Nothing was out of place yet everything had changed.

The carpet was scarlet, with the same blue leaves found in the family crest. As he walked over it he remembered all those occasions when the maids had been on their hands and knees with a brush and a pail of spent tea leaves. Had Lorna been one of them?

In his mind he saw her all those times when he'd deliberately ignored the staff. She nodded to him in the hall. She smiled at him when he was entering his library as she left it. She was here, dusting the Chinese urn on the hearth or the potpourri pot on the bookshelf. She diligently brushed away nonexistent dust from the sofa and the wing chairs arranged in front of the fireplace. Or maybe she even emptied the ashes, getting soot on her cheek.

The curtains on the three tall windows had been opened, the view the approach to Blackhall. He knew that just beyond the copse of trees to his right, hidden from his view, was the cottage.

How many times had he stood there in the last month wondering if Lorna was well, if she needed anything, if she was happy with her decision to return?

Now she was in his bedchamber, being settled into the tall and wide bed that had belonged to Russells for generations. His son would rest beside the bed in his cradle, an heirloom that Lorna had seen fit to alter. Where before it had been utilitarian and almost ugly, now it was beautiful.

What else would she change at Blackhall?

Even now he could feel the wall thinning between him and other people until he could almost see through it. He was going to be weakened. He could almost feel the target on his back, the stuttering of his heart as it readied for the moment it was shredded.

He had to do something, anything, to protect himself.

Chapter 20

$\mathcal{L}$orna didn't sleep well that first night, since Robbie insisted on eating every two hours.

The first time she got up, she sat on the edge of the giant bed and fed him, then tried to find the nappies. She finally located all of Robbie's clothing in an armoire in the dressing room where she'd also found Alex, sleeping on a cot that didn't accommodate his height or breadth easily. His feet were hanging off his impromptu bed, uncovered. She stopped herself from rearranging his blanket. He might be her husband, but they were little more than strangers.

She got what she needed and crept back into the bedroom. Once Robbie was changed and dry, she put him into the cradle again, dozing until he woke once more. That was the tenor of her night: sleep, feed him, change him, sleep, repeat.

She was in no mood for Matthews's rudeness just past dawn.

Lorna knew Alex's valet, but she didn't like the man. Matthews was too officious, too conscious of his position as the duke's personal servant, a role he bragged about endlessly.

Now the valet was staring at her as if she'd committed a sin worse than spilling wine on a priceless carpet. Perhaps she had; she'd married the duke.

"Where's His Grace?" Matthews asked, taking in the cradle and Lorna's disheveled appearance in one glance.

Pulling up the sheet, she covered the bodice of her borrowed nightgown and forced a smile to her face.

He, of course, was sartorially perfect as always.

His face was round, almost pudgy, with a double chin. He'd always appeared brown to her, with his thick brown hair and brown eyes that were always narrowed. He had a barrel chest with short legs and a curious way of walking. She often wanted to ask him if he'd ever been at sea because he had the rolling gate of the sailors she'd seen in Inverness.

She and Matthews didn't converse, however. She wasn't on his level, a fact he'd made perfectly clear when she was on staff.

"He's in the dressing room," she said.

The man was an inveterate gossip, passing along all sorts of stories. He didn't really care if they were true; what mattered to him was whether they were salacious. Or if he'd learned the tale before anyone else. He would, no doubt, pass along that the duke had been sleeping on a cot.

She might as well tell him the rest.

"His Grace and I were married yesterday," she said.

He stopped halfway to the dressing room but he didn't turn around. Had she startled the man into apoplexy? She doubted it.

Matthews slowly turned, looking her up and down in a contemptuous perusal.

"You're the Duchess of Kinross?"

She was grateful for the Dowager Duchess's warnings, but she honestly hadn't thought that a member of the staff would be the first to ridicule her.

Although she didn't know anything about being a duchess or a wife a day ago, she hadn't known anything about being a mother, either, and she was managing that well enough.

"Yes," she said, "I'm the new duchess."

Matthews didn't say another word, just marched across the expanse of the room and into the dressing room, closing the door harder than necessary. Didn't the fool care if he woke the duke?

Evidently, he didn't care about waking the baby, either.

Robbie let out a startled wail. She sent an annoyed glance in the valet's direction before picking up her son and bringing him into the bed with her. Arranging the covers in a mound to give her some privacy in case Matthews came storming out of the dressing room, she put Robbie to her breast.

He fussed for a bit, making her wonder if he could feel her irritation. Or maybe he was sensitive to her fear.

She didn't want each day to be marked by confrontation. She didn't want to have to justify her existence each time she encountered someone like Matthews. Would the rest of the staff behave in a similar fashion? Nan hadn't, but then, she'd been the truest friend imaginable.

Robbie finally settled down. For the next ten minutes she was left in peace with her son, the problems of her new position pushed aside for more elemental concerns. Would she be a good mother? Was he getting enough milk? Was she doing this right?

She concentrated on Robbie's intent, determined

infant face, seeing in his focus more than a hint of his father. Would they be the same in temperament? What would it be like to rear someone like Alex? She needed to ask the duchess.

A sound made her glance up to see Alex standing there, appearing ducal. His black suit showed off his snowy white cravat. He was freshly shaved, hair brushed and shining.

She, no doubt, looked like a maid who'd worked all day, more than a little messy and in need of a wash and a change of clothing.

As if he'd heard her thoughts, he spoke. "We have to arrange for a lady's maid for you."

"Good heavens, no."

One eyebrow went up, an expression she'd seen the duchess wear. Part incredulity, part irritation, it gave her a clue to what he was thinking.

"I haven't the slightest interest in having a lady's maid. I would probably offend her on an hourly basis. 'What are you doing nursing your child? Why isn't he in the nursery? You should be thinking of your wardrobe rather than your son.' I have absolutely no intention of being dictated to by another person."

"Has anyone dictated to you?"

His eyebrow regained its normal appearance as he walked toward her. He sat sideways on the edge of the bed, one knee drawn up, and reached out with one hand, stroking a finger over Robbie's cheek.

"He's hungry this morning," he said.

"And all night."

"Were you up all night?" he asked.

"Don't sound so surprised. Your son is a voracious eater. Every two hours he wants another feed."

His palm cupped the baby's head tenderly.

"You didn't answer me. Has anyone dictated to you?"

"No," she admitted. "Although Matthews is in a snit."

"Matthews is always in a snit," he said, smiling. "You just have to learn to ignore him."

"He shouldn't be allowed to be . . ." Her words trailed off because she realized his knuckles were gently stroking the edge of her breast where Robbie's fist was resting.

He glanced up at her. "He shouldn't be allowed to be what?"

She patted his hand, then gently removed it from her breast. He didn't say a word, but his smile vanished.

"Rude to you," she said. "Mrs. McDermott would never allow it. She certainly doesn't with the maids."

He rested against one of the mounds of coverlet and pillows, looking indolent and too attractive. Didn't he have some work to do this morning?

"Do the maids wish to be rude to me?" he asked, once again smiling.

He really was devastatingly handsome and too aware of it, too. At the moment he reminded her of Thomas, which was not a compliment. At least he hadn't tried to seduce every single maid at Blackhall. If he had, the girl would have run back to the servants' quarters and let slip the secret in a matter of minutes.

"All the maids are madly in love with you and you know it."

The eyebrow rose again. "Are they?"

Robbie was nearly asleep, his mouth slack on her nipple.

"You know quite well they are."

"I don't," he said, watching his son. "Nan could be

your lady's maid. If she'd want the position. It pays much better, plus the two of you are friends."

Surprised, she studied him. "You would allow that?"

His eyes met hers.

"I don't want to make you miserable, Lorna. I want you to be happy. You need someone to help you. Why not Nan?"

She could have kissed him. In that next instant, she actually thought of doing it, of bending over Robbie and touching her lips to his.

She waited too long because he abruptly stood.

"I have to go to Inverness," he said. "I'll be gone a few days. Is there anything I can get for you there? Or anything you need now?"

She shook her head, raised Robbie to her shoulder and occupied herself with her son's care.

She wasn't upset that he was leaving her. Of course she wasn't.

"I'm going to put the notice of our marriage in the newspapers," he said.

"Is that why you're going?"

"No. I have business with the Scottish Society."

She recognized the name, the same group he'd hosted the night of the fancy dress ball. Curiosity wasn't an admirable trait, at least that's what Mrs. McDermott always said at her morning lectures. What balderdash. How could they not be curious about the Russell family?

How was she supposed to quell her curiosity now?

Before he turned and left, she stretched out her hand as if to touch him, but he was too far away.

Oh, how did she say it? How could she possibly form the words? *Tell me what business. Talk to me about your day, what you've planned, who you'll meet. Do you like to travel? Will you take the same carriage I rode in yesterday? Are you a sound sleeper? Did you not hear Robbie last night?*

What came out was a silly question, but she didn't call it back once it was uttered.

"What is your earliest memory?" she asked him.

He glanced at her then turned. "Why?"

She smiled. "Must there be a why all the time? Could I not simply wish to know?"

"I was five, I think. I was given a pony for my birthday."

Her smile broadened. "I was given a quizzing glass. I spent hours staring at the magnified world."

"I'm surprised you weren't given drawing materials."

"That was my sixth birthday," she said. "A box of watercolor paints and brushes. It had three drawers and a lock and key with the most wonderful colors."

"Do you still have it?" he asked, coming to sit on the edge of the bed again.

She shook her head.

"So your box of paints was lost in your travels?"

She nodded. "I think I left it behind at our lodgings in Perth. I like to think that someone found it and was able to use it."

"Why did you want to know my earliest memories?"

"I'm curious about you," she said, giving him the truth. "What's your favorite color? Do you have a favorite song? Poem? Play? Food? Book?"

"The last treatise by Sir David Burton," he said. "A fascinating study of the polarization of biaxial crystals and double refraction. And you?"

"The poetry of Elizabeth Barrett Browning," she said. "A very romantic volume."

"I like roast beef, but I'm also partial to chocolate biscuits."

"Spice scones for me, please," she said, smiling.

"No favorite song. At least I don't think so. I shall have to think on it. What about you?"

"Something my mother sang to me when I was a child," she said. "I don't know the name of it, but it was about a little boy who wanders down a path into a flower garden, gets lost and then found."

"Blue."

"Yellow," she said. "Although, I do like blue and yellow together."

"They make green," he said.

"If they're combined," she said, "one into the other. But if they're aligned next to each other, they're quite pleasant."

"You're the artist," he said.

She was startled by the comment. "I haven't worked in days and days."

"You're a new mother," he said. "You're supposed to be that and nothing else for a few days, I think."

"Ah, ducal wisdom."

"Of course," he said, and grinned at her.

In that instant she saw a hint of the boy he'd been and one that Robbie might emulate. Her heart swelled as tears came to her eyes.

"Thank you," she said, determined not to cry even though she was suddenly feeling weepy. "You've been so kind. Thank you for taking such good care of me, and for Nan, and for being so tender with Robbie. Thank you for letting me name him Robbie and for giving me your bed."

He looked as if he would like to say something, but didn't.

"I'm your husband," he said. "I should do all those things."

She nodded, chagrined when she felt a few tears falling down her cheek.

SHE WAS WEEPING and something twisted inside him. One tear, that's all it took to make it feel as if a knife were thrusting into his belly. Suddenly he wanted to answer every question she asked and more, eager to share himself with another human being when he hadn't done that in . . . Had he ever done that?

She sat among the pillows looking luminous, like a painting he'd once seen in Italy. *Madonna of the Milk*, he thought it was called, by Verrocchio. Unlike the painting, there'd been no angels in the scene, but she hadn't needed any.

Bending, he brushed a kiss along her forehead, an avuncular gesture and one he intended to last only seconds.

She raised her head. She reached up, leaned toward him, and suddenly his lips were on her mouth. He was kissing her, deeply, leaning down, one hand bracing himself on the headboard, the other thrusting into her hair. He heard Robbie from far away, felt himself harden, wanting her with a desperation he'd never felt for anything, anywhere, at any time.

What the hell was he doing?

Kissing her. Dear God, her lips were warm to hot, her tongue dueling with his.

She was a day away from giving birth.

He wanted her.

She was a new mother.

He was losing all control.

He stepped back, staring at her, wanting to apologize, but words escaped him. He didn't think he could talk at the moment. Was she going to notice that he'd not been unaffected by the kiss? How did he explain being a randy monster under these circumstances?

He'd never lost his mind around a woman. The last time had been on that stormy night last year.

He needed to leave, now, but he wanted to stay there for hours watching Lorna and his son. She held him so tenderly, but with such competence. Shouldn't a new mother have fumbled a little, been uncertain? She hadn't been. Each one of her movements was unhurried and patient. When Robbie fussed, she simply smiled and rubbed his back, crooning to him softly.

The sight of the two of them made something open up in his chest, as if he were being carved from the inside out.

He wanted to stay and that's exactly why he left.

BEFORE DESCENDING THE stairs, Alex made his way to his mother's apartments. The door was open, as it often was.

"How is Lorna? And the baby?" she asked, turning to smile at him. She put down the copper atomizer she'd been using to spray the ferns and walked toward him.

"He was up all night," he said, a little surprised that he hadn't heard Robbie.

"That's to be expected. You were the same. Demanding from the very first."

"How do you do it?"

"Do what?" she asked with a smile.

"How did you ever get over my father's death?" he asked. "Or Moira's and Douglas? How do you wake up every morning, go about your day, and find something to interest you? How do you endure the pain of losing them?"

"Oh, Alex," she said, walking to him. She grabbed his arm and pulled him into her sitting room, leading him to the settee. "What's brought this on? Robbie's birth?"

He didn't know. He only knew that this morning, sitting on the edge of the bed and watching Lorna and Robbie, he'd been hit with a knowledge he'd never before had: pain was waiting for him. Pain of such magnitude that he wasn't sure he could bear it.

"What choice did I have, my dear Alex?" She sat beside him, holding his hand between hers. "I used to pray for death," she confessed.

At his frown, she smiled. "That only lasted for a week or so. Until I realized that you still needed me. I couldn't go to my bed and stay there. But there were times in the next few months when it was too tempting to do exactly that."

He never wanted to cause her pain and shouldn't have asked the question. He should have dealt with his feelings the best he could rather than bothering her.

Nothing was the same. Up was down and left was right. His world had been turned inside out, but the worst of it was the hint of something terrible just beyond the horizon.

"I once had a dream," she said. "Your father was alive. He was sitting on that bench near the conservatory."

"I know the one," he said.

"He asked me what I was doing with my life. I didn't get a chance to answer before he vanished. Or I woke up. I can't remember which." She smiled. "That dream made me think. I knew I was going to mourn him for the rest of my life, but what else was I going to do with the time?"

She studied the windows and the bright sun streaming into the room. Ever since he was a little boy he'd equated sunlight with his mother. She liked sunny rooms. She loved taking walks on a bright summer day. She smiled and the room lit up.

"I've often wondered if gloaming is similar to how ghosts view the world," she said.

Alex turned and studied the view through the mullioned windows of her sitting room. Night came late in the Highlands in the late spring and full summer. Even in the winter months the gloaming lingered, stretching out its gray fingers to encompass Blackhall and soften the world. Now, however, there was only bright sunlight, the morning still in its infancy.

"Ghosts?" His mother's words surprised him. "Do you believe in ghosts?"

"We live in Blackhall Castle, my dear son. How can I not believe in ghosts? There's the Green Lady in the west tower and the Sad Priest in the chapel, to mention only two."

"The result of hysterical servants," he said. "I believe some of those stories were gleefully spread by previous occupants of the castle. If everyone who died at Blackhall became a ghost, we'd be overrun."

"Not everyone becomes a ghost," she said, her tone perfectly reasonable, as if their conversation were based on a rational idea.

"What's the criterion for becoming a ghost?"

"Perhaps they were unhappy in life," she finally said. "Or desperately wish to communicate with the living for some reason."

"Why? To say good-bye?"

"Perhaps."

For a moment he wondered if she'd consulted one of those charlatans who promise to contact the dearly departed.

"Do you think my father is a ghost?" he asked gently. "Or Moira or Douglas?"

"No," she said, "I don't. Sometimes, though, I wish they were. Each one of them. Isn't that selfish of me? I should wish them everlasting happiness in Heaven. The truth is, I'd welcome being haunted by my darling Craig and my children." She turned and stared directly at him. "But I can't live in the gloaming, Alex. Not like you have."

"What do you mean?"

"Ever since you were sixteen, my darling son, you've been holding yourself aloof from everyone and everything. You've been trapped between the living and the dead. As if you were afraid to completely give yourself up to life. As if having feelings of any kind terrified you."

He started to say something but she raised her hand to silence him.

"I'm not calling you a coward, Alex. Your reaction was understandable, but now I suspect you're thawing. The sensation is not unlike when your toes go numb from cold. The first feeling is a burning pain."

"And if I don't want to feel that much?"

Her smile was tender. "That's your decision, son. I would hope you choose not to live in the gloaming, but to choose the daylight. To love, fully, completely, and absolutely. You will be hurt. You will feel pain. But, oh, the rewards are worth it."

She left him without anything to say.

He'd never thought his life to be lacking. He had

work he enjoyed and that gave him purpose. He had a family he loved. He had responsibilities and acquaintances. He'd been happy. At least he thought he had. Until a few weeks ago he would have ridiculed anyone who said otherwise.

"I'm going to Inverness," he said, standing. "I have to submit my treatise."

"How long will you be gone?"

"A few weeks, perhaps longer."

He'd half expected her to argue that now was not the time to leave Blackhall, that he had a new wife and a new child who needed his presence. All she did was sit and look up at him, her eyes soft and kind and seeing too much.

He stood and left her before he could offer any excuses for his behavior.

What the hell could he say? That his wife terrified him? That his reaction to Lorna was uncontrolled and wholly unlike him?

All true and nothing that he could possibly explain.

Chapter 21

$\mathcal{F}$or the first time in her life Lorna used the bellpull to summon one of the staff. As she waited, she changed Robbie, then carried him into the dressing room, where she put him on the cot his father had slept on the night before. He fussed for a few minutes before settling down into sleep with his fist in his mouth.

She made quick work of using the facilities in the bathing chamber, then washed her face and hands before picking Robbie up again and cradling him in her arms.

Matthews was nowhere to be found. He must have slipped out the door located on the other side of the bathing chamber. Hopefully, the next time they met his demeanor would be more polite. If he wasn't, she'd have to deal with him somehow. How she handled Matthews might well form the basis of her relationship with the rest of the staff.

With one hand, she grabbed a few of Robbie's sacques and nappies from the dresser and made her way back to the bedroom.

She knew this room well from having dusted it every day. Every week she and another girl rolled the mattress from the top to the bottom of the bed, then turned it sideways twice to make sure the goose down was properly distributed.

She'd gotten on her hands and knees and brushed the dark blue carpet with its pattern of white crest and thistles with a boar bristle brush. She'd stood on a ladder to clean the two chandeliers. She knew every nook and cranny, every deep blue and gold curlicue of the valances, every fold of the blue bed curtains.

Now it was her room and the realization terrified her.

A knock made her leave the bed and go to the sitting room door, opening it to find Abby standing there, hand raised to knock again.

Abby was one of the older maids who had been at Blackhall for a decade or more. She was quick to share what she knew about any task and her round face almost always bore a smile. She came from a tiny village not far from Inverness and she was forever telling tales of the inhabitants of the village, to the point that Lorna felt as if she knew those people she'd never met.

She couldn't help but wonder if Abby would tell stories about the people of Blackhall.

Abby's eyes widened at the sight of her. She took a few steps back, her gaze traveling from Lorna to sweep the room behind her, coming to rest on the baby in her arms.

"You've had the child, then?"

Lorna nodded. "Robbie," she said, glancing down at her son. "And I've married."

Evidently, the footmen hadn't told anyone of carrying her inside Blackhall. Nor had Peter or Nan said anything to anyone. Nor had Matthews had enough time to carry his stories the length and breadth of the castle.

"I've married the duke," Lorna added.

Abby's eyes widened even farther but she didn't respond.

Was that how it was going to be, then? She'd be faced with a silent staff? She would be just like Alex walking through Blackhall, averting her eyes for fearing of seeing something on the faces of the servants?

No, that wouldn't do.

What did she say to put Abby at ease? She didn't know. How had the duchess always made her feel comfortable? She asked about personal things, that was how. She remembered details about her life, things she'd told her on previous encounters.

"How is your tooth?" she asked.

Both Abby's eyebrows winged upward, but she answered nonetheless. "Better. Mrs. McDermott said I should put some oil of cloves on it and it helped a little."

"I could make up a poultice for you," Lorna said.

"You would?"

"I just need to gather up my supplies."

"You needn't bother," Abby said. "You're a duchess now." She frowned at Lorna. "Are you sure you're a duchess?"

"I am. I don't feel like a duchess, although I'm not altogether sure how a duchess is supposed to feel."

"Special," Abby said, surprising her. "Especially if you're married to the Duke of Kinross."

She'd forgotten. Abby was one of those maids who was forever sighing after the duke. Since she'd been in that group, she couldn't be critical. What would Abby say if she heard that the man was far more than his appearance?

"I need to see Nan. Would you take word to her?"

Abby surprised her again by shaking her head. "It's

Mrs. McDermott you need to see, Lorna. Your Grace." Abby frowned again. "She's the one with the authority to pull a maid from her tasks."

There was more to this duchess thing than she'd considered. She needed to study everything from a different point of view.

When Abby left, she put Robbie down in his cradle and sat on the edge of the bed. She wasn't tired. Giving birth hadn't exhausted her as much as enlivened her. She wanted to do something, but what did a new duchess do?

She slid from the bed and walked to the dressing room and opened the armoire. There, beside Alex's starched shirts, were her two dresses. How Matthews must dislike their juxtaposition in such a ducal place. She was surprised he hadn't used her garments as polishing rags for the silver buttons on Alex's suit jackets.

They married for one reason: to protect their son. Why didn't everyone realize that? Alex felt nothing for her. If she was feeling anything, it was gratitude. That's all.

She would have to make arrangements to gather up all her herbs, bottles, and equipment. Some of them were dangerous and couldn't be left out for anyone to find. In a few days she would take a carriage—or should it be a wagon?—back to the cottage. Perhaps Peter could go with her. Or maybe it would be better to keep everything at the cottage.

Her figure was still not what it had been. Louise said it would take a few weeks until it was. What should she wear for her meeting with the housekeeper? In the end there was no choice. She changed her nightgown for another one her mother-in-law had furnished her with a matching wrapper. It was a lovely yellow with pretty flowers embroidered on it.

How strange to dread meeting with Mrs. McDermott. Was it because the housekeeper had lectured them all about proper decorum around the Russells? *Remember you are being paid a fair wage to treat their belongings with care. Don't, above all, behave above your place. You are on staff at Blackhall Castle. Remember that and be proud. A great many people would like your position.*

Or did her dread have anything to do with how the housekeeper treated her at the cottage? The woman's disapproval had been palpable. Surely the housekeeper would approve now that Reverend McGill had married them.

Robbie fussed at that moment, as if to correct her assessment of the situation. She'd done one thing right. This perfect child was proof of that. She went to the cradle and gazed down at him. He didn't open his eyes, just made a face and fell back asleep.

How like Alex he appeared. Would he grow up to be as devastatingly handsome? Pray God life would be kinder to her son than it had been to his father. The duchess's words came back to her.

He's brooding and a loner. He has a sorrowful past and he's handsome. What better target for their gossip?

How many times had she seen him from the conservatory and wanted to put her arms around him in comfort? Or make him sit down so she could massage his shoulders? Or bring him a cup of tea? Or urge him to quit his office to go and rest?

She wanted to care for him, talk to him, share his thoughts and fears, and reassure him. She wanted to be the person to whom he came to argue a point, test his reasoning, and reveal his discoveries.

In the night, he'd turn to her and love her until they both lay gasping and blissful. In the daytime, he'd think of her and remember those moments. Or perhaps he would even seek her out in order to test his memory and hold her for a time.

Perhaps what she felt for Alex, Duke of Kinross, was a bit more than gratitude. She had a choice, though, didn't she? To let those emotions live and flourish or quash them as soon as possible.

She'd never been promised a lifetime of happiness, but she'd had one night with Alex. Memories of that night would have to last a long time, maybe even a lifetime.

Suddenly, one of the double doors of the sitting room swung inward so hard the handle hit the wall.

She glanced up to see that it wasn't Mrs. McDermott but Mary striding toward her, dressed in a dark maroon riding habit with a crop in her hands. She was slapping the whip against the floor as she walked, the black plume in her hat bouncing almost like a warning.

Lorna glanced back toward the cradle, grateful that the sounds hadn't disturbed the baby. She walked out of the bedroom, leaving Mary to follow her.

Mary's cheeks were mottled with large pink splotches. Her eyes narrowed as she stopped only feet from Lorna.

"You can't be the Duchess of Kinross. You're a maid."

She didn't respond, having learned that silence was the quickest way to avoid an argument. Besides, what could she say? To Mary, she'd always be a maid and nothing more.

"He couldn't have married you," Mary said, her voice dripping with contempt. "You'll bring the mighty Russell family down. The whole of the empire will ridicule him and the entirety of the family."

She really should have remained silent, but she couldn't help herself.

"But he did. What galls you, Mary? That he married me? Or that it wasn't you? Or do you think your sighing after Alex hasn't been noticed by the staff?"

The spots on Mary's cheeks became a darker pink and traveled down her neck. Lorna wondered if the woman was going to have a fit.

A movement out of the corner of her eye had her glancing toward the door to the corridor. The duchess stood there, taking in the two of them.

"Have you come to offer congratulations to Lorna?" Louise asked, moving into the room. Her face was unsmiling, the expression in her eyes one that Lorna fervently hoped was not directed at her.

"No, I've come to tell her that Alex has left Blackhall. She drove him away, Louise."

Lorna kept her face still. Hopefully, Mary couldn't read the anger she was feeling. How dare she say such a thing? At that moment Robbie fussed. She turned and silently went to tend to her child, grateful for the excuse to leave.

"HOW COULD YOU have let something like this happen, Louise? Alex has gone. He only married her to keep her brat from being called a bastard. I'll bet it's not even Alex's child. And now she's driven him away."

Was there no way to silence this woman?

"Have you any idea what the countryside will say? Alex will be a laughingstock. Society will shun us."

She really should walk away now before she said things she'd regret. The problem was, she'd imagined saying them so many times since Mary had first come to live at Blackhall that the words were straining to be said. She could envision them jumping to her lips, each one of them coated in glee.

"She's nothing but a maid!"

Mary had never been particularly observant on the best of days. She was blithely continuing her diatribe, leveling insult after insult on Alex, on her, and on Lorna, whom she'd verbally assaulted only minutes earlier.

"Alex could never marry you," Louise said when she could get a word in edgewise. "So there's no sense in yearning after him. There are laws that forbid it. You're Ruth's sister."

Mary's color was high, almost the match of her riding habit.

"He didn't have to marry *her*," she said. "She's a trumped-up whore. We'll be laughingstocks, Louise."

"Then perhaps you should contemplate leaving Blackhall."

Mary's sudden look of surprise was only mildly gratifying.

"You can go and live in Edinburgh, perhaps. Or if you're better suited to London, I'll give orders to make the house there ready for you. You're family, Mary, and you'll always have a home with us, but maybe not at Blackhall."

"This is my home," Mary said, clenching her hands on the crop.

Louise's smile felt odd, as if her facial muscles didn't want to obey her will.

"If you remain here, you'll have to accept Lorna

as Alex's wife. She is the new Duchess of Kinross. As such, she has my full support as well as my affection. "

Mary didn't say another word, but turned and stormed out of the sitting room and down the corridor. Louise half expected her to stop and deliver another insult, but the woman blessedly disappeared from view.

With any luck, Mary would choose to live in London, since that was the farthest distance from Blackhall. That would be the best solution, but she knew Mary. The woman hadn't made it easy on anyone since the day she arrived. There was every chance all of them would be forced to endure her pouting and tantrums in the future. It might take another confrontation or two before Mary finally left.

She sighed and headed for the ducal bedroom, determined to first apologize to Lorna and then to spend time with her grandson.

Chapter 22

$\mathcal{H}$e'll come back, you know," Louise said.

Lorna glanced at her mother-in-law. They were sitting in the family parlor, a pleasant room facing the expanse of lawn at the back of Blackhall. The castle was perched on a hill overlooking Loch Gerry, the piney woods between the two.

The green curtains matched the outdoors, spring coming to the Highlands gradually but with triumphant bits of color on the landscape.

The two settees facing the fireplace were each upholstered in a subdued green and gold pattern. Louise had moved the table between them and now Robbie's cradle sat there. Not that her son was anywhere but in his grandmother's arms when Louise got the chance to hold him.

"Will he?"

She'd become fond of Louise in the last weeks, enough to hide her real thoughts. She wasn't the least bit certain Alex was going to return to Blackhall. Oh, he might come back for holidays or to see his mother. But for her? No. Or his son?

The three interminable months had passed in a pleasant routine marked by moments of grief.

After a while it was like there never had been a

Duke of Kinross with blue-green eyes at Blackhall. There was only Robbie and Nan, the duchess, and caring for her child.

"Yes, he'll come back, and soon, I think," Louise said, glancing down at Robbie.

He always fell asleep quickly in her mother-in-law's arms, as if he knew that it was a place of safety.

"He's been gone a long time, Louise."

The other woman nodded then glanced at her.

"I know." Louise sighed. "He did the same with Ruth after learning of her infidelity. If she was at Blackhall, he stayed in Edinburgh. When she went to Edinburgh, he returned to Blackhall. This is different, however."

"How?"

Louise didn't say anything for a time. Robbie lay on his tummy on her lap. His legs kicked out as he made sounds she'd come to think of as Robbie language. From time to time he would push his chest up and stare at Lorna as if checking to make sure she hadn't gone anywhere.

He had, blessedly, started sleeping six or seven hours at night, letting her sleep as well.

When Louise wasn't talking to her, she was engaged in conversation with Robbie. He, in turn, would answer her with oohs and aahs, grabbing for one of her necklaces or her sparkly earrings.

He was a happy baby, one who smiled often. In the last weeks he'd grown so much, changes Alex hadn't seen.

Blackhall might be his home, but he had other properties in Inverness, Edinburgh, and London. He could live anywhere.

"Should I move to Inverness? Or Edinburgh?"

"You're certainly welcome to live anywhere you wish, but know this. I'm following you. I am determined to be Robbie's grandmother, and wherever you go, I go."

"I won't go anywhere," Lorna said. "I consider Blackhall my home, as much home as I've had in the last ten years."

The two women smiled at each other, the moment punctuated by Robbie speech.

"I do wish Mary would choose somewhere else other than Blackhall to live," Louise said. "I'm surprised she hasn't followed him."

"She looks at me as if she hates me."

"She probably does," Louise said, surprising her. "She knows she isn't welcome in my private apartments anymore. I haven't left any doubt in her mind that I disapprove of her behavior."

Lorna avoided Mary whenever possible, a technique her new mother-in-law openly facilitated.

The two of them had taken to eating dinner together in Alex's sitting room, one of the few rooms in the castle Mary couldn't invade. To ensure that was the case, Peter stood guard at the outside door, a position that one of the footmen always maintained at night. In fact, a great many footmen were always abroad after sunset, which she hadn't realized until after her conversations with Mrs. McDermott.

She'd dreaded the initial meeting with the housekeeper, but she shouldn't have. When she'd met with Mrs. McDermott a few weeks ago, the woman was as warm and personable to her as a new duchess as she had been to the scared girl applying for the position of maid years before.

Evidently, it was only when she was living at Blackhall in an unmarried, pregnant state that Mrs. McDermott disapproved of her.

"You'll be a fine addition to the Russell family," the housekeeper said.

Then she'd done something surprising and touching, a gesture that had brought tears to Lorna's eyes. She'd bent forward and kissed her on the cheek.

"You were always one of my favorites, Your Grace."

Unspoken were the words: as long as she didn't allow the duke to keep her as his mistress. Just like that, the interlude when she'd lived at the cottage was to be forgotten and never mentioned again.

Of course, there wasn't a problem with Nan being released from her duties to be her lady's maid. Mrs. McDermott had even offered to train Nan.

Lorna had wanted to ask: who would train her to be a duchess? Evidently, she wasn't to be a wife, because her husband had left the day after their marriage.

"The only good thing about Alex being in Edinburgh," she said, "is that Matthews isn't here."

Louise smiled and nodded. "People who look at our lives from the outside think that it must be wonderful to have servants at our beck and call. What they don't know is that we're at the mercy of those same servants, and some of them can make life miserable."

"I hope I never did."

"Present company excluded, my dear. You were always a bright spot in my day. And still are."

Robbie took that opportunity to make a crowing sound, his legs and arms kicking out. They both laughed.

"Alex doesn't love easily. I think that's a lesson life itself has taught him. Don't trust, don't reveal your emotions, because you'll either lose those you love or they'll disappoint you. He wears an armor around himself."

Looking up, she smiled at Lorna. "When people disappoint him, as they invariably do, he feels justified in his distrust. When they don't, like you, I believe it makes him acutely uncomfortable."

"And you think that's why he's staying away, because I make him uncomfortable?"

"Oh, yes, and he's probably miserable."

Should Louise sound so amused?

Robbie fussed and her mother-in-law crooned softly to him, putting him on her shoulder. Lorna noticed that she'd taken the precaution of removing her earrings. As Robbie batted at her hair, she glanced over at Lorna.

"Alex tries to measure life, Lorna, and there's no way it can be. If he hadn't been so fascinated with fingerprints, he would have found some other similar avocation. He wants everything in order. Life is messy."

Robbie's fists suddenly flailed in the air, summoning Louise's smile. She patted his back with the skill of a longtime mother.

"You've upset him from the beginning. You weren't what he expected."

"I've just been myself," she said in her own defense.

"Of course you have, and I wouldn't change you in any way."

Lorna didn't know what to say to her mother-in-law. A good thing Louise didn't appear to expect an answer. In the last year she'd bedded a duke, become pregnant, become a duchess, and given birth. Yes, life was messy.

Would life get any easier when Alex returned?

ALEX HAD SPENT six weeks in Inverness, rationalizing that he needed the time to take more specimens. At the end of the six weeks, he moved on to Edinburgh, one of his favorite places in Scotland. The time was spent in laborious pursuits, cataloging all the prints they'd amassed in Inverness plus taking new prints in the markets and the stalls of Edinburgh.

He was a bit of a celebrity, one of dubious fame. Word had spread of the duke wanting to coat your fingertips with soot. He didn't have to pay anyone to let him do it after he explained his project. He wasn't intent on taking all the fingerprints of every soul in Scotland, just a representative amount of people from various occupations.

"My mother has sat for her prints," he said. "As well as other members of my family. There's a record of them now, and there will be one of you."

"And what would you be wanting them for?" one man asked.

He didn't tell the man that he hoped to turn over his collection to the authorities one day. That was for years down the road.

"I study them," he said. "So far I've never found a similarity between one individual and the next. I'd like to see if twins are identical. Or if people from the same area have features that are the same."

The man had wandered off after his prints were done. No doubt he'd headed for the nearest tavern to tell his tale about the odd duke.

Jason was an ideal assistant, one with a thirst for knowledge and a yen for travel. Edinburgh was fascinating to him, from the castle on the rock to the tales of the underground city. When he could, he gave Jason a few hours to explore on his own, only for the young man to return filled with some new tale of the city he'd learned or something wonderful he'd seen.

Another of Jason's assets: he never once asked why they were remaining in Edinburgh or when they were returning to Blackhall.

The days were filled with activity. The nights were barren. He worked until he could no longer see the swirls and patterns of the various prints. He'd finalized his catalog system and put Jason in charge of ensuring that every card was in its proper position. Each person's prints were not only listed in the catalog by name, location taken, and occupation, but by significant features of the print itself. This way, he had a way of cross-referencing the print.

He kept himself frenetically busy, to the extent that he accomplished what he'd planned for the next two years. He met with members of the Scottish Society who lived in Edinburgh and attended lectures. He avoided social occasions for two reasons: he didn't enjoy socializing all that much, and news of his wedding had probably leaked out. He didn't want to explain why he was in Edinburgh and his wife was at Blackhall. Lorna didn't deserve the gossip.

Nor did she deserve a husband who was acting the fool.

His mother hadn't come out and called him a coward but that's exactly how he was behaving.

Lorna hadn't written him. He hadn't heard from her in all the time he'd been away from Blackhall. He'd only known her a month. A month and one night. Not long enough to affect him in this way.

He might as well be invisible to her.

That thought was, at first, oddly painful, then simply annoying.

Nor had his mother sent him a note. It was as if he'd dropped off the face of the earth and the two women couldn't be bothered.

He didn't know what was more irritating: that no one seemed to notice he was gone or that his conscience was telling him that's exactly what he'd wanted.

Matthews was even hinting at going home, and Edinburgh was a joy to his valet. There were countless shops from which to purchase innumerable items Alex didn't need, as well as tailors to visit and hold out the carrot of the Duke of Kinross's trade.

The Edinburgh house was exceedingly comfortable, the staff excellent in the execution of their duties. He did the same thing he'd done in Inverness, finding himself studying the maids, of all things, and wondering at their lives. He addressed the housekeeper in Edinburgh just as he had in Inverness, no doubt surprising both women with his sudden interest in the servants. Were any of them suffering any hardships? Were their wages enough? Could he have a list of their names?

He'd even taken to nodding to each servant as he passed and addressing them when they met. After the first few times, when they only curtsied, wide-eyed, they'd always responded with a smile and a greeting.

About damn time he started noticing things.

Matthews was an exception. Alex tried to turn a deaf ear to his valet and his gossip most of the time, but one morning he found himself acutely interested in what Matthews had to say.

"I've heard from Miss Taylor, Your Grace. A great many things are changing at the castle. Your mother continues to dote on your son."

Matthews watched him carefully as he delivered

that news. Alex closed his eyes, wished the man would finish shaving him silently but knew that would be too much to ask.

"Since when does my sister-in-law correspond with you, Matthews?"

"Miss Taylor wrote me to ask if I would purchase a few items for her."

"How did she know we'd moved on to Edinburgh?"

When the valet remained uncharacteristically quiet, he opened his eyes and stared at Matthews.

"I might have dropped her a note to let her know, just in case the Dowager Duchess needed to reach you, Your Grace."

"You are neither my secretary nor my confidant, Matthews. I'm capable of informing my mother of my whereabouts. I don't need you doing so."

Matthews bowed stiffly. "Yes, Your Grace."

"What else did Mary write?"

Matthews smiled, and Alex knew he'd fallen into the valet's trap. He closed his eyes again and vowed not to react to the man's further news.

"Your wife refuses to use the seamstress who served the previous duchess, Your Grace. Evidently, the seamstress doesn't approve of your wife's taste."

He noticed that Matthews was careful not to call Lorna "duchess." Did the man think she didn't deserve the title? His valet was a snob, not the first time Alex had made that assessment.

"Your suite smells of nappies, Your Grace. And I understand your new wife has washed out baby garments in the bathing chamber and hung them in the dressing room. When Miss Taylor suggested that the laundress would be better suited to care for the child's garments, she was rebuffed by that woman your wife chose as a lady's maid. She's ill-prepared for the position, sir. She has no training, and scorched a dress when she tried to press it."

Alex remained silent, not giving Matthews any encouragement.

"Your wife has been exceptionally rude to Miss Taylor, sir. In addition, the poor woman has been ignored by the Dowager Duchess, who seems to have forgotten their earlier friendship. Well, what can you expect?"

He sat up abruptly. "Are you finished?"

"For the most part, sir, but—"

He cut Matthews off with a glance, grabbed the towel from the man's hand and wiped his face.

Mary was an annoying harridan who constantly repaid his generosity by gossiping behind his back. Unfortunately, she'd found a kindred soul in Matthews. The two of them would make Lorna's life miserable if they could.

His behavior had, no doubt, given Mary the idea that she could tell tales about his wife with impunity. Had the rest of the staff gotten the same impression?

Damned time he returned.

Why was he suddenly pleased by his decision?

LORNA DISCOVERED THAT being a duchess was a great deal more difficult than anything she'd assumed. A duchess had duties just like the staff, some more onerous than others.

Her mother-in-law had turned over Blackhall's ledgers to her when Robbie was two and a half months old.

"The steward does the actual entries," she was told,

"but it's important for you to oversee all the expenses. If something seems outrageous to you, you need to tell him."

She'd been speechless at the responsibility, and when she tried to demur, the Dowager Duchess merely smiled and shook her head.

"It's something I've been waiting to do for ages, my dear. It's your duty now."

She was to meet with the steward every week, plus meet with Mrs. McDermott to adjudicate any disputes among the staff, another duty of which she'd been ignorant. She had to decide upon the meals, any additional positions, and make suggestions for castle repairs that would go to the steward and from him to the duke for final approval.

Lorna straddled an odd line with the staff. They all seemed friendly but reserved. She wanted to be like the Dowager Duchess, who noticed each person who served her and treated everyone with respect and dignity.

She couldn't say more than hello to Abby, for fear the girl would launch into a long-winded conversation. That would lead to the girl being lectured by Mrs. McDermott, requiring her to either intercede— which wouldn't be wise—or ignore the fact that one of her former friends had been put on probation, an even more difficult choice.

She had to be very careful, something she'd never before considered.

Nan was her conduit to the staff and told her anything that went on in the servants' quarters that she thought Lorna needed to hear.

It was from Nan that she learned Mary was telling tales again. Alex, Mary said, had found a mistress in

Edinburgh, which was why he was gone so long. He didn't want to return to Blackhall to the woman he'd been forced to marry. He was desperately unhappy that his new wife had been a servant, enough to stay as far away from the castle as he could for as long as possible.

Unfortunately, since she didn't know any different, Mary's gossip hurt, no doubt as it was intended.

When was Alex coming home?

"WE'RE LEAVING TOMORROW," Alex told Matthews that night.

Something eased in his chest as he instructed the valet to make arrangements. He'd inform Jason in the morning and do the last of his errands.

He was going home. About time.

Sitting on the edge of the bed, he took a few sips of whiskey. The effort to sleep didn't work very well. Most of the time he lay in his bed, staring up at the ceiling, the events of the last year playing in his mind.

When he did sleep, he dreamed, scenes he didn't give himself permission to envision awake.

Tonight was just like any other night except that he was awakened in the wee hours by a lamp shining in his eyes. "Well, at least you don't have a woman with you," Thomas said.

Alex threw his forearm over his eyes, trying to come to grips with the notion that his uncle was standing in his bedroom.

"Have you taken to drinking yourself to sleep, then?" Thomas asked, examining the bottle on the bedside table.

"Why the hell are you here? To chaperone me? To judge my morals? A little ridiculous, coming from you, don't you think?"

"I've never married," Thomas said.

"No, but you have five little Thomases around."

"But had I married," his uncle said, ignoring his comment, "I wouldn't have left her the minute I married her."

A chill raced through him. "Are they all right?" he asked, sitting up.

Thomas leaned against the door frame, arms folded. "Do you care?"

"Are they all right, Thomas?"

"Yes, no thanks to you. Your child is growing. He'll probably have learned to walk before you return home. He knows me. He even smiles when he sees me. No doubt the first word out of his mouth will be 'Thomas.'"

Alex grabbed his robe and put it on. "Is that why you're here, to regale me with tales of how avuncular you are with my son? What about my wife? Do you charm her, too?"

"I'm too damn tired to hit you, but just so you know, I want to. I've grown to quite like your wife, which is more than you can say."

"You don't understand."

"Oh, I do. You're a damn fool, and I fault myself that I've never noticed it before. You were a damn fool with Ruth and you're a damn fool with Lorna, only for a different reason."

Alex grabbed the bottle of whiskey and poured two fingers into the glass on the table.

"You were a fool to put up with Ruth's behavior, but I'll bet you never said a word to her, did you?"

"What difference would it have made?"

"Who knows, since you never bothered to try? Sometimes, I wonder if she bedded anything in pants just to get a reaction from you. Something that said you weren't a cold fish after all."

"I'm not a cold fish, damn it."

"Evidently not with Lorna, or you wouldn't have become a father. Maybe you're right. I don't understand why you're doing everything you can to destroy what she feels for you."

He took a sip of the whiskey and immediately wished he hadn't. It burned down his throat. Worse, it reminded him of too many nights of hoping for oblivion, only for it to escape him.

"She won't hear a word spoken bad about you. She says that you and she weren't a love match, that you married her only to give Robbie a name. That she understands why you don't want to return to Blackhall. I'm glad she does because neither your mother nor I do."

He didn't have anything to say to that, and he should have. He'd expected this confrontation, in a way. Actually, he'd thought it would occur when he returned to Blackhall and that it would be his mother who lectured him. He'd never anticipated that it would be Thomas or that his uncle would seek him out in Edinburgh. That he'd done something even Thomas found reprehensible was almost laughable.

He wasn't sure he could explain to either of them. Or even to himself.

He wasn't the same person around Lorna that he'd always known himself to be. He had no control, witness what had happened the first time he kissed her. And he found himself wanting to kiss her whenever he saw her.

He'd lost his focus. Every time he took someone's fingerprints, he found himself trying to recall the day

Lorna had sat before him encapsulated by sunlight. He didn't know if he was remembering or forming a picture in his mind of what it had been like, the bright rays finding the gold threads in her hair, her glorious brown eyes enlivened by humor. Her cheeks had turned pink as he regarded her and then held her hand as he'd taken her fingerprints.

No, he was certain no one would understand.

Time hadn't made the situation easier. Nor had distance. The longer he stayed away, the worse his affliction became. Even whiskey couldn't take her image away. Or make him stop wondering about her and Robbie.

She wasn't the first woman he'd ever bedded, even though that one and only occasion with her had been . . . What could he call it? Incredible? Spectacular? Memorable? Every minute of that night was emblazoned on his memory.

Did she miss him? Had she missed him all these months? He'd counted the days, tried to keep himself occupied, took over six hundred fingerprints, studied what they'd amassed, and checked the clock at least a dozen times an hour.

No time had ever passed as slowly.

"It's time you came home," Thomas said.

"Yes."

Let Thomas think it was his powers of persuasion that had convinced him. No need for his uncle to know that his valises were packed and the coachman had already been alerted to be ready at dawn for their departure.

All that awaited him was his arrival at Blackhall.

He would be calm and unexcited when entering his

suite. If she asked him why he'd remained away for so long, he would be vague.

Perhaps she wouldn't ask.

Perhaps she hadn't cared.

Perhaps—and this was a thought that chilled him— she appreciated his absence and would dread his return.

She was, after all, Lorna, and she'd made no secret of her thoughts about him.

She'd looked straight at him in the midst of labor, gritted her teeth and exchanged vows, all the while leaving no doubt that she did so only for the sake of her child. Earlier, she'd imperiously pointed to the door of her pitiful room, demanding he depart when it was all too evident she needed help.

She didn't want him.

He'd never before been at the mercy of another human being. She could smile at him and ease his heart. Or act as if she hadn't noticed he was gone.

The problem was, he didn't know which it would be or how he would respond. No, he was definitely not himself. Nor had he been ever since meeting her.

Chapter 23

$\mathcal{M}$atthews was sullen yet obsequious all the way back to Blackhall. What his valet didn't realize was that of all the servants at the castle, he was perhaps the most expendable. Alex could shave himself and didn't need someone to care for his garments or to dress him, and Matthews's increasing penchant for gossiping was annoying.

His arrival was without ceremony, or welcome, for that matter. He entered the foyer of the castle, taking in the soaring space, the staircase, the rooms jutting off to the left and right.

A uniformed maid bobbed a curtsy in his direction. He made a note of her face, met her eyes, and nodded back to her. Mrs. McDermott's wishes be damned, he was going to pay attention to Blackhall's staff.

He walked into his sitting room to find that it didn't smell of nappies at all. Instead, he could detect a hint of cinnamon and something floral. He dispensed with his coat, hat, and gloves, tossing them onto the settee.

"She doesn't seem to be here, Your Grace."

He stopped and turned, gathering up his patience before he spoke to his valet.

"My wife isn't to be referred to as 'she,' Matthews. Nor is she to be called 'your wife,' especially not in that tone. When you refer to her, you will do so as 'the duchess,' do you understand?"

Matthews drew himself up, his shoulders rigid beneath his spotless black jacket.

"Your Grace," he said, bowing slightly and gathering up the coat, hat, and gloves. The gesture wasn't an admission of error as much as a faux gesture of humility.

Alex wasn't fooled.

He waved his hand in Matthews's direction, a sign that he wasn't to be followed, and strode to the bedroom door.

Nan was sitting before the fireplace, stitching a garment. Her face was a study in concentration, her lips pursed together and eyes intent on her task.

The cradle sat beside her, far enough from the fire to be safe but close enough that his son wouldn't be cold. Although it was May, spring came grudgingly to the Highlands, keeping a chill to the air.

Nan glanced up as he entered. Her smile was instant and welcoming. He wanted, in an odd way, to thank her for that.

"Is he sleeping?" he asked, softening his voice as he approached.

"At the moment, no, Your Grace. He's trying to decide whether or not to chew his hands or examine his feet."

His son's cradle had been replaced by a larger version. So, too, had the newborn he'd last seen. Robbie had doubled in size. The baby's eyes fixed on him, investigating him; his face crumpled then smoothed out, almost as if he changed his mind about crying about this strange man standing over his bed.

Nan gestured toward the other chair. "If you'll sit, I'll get him."

He was perfectly capable of taking his own son from his cradle, but he did as she asked.

"He's grown," he said after she placed Robbie in his arms.

"That he has," she said. "He's a big eater, is our Robbie. He has the appetite of a Highlander. At least that's what Lorna says."

"He has brown eyes," he said. "They were blue when he was born."

"They sometimes change like that. He's got Lorna's eyes, but, begging your pardon, Your Grace, the rest of him is just like his daddy."

"He has dimples."

Nan only smiled at him.

His son looked up at him as if he were saying, *And what have you been doing, gone all this time?*

He hadn't been around infants often, but it seemed to him that his son, even at this tender age, was advanced. Surely no other infant could gaze out at the world with such an intent gaze or have such intelligence shining through his eyes.

Robbie gripped his finger, and it was as if the baby held onto his heart instead.

He'd never before felt what he did now. He would do anything for Robbie, would move mountains to ensure his safety, would hire anyone to teach him what he needed to know about life.

Why the hell had he stayed away for so long?

"Where is Lorna?" he asked, glancing at Nan.

She looked away, a sign that she was probably going to lie to him. But either he'd misjudged her or she changed her mind, because she turned back, stared straight at him, and answered.

"She's gone to the cottage, Your Grace. She can't be

away from Robbie all that long, however, so she should be back soon."

"Why the cottage?"

"She still goes there to make her cures. It's a good place to keep all her bottles and herbs."

The baby gurgled at him, and when he bent his head to kiss his son on the cheek, Robbie struck him on the nose with his fist.

There was the off chance that his mother would do exactly the same.

He tucked Robbie into the cradle, folding the blanket at his waist.

Nan had put down her mending and watched him with Robbie. Now she picked up the garment and occupied herself with the next stitch.

Something Matthews had said in Edinburgh jogged Alex's memory.

"Has the seamstress been to see her? I've given orders that Lorna's to have a new wardrobe."

Nan glanced to the left then the right before looking straight at him.

"Has she refused it?" he asked.

"Not refused, exactly, Your Grace, but she and the seamstress had different thoughts about the matter."

Nan bit off a thread and gave a seam intense scrutiny.

"Tell me," he said.

She looked at him, then back at the dress.

"Well, Your Grace, the seamstress seemed to think that a great many ruffles and flounces were called for, with wide hoops and trailing sleeves. Lorna was having nothing of it."

"So she's had nothing made?"

"Well, she has, Your Grace, but not from the seamstress. They were both at the knag and the widdie. The seamstress was all for making Lorna into something she's not, and Lorna wasn't bending an inch." She sighed. "Even your mother got involved, but neither was budging. I think the whole thing started because of Miss Taylor, myself."

"What did she do?"

Robbie snuffled a little. He glanced down to find his son grimacing in his sleep. Was that Robbie's opinion of Mary? If so, his son had already developed great taste.

"She told the seamstress that Lorna looked the part of a servant and that her wardrobe was 'trittle trattle.' "

"I don't suppose Lorna appreciated her clothes being called rubbish," he said, wishing he'd come home sooner.

Staying away had accomplished nothing more than to make him miserable. It certainly hadn't eased tensions in his home.

"According to the seamstress, Your Grace, Lorna was a fool to nurse Robbie. It ruined her bosom and made her appear coarse in anything she wore."

"She said that?" He was beginning to dislike the seamstress as much as Nan evidently did.

She nodded vehemently. "Then she kept saying how Miss Taylor had a sense of style and so did the former duchess, if you'll pardon me for bringing her up. But Lorna didn't because she'd evidently never dressed as anything but a maid."

"Did she?"

"Of course, Miss Taylor heard all these comments and couldn't wait to pass them around, which got back to Lorna, of course. She told the seamstress that she didn't see why you should have to pay for her being insulted and she dismissed the woman."

"Then what happened?"

She left the dress in her lap and smiled at him, a charming gap-toothed smile that had him smiling back.

"Well, Your Grace, there's a girl on staff named Hortense. She's the one who helped Lorna with the gown she wore to the fancy dress ball. She's not a very good maid, but Mrs. McDermott puts her to work in places where she can't break anything. She cleans the baths or helps the scullery maids. She isn't allowed in the parlors or the sitting rooms."

"And she's the one who's sewing Lorna's gowns?" he asked, bemused.

"Oh, yes, Your Grace. Lorna asked Mrs. McDermott if Hortense could be her seamstress. Hortense loves sewing and is beyond pleased to get this chance. She's been working on Lorna's wardrobe ever since."

There'd been a whole world beneath his nose and he'd never noticed. First, Lorna. How the hell had he missed her? Then Nan, who was as voluble a creature as he'd ever met. When had she ever been silent? Now Hortense, who broke things.

He'd learned more about the inner workings of Blackhall in the last few months than he'd known all his life.

He stood. "You think Lorna's at the cottage, then?"

She nodded.

He left the castle, heading for the cottage, fighting the wind as he walked. A gust hinted at the recently departed winter. He only pulled up the collar of his jacket and continued on.

The sight of the cottage around the curve of the road made him quicken his pace. No smoke was visible from the chimney. Nothing moved in the windows. The building seemed empty, almost bereft without an occupant.

Where was Lorna?

He didn't allow the sinking feeling in his chest to stop him, but continued to the front door. He pushed in the latch and entered, feeling the chill seep around him. At least here he didn't have to battle the wind.

"Lorna?"

The cottage was empty, the rooms so silent that when she answered him he was surprised.

"I'm in here."

Her voice didn't sound right. When he entered the bedroom he knew why.

Her face was streaked with tears.

Striding across the room, he took her into his arms, wrapping them around her tightly.

Her black cloak was nearly threadbare, not enough protection for the chilly spring wind. The hood had fallen, leaving her hair loosened from its bun and framing her face. Her nose was pink and her eyes red-rimmed.

He hadn't imagined a homecoming like this. Was she crying because he'd returned or because he'd stayed away so long?

She burrowed her forehead against his chest, her words muffled against his jacket.

"What is it, Lorna?"

She raised her head. "That," she said.

For the first time, he noticed the destruction. Several of the bottles had been broken, shards littering the table. Most of the herbs had been tossed to the stone floor. Even the mortar and pestle had been damaged. The cracks in the surface of the pestle looked as if it had been thrown.

Someone had done the damage deliberately. The only question was: who?

She didn't move, merely pressed her cheek against his chest. He hadn't been able to stand so close to her for months, had never before felt her tremble lightly in his arms.

"Are you cold?"

"Not now," she said, the words muffled.

"I'll find out who did this."

When he first held Robbie, he felt a surge of love, coupled with the need to protect his precious child. The emotion came back to him now in a way that was startling.

Lorna was resolute, independent, and determined to fight the world single-handedly. He'd never considered that she might need him. Nor had he ever anticipated that he would feel this way when she did. He wanted to shield her from the world. He wanted to defend her against anyone who had the audacity to challenge her. He wanted to soothe her, dry her tears, and take away the reason for them. He wanted to ease her heart and smooth her path.

He wanted to do these things not from a sense of duty, but to please her.

They were united in a single purpose: to rear their son and give Robbie the best life they could. But as he held her within the shelter of his arms, Alex also wondered if they might share something else. The need to feel whole, to trust, and to give and receive comfort.

She glanced up at him, her nose pink from crying, her brown eyes deep with tears.

"It's all right," he said. "I'll make it right."

What she would've said next was lost because he bent his head and touched her lips gently with his. He hadn't meant to kiss her, but the memory was always there in the back of his mind. Perhaps time had exaggerated the sensation of kissing Lorna. The experience had been blown out of proportion.

Now he surrendered to temptation.

He tilted his head slightly to deepen the kiss. She made a sound in the back of her throat. When he would have pulled away, she reached up and grabbed his jacket, pulling him to her.

No, it wasn't his imagination. Nor had he exaggerated anything. She opened her mouth beneath his, their tongues dueling. Lights danced behind his eyelids. Desire surged through him, heating his extremities, hardening him and reminding him how long he'd been celibate.

He wanted to taste her everywhere, find that spot at her neck that had made her moan so long ago. Or place a kiss at the base of her throat. Or whisper things he wanted to do to her and hear her shocked gasps.

Breathing hard, he forced himself to step back. Would she know how aroused he was?

She blinked up at him, stretching out her hands to touch his chest.

"I'm not cold now," she said.

He smiled down into her upturned face. "That's why I kissed you, of course."

"Of course," she said. "A very kind gesture. Thank you."

They smiled at each other, the first time they'd ever been in perfect accord. No, that wasn't true, was it? After Robbie's birth they'd sat together, watching as their child slept. The night had been silent, the atmosphere almost magical. Not unlike this moment in an empty cottage.

"I've wanted to do that for months," he said, feeling the need to tell her the truth.

"I've wanted you to."

What the hell did he say to that?

"I'll find out who did this."

"It doesn't matter," she said.

"Of course it does."

She shook her head. "Some of the herbs were difficult to find. Some of them were specimens I've had for a few years. They would be hard to replace. So it doesn't matter if you find out who did this. The damage has already been done."

"Someone did this to hurt you and I'm not going to tolerate it."

Her eyes widened.

"Because I'm the Duchess of Kinross."

He managed to hold onto his temper. "No, because you're Lorna. You shouldn't be punished for being the Duchess of Kinross."

"Why not? You've done a good job of it. A most excellent job, as a matter of fact."

She swiped at her hair, made a face, and then used both hands to arrange it into a bun. Her hair finally done, she frowned up at him.

"What are you doing here?"

"I live here," he said.

"Not for nearly half a year."

"It wasn't that long."

She gave him a look that felt like it scorched.

"Very well, it was too long."

"Did you address the society?"

"Yes."

"Did it really take all that time?"

He'd never had the need to explain himself. But, then, he hadn't often done something as egregious as his recent behavior. She was absolutely right. He'd given her every reason to be angry. How did he tell her the truth?

"Were you seeing a woman?"

"What?"

Of all the questions she could have asked him, that one was the least expected.

"Mary said you had a mistress."

"Mary talks too damn much."

"Do you?"

"Have a mistress?" He speared one hand through his hair. "Does it matter?"

"Yes, I find it matters very much."

"I did once," he said. "She found someone new."

"Did you see her when you were gone?"

"No, I didn't see her. Or any other woman, for that matter. Jason and I managed to concentrate on our work without any female interference."

"Even after all that time?"

Did she really believe that he would be interested in anyone after her?

"Even after all that time."

She shook her head as if reprimanding him.

"I was taking fingerprints," he said, feeling the need to explain. "I needed the time."

"No, you didn't."

"Are you trying to dictate my work, Lorna?"

"No, I'm trying to get you to be honest. You regret our marriage, the necessity of our marriage. You might even regret Robbie for all I know. You left to go and nurse your wounds. Or escape me."

He was embarrassed, feeling vulnerable, confused about his emotions, and wanting to kiss her again. The perfect time for an argument.

"I had work to do," he said.

She only sent him a look.

He decided that he wasn't going to win that argument so he changed the subject.

"I'm coming back here with my fingerprint kit," he said, scanning the room.

Her frown was question enough.

"There might be some fingerprints on the glass."

"Do you think you can find out who did this?"

"There's a good chance," he said.

"I'd like to come with you," she said, "but I have to feed Robbie first."

"Then we'll attend to our son before coming back here."

He held her hand as they left the cottage. He wanted the connection with her. He wanted to kiss her again, but for now he'd settle for her hand in his.

The walk back to Blackhall was made in silence. He doubted they'd be able to hear each other over the wind anyway, even if he could find something to say.

He was beset by confusion, by the realization that he'd erred, and badly. He shouldn't have remained away.

Once back at the castle, he followed Lorna up to the ducal suite.

"Has he been fussy?" she asked.

Matthews appeared in the doorway to the sitting room. The valet stared at Lorna, his face a mask of stiff disapproval. He only altered his expression when he realized Alex was watching him. Bowing slightly, he disappeared.

"Only in the last few minutes," Nan said with a smile. "Almost as if he knew you were coming."

"Go and have your tea."

"Are you sure?" Nan asked, glancing toward the dressing room. "Matthews is here."

"What does that mean?" Alex asked.

She turned to him. "He hasn't been the most pleasant person to Lorna, Your Grace. Her first day here he made it clear he was an enemy, not a friend. Now that he's back I'm sure he'll find a way to insult her again."

"I'm here," he said, feeling an odd need to prove his loyalty was at least the equal of Nan's. "I won't tolerate his bad behavior. Has anyone else at Blackhall been rude?"

"You have, Your Grace."

That certainly put him in his place.

He didn't know how to define the emotion washing over him. Was it shame? Surely not. He hadn't done anything for which to be ashamed. Surely there was another bridegroom who'd deserted his bride the day after she'd given birth?

She stared straight at him, as if defying him to discipline her.

He'd never been chastised by a maid. No, that was wrong, wasn't it? Lorna had done the same. What kind of punishment could he mete out to her now for telling the truth? Or for being so loyal to Lorna?

The women in his life were rendering him speechless. At least his child was a boy. He looked forward to having reasonable and rational conversations with his son in the future.

"I'm here now," he said. "I have no intention of leaving again."

Nan looked at him as if she didn't believe him. Words wouldn't matter right now, would they? What counted were his actions.

She nodded, once, then left the room.

"Why didn't you tell me about Matthews?" he asked when Nan was gone and Lorna was settled in the overstuffed chair.

"What was I supposed to do, Alex? Whine that your valet hasn't been nice to me? You've known him a great deal longer than you've known me."

He was trying to wrap his head around that statement when she unbuttoned her dark blue dress, revealing a shift that was devised to separate in the middle.

"You aren't wearing a corset," he said.

"No." That was all. No explanation. No embarrassment.

He'd thought her natural before, but now she'd acquired a smooth competence in nursing their son. She smiled down at Robbie, her left arm cradling him, her right hand gently guiding him to her breast.

She ignored his presence, the two of them a complete unit that didn't require an outsider—him.

It had never occurred to him that he'd ever feel unwanted at Blackhall. The castle was his home, his heritage. He knew every nook and cranny, had played as a boy in every unused room. He'd explored the attic and the dungeon, knew the secret of the revolving bookcase in the library, had even carved his initials on the keystone of the gate. Yet ever since he'd walked in the door, he felt the aura of disapproval, as if the bricks were turning their backs on him.

He'd made a mistake, a bad one, and he was going to have to pay the price for it. How his punishment would be meted out, he wasn't sure, but he was certain it would come.

He had to do something about Matthews and any other servant who'd seen his departure as reason enough to make Lorna's life miserable. But he couldn't expect them to treat Lorna with respect if he hadn't.

She put Robbie to the other breast, remaining silent, increasing his discomfort. He wasn't familiar with this feeling, but it was one he'd experienced with her from the beginning. She kept him off balance, did things he didn't expect, and acted in ways he couldn't possibly anticipate.

He'd never met a woman like her.

"What else has happened since I've been gone?"

"Nothing," she said. A note in her voice bothered him.

"Nothing?"

"Not one thing, Alex, that would interest you. Robbie learned to sleep the night, your mother and I've become friends, Nan has become a genius at removing stains from my clothes, and the days have been very pleasant."

"Perhaps I should leave again, then," he said.

To his surprise, she took his words seriously.

"Who am I to tell a duke how to behave?"

"A duchess. That's who you are."

"I haven't the slightest idea how to be a duchess," she said. "I wasn't trained in my role as you were. I don't know how to be a wife, either. You have the advantage on me since you were a husband before."

She smiled at him, and he had the thought that she'd watched Matthews too closely. They'd both mastered the art of looking pleasant while wishing him to perdition.

Chapter 24

$\mathcal{H}$e left Lorna and made his way to his office, where Jason had moved all their new files. His assistant had placed his kit and the box containing Lorna's present on his desk. He stared at the box and wondered if he'd been a fool to have been so preoccupied with finding the perfect gift for her.

The four drawers of the walnut box contained a selection of watercolors, brushes, and other tools he'd been assured were sought after by artists. He'd found it after an entire week spent going from one shop to another.

She'd probably refuse it.

Lorna had confronted him before when she was angry, but she'd acquired something between that first occasion and now. Maybe it was confidence, because she hadn't looked the least bit uncertain as she sat there spearing him with words while nursing their child.

The damnable thing was that he deserved everything she threw at him. And probably more.

A few minutes later he and Jason walked down to the cottage.

"We've had mixed success with fingerprints on glass, Your Grace," Jason said when he surveyed the scene of destruction.

"Let's hope our luck changes."

They carefully collected shards of glass with tweezers, dusting any potential area with soot he'd put through a filter. By the end of the hour they'd found three good specimens he would try to match. Using cotton cloth coated in an adhesive, they managed to lift the prints from the glass.

Once back in his office, Alex placed the cloth sections on his desk, arranging the cards from the residents of Blackhall, servants and family alike, in a pile nearby.

"You didn't wait for me."

He glanced up to see Lorna standing at the door. She'd changed her dress, but it wasn't much of an improvement. This one, too, reminded him of her servant's uniform, a dark blue garment with white cuffs and collar.

"When is Hortense going to finish your wardrobe?" he asked.

"You know about her?"

"Nan told me. And the whole story of the seamstress and Mary."

She sighed. "It was a bit of nonsense," she said. "Hortense is ready to do the final fittings sometime this week. Now tell me why you went to the cottage without me."

"In light of our recent discussion, I thought it best to absent myself from your presence."

"You sound pretentious when you're annoyed."

"I beg your pardon?"

"Just like that," she said, entering the room. "Are you annoyed?"

"No. Yes. Perhaps."

She took the chair next to his desk and without

asking permission, picked up the first of the cards in the pile.

"Mrs. McDermott?"

"I'm beginning with the household staff."

"She wouldn't have done anything. Why are you annoyed?"

She was like a terrier. Once she had her teeth on a subject, she didn't give it up easily. Since he was the same way, he identified the trait easily enough.

"You annoyed me." He studied her for a moment. "Why do you look so surprised?"

"I wasn't the one who remained away for so long. Why do you have the right to be annoyed? Because you're a duke?"

"Now that question is annoying."

She selected the next card. "Mine?"

"I have to rule you out," he said. "Some of the prints I've taken could be yours."

She nodded. "Mary was adamant that you'd left me for another woman. That you'd left because you were hideously embarrassed that I'd been a servant. And that you remained away because you only married me to keep Robbie from being a bastard and regretted the decision."

He was going to have to do something about Mary, too.

"You should try to avoid her."

Lorna's laughter brightened the room.

"I do try to avoid her, Alex. You, yourself, should know how nearly impossible that is."

"Then you shouldn't listen to her."

"If you hear a lie often enough, Alex, you begin to wonder if it's the truth."

"I'm sorry," he said. The apology startled him, but once he began, he continued. "I shouldn't have remained away. Once my business with the society was concluded, I should have come home."

"What was your business with them?"

He wasn't accustomed to sharing the details of his life with others, but he found it surprisingly easy to do with Lorna. She listened to him explain his treatise and why he thought someone had stolen his ideas.

"My father had just published a book when he encountered another botanist with the same subject matter," she said. "He said it happened often in science that more than one person has the same idea at the same time. Couldn't it be that way with your discovery of fingerprints?"

"The society will have to make that conclusion. I've done what I can."

She tilted her head and regarded him. "Is it all that important that you're the first? Wouldn't it be just as valuable if you could add to the science?"

He considered the matter.

"Yes, it's important to be the first," he said.

"Why?"

"Because it's mine."

When she didn't say anything, he bent down and retrieved the box he'd put beside his desk.

"I got this for you," he said.

She frowned at him, but she took the gift, placing it on the top of the desk beside her. It took her only seconds to open it, revealing the walnut artist's box with its gold fastenings and four drawers.

When she opened the top, she didn't say anything, but her eyes widened. She remained speechless as her fingers danced along the sable brushes. One by one she removed the pots of watercolors, opened the top of each and examined the paints.

Still, she didn't speak.

This was not the first gift he'd ever given a woman. He once had an arrangement with an Edinburgh jeweler where the man reminded him of birthdays and anniversaries.

Perhaps he should have brought her something sparkly. Evidently this humble artist's box didn't impress her.

"You said you lost yours in your travels. I thought I'd replace it. You don't have to accept it, of course. I'll have it returned to the shop."

He reached out to take the box from her.

"No," she said. "No."

He waited, but she didn't say anything further, merely stroked her fingers over the fittings, opened and closed the drawers, took out the charcoal pencils and studied each one with great care.

"You heard," she said. Her gaze lifted to his. "You heard me tell you about my box."

"Of course I did."

"A great many people don't listen when you talk to them. You did."

He didn't know what she wanted him to say. Why wouldn't he listen to her?

"There's even a princely purple," she said, looking at the paints again. "Your color."

"My color?"

"Ever since I was a little girl, I've seen people as colors. Your mother, for example, is a delicate pink, almost like the Russell rose. Nan is a bright yellow.

Reverend McGill was orange, almost the color of flames. Mrs. McDermott is a warm, fluffy gray. Matthews—" She abruptly stopped.

"What is Matthews?" he asked, curious.

"A yellowish green," she said after a moment. "Almost a sickly color."

"And I'm purple?"

She glanced at him and smiled. "A dark purple that's almost blue. As I said, a very princely purple."

He didn't know what to say, but she wasn't finished.

"You couldn't have given me a better gift, Alex. Thank you."

The quaver in her voice made him think of tears, but her lips curved into a charming smile, one that made him stand, bend down, and kiss her.

His mouth touched hers gently, lingering for a moment, simply experiencing. Her lips were soft, warm, and welcoming, encouraging the desire that surged through him.

The sensation that followed was disturbing. Not the lust that he anticipated, or the wish that he could take her to his bed, which he was thinking whenever he was in her presence. No, this need was new, different, and more than a little startling.

He found himself wanting to confide in her, to ask her opinion, to tell her his secrets. He'd never before felt compelled to do that with anyone.

He finally sat again, his attention on his pen, straightening his blotter, and rearranging the inkwell in the exact center of his desk.

"Thank you," she said again, reaching out and placing her hand on his wrist.

He felt her touch through the cloth. Glancing over

at her, he wanted to tell her how she made him feel. Young, perhaps. Certainly untried. He wasn't Alexander Brian Russell, ninth Duke of Kinross, around her. He was only Alex.

"I remember when you took my fingerprints here," she said, glancing around his office. "It was a Tuesday and you were wearing a blue shirt with one of your black suits. This one had silver buttons. You'd cut yourself shaving and you had a small plaster on the side of your chin." She smiled at him. "Do you shave yourself or does Matthews do it for you?"

Had she always had that mischievous twinkle in her eyes? Her face had thinned, the angle of her jaw somehow arresting. She was, if anything, more beautiful for having given birth. Her hair had acquired a luster that made him want to study it in the sunlight, see how many strands were gold, how many brown.

He stared at her for so long that he almost forgot the question.

"Matthews," he finally said.

She nodded. "I thought as much. That's what he said, although I've learned to take only about a third of what he says as gospel."

"Matthews told you?" he asked, surprised.

"Not me. The staff. He tells everyone about all his many duties. He fusses a lot about your clothes, how you abhor stains and won't wear a shirt if the cuffs are frayed. He has to order a great many shirts for you, I understand, unless that's another exaggeration."

He sounded like a peacock, a Beau Brummell of the Scottish Highlands.

"What else did he tell you?"

"You like a certain brand of English perfume. Well, not perfume, exactly, but cologne for men. He doesn't care for it, himself, but he concedes that it's your choice, after all."

"Does he?"

"Abby says that there's an expression in her village about a man like Matthews: he thinks he's big, but a wee coat fits him."

"That sounds like Matthews," he said. He never realized that the man was telling people things he'd rather not share with everyone.

At his look, she smiled. "You have to understand, Alex, that even your brand of cologne is of interest to the staff. They're fascinated about you. A sighting is enough to keep one of the maids tittering for hours."

He sat back in his chair and regarded her.

"Did you titter?"

"I imagine I did, but not as much as Mary."

"I beg your pardon?"

Her smile deepened. "Oh, come now, Alex. Don't pretend you don't know."

"Know what?"

"Even the staff knows that Mary adores you."

"She's my sister-in-law."

"Who would like to be more," she said.

"I beg your pardon?"

"Haven't you ever seen the way she looks at you? Or follows you with her eyes? She nearly salivates. She's madly in love with you."

He'd never blushed in his life, but he found himself extremely uncomfortable.

"I think you've misjudged the situation. I think of Mary as a sister, nothing more."

She shook her head. "Then you should pay more attention, Alex. Why do you think she's so hateful? Even your mother understands that Mary is jealous."

She glanced at him, all warm brown eyes and fascinating mouth. He really wanted this conversation to be over. He wanted her gone. He needed her gone.

He knew, suddenly, why he'd stayed away for so long. Not to do his work, although that sufficed as an excuse. His surprising wife posed a threat to his peace of mind, if not his way of life. She made him feel too much. All sorts of emotions were knocking on his door, emotions he'd been able to control before Lorna came into his life. The threat was there that he would feel even more.

She was going to make him suffer. He knew it.

What was it his mother had said? He had a choice, to live in the gloaming or move into the daylight. He'd stayed in the shadows so long, he wondered if he could make the change.

Did he even want to?

The answer to that startled him.

With all his heart.

Chapter 25

$\mathcal{L}$orna stood and made her way to the dressing room door. She'd heard voices there earlier but nothing for a half hour or so. She sincerely hoped that meant Matthews had left. She didn't want a witness to her possible humiliation.

Slowly, she grabbed the door latch and pushed in. The room was dark, enough that she couldn't see a shape on the cot. Was he there?

"Alex? Are you asleep?"

"No," he answered.

"You don't have to sleep in here," she said. "I can't imagine that cot is comfortable."

"It's not."

"Come and sleep in your bed."

"I don't want to disturb you."

She couldn't help but laugh at that. "Robbie will be up in a few hours. You're the one who'll be disturbed. But until then you'll be able to sleep on a real mattress."

Without waiting for his answer, she turned and walked back into the bedroom. If he followed her, well and good. If not, there was nothing more she could do tonight.

He stood in the doorway attired in a long dark blue dressing gown.

"I don't sleep in a nightshirt," he said. "I detest the things."

"Oh."

What on earth did she say to that? He'd be naked. Now was the time to tell him to turn around and go back to the dressing room. Instead, she remained silent, watching as he walked toward the bed and stood on the other side. His gaze hadn't left her face.

She removed her wrapper and stood there in her nightgown.

"We've never shared a bed," he said.

"No."

"Only a settee."

"Not even that," she said, a smile blossoming on her lips. "I believe Mrs. McDermott calls it a fainting couch."

"Damned uncomfortable thing."

"Yes."

"I don't snore. Do you?"

"I don't know," she said. "I don't think so, but I might."

"I'll endeavor to ignore it if you do."

"How do you know you don't snore?" she asked, mounting the steps and climbing into the bed. "Have you been told you don't by other women?"

"Matthews," he said.

She wasn't sure she believed that, but she didn't press the point.

Robbie made a sound in his cradle.

"We shouldn't talk," Alex whispered.

"Nonsense," she said in a normal tone. "He has to learn to sleep through anything. Either that or the first time there's a storm he'll be terrified."

"How did you get to be so wise?"

She laughed, charmed by the question. He began to undo the belt of his robe and she deliberately glanced away.

"I'm not wise," she said. "I do have uncommon common sense, at least that's what my father said. Nan thinks otherwise, however."

"Here we are, brought down by the staff."

She turned to see him sliding into bed, bare-chested. The last time she'd seen him naked he'd been draped in shadows. Now the lamp on the bedside table revealed his muscled arms and the light dusting of black hair on his chest.

She wished she hadn't averted her eyes. She should have seen him completely naked.

"Is this your way of thanking me for the box?" he asked, reaching over to extinguish the lamp.

"No, Alex, it's not a way to thank you for the box."

"Why do you sound so annoyed?"

"Not everything has a price."

"I didn't mean it that way," he said.

"I'll move to another room in the morning. I think that would be best."

She slid down beneath the covers, rearranged her pillow, and tried to think of anything other than the fact he was so close.

"Did you and Ruth sleep together?" she asked.

"No, but this marriage is nothing like that one. Stop trying to find similarities between them."

Well, that certainly put her in her place, didn't it?

"Because I was a maid and she was the daughter of an earl?"

She turned again, facing away from him. He placed his hand on her waist, drawing her back.

"I never wanted to sleep with her," he said. "I never

wanted to sleep with anyone else," he added, sounding chagrined at the admission. "Not until now."

She wished she knew what to say to that. Finally, long moments later, she said, "I've never slept with anyone. I didn't have brothers or sisters."

"I did," he said.

"I know," she said, placing her hand on his where it rested on her waist. "Do you miss them?"

"Every day," he said. "Especially Moira. She and I were only thirteen months apart. We fought a great deal. You remind me of her a little."

"I do? Why, because we fight?"

"No, because you have the same spirit as Moira. She was brave and daring, just like you."

"I'm not brave and daring."

"Oh, but you are. Who else would have come to a fancy dress ball?"

There was that.

"You went off to live in Wittan by yourself, braving the censure of society."

"That's because I was foolish. I didn't know I'd be so reviled. But I had no other choice."

They each remained silent.

"Thank you," she said a few minutes later. "For the box. It's the most wonderful present you could have ever given me. Other than Robbie, of course."

Their son snuffled in his sleep, a reminder of the bond they shared.

"I don't want you moving to another room," he said.

She didn't have an answer for that, either.

"Sleep," he said softly in her ear.

She smiled again, patted his hand, and allowed herself to do just that.

"YOU'LL WEAR OUT the carpet, Mary," Thomas said, taking a sip of his whiskey as he watched the woman pace Blackhall's library.

He could, as the expression went, tune his pipes to Mary's wailing about Alex's marriage. She had been complaining about it for months now, and it wasn't getting easier to stomach.

He really should go back to London. He'd created his own identity there. He was the Earl of Montrassey. No one knew him as the uncle of the current Duke of Kinross, nicely sliced out of any hope for the dukedom by an almost illegitimate infant.

"Look at it from my angle, Mary. If I can condone the marriage, with all its ramifications, then surely you can."

She stopped her pacing long enough to send him a fulminating glance. "She's a maid, Thomas. Do you condone someone like that being the Duchess of Kinross?"

"It doesn't matter what I think, Mary. Nor does your opinion matter one whit in this instance. She is the Duchess of Kinross and nothing you or I could say will change that."

"He should never have married her," she said.

He silenced his first response. Alex could never have married *her*, which he knew was her secret hope and wish. She'd had the bad luck to be Ruth's sister. However, if she hadn't been Ruth's sister, she'd never have come to Blackhall in the first place.

He'd often thought they'd all have been better off if she hadn't.

Mary was a chattering little bird, as he'd occasionally thought of her. She gathered up information the way a nesting female collected twigs, fitting all the divergent pieces together to create a story here, a story there. Then she sat on a branch or, in her case, a chair in the parlor, and shared what she knew with anyone who was unfortunate enough to pass by. Maid or footman, housekeeper or the Dowager Duchess, it mattered not. Mary spread her tales.

One of her favorite sources of information was her own maid, Barbara, a rather scrawny female with an unfortunately long nose and thinning hair graying at the temples. Whenever he encountered her, he had the impression that the words she spoke had no resemblance to what she was thinking. Even her "Good morning, your lordship" was laced with a tone that made him think she was wishing him to perdition. No, the disgust in her gaze was tangible enough to feel.

Barbara was the perfect foil for Matthews, another obsequious servant at Blackhall. The two of them were like adders, slithering through the corridors and rooms of the castle, striking at any poor little mouse-like creatures they discovered.

He disliked them both, and wasn't altogether fond of Mary, either.

None of his hints had fallen on fertile ground so far. She was still pacing and still grumbling.

He'd come into the massive library to procure a book, something to occupy his mind, only to be waylaid by Mary. The woman was still pacing and still grumbling, unwilling to accept a fait accompli. Alex had married again.

Sooner or later she had to acknowledge that fact.

Granted, the marriage had been startling, but he didn't reveal the depth of his surprise to Mary.

Alex didn't trust the world, and why should he?

He'd been shown exactly what could happen in life at an early age. No wonder the boy had shuttered himself off from emotion, from feeling. If Lorna had broken open Alex's self-imposed cocoon, then he'd salute her.

Mary, however, was having none of that. In the true fashion of others of her ilk, she only saw the world through the prism of her own feelings. What she wanted was paramount. What she felt or thought was more important than what anyone else could possibly feel or think.

She was excessively tiresome in her selfishness. Not to mention excessively boring.

"She brightens him, Mary," he said.

Anything he said would simply bounce off the woman, so why not barrage her with the truth? He'd seen the change in Alex himself over the months. His nephew had been infuriated, curious, angry, and then bemused. He'd been bested without even knowing he was in a contest of wills.

"I believe that the dear boy is on his way to being happy. Surely you don't begrudge him that?"

"Happy?" She rounded on him again. "Why did he remain in Edinburgh for months? Why did he only now come home? Or do you consider it normal for a bridegroom to marry and immediately leave his bride?"

Alex's actions had been strange, but perhaps understandable. They were the last dying gasps of a man who was fighting the inevitable, just like he was.

Hadn't he done the same thing by coming home to Scotland this last week? He'd escaped London with a feeling that the Hounds of Hell were on his heels because a certain woman named Gloria was tightening the noose with a smile, the sound of her laughter, and the sparkle of her blue eyes.

When Louise had sent him after Alex, he went with the full understanding of how his nephew felt. What he didn't know was how to convey it to Mary.

"No doubt he'll fill the nursery," he said. "Louise will be ecstatic."

"She was complicit," Mary said. "She's as bad as Lorna."

He stared at her, the whiskey in his hand forgotten. His sister-in-law had his undying admiration, not to mention a genuine fondness. She'd adored his brother Craig, which had been obvious to a blind man. After his death and the deaths of her children, she refused to fall back into self-pity but had rallied to become the heart of Blackhall, beloved by everyone. Except, perhaps, this sour-faced, sour-hearted woman.

"I won't hear anything said against Louise. You should have better sense than that, Mary."

"She conspired to marry that creature to Alex."

"Watch your words, Mary."

"Why should I? The whole world will be talking about it soon enough. Did she care? No."

Louise had opened up her home to Mary with no reservations, and this is how the damn fool repaid her kindness?

"Something should be done."

The tone of her voice struck him as wrong. He sipped at his whiskey, watching her. She had resumed her pacing the length of the library, turning, and retracing her steps. When she passed by the fireplace and the wing chair where he was sitting, she didn't even seem to notice him. Her brow was furled with concentration, her lips thinned.

"Why are you so angry now? Because Alex has returned without a bill of divorcement? Or because Alex returned at all? Did you have fond thoughts of joining him in Edinburgh?"

She looked startled at his words. Could that be the reason? Damn fool woman. Did she honestly think Alex gave a fig about her?

"Something should be done," she repeated.

"What do you plan on doing, Mary?"

That question stopped her. She glanced at him, her smile a poor rendition of a genuine expression.

"I don't know what you're talking about, Thomas. Whatever could I do? Alex is married, isn't he? A union until death. At least in my poor sister's case."

Mary hadn't cared about Ruth all that much, he remembered, being so occupied with carrying tales about her infidelity to anyone who listened. Now, however, Ruth had ascended to the role of saint in Mary's eyes.

"Don't you want Alex to be happy?" A foolish question, perhaps, to ask of someone so occupied with her own thoughts and feelings.

"Of course I do," she said brightly.

A lie if he'd ever heard one.

She blessedly left the room a few minutes later, taking his peace of mind with her.

He didn't like the feeling he was getting. It felt like an itch in the middle of the back of his neck, a hint that something was wrong and that he might be in danger.

A talk with Alex in the morning wouldn't be remiss. While he was at it, he'd speak to Louise. Perhaps there was a way to rid themselves of the busy bird in their midst, a bird with talons and a razor sharp beak.

Chapter 26

$\mathcal{A}$lex woke to the sound of rain and wind against the window. The curtains hadn't been closed completely, revealing flashes of lightning assaulting Loch Gerry. He was immediately grateful for two things, that he wasn't out in it, and that the storm had awakened Lorna.

Her hand was flat against his chest, a connection in the darkness.

He turned his head, wished he could see her, but he wasn't about to light the lamp for fear it would wake Robbie.

Reaching out, he cupped her face, feeling the edge of her smile against his palm. He rose up on an elbow, bent, and kissed her softly, an exploratory kiss, one in which he tested his welcome.

Her hand reached around his neck and pulled him to her.

"Alex," she said softly.

Slowly, he pulled down the sheet, giving her time to protest. She didn't say a word, didn't jerk the sheet from his hand. Nor did she roll away in speechless repudiation.

His hands slid over her nightgown, riding along the soft, womanly curves. He remembered her well. His fingers recognized the indentation of her waist, the flare of hips, the long, long perfection of her legs.

The rain-cooled air should have been chilly, but he felt like a furnace roared inside him. He'd dreamt of this moment, of seducing Lorna. More than once he'd awakened heated, feeling like he'd been celibate for decades and both wanting and needing her.

His cock hardened. His hands shook as he unfastened the buttons on the placket of her nightgown. He wanted to tear the garment from her but only slipped his hand inside the garment, feeling her breasts hard and filled with milk.

She made a sound when he stroked his fingers over one nipple and then another. Bending his head, he softly licked each before placing his mouth on hers.

Lorna deepened the kiss, her tongue dancing with his, her hands framing his face. Her fingers speared through his hair and kept his head still for her assault.

His heart was racing. His cock hardened further.

Suddenly Lorna sat up, ridding herself of the nightgown, the lightning outside momentarily revealing curves and shadows before vanishing and taking away his sight.

She surprised him by exploring his chest, hips, then plunging her fingers into the nest of hair at his groin. He could swear he swelled even more when she wrapped her hands around him, stroking from base to tip.

When had she learned to do that?

Her kiss was carnal and alluring, making him forget everything but this moment and her. The shape of her, the smell of her, the softness of her skin and the curves that commanded his hands to touch and stroke, remembering another stormy night.

His memory hadn't been enhanced by time or imagination. Tonight was just as magical as the night a year ago. She was just as fascinating, but this time she wouldn't disappear. He could hold her in his arms and know that she would be there in the morning.

He was the one who had vanished. That thought hit him with the force of a blow.

He was the one who'd fled from her. Had he been afraid or just cautious? Had he known that this one woman would change the life he'd always known? Not only his life but his view of it. His very character would be altered.

How did he make up for being a fool?

She'd welcomed him with grace. Granted, she'd questioned him, but that was all. She hadn't punished him with silence or petulance. Instead, she invited him into her bed and now welcomed him with open arms.

Slowly he rolled over, taking her with him, his hands on her waist guiding her into position over him. He widened his legs and drew up his knees, creating a cradle for her.

"Alex?"

"It's better for you to be on top," he said.

She bent over him. "Is it?" she asked, the words infused with something magical, given the husky nature of her voice.

"I've been told it would be easier for you after giving birth."

She froze in position, her hair draped over him, her breasts grazing his chest.

"And who would be telling you that?"

Torture. She was torturing him. Did she know it?

His hands were still on her waist. Guiding her into

position, he rose up a little. When she lowered herself onto him, he closed his eyes, adrift in the sensation.

"Who told you that?" she asked, her lips against his cheek.

"Someone I consulted," he said, the words difficult to speak, even in a whisper.

She rose up a little, then down again. If she was experiencing any discomfort, she didn't show it. He, on the other hand, was poised on a twin precipice of delight and agony. He had the disconcerting thought that she'd taken command.

"You talked to someone about bedding me?" she asked, her voice taking on an odd tone.

He shouldn't have said anything, but now that he had, he needed to explain.

"I sought out an expert."

"What kind of expert?"

She sat up, which had the effect of seating him fully inside her. He wanted to savor the feeling but needed to answer the question.

"A woman of ill repute? A prostitute?"

His hands gripped her hips, wanting her to move, but knowing that he was doomed to finish this conversation first.

"A doctor," he said. "I wanted to ensure that the first time after Robbie's birth would be pleasant for you."

She lowered herself over him, brushing a kiss against his lips, her knees tightening on either side of him.

"Why didn't you just ask me, Alex? There are certain herbal preparations that would have been ideal for this moment."

There was another note in her voice now, a hint of amusement. He was, no doubt, a fool. At the very least, a randy fool who was at the mercy of a woman who'd become a siren in his absence. No, she'd always been that, hadn't she? Somehow, the confidence she demonstrated as a mother had transferred to the woman.

Lorna Gordon Russell was not to be underestimated. As she slowly rose and lowered herself over him, he realized that he'd been wrong.

He wasn't seducing her. She was seducing him, and doing it so well that ecstasy was spiking through him, deadening his mind and making him an atavistic creature intent on only his needs and wants.

He pulled himself back from the brink, focusing on Lorna. Her breath was coming faster, her skin was heating, and she was making soft sounds in the back of her throat. His fingers danced between them, stroking her, urging her to completion so that she finished before him.

He didn't know how long he could hold out.

With her, he had no skill, only need. With her, he was impatient to desperation.

She suddenly slumped forward, her breasts pressing against his chest. Her hands clenched his shoulders as she tightened like a fist.

She was hot and tight, stretching around him. He wanted to bring her pleasure even if meant waiting, and the last thing he wanted was to wait.

He ducked his head to trail his mouth down her throat, feeling the rapid pulse beat there. He was lost in the sight and smell of her, the soft moans she was making as she wrapped her arms around his neck. She sighed into his mouth.

Abruptly, vibrations traveled through her as her whole body clenched. A second later he had no choice but to come with her, his hips rising, every muscle and nerve focused on completion.

He hoped to God that she'd found pleasure in their joining because he could no longer hold back. He'd never before felt anything like this, endless pleasure that catapulted him from one wave of sensation to another. His body bowed, every muscle tightening as he erupted inside her. Lights danced behind his lids, each sense centered on the feel of her constricting around him.

His breath left him along with his strength. His eyes were probably rolled back in his head.

A last thought before his vision grayed and bliss overwhelmed him.

HE HAD DIED and gone to Heaven, returned, and now lay here staring at the ceiling, incapable of speech.

No wonder that stormy night had happened. He was surprised that it had ended. He remembered thinking that he wanted to continue, wanted a rematch, wanted to make love to this woman until the dawn came. If some of the servants interrupted them, oh well. Perhaps it was time they learned a little about the facts of life. Perhaps it was time they learned some biology.

What had stopped him then? Oh, yes, he'd insulted Lorna. He couldn't believe she'd been a virgin. He'd allowed his distrust of all things and all people to interrupt what might have been a marathon lovemaking session.

He turned his head slightly. Lorna was on her side, her face toward him. She had the most beautiful lashes. Her face was pink, her lips well-kissed and swelling slightly beyond their borders.

What had she done to him?

She had ruined him for any other woman, that was certain. Any idea of ever being unfaithful to Lorna was not only distasteful but would be stupid in the extreme.

He had his psyche, his siren, the woman who affected him as no other woman could right here in his bed. His wife. His surprising, delightful, fascinating wife.

His laughter woke his son.

SHE AWOKE WITH a kiss and the soft brush of a fingertip along her cheek.

Her eyelids fluttered open, then closed at the sight of Alex's smile. For a brief second she allowed herself the luxury of thinking there was something in his eyes other than humor.

"Robbie's hungry."

"Umm," she said. "He's always hungry."

"Will he always be up every few hours?" he asked.

"I'm surprised he didn't wake earlier."

Sleep beckoned, but she dragged herself upright, eyes still closed.

"He's a duke's son," she added. "Very autocratic and demanding."

She slit open one eye then the next, her head back against the headboard. Robbie was beginning to cry in earnest now, but before she could swing her legs over the side of the bed, Alex was at the cradle.

"Come here, little man," he said, scooping the baby up in his arms.

Alex must have opened the curtains earlier because sunlight streamed into the room, a ray of light catching him in its beam. He stood there, attired in his robe, arms cradling their son, emotion softening his face.

"Let's go find your mother, shall we?"

He turned and stopped, glancing at her.

Time stilled, the space emptying between them. She sat there, her eyes filled with tears. He stood there, arrested by something he saw. The seconds ticked by filled with unspoken emotion.

She loved him. She'd been attracted to him from the first moment she'd seen him. She'd felt lust and desire and passion in his arms. He'd annoyed her and made her angry. He'd hurt her but also stirred her, impressed her, and summoned her admiration.

Somehow, in the weeks and months that had passed, despite everything, she'd fallen in love with him.

Slowly, he began to walk to her. She unbuttoned her nightgown. He gently placed Robbie in her arms but he didn't move away. Instead, he stood there, only inches from her, so close she could see each individual bristle of his morning beard, the rapid pulse beat at his throat, and hear his accelerated breathing.

She put her child to her breast and he watched.

She shouldn't be feeling this, not now. How could she be catapulted into desire so easily?

Could she hint for a kiss? She closed her eyes, trying to ignore him, only to open her eyes wide when she felt the touch of his fingertip on the slope of her breast.

She glanced at him, but his gaze was fixed on her nipple, on the sight of Robbie eagerly suckling.

"I never thought that the sight of a mother nursing her child would be so beautiful," he said. "Thank you for that."

He so easily stripped words from her. She didn't know what to say to that comment. But, then, she'd often sought refuge in her drawings when language failed her. Perhaps she needed to draw him as he appeared now, blue eyes intent, his face molded by concentration, his lips curved into a half smile.

"Nor did I ever know it could be so arousing."

She couldn't look away. Trapped by his gaze, she let him see everything she was feeling: confusion, wonder, desire, and love.

"I most definitely don't want you moving to another room," he said. "Stay here with me."

Perhaps she should have questioned him further. Or asked him if what she saw in his eyes was real. Instead, she only nodded, watching as he stood and made his way to the door.

Once there, he turned. They shared a look again, one that made her heartbeat escalate.

Robbie fussed at that moment, as if annoyed that her whole attention wasn't on him. She glanced down at her son, and when she raised her head again, Alex was gone.

She stared at the closed door for a long time.

Chapter 27

$\mathcal{L}$orna made their bed herself, straightening the coverlet and fluffing the mattress. She stopped twice to hold Alex's pillow against her face, breathing deeply. She felt foolish and nearly overcome with emotion.

She was a duchess, married to a duke, but not any duke. Alex. This morning, waking to his smile, had been glorious.

"Lorna?"

She came back to herself to see Nan standing in the doorway of the sitting room, smiling as brightly as the summer sun. The change to lady's maid had been good for her. Not only was she given more status in the eyes of the staff, but she'd also received an increase in pay and a larger room.

"Are you ready?" Nan asked, removing her shawl. "I'll bring in the dresses if you are. Here or in the sitting room?"

She peeked into the cradle to see Robbie still asleep. "In the sitting room," she said. "I don't want to wake him unless I have to. The little darling slept the whole night."

Closing the door softly, she entered the sitting room to find that Nan had rearranged the chair and the table, giving them room in front of the settee.

A few minutes later Nan and Peter entered the room nearly buried by garments. Nan instructed the footman to put them on the nearby chair.

"I don't remember that many," Lorna said after Peter left.

"I've never seen Hortense work so hard," Nan said. "At every meal, she doesn't stop talking about patterns and fabrics. She even asked Mrs. McDermott if it would be possible to travel to Inverness to obtain some bolts of the newest material."

"What did Mrs. McDermott say?"

She wasn't as sanguine as Alex and Louise about people's opinions. Besides, most of the staff had been friends of various degrees at one time.

Nan smiled. "That whatever you need Hortense to do she's to do. You are, after all, the Duchess of Kinross. And quite a heroine to all the maids."

"Whatever for?"

"All the girls believe that if it can happen to you, then they have a chance for happiness, too. Mrs. Mc-Dermott even lectured them." Nan's expression suddenly changed, as if she just realized what she'd said.

"On not acting the harlot?"

"She didn't mean it that way, Lorna. She just wanted to caution the girls that there isn't a happy ever after ending in everyone's story."

"Mrs. McDermott is right," she said. "I've been lucky, haven't I?"

"You would have managed, somehow," Nan said.

Lorna glanced at her. "You've been so loyal and generous, Nan. I couldn't have a better friend than you."

"Even when I speak my mind?"

Lorna smiled. "Especially then. You've always given me wise counsel."

"You didn't always listen."

"No, but if it hadn't been for you, we wouldn't be here now, would we?"

Nan answered the knock on the sitting room door. Hortense stood there, holding a tray, her eyes wide, her narrow face white with panic.

"I was asked to bring this up, seeing as how I was coming," she said.

Every item on the tray was clinking against something. If they didn't intercede quickly, Hortense was going to lose her grip and create yet another disaster.

Lorna cleared the table in front of the settee just as Nan grabbed the tray to keep everything from tumbling to the floor.

What was Mrs. McDermott thinking?

Hortense was tall and spindly, with a habit of leaning forward so that she looked like an egret hunting food. Although Hortense was at least ten years older, Lorna always felt the urge to protect her. Perhaps it was her air of innocence, as if she woke wide-eyed and naive each morning. Or her way of laughing like her own amusement surprised her. Her sweet disposition made her a favorite among the staff, and she was so happy with this opportunity to show her sewing talent that it was a pleasure to be around her.

"I'll just go get my basket, shall I?" she asked now, looking relieved to be divested of the tray.

In seconds she was out the door, leaving Lorna to smile at Nan.

"She's very sweet," she said.

Nan nodded and handed her the plate of biscuits. Lorna didn't hesitate and grabbed two.

"She is. She's also the very worst maid."

"But an excellent seamstress," Lorna said.

She sat and watched as Nan poured the tea and handed her a cup. Robbie cried out in the bedroom. She put her cup down and was on her feet, tea forgotten.

ALEX GOT TO the stables early, the better to burn off the energy coursing through him. He entered cautiously, pleased when he realized he'd arrived before Mary.

His mount was Samson, a stallion he rode when he could. Although Mary was a fine rider, he'd given orders that she not be allowed to ride the horse.

A reaction he hadn't analyzed until now. He was normally a generous person, or at least he wanted to be considered generous. Yet it annoyed him when Mary took advantage of that largesse or assumed that because he had given her A, then B should be hers as well.

Mary assumed that everything was hers. She was like Loch Gerry when it occasionally flooded, spreading over the glen until it turned into a marsh. There were no boundaries in her world.

Was that why she'd made Lorna miserable? Because she was jealous? He couldn't accept that Mary had any feelings for him. He thought she'd simply decided to acquire him like she had the mare she rode, the wardrobe she wore, or the suite she occupied.

What the hell was he going to do about his sister-in-law?

The day was looking to be warmer than yesterday. The wind had calmed, leaving a perfect spring day to appreciate. These quiet moments were few and stolen from his responsibilities and the crowd of people at Blackhall.

The route he took was one familiar to him, through the woods, down a barely marked path to an outcropping over the loch, then backtracking a little to the road that led to Wittan Village. He took the road to the right to inspect the land around Blackhall and the herds of Highland cattle. Today he would carve some time out of his schedule to visit with a few of the crofters who made their living on Blackhall's tillable land.

In a few hours he would be back home, soon enough to see Lorna. Otherwise, she would think him a besotted idiot.

What a fool he'd been to remain away.

SHE TENDED TO Robbie. He wasn't hungry, since he'd eaten less than an hour earlier. She changed his nappy and rocked him while sitting on the edge of the bed. When she heard a scream, she put Robbie in his cradle and ran into the sitting room.

Nan was on the floor, her back arched and limbs flailing.

"What happened?" Lorna asked, falling to her knees beside her friend.

Hortense stood there weeping and wringing her hands.

"Tell me, Hortense. What happened?" Lorna turned Nan to her side. Blessedly, the seizure appeared to be easing.

"I don't know," Hortense wailed. "I don't. We were just sitting there talking, waiting for you, and all of a sudden she fell over."

Lorna had never seen that with Nan before. People don't normally have seizures without a history of them, she thought, and scanned the tray. She'd had two of the biscuits and nothing had happened to her.

"The tea?" she asked. "Did she drink any of the tea? Did you?"

When Hortense looked at her wide-eyed, she blew out a breath, exasperated with the other woman.

"Tell me, Hortense!"

"I had two biscuits, but not the tea."

She placed her hand on Nan's back, felt the easing of the muscles. In Inverness the innkeeper's daughter had a seizure. The girl's mother said that she always knew the episode was over when her daughter's back was no longer in spasm.

What Hortense said just registered with her.

"You didn't have the tea?" she asked, reaching for the pot.

She pulled off the cozy and removed the top, sniffing. Even before she raised the pot to her nose, she smelled the distinctive licorice scent of monkwood.

"How much did she drink?" she asked, fear coloring her voice.

"I don't know," Hortense said. "One cup maybe?"

There was a cup on the tray. She raised herself up and peered inside. Half the tea was gone.

If it was monkwood, Nan had already drunk enough to be dangerous. The seizure was over, but her coloring was terrible. Her lips were turning bluish.

There wasn't much time.

Lorna walked over to Hortense and grabbed her by the shoulders.

"You have to be brave now. I have to go to the cottage to get some medicine for Nan. You have to stay with her. Ring the bell and get the duchess in here to help you and care for Robbie. All right?"

"All right."

"Don't drink the tea. Don't let anyone else drink it, either."

"Shall I pour it out?" Hortense asked.

"Don't touch it," she said. "It's poison."

She began to run, hoping she wouldn't be too late.

ALEX HADN'T MADE it out of view of the castle before he heard a shout. He turned in the saddle, hoping it wasn't Mary. Instead, Jason was racing toward him, his assistant's normally pale face florid with effort.

"Your Grace! Your Grace! Come quick. She's been poisoned!"

His heart chilled in that instant.

"What's happened?"

In the next few minutes he realized that Jason, while near perfect in a calm environment, lost his head in a time of crisis.

"She fell to the floor. Had a fit."

"Who? My wife?"

Jason took a few deep breaths before answering, moments ticking by so slowly he almost dismounted and shook the young man.

"No, Your Grace. Not the duchess. Nan. She's had a seizure and the duchess said she was poisoned."

Alex turned Samson and raced back to the castle. At the kitchen entrance, he dismounted and handed the reins to a startled maid before taking the servants' stairs two at a time.

His mother was in his sitting room, kneeling on the floor beside Nan. Another woman stood in the corner clenching her two hands together and staring at the scene.

"Where's Lorna?" he asked.

His mother glanced up at him only for a second before her attention returned to the unconscious woman on the floor.

"At the cottage," she said.

He raced back down the stairs, wishing his staff weren't so responsive. Samson had already been turned over to a footman and was halfway to the stables. He grabbed the reins out of the man's hands, said something he hoped was halfway coherent, mounted, and raced down the road.

Halfway there, he saw her. Lorna hadn't even grabbed a shawl in her haste to help Nan.

"Give me your hands," he said when he reached her.

Her face was white, her mouth pursed. He'd only seen the fear in her eyes once before, when she was being verbally assaulted by Reverend McGill.

"Give me your hands," he repeated.

When she did, he pulled her up to sit in front of him on the saddle.

"Tell me what happened," he said, putting his arms around her.

"Nan had some tea before the final fittings. She had a seizure only minutes later."

Something in her voice disturbed him.

"What is it, Lorna?"

"The tea smelled of monkwood. It has a distinct odor."

"It's poison?" he asked.

"Deadly poison," she said.

They exchanged a look. "Did you drink any of it?"

"No," she said. "But I might have. I had to go check on Robbie."

"What's in the cottage?" he asked when they reached their destination. He lowered her to the ground, tied the reins to the door latch, and followed her inside. "Your herbs were all destroyed."

"Not all of them," she said. "There were some in a special place."

"Do you think you can help Nan?"

Lorna turned and faced him. In the last few minutes, anger had replaced the fear in her eyes.

"My father wrote about monkwood poisoning. There's a cure for it. I think I still have what I need."

She walked into the bedroom, pulled open the armoire and withdrew a small chest that she put on the bed. Beneath the bed there was another chest, which she also retrieved. Opening both, she selected three cork-stoppered bottles and put them into a cloth bag.

He followed her as she left the cottage and waited beside his horse. He mounted, then pulled her up beside him once more, tightening his arms around her as he gave Samson his head.

They didn't speak. He didn't know what to say. What if Nan didn't survive? What words could possibly ease the moment?

When they were back at the castle and in the sitting room, Lorna unpacked the bag and put the bottles on the table. Two contained leaves of some kind, the third a white powder.

In their absence his mother had retrieved Robbie from the bedroom and now stood with him in her arms, rocking from one foot to the other. Peter had placed Nan on the settee and was standing behind it, biting his lip. Jason stood with him, along with the other woman.

Alex didn't know whether to dismiss all of them or allow them to remain there in the room in what might be Nan's last moments.

"What can I do?"

"I need hot water," she said. "And a little whiskey."

He glanced at Peter, who nodded and left the room for the hot water. Alex, meanwhile, poured a tumbler of whiskey from the sitting room sideboard and handed it to Lorna.

Lorna mixed the white powder with the whiskey then knelt beside the settee.

Nan's face was a curious gray, her lips a bluish color.

"Help me raise her up."

He moved to the settee, sat at Nan's head, and lifted her shoulders. He thought she was unconscious but she moaned when Lorna pressed the glass to her lips.

"You have to drink this, Nan. I know it's vile but you have to."

He thought it was Lorna's will alone that got the concoction down Nan's throat.

When Peter returned bearing a steaming tea-kettle, Lorna pressed half of the leaves from both of the bottles into the boiling water. They all stood silently watching Nan as the brew steeped. When Lorna deemed it ready, she poured some of the green mixture into the same glass, then cooled it by adding more whiskey.

"She won't like this one, either," Lorna said, glancing up at him. "The cure is said to taste like briars mixed with horse excrement."

His mother's laugh surprised them all. When he glanced at her, she shrugged, still making that rocking motion to soothe Robbie. His son was gnawing on one fist and drooling all over his mother's expensive dress. She didn't appear to care one whit.

"I do bless the day you came into our lives, Lorna," his mother said. "You're a breath of fresh air. You'll save her. I know you will."

Once Nan finished the glass, her color was a little better. The bluish tint to her lips had disappeared. She looked more herself, but ill.

"How long until you know if the cure worked?" Alex asked.

"Not for a day or two. If she doesn't have any more seizures, she should recover."

"Is there anything I can do?" Peter asked, stepping forward.

Had Peter developed feelings for Nan? It was a question he would never have asked himself a year ago.

"Say a prayer," Lorna said, studying her friend. "Or a dozen of them."

He would say a few as well, of thankfulness that Lorna hadn't drunk any of the tea. Who would have saved her if she had? He certainly didn't have the expertise, and by the time a physician could be called it would have been too late.

While he was at it, he'd say another prayer, that he found the person responsible before anything else could happen.

THEY TUCKED NAN into the guest room near their suite with Hortense to care for her. The woman had strict orders to alert Lorna if Nan developed a fever or if her appearance changed in any way.

Alex had sent for the physician as well. The doctor might not know about herbs and their poisonous properties, but he would be able to help Nan if she had another seizure or if her condition worsened. He probably wouldn't arrive until morning, which meant there was nothing more to be done but return to their suite.

Lorna peeked into the bedroom to find Robbie asleep and her mother-in-law dozing next to him in the overstuffed chair. She closed the door and faced Alex.

"They're both asleep," she said. "But not for long. Robbie needs to be fed."

"But for now we have time to talk." Alex stood by the fire.

She didn't ask him what he wanted to discuss. The questions had been fomenting all evening. She sat on the wing chair in front of the fireplace, stretching her hands out in front of her. Someone had tended the fire earlier and it crackled merrily, as if the flames were talking to each other.

"Will she live?" Alex asked.

She nodded. "I think so. Whoever put the monkwood in the tea didn't know how many leaves to use to cause death."

"But they'd known that monkwood is dangerous."

"Most people know that," she said. "It's like foxglove. People have heard that it can be used for good but that too much can kill."

He sat next to her in the adjoining wing chair.

"I need to talk to Mrs. McDermott. I don't want any trays left unattended. And from now on, only the staff regularly assigned there is to be allowed in the kitchen."

"I don't think the poison was meant for Nan," she said.

"Nor do I."

She glanced at him for a moment before she went back to studying the fire.

"Your uncle came to the cottage one day," she said. "He wanted to know about my herbs."

"You think Thomas would have done such a thing?"

"No," she said. "I don't. He's been genuinely kind to me these past months. I find him charming. He might be a libertine, but I doubt he's a murderer."

Alex didn't say anything, but his face changed, molding itself into stern lines. For just a second she saw how he might appear in thirty or forty years. That is, unless he allowed some happiness into his life.

"He was complimentary of you when he came to Edinburgh," he said.

"Was he?"

She glanced at him again, caught the glint in his eyes and shook her head.

"I'm not Ruth, Alex."

He didn't answer her.

"Oh, for pity's sake, Alex, stop it. I will not be compared to Ruth. Not in any way."

"What does that mean?"

"She was a great deal more understanding of you than I am."

"Again, what does that mean, Lorna?"

"According to your mother, the two of you chased each other all over Scotland. I have no intention of tolerating that kind of behavior. I think it only fair to warn you that if you desert me again, I'll sue for a legal separation."

"I beg your pardon?"

"The Matrimonial Causes Act," she said, closing her eyes and laying her head back against the chair. "I believe it was passed a few years ago."

"Who told you about the Matrimonial Causes Act?"

His voice sounded strange, but she didn't open her eyes.

"It's your choice," she said. "Either you're a husband or you're not. I know you only married me for Robbie's benefit. But our son deserves to see his mother treated with respect and decency. Leaving me for so long was neither."

"No, it wasn't," he said, surprising her. "I should have been here. I should never have left you. But I didn't only marry you for Robbie's benefit."

She opened her eyes and studied him.

"I know we do well together," she said, feeling her cheeks warm.

"Do well together?" he asked, a strange smile playing around his lips. "That's one way to put it."

She was not going to ask what he would call what happened to them when they kissed or touched. She knew she lost any awareness of her surroundings, even the sense of who she was. Perhaps it was safe to say she lost her mind around him. Was it the same with him?

She didn't ask and he didn't volunteer any additional information.

"Why now?" he asked. "Why mention the Matrimonial Causes Act now? You had plenty of time in the last day or so."

"Because of Nan," she said. She turned and looked at him steadily. "Because, for a little while, I thought she would die. Then I realized that someone wanted me to die. For marrying you. It seems to me that if I'm in danger for being your wife, I ought to at least be treated as one."

He didn't respond.

She stood, keeping herself silent. She knew who wanted her gone from Blackhall. So did Alex. Was he going to do anything about Mary?

How he treated this situation might well decree their future and the rest of their married life together. What had Louise said? Something about life being too short and to grab her happiness where she could.

Someone wanted to ensure her life was cut short now.

Chapter 28

Alex sat at his office desk, trying to concentrate on the fingerprint cards before him.

He put down his magnifying glass and stared out at the view of the morning from his office. It was no use. He couldn't concentrate.

The day was a gray one. Mist huddled on the ground like earthbound clouds and clung halfway up the trees. The top branches were black against the white, dead sticks waiting for a touch of green.

He and Jason had each taken half the cards belonging to the staff and were going through them to find a match to the fingerprints they'd lifted from the cottage, in what he was mentally calling Lorna's apothecary.

His contribution to the task was almost nil. His mind was on Lorna's words from the previous night.

He'd slept on the damnable cot again, his dreams fitful things no doubt fueled by the events of the evening. He was worried about Lorna's safety, incensed by the thought that someone would dare to try to harm her, and trying to push his suspicions away, at least until he had proof.

An excellent reason to press on with this task. He picked up the magnifying glass again and took the next card to examine.

She thought he'd just married her for Robbie's sake. Not only that, but she'd leveled a look of such disgust on him that he'd physically felt it. It was one thing to be lectured by Thomas, who was a profligate satyr. Quite another for Lorna to excoriate him with a few words.

He felt more inept than he'd felt for years. Or ever. What did she want from him?

The truth?

She was right. That was the damnable thing about the whole situation. She was absolutely right. He didn't have any grounds to mount a defense. His actions had been indefensible.

He'd been behaving exactly like he had all his life, burrowing inward, hiding himself, revealing nothing.

I'm not Ruth. No, she wasn't. Lorna wouldn't escape Blackhall for the entertainments of the city. She wouldn't take lovers, of that he was certain. Nor would she allow him to remain in his office, immersed in his prints, if there was something on her mind.

Look what had happened last night. He didn't doubt that she meant what she said. Scandal be damned, she might just sue for separation if he ever left her again. She was right about something else. They were good together. Better than he had envisioned.

For the first time in his life he knew he hadn't lived up to the expectations of his family. Not only those of his father, by example, but his mother and uncle. The discordance of that thought had him standing, walking to the window, and fighting back the urge to flee.

He couldn't escape himself, yet he'd certainly tried to do that, hadn't he?

He had three problems at the forefront of his mind. One: Lorna and their relationship. He needed to define it, capture it, and understand it. Two: how did he keep his new family safe? Three: if Mary was behind the attack, as he suspected, how did he handle her?

Disturbed, he went back to his work and was almost instantly rewarded with a match. Fifteen minutes later he found another. Jason surprised him with an announcement that he'd found not just one match, but two.

He motioned Jason to his side. He slid the set of prints he'd taken from the shards of glass in the cottage next to the cards.

"You look at the ones I found and I'll check yours," he said.

They each spent a few minutes examining the cards.

"There are definitely four matches, sir," Jason said.

He agreed.

"People among the staff, sir?" Jason sounded as incredulous as he felt.

He glanced up at his assistant. "Turn over the cards."

Jason reached out and with his long-fingered hand turned over each card to reveal the names. His silence was as pointed as any comment he might have made.

"What are you going to do, Your Grace?" he finally asked.

He wasn't surprised at the question. Jason had always impressed him with his quick understanding of the facts.

Four people besides Lorna had touched the bottles from her apothecary. He was one of them, which was understandable. He'd originally unpacked the trunk for her. One of the remaining three people had destroyed what they could and stolen the herbs that had nearly killed Nan. He didn't know if it was the same person or if two different people were involved. It was all too possible that someone had stolen the herbs from the cottage before the damage occurred.

He was just going to have to find the answers.

"I'm going to go and see my uncle," Alex said, partially answering Jason's question. He knew what he was going to do with the other two individuals as well, but Thomas's answer was the first one he'd hear.

LORNA AWOKE FEELING groggy, almost heavy, as if she were grieving and weeping tears that couldn't be seen. She hadn't felt that way since after her father died.

Alex had only been home a few days and their marriage was already crumbling.

He'd remained in the dressing room all night. Had she erred in confronting him? Something had snapped when he mentioned Ruth. She hadn't planned on saying what she had, but did he seriously expect her to silently acquiesce to his absences? That wasn't her definition of a marriage. Nor was she going to be the kind of wife who simply accepted any bad behavior on his part because he was the Duke of Kinross. He was her husband, which was at least as important.

She might not have the pedigree that Mary thought was so necessary to being a duchess, but did that really matter? Wasn't her behavior more important than her heritage?

She hadn't exactly behaved in a proper manner, either, or the Duke of Kinross wouldn't have felt it necessary to marry her when she was in labor. Very well, she wasn't a proper duchess. What about being a wife? In order to be a proper wife was she supposed to simply remain silent and meek?

She doubted she'd be able to alter her character

enough to fit into that role. Even as a maid she'd had to bite her tongue more than once. At night, Nan, who was the most amenable of people, had to listen to her complain about their rules.

No, she was destined to be just who she was, a deplorable duchess and a demanding wife. What about Alex? Did he think himself exempt from any kind of standards of behavior?

She fed Robbie and dressed, all the while trying to decide who she was more annoyed at: Alex or herself.

Taking the baby with her, she went next door to see Nan. To her delight, her friend was sitting up in bed. Although pale, she appeared to feel better than she had yesterday afternoon. She even smiled when Lorna opened the door and peeked inside.

"I'm so glad it's you," Nan said. "Hortense has threatened me with gruel, can you believe it? I'm genuinely hungry, but she said she couldn't bring me anything but broth. Broth?"

"It would be better for you," Lorna said, moving to sit on the chair beside the bed. "Your stomach is bound to be upset."

Robbie reached out for Nan and she grabbed his plump little hands.

"Hortense said that someone poisoned the tea. Is that true?"

She nodded. "I don't know who," she said. "But I know what they used. Monkwood."

Nan's eyes widened. "The same monkwood that can kill you?"

Lorna nodded again. "The very same. I gave you an antidote, and I'm grateful that it seemed to have worked."

"So am I," Nan said, leaning back against the pillow.

A moment later she spoke again. "They could've killed all three of us."

"I don't think they cared how many people they killed as long as I was one of them."

Nan glanced at her. "Someone doesn't want you to be the Duchess of Kinross. But why now?"

"Because Alex has come home," she said. "Maybe she thought he would come back and tell me he was going to divorce me. Or throw me out of Blackhall. I don't know."

"Mary," Nan said.

"I think so."

"What are you going to do?"

She had slept fitfully the night before with her worry about Nan, her confrontation with Alex, and her suspicions. Daylight hadn't brought her any answers.

"I don't know at the moment," she said.

Robbie was fussing a little, so she put him on her shoulder and began to rock back-and-forth in the chair. The soothing motion soon led to him sleeping, his head lolling against her neck.

"No one saw her put the monkwood leaves in the tea," Lorna added.

"If she really did it, Lorna, she'll do something else."

"That's what I'm afraid of. I'm going to move all my remaining herbs to a locked room somewhere here in the castle. Or maybe I should just destroy them."

What a pity, since some of them had taken her father years to collect and others were rare. They were the only important things she owned, but if she had to destroy them to prevent others from using them for ill, she would.

When Hortense arrived, Lorna approved of the broth that she had brought from the kitchen.

"Mrs. McDermott made me promise that I wouldn't stop on the way anywhere, Lorna. Your Grace, I mean. I was to come straight here and not let anyone near the bowl."

Evidently Alex had already instituted his measures.

"Good," Lorna said.

Turning to Nan, she smiled. "If your stomach can tolerate the bone broth, I promise to bring you something more substantial later."

Nan only made a face.

The sun had finally decided to make an appearance, burning off the mist and chasing away the bank of clouds.

She didn't want to return to the sitting room. Nor did she want to be with anyone. She was in a strange, almost sad mood. Without much encouragement she could burst into tears. Not exactly a time to be with a companion. Instead, she was going to get a little fresh air, and it wouldn't hurt Robbie, either.

She bundled up both of them, using one of her long woolen scarves to devise a way to carry Robbie. She tied it around her waist then above her shoulders, knotting it at the front. She spread the scarf open and lifted Robbie inside. He seemed to think it was great fun, his brown eyes sparkling up at her. Whenever she looked at him, it was like something was squeezing her heart. Except for the color of his eyes, he resembled Alex so much.

Robbie was beginning to recognize certain people. He'd smiled his first smile. His gurgling sounded like laughter. He was lifting his head up and surveying the world like he was pleased with what he saw. Soon he would be crawling and then walking. All of Blackhall would be his domain.

She, too, had changed in the intervening months. She was no longer willing to simply dream dreams. She wanted to see the world as it was, but be happy with it, too. She wanted to be loved. Surely that wasn't too onerous a wish.

She made her way to the first floor without seeing anyone. She didn't know about other great houses, but Blackhall had a certain rhythm to it. A pulse beat, perhaps. Most of the daily activity happened between dawn and eleven. Then, people gravitated to the servants' dining room for an early lunch. The castle seemed to doze a little between lunch and when the cleaning of the upper rooms began at one. From then until four or five, the staff were busy with their tasks. Conversation could be heard in the stairwell, along with occasional laughter, but never near the family quarters or in the public rooms that might be occupied.

They were a discreet group, the staff of Blackhall Castle. Most of them had come from Inverness with a few from nearby villages. The pay was good, the working conditions better than the factory jobs that sometimes lured a girl back to Inverness. Not only did they have hot water in their rooms, but they were fed delicious meals. Nor did Mrs. McDermott expect anyone to work twenty hours a day. Granted, the housekeeper was strict, and she did have certain standards that she expected the staff to follow, but work was normally complete before dinner, and afterward the time was theirs.

But there was little at Blackhall in the way of entertainment.

Perhaps she should institute a staff party once a month or a visit to Inverness. The logistics of doing either seemed enormous, but she was determined to try. Even if they were without the entire staff for a half day, surely they could manage. If she had to, she'd take Thomas his tea tray herself. That is, if he was at Blackhall. He was spending more and more time in London lately.

She opened one of the rear doors of the castle. Another advantage to having been a maid. She knew where all the exits and entrances to the castle were, along with hiding places, secret passages, and servants' cubbies.

Robbie began to fuss. Maybe he didn't like the little wool hat that Nan had knitted for him. Or the matching mittens of blue that prevented him from gnawing on his knuckles, a favorite pastime of his.

She hummed a little tune, which seemed to soothe Robbie. He enjoyed her singing to him, probably because he didn't know what the difference was between being able to sing on key or not. Nor could she play the pianoforte. Her father had never considered learning a musical instrument to be as important as memorizing the genus and family of hundreds of herbs and plants.

Louise didn't play, either. "I did once, my dear," she said one evening at dinner. "I simply gave it up because I didn't enjoy it. I've decided to only occupy myself with things I truly enjoy."

"You hate needlework," Lorna countered.

"Ah, yes, I do, but that isn't an occupation. That is penance. I force myself to consider those sins I've committed that day and vow to try to be better. You'll notice that I do needlework every day."

Lorna had nodded.

"That's because I've sinned every day. Either I'm thinking uncharitable thoughts or I'm too impatient or I've said something I shouldn't have."

"I think you're perfect," Lorna said.

The Dowager Duchess's eyes had filled with tears and she leaned over to hug Lorna. Not the first time the sweet woman had done so.

Her mother-in-law was one of the best things about living at the castle. Being able to look at Alex anytime she wanted—as long as he was at Blackhall—was another. Bedding him was certainly at the top of her list.

Occasionally, he surprised her with an indication that he was thinking about her. The day he returned, for example. Or his anger on her behalf about Matthews. Last night he seemed to truly care that someone had wished her harm.

He wasn't an easy man to get to know.

She took the path that wound around the west wing and down to the outcropping over the loch. Veering to her left, she kept on the barely trod path, knowing the way well from her half days off. With no relatives to visit, she'd often come exploring this way.

Today no one had come rushing out of Blackhall to advise her, admonish her, or otherwise lecture her. For a little while she would be alone. Those moments had been rare ever since giving birth.

The roads around the castle were paved with macadam, something she'd seen on only the wealthiest estates. The Russell wealth was evident in other ways: the staff of gardeners required to maintain the lawns, the greenhouse, and the various gardens. Two carpenters and three masons were employed on a continual basis. Their renovations seemed to be ongoing, from the original tower to the docks on Loch Gerry. Add in the servants in the kitchen and those required to clean the castle, and the staff numbered over seventy, all of whom had to be fed, housed, garbed, and paid.

She knew exactly how much it cost because of her weekly meetings with the steward. Until becoming a duchess she had no idea how much work one did.

The landscape was gray with occasional touches of green. Here and there, as if to tease her, she saw a touch of yellow or a surprising slash of red. Spring had come to the Highlands, but so reluctantly that it was tiptoeing across the landscape and cloaking its arrival beneath a curtain of fog.

The movement of her walking lulled Robbie to sleep. She glanced down at him and smiled, enchanted with the perfection of his baby face.

If something couldn't be done about Mary, perhaps she should be like Alex and run away from Blackhall.

Would he even notice that she'd deserted *him*?

Chapter 29

*Y*ou think I would do such a thing?" Thomas asked.

His uncle was sprawled in a chair in the library, a glass of whiskey in one hand, a book in the other. The book surprised Alex, the whiskey didn't.

"Someone destroyed her apothecary," Alex said. "Your fingerprints were on the bottles."

"What you're not saying, nephew, is even more insulting. Someone also tried to poison Lorna. Do you think I would do something like that?"

His uncle was angry, but he hid most emotions behind a placid facade. Most people wouldn't have noticed the stiffness of his smile or the edge to his voice.

A curious thought struck Alex. Was he like Thomas in that way? Were they both so damned civilized that they buried their emotions down deep where they wouldn't cause any problems?

His were clawing their way to the surface of late.

"It doesn't mean that the person who destroyed her apothecary also stole the herbs," he said. "Two people could have been involved."

"I wasn't," Thomas said, sitting up and reaching for the tumbler of whiskey he'd put down. "On either count." He took a sip, placed the glass back on the table, and glanced up at Alex. "Of course I can't prove that to you."

"You were there, though," he said.

Thomas nodded. "I admit that freely. I went to see her, to try to figure out why you were determined to ruin your life by having her live at Blackhall. I was fascinated with all her herbs, but she slapped my hand when I would have opened a few bottles."

"Perhaps it's time you moved to the house in Inverness," he said.

Thomas smiled. "Before you allow your anger to blind you, I'll admit I figured out her attraction soon enough. She has something, your Lorna. She's her own person. She's not one of those women who change her opinion as often as her dress. She looks you in the eye. You grow to respect her as I have." Thomas took another sip of his whiskey. "And I like her. I can't say that about many women I know. I wouldn't do anything to harm her."

Alex turned to leave, only to be stopped by Thomas's comment: "Do you have any idea how damned lucky you are?"

He glanced back at his uncle.

"Most people don't in your situation. They're concerned with the annoyances of life, not the blessings. Take my advice, Alex, don't ignore your wife. Or your son. A great many men would envy you."

"You included?"

His uncle inclined his head, the smile slipping from his face. "Maybe once," he said. "Not at the moment. Maybe you've spurred me to pursue my own Lorna."

"Are you contemplating matrimony, Uncle?"

"Why not? I can't be a greater fool than you've been. You've shown me what not to do."

Alex studied his uncle for a moment. "Do you resent Robbie?"

"Why on earth should I?" Thomas smiled again. "Ah, I understand. Am I supposed to be jealous that the infant has usurped me? I never wanted to be your heir, Alex. I'm too bloody indolent to be duke, while you're a better one than I could ever be. Take a bit of advice from a bachelor, however. Devote a little of that energy toward your wife. Lorna deserves at least that."

In lieu of a response, Alex turned and left the room.

THE SCENE WITH his valet was as fraught with drama as Alex had dreaded. Matthews admitted, finally, to his vandalism. However, he staunchly refused to take any responsibility for Nan's poisoning.

"I would never do such a thing, Your Grace. I understand if you'd like me to apologize to your wife. The duchess."

"I don't give a flying farthing for your apology, Matthews. I just want you gone from Blackhall."

Matthews's face drained of color. His hands shook as he held the pair of Alex's silver brushes.

"Sir? I'm dismissed? Haven't I given you years of service, Your Grace? Should I be dismissed for a solitary error of judgment?"

"That error of judgment was perpetrated against my wife, Matthews."

"I didn't harm Her Grace, sir. I would never have done that."

"No, you only destroyed what she considered valuable. That's enough of a crime to warrant your leaving my employ. Make sure you're gone by sunset."

He turned and left the dressing room, entering the sitting room to find it empty. Nor was Lorna in the bedroom. Robbie was gone as well. They weren't in Nan's room, but he was gratified to see that Nan and Hortense were talking about something. Their conversation evidently involved clothing because a selection of garments were draped over the end of the bed.

He left as soon as he could, the only clue to Lorna's whereabouts a comment from Nan.

"She said she needed a little fresh air, Your Grace."

His mother often said the same thing, so he did what he considered logical, followed the path around the conservatory, past the formal garden, the west wing, the French garden, and then back to the main building. Lorna wasn't outside.

Nor was she in the east wing, the conservatory, any of the parlors on the first floor, the library, the kitchen, or the dining room. Out of an abundance of caution he checked the dungeon, but she wasn't there, either.

By this time he'd asked for the assistance of two footmen and the majordomo. His efforts ended at the stables, but she wasn't there, either. Recruiting two stable boys, he entered the woods and began to follow a path he hadn't been on since he was a boy.

He pushed down his fear with some effort. Panic never helped any situation, especially this one. But the thoughts kept assaulting him: what if she'd been harmed? What if someone had taken them from Blackhall? What if they were in danger?

A half hour later he found her, sitting on a log in Devil's Marsh, contentedly nursing Robbie. She couldn't have found a more dangerous place.

The name for a marsh was *fideach* in Gaelic. But the locals had labeled this particular bit of land the Devil's

Marsh for all the deaths that had occurred here in the last hundred years.

Grasses covered most of the area, with little lakes in between. Some areas appeared solid enough to take a man's weight, but others were deceptive. One wrong move and a body could disappear from sight, never to surface again.

Pockets of mist rose in the air, nearly obscuring the remains of tree trunks and branches sticking out of the water. One false step and she would have been sucked to the bottom.

Yet there Lorna was, calmly nursing their son in the one place he'd never thought to find her.

"It's a damn treacherous place to be," he said, his voice echoing oddly.

He picked his way to her, wanting to shake her for the fear she caused him. That, too, was the price of love.

Evidently oblivious to his mood, she turned and glanced at him.

"I know my way around a marsh, Alex," she said. "And this one as well. I used to come here when I had a free moment. It's relaxing."

"Relaxing? Are you daft? People have died here, Lorna. The ground appears solid until you put a foot on it."

"I'm safe as long as I don't go any farther, Alex."

"Yet this is the place you choose to bring Robbie?"

"Is that why you're so upset? Because Robbie is with me?"

"No, damn it."

She calmly closed up her dress and placed Robbie on her shoulder. His son looked up at him and smiled. Could an infant be amused?

Perhaps Robbie was ridiculing him for his worry

now when he'd remained away for so long. A thought so chastising that it had the effect of banishing his anger. He hadn't acted all that protective, had he?

"Why have you come here?" he asked, sitting on the log beside her.

Robbie slapped at him with his fist, and he grabbed it, kissed the boy's knuckles, then immediately felt foolish for doing so.

Lorna's eyes seemed to warm as she glanced at him.

"I used to come here on my half day off," she said. "I'd wager that you explored it as a boy."

"I was shown how to navigate it by our gillie," he admitted.

"I can't imagine that your parents were happy with you for exploring Devil's Marsh."

"They weren't. My father said something in Latin, as I recall. Something to the effect that some fools outgrow their stupidity and he fervently hoped I was one of those. My father's word was law and I respected him greatly. The worst thing was disappointing him. I didn't learn, until much later, that he'd done the same thing as a boy."

"I hated disappointing my father, too," she said. "He would get that look on his face, one that meant I'd done something wrong. I couldn't bear that expression."

"What had you done?"

She shrugged. "It almost always had something to do with a sketch. Or I wasn't patient enough while he was studying something. Or I'd wandered off on my own. I did that a lot." She gave him a smile. "You've explored every inch of Blackhall land, haven't you? I'd be willing to wager that you've carved your initials into more than one tree in the forest."

He shook his head. "That would be wanton damage,"

he said. "But as far as exploring, yes. What kind of Russell would I be otherwise?" He glanced around him. "My ancestors died for this land. They held onto it at great cost to themselves. It's in trust now for Robbie."

"Did you have a dog as a boy?" she asked.

He glanced over at her, smiling.

"I've always had a dog or two," he said. "Why do you ask?"

"For some reason I see you with a dog," she said. "One of the larger ones with long hair and intense intelligent eyes."

"I had a dog like that once. Her name was Persephone. My sister named her. She'd been studying Greek gods and goddesses at the time, I think."

"I never had a dog," she said. "My father promised me that if we ever settled down into one place we would get one."

"Did you?"

She shook her head. "No, by then he was too sick."

"I should get Robbie a dog."

"Wait a little while," she said, smiling. "At least until he can walk."

She turned and looked out over the landscape. "I'm sorry if I worried you, but I had no other place to go where I could be guaranteed of privacy. No one comes here."

"Then I apologize for interrupting you. I do, however, have the whole of Blackhall searching for you, so it's best if we return."

"You do?"

"Everyone from the majordomo to the stable boys. Nan is the only one exempt from the search, although I daresay my mother is doing her best to find you as well."

"Oh dear. Why?"

"Why?" he asked. "Why?" He shook his head then answered her. "Because Nan was poisoned and it's only a miracle that you weren't. Because I've got a damn basket of adders back at Blackhall and I've done a lousy job of being a husband. Because. Just because."

"All right," she said, looking bemused.

"All right?"

She nodded.

"Damn, that was easy."

"You made a lot of sense."

"I dismissed Matthews," he said, reaching out and patting Robbie on the back. His son swiped at him with his fist again, summoning his smile. "His were one of the sets of prints we found. When I pressed him, he admitted destroying your apothecary. I don't know if he was the one who put the monkwood in the tea."

"I always thought it was Mary," she said.

"I found her prints as well." He debated telling her about Thomas and then did.

"Thomas didn't do anything," she said. "I can almost guarantee that."

"That's right, you find him charming." He tried to conceal his envy but it must have escaped.

Her laughter startled him. So, too, Robbie's sudden grin.

"What's so amusing?"

"You," she said. "If I didn't know better I'd think you were jealous. As if you have any reason to be."

She shook her head, still smiling.

What did he say to that? What did she think of him? Did he really want to know?

"What do you think of me?" he asked, daring himself.

She tilted her head and regarded him in the same way he often studied a rendering of a set of fingerprints, looking for a pattern in the swirls, something to indicate in which category he should file the specimen.

"I used to worship you from afar," she finally said. "I'd sit in the conservatory and watch for you every night."

"You couldn't have," he said.

"Why? Because you didn't know I was alive? I studied you the way my father used to examine a flower. What is the shape of its stalk, its stamen, its petals? How does it react to nature? What is its environment?"

"I never knew," he said.

"You weren't supposed to know," she said. "If you had, I would no doubt have been lectured by Mrs. McDermott, or even let go."

"Is that why you came to the ball that night, because I was someone that interested you?"

Her smile deepened. "I wasn't just interested in you, Alex. I was fascinated with you. I wanted to stare at your face for hours at a time. I wished that I'd taken up portraits because I ached to paint you. It was more than interest. Perhaps it was obsession. The day you took my fingerprints was the happiest day of my life."

She smiled at him, such a lovely expression that it froze the moment. He would always remember her smile, the day, the place, and the hard thumping beat of his heart.

Mist rose up behind her, framing her face. She was even more beautiful now than she'd been a year ago. More enchanting because he'd been shown her mind, her heart, all those qualities that made her Lorna and therefore special.

"And then you turned into a prig," she said, startling him.

"You called me a prancing mouse that night."

"I was dreadfully hurt by your words. You're lucky I didn't think of something else revolting to say. A prancing mouse isn't that bad, actually."

"It was a unique insult."

"What are you going to do about Mary?"

"Send her away," he said. "She's been offered the use of the London house as well as the other properties and always turned them down. I'm afraid the time has come for me to choose where she's going to live. Anywhere but Blackhall."

Her silence concerned him.

He stood and held out his hand. Instead of giving it she handed Robbie to him. He wasn't as adept holding his son as she was, but they managed well enough.

"What are you thinking?" he asked as they began to walk.

He genuinely wanted to know, a fact that would have startled him before he'd come to appreciate Lorna's mind, her way of thinking, and her streak of pragmatism.

"I think it's unfair that someone should be rewarded for being evil," she said.

He stopped in the middle of the path and regarded her.

"If she goes off to live in a village somewhere, no one will condemn her," she began. "They'll probably think they have someone of stature living there. After all, her father was an earl and her sister married a duke. I doubt the local minister will charge her with being a slattern and befouling the air of the village simply by living there."

It was his turn to remain silent.

"Yet she tried to kill someone. At the very least, she tried to hurt someone. Even Matthews had to pay the price for destroying . . . what did you call it, my apothecary?"

"It seemed an apt term."

"I like it," she said. "Matthews lost his position. What price does she have to pay for her monstrous actions?"

"I never gave her cause to feel anything but sisterly affection for me."

"You don't have to give a woman cause," she said, smiling up at him. "All you have to do is glance at them."

Her expression had his heart thumping in his chest.

Something had happened to him. Did she have an herbal remedy for him? Was there something he could ingest or rub on his chest? Some medicament that would cure what he had?

Did he want to be cured?

He wasn't going to name it. He didn't want to slap a label over it. He knew, all too well, what he was feeling, and he couldn't banish it or manage it.

He'd never been at the mercy of his emotions before, but now he was.

Need could be regulated. Cravings could be mastered. Except this one.

He craved seeing Lorna like he sometimes wanted a few of cook's raisin scones or the peat smokiness of a good whiskey. No, more than that. She was a lungful of fresh air, a glass of sparkling water. She was sunshine and growing flowers, laughter and hope. She was all those things necessary to his life and important in it.

When had that happened?

The force of what he felt was petrifying.

He might as well surrender now. Fighting it any longer was futile.

He wanted her, the whole of her, her laughter and her thoughts. He wanted her to share herself with him and wanted to do the same with her, the first time he'd ever felt that way about a woman. But, then, Lorna was unlike any woman he'd ever known.

Her hair was touched with sunlight until it glinted like gold. She didn't mind getting dirty and thought that mud was just another of nature's miracles. She carried Robbie around like one of those marsupials he'd seen on his visit to Australia, perfectly natural in motherhood. She'd transformed his mother into someone who laughed more often than she looked sad, who expressed joy in a quick smile and in whose eyes he saw a radiant happiness he'd never expected to see again.

And him? What had she done to him?

She reminded him that he was a man first, then a man of science, duke, property holder, and all the other attendant roles of his position. She taught him that being a father was not passing on lessons as much as accepting and giving love.

He was always going to worry about her and be afraid for her. She was going to make him question his own thoughts. He knew, without a doubt, that there would be times when she'd annoy him. They would probably get into rousing arguments because she'd never back down. She had the unique capacity to hurt him.

Yet with her, he'd experience everything life had to offer.

He'd never be able to hide again.

How could he rearrange his world to best please her?

He wanted his wife, and not simply in his bed. He wanted to hear her laugh, see her smile, and notice that her eyes were sparkling with humor.

Had he ever been affected by someone the way he was Lorna? Had his emotions ever been wrapped up in another person's happiness? He didn't think so. Had he ever been a fool the way he was around her? That was an easy question to answer. No.

Lorna had opened up his heart and he'd never known it was closed.

Chapter 30

*B*ack in their room, Lorna watched as Alex placed Robbie in his cradle. The baby gurgled up at him, fists and feet punching the air.

The two of them, father and son, regarded each other for a moment before Alex glanced at her.

"I can't get over how much he's grown."

"Your mother said he'll be walking early if he's anything like you."

He only shook his head, turned back to the cradle, and tucked the blanket over Robbie's feet. The baby promptly kicked it off.

"He'll probably be stubborn, too," she said, smiling.

Alex startled her by reaching out, hooking his hand behind her neck and gently stroking the skin there with his fingers.

"Do you still feel the same?" he asked. "Are you still fascinated?"

"I was madly in love with you," she said. "I think now that it was just lust."

"There's nothing wrong with lust," he said.

"Not if it's coupled with something else. Otherwise, it's just like a plate of chocolate biscuits. You can't live on chocolate biscuits. You'll get sick from them and of them. You have to have meat and potatoes and greens."

She studied him.

"I admired you like you were a prince. I thought you the most handsome man I knew. Then I thought you the ugliest."

He would have walked away had she not extended her hand to him.

"Now I know the truth," she said.

"And what is that?"

"Oh, don't sound so ducal, Alex."

"I cannot help the way I sound."

"Of course you can. You get all stuffy and pompous if someone barely bumps against your consequence. You're the Duke of Kinross and they, by God, better know it."

"That's the truth?"

"No. The truth is that you're flawed and human. You make mistakes and you're not perfect. But that's all right."

What would he say to know that she loved him even more with his flaws?

"You aren't perfect either, Lorna Gordon Russell. Nearly so, but not completely."

She smiled at him. "No, I'm not. I'm certain I could prepare a list of faults if you'd like."

"No need," he said, smiling back at her.

When his lips touched hers, she closed her eyes, feeling the liquid sensation she always experienced when he kissed her. Her fingertips tingled and her knees weakened.

He tilted his head to deepen the kiss and she sighed into his mouth. Words might separate them occasionally, but this—this magic that happened when they kissed—was blessedly always the same.

When he pulled back, she blinked up at him.

"I suppose there's a lot to be said for meat, potatoes, and greens," he said. "But chocolate biscuits are still good as well."

He kissed her again and the world fell away. It was just the two of them on an island they'd created, a small slice of the world made intimate and private.

When he drew back they were both breathing fast. She would have led him to their bed if he hadn't spoken.

"I have to talk to Mary. Will you promise to stay inside the castle until she's left?"

With his words, he brought her back to the world as it was, not as she wished it could be.

She nodded.

"It might take a day or two to arrange everything, but I'd feel better if I had your promise."

"Yes," she said. "I promise."

He nodded, grazing his knuckles over her heated cheek.

"Thank you," he said softly, and bent to kiss her again.

When he left her, she had the thought that she should go with him, an extra layer of protection against Mary. The sooner the woman was gone from Blackhall, the better.

ALEX WAITED FOR Mary to arrive, having summoned her to the library. This room was at the heart of the main building, part of the original castle that had been renovated all those years ago.

Two curving iron staircases led from either side of the room to the second floor. In the middle, framed by a series of windows overlooking the grounds of Blackhall, was a large octagon-shaped well.

He'd entertained the Scottish Society for Scientific Achievement here a year ago, filling the space with twenty-four chairs and a podium that had been erected where his desk now stood. The speakers had taken turns describing the inventions and discoveries that marked the previous year. At the end of the meeting, the winner of the annual award had been presented and then the members attended the fancy dress ball.

He hadn't won when he'd anticipated being feted for his work. Yet the night ended in a way he hadn't expected, beginning a chain of events leading to this moment.

Sitting at his desk, he watched the door, wondering if Mary would confess to what she'd done. He doubted it. Mary blamed others for her mistakes. She refused to admit she was ever wrong. Yet for all her annoying faults, she was devoted to the proper treatment of animals. She was also generous to those she cared about, limited though the number might be.

She was, like most people, a mixture of good and bad traits. Unfortunately, her bad traits were tipping the scales.

"You wished to see me, Alex?"

He glanced up to find Mary standing in the doorway.

"Come in," he said. "Close the door."

She smiled, the expression annoying him down to his toes. She looked like a cat who'd just killed a bird and left it behind to impress the other cats as to her hunting skills.

He motioned for her to sit in front of his desk, but didn't rise, as would have been proper or polite. She frowned in response, but moved her skirts to sit, her eyes on his face.

"Matthews said you've fired him, Alex," she said

before he could speak. "I do hope that's not true. He's a good valet. I hope you reconsider. You shall, won't you? As a favor for me?"

"Matthews is no longer welcome at Blackhall," he said, breaking in before she could embark on a soliloquy of the valet's virtues. "Nor are you," he added when she fell silent.

Her eyes widened but she didn't speak. A blessing, and one he hadn't expected.

"I've decided to set aside an amount for your use each year, to be paid by my solicitors. In addition, I will purchase a residence for you in the village of your choice, as long as it's a substantial distance from Blackhall."

He wasn't going to allow her to stay at any of the Russell properties in Inverness, Edinburgh, or London. Nor was he going to support her lifestyle there. Yet he wasn't going to do to her what society had done to Lorna, isolating and ostracizing her.

"You can take your maid with you if she's willing to go. I'll pay her salary as well."

"You're sending me away?"

"Yes."

He expected the next question, but he hadn't anticipated the vitriol with which it would be asked.

"That whore you married did this, didn't she? She convinced you to send me away. Is she that jealous? Does she know the special bond we share?"

"We share the bond of my marriage to Ruth, Mary, that's all."

"No," she said. "You love me. I know you do. All those meals we've shared. All those times we've talked. You can't marry me. I understand that. But you could come to my room."

She sat back, smiling at him in what was probably her version of a come hither expression but was more like a simper. She reminded him, curiously, of Ruth in the last year of their marriage, before she'd become pregnant with a baby of dubious heritage.

"You could divorce her now. The child wouldn't be a bastard. He'd still be your heir."

He stood, rounded the desk and kept walking. If he stopped, he might be tempted to haul her up from the chair and throw her out of the library.

At the door, he turned to her. "You've misinterpreted kindness for affection, Mary. At the moment, I have no feelings for you except disgust."

"You can't do this to me," she said, tears making her voice quaver. "This is my home."

"On the contrary," he said. "This is *my* home. You've been a guest here, but the day you tried to harm my wife, Mary, you outstayed your welcome."

She stood and faced him, her hands gripping the fabric of her skirt.

He opened the door and stood there, hoping she left before saying anything else. His self-control was hanging by a thread.

"Why are you doing this to me, Alex?"

He stared at her, wondering how he'd tolerated Mary at Blackhall for the last three years. Her emotions were on a continuum ranging from arrogant confidence to self-pity.

"Do you deny you put monkwood in Lorna's tea? That you tried to poison her?"

"I don't know what you're talking about."

"I'm not going to debate the issue with you, Mary. I just want you gone."

Her face changed. The smile vanished and an expression entered her eyes that almost made him take a step back. In that moment he realized that Mary wasn't simply deluded, she might possibly be evil.

"I only did what she did, Alex. That whore has poisoned your mind."

He stood silent as she sailed out of the room, a thin smile on her face.

Chapter 31

*L*orna put Robbie down for his afternoon nap and crept out of the bedroom, closing the door softly behind her.

Grabbing the book she'd taken from the library earlier, she tucked herself into one of the wing chairs in front of the fireplace and savored the quiet. It wouldn't last long. Robbie seemed to know when she was gone. But for the time she had, she was going to enjoy every second.

Instead of reading, however, her mind replayed the scenes in the past few days. Not only the frenetic activity to save Nan, but also the times with Alex. She hadn't expected him to be so protective, not just of Robbie, but of her.

How was his meeting going with Mary? Would the woman finally leave Blackhall?

How could someone try to deliberately harm another person? She remembered asking her father that question after one difficult afternoon. He'd been sitting with an old woman outside her cottage, taking down notes as she expounded on various formulas she'd devised through the years. Lorna noticed that he was watching the woman with a curious look, one she'd rarely seen. Only then did she pay attention to what the woman was saying. She used her knowledge for ill as well as good. If someone slighted her, she gave them a stomachache that lasted for days. If they cheated her at market, she sold them a salve that made their skin break into a pustulelike rash.

Later, when they made their way back to their lodgings, she asked her father why he hadn't spoken honestly to the woman, telling her that what she was doing was wrong.

He'd answered her in a subdued voice. "She would never have seen the truth, Lorna. Some people don't. They think they're not harming others as much as helping themselves. They never see their actions as aggression as much as protection, but the result is the same."

Had Mary seen her actions as protection? Had she thought that by eliminating her she'd win Alex?

Mary wouldn't have been pleased to know that she understood. For two years she'd yearned after Alex, knowing that nothing would ever happen between them. She could almost feel sorry for the woman except that Mary had almost killed Nan and wanted to harm her.

But as far as her fascination with Alex, yes she could well understand that.

Whenever he kissed her, she lost all her thoughts, all her abilities to tell the day, the time, the place. She was simply Lorna and he was Alex and nothing else mattered.

Really, he had to stop doing that.

Please, no. Never stop.

She was probably seeing something that wasn't there again, just as she had earlier. But wouldn't it be wonderful if she weren't? If what she wanted so desperately was coming true after all?

Alex would love her. She'd be free to tell him exactly how she felt about him now. Surely he could see how much she loved him?

"I beg your pardon, Your Grace," Peter said from the doorway. "There's a letter for you."

One of these days she would get used to being called "Your Grace," especially by people she used to work with, but she wasn't comfortable with it now. Yet she knew if she asked Peter not to call her that, he would balk, turn red, and stammer.

The problem was hers, not his.

She stood and walked toward him, taking the envelope from the silver tray he extended.

"And I'd like to thank you, too, Your Grace."

"What for?"

Peter smiled brightly. "I'm to be apprenticed to Mr. Stanton. He says that he has lots of work for me and I'm to learn the trade."

She knew Stanton. The carpenter was employed at Blackhall, lately working on the restoration of the Great Hall.

"It's because of the duke's recommendation, Your Grace, but he'd never have known about my work unless you pointed it out to him."

"No, it's because your work is beautiful. But is this something you want, Peter?"

He nodded emphatically, his blond hair flopping on his brow. "Yes, ma'am. The duke says I have a lot of talent that shouldn't go to waste. I'm to start next Monday."

"Then I'm glad for you," she said.

"It's more money than a footman pays, Your Grace. I'd have enough to put by for the future."

"A wise decision. Perhaps you'll be able to take a wife shortly," she added with a smile.

She hadn't missed the relationship that had grown between Nan and Peter, although neither of them spoke of it.

"Do go and tell Nan," she said.

His smile was sudden and shy, making her want to hug him.

"Is she feeling better, Your Grace?"

"She is. She's able to sit up and eat something and is already planning her escape. I know she'd be pleased to see you."

He nodded again, causing that one lock of hair to acquire a life of its own. She watched as he left the sitting room and walked a short distance across the hall, where he placed the salver on a table. He stood in front of the room Nan was currently occupying and slicked his hair back with one hand before examining his jacket, trousers, and shoes.

Smiling, Lorna closed the door and opened the letter.

Once she read the contents, she moved to one of the wing chairs in front of the hearth, sat down and stared for a moment at the cold fireplace. Evidently, Peter had not been the only one to benefit from Alex's interest.

Your Grace, the letter began, *we would be excited to publish your late father's definitive work on Scottish herbs and flowering medicinal plants.* There was more, about dates and times that might be convenient to discuss further plans, compliments about her drawings, and praise for her father's knowledge.

Her heart felt as if it had expanded to fill all the empty spaces since her father's death.

She hadn't missed his book. When had Alex taken it to a publisher? When he'd been in Edinburgh? He hadn't said anything, but then he wouldn't, would he? Alex did things without fanfare or the need for recognition. He simply moved mountains or made cottages available or banished troublesome relatives.

She pressed the letter against her bodice with both hands and bowed her head.

Please, don't let it be just something I want to see. Please let him love me, too.

The Reverend George McGill would say that she had no right to pray, that God would be sickened by her implorations, sinner that she was. But while the Reverend George McGill might be sanctioned by the Church of Scotland, the man did not have a charitable thought in his mind. Even officiating at her wedding hadn't softened his heart.

She glanced over at the door as it opened, glancing away when Alex entered the room. She was on the verge of tears and that was hardly the reaction he deserved.

"Lorna? Is everything all right?"

She nodded wordlessly, trying to compose herself. When he crossed the room to her side, she handed the letter to him.

"Thank you," she said. "Thank you for this."

He lifted his eyes from the letter and smiled, revealing both dimples.

"It's a beautiful book, Lorna, and deserves to be published."

"It wouldn't be but for your involvement."

"I don't believe that," he said, taking the adjacent chair. "I think it would have eventually found a home."

"Not as quickly without the support of the Duke of Kinross," she said. "Thank you, Alex, it was a wonderful gesture."

He placed the letter on the table, reached out, and took her hand.

"I find that I want to do a great many things for you, Lorna. I think we should have an apothecary here at Blackhall. You could keep your herbs there and make up your potions."

"Neither potions nor cures," she said with a smile. "Just aids in healing. That's all."

"Then aids in healing," he said, studying her hand.

"You would do that?"

He nodded. "And anything else you'd want." He examined her fingers with great intensity. "I'm not used to being uncertain," he said, surprising her. "And I am around you. It's disconcerting."

"Why do I make you feel uncertain?"

"Damned if I know," he said, then apologized for his language. "See? I don't normally swear."

He smiled, a curious self-deprecating expression. "I had you judged as one thing, but you weren't that at all. Instead, you're a devoted mother, a loyal friend, a healer, and an artist. You tell me about things I've never known in my own home. I've even started looking at the world differently. I see something growing beside the road and wonder if it has healing properties. I hear someone complain about their arthritis and think that your balm would help them."

"Is that why you stayed away so long?" she asked softly. "Because you don't like feeling uncertain?"

He looked at her, his gaze intent.

"No," he said. "I stayed away because you scared

me, Lorna. I didn't want to feel so much for anyone, let alone someone who confused and constantly surprised me."

She couldn't help but smile at him. Happiness bubbled up inside her, crowding out every other emotion.

Pulling her hand free, she stood and moved in front of him. Thank heavens she was only wearing her at-home petticoats. She removed them easily and kicked them out of the way.

"What are you doing?" Alex asked, but she noted that there was a twinkle in his beautiful eyes.

"Just testing a theory," she said, crawling into his chair.

She placed a knee on either side of his legs, pulled her skirts up so the material wasn't trapped beneath her, and sat.

"What theory would that be?" His mouth quirked in a half smile.

Raising up on her knees again, she brushed the backs of her hands against his cheeks, feeling the stubble against her knuckles.

"If you were as sensitive to my touch as I am to yours."

"You could ask me," he said.

"That's true. But it's so much better to test a theory, don't you think? You're a proponent of the scientific method, I believe."

She placed her lips gently against his, but pulled back when he would have deepened the kiss.

Placing her cheek against his, she kissed his earlobe, then explored the curve of his ear with her tongue.

"Lorna."

"Umm," she said, dipping to place a kiss against the side of his neck.

The pulse there was beating furiously.

She smiled.

"Do you have your answer yet?"

"No," she said, bending forward to begin to unfasten his shirt. "You're always so perfectly attired. Are you going to hire someone to replace Matthews?"

"Must we talk of valets?" he asked.

"No," she said, brushing a kiss on each eyebrow. "We mustn't. Close your eyes."

"Why?"

"I want to kiss your eyelids."

"Why?" he asked.

"I want to kiss every part of you."

"Lorna."

"Umm. Close your eyes."

He finally did, and she placed a gentle kiss on each eyelid, then his nose. She hovered over his mouth for a moment before resting her lips against his.

His hand at the back of her head meant she couldn't escape this time. Not that she truly wanted to, not when his talented tongue began to dance with hers.

What was there about a kiss that seemed tied to the core of her? When he kissed her, she felt it deep inside, as if her body awakened with a jolt.

Her fingers slid through his hair to his neck.

She'd never felt so alive as when she was kissing Alex. Or looking at him. Or being around him.

She had never thought that anyone could ever matter as much as her child, but he did.

Her body was heating from the inside out. She moved closer, wanting to touch him everywhere.

His fingers were unbuttoning the buttons of her dress.

She pulled back to help him.

"Is this a new dress?" he asked, intent on his task.

"Yes." She didn't want to discuss her clothes at the moment, especially when she was desperate to remove them.

"Very well," he said, his voice harsh. "I won't rip it off you."

She wanted to be naked in his arms. Take her here or on the floor, on the settee or wherever he wanted.

Because she was still nursing Robbie, her corset had been adapted, cut low. The lace-trimmed shift was new, something Hortense had cleverly devised to allow her freedom. Slipping the two buttons loose from their loop revealed both breasts.

Her areolas were large and dark, the nipples erect and hard. Alex used both hands to stroke her soft skin, one breast at a time. She raised up and he touched one nipple with the tip of his tongue. She closed her eyes at the sensation, pressing both hands against the back of his head.

A shudder escaped her when he slid one hand beneath her skirts, slipping into the split of her pantaloons and cupping her.

Had they locked the door? Shouldn't she care more about their privacy? If someone walked in he'd be shocked, but that would be his fault.

Desire swirled through her, heating every inch of her skin. Alex moved his fingers, her slickness easing his path. She could feel the pulsing inside her as her body readied for him, needed him.

"Do you want me?" he asked against her mouth.

How could he ask that?

"Yes," she said, the word pushed out from between lips that felt swollen.

His finger stroked her with a slow intimacy. Anticipation made her tremble. Her breath halted then began again as if she had forgotten how to breathe. Instead, every sense was concentrated on what his hands were doing.

"Kiss me, Lorna." She could feel his smile and gently bit his bottom lip.

Need shuddered through her along with anticipation. What would he say next? What would he do? Where would he touch her? Would he allow her to reach down and unfasten his trousers?

She matched his smile as she did exactly that, freeing him to fill her hand. She'd never contemplated doing what she was doing, never thought to mount him while sitting on a chair.

"Lorna?" He pulled back. "It would be more comfortable in our bed."

"No," she said. "Here. Now. Besides, we might wake Robbie." She reached down and held him, stroking her fingers over his length.

"Do you want me?" she asked, daring herself.

He smiled, his lips curving, deepening his dimples, adding a sparkle to his beautiful blue-green eyes.

Instead of answering her, he pulled her down for another kiss, all the while sliding his hands below her skirt. She heard her pantaloons rip and didn't care. His palms cupped her buttocks, lifted her up.

She lowered herself over him as he guided himself into her.

His lips skimmed along her jaw as he murmured her name. She held herself still, savoring each sensation as he slid inside, hard and hot. Lightning tingled through her body. Liquid fire followed in its wake as he stroked her breasts with his fingers.

She lowered her head against his shoulder, her lips

against his neck, her teeth gently grazing his skin. Her hands lay weakly against the arms of the chair. He moved his hands to her waist, lifted her slightly, then lowered her onto him once again.

The slow invasion was gentle, tender, and devastating.

Reaching up, she wound her arms around his neck, placed her mouth on his and held on.

Her breathing was fast and shallow; her heart was thundering. Her thoughts were centered only on him.

Pleasure surged through her, stealing her breath, curling her toes and fingers. The sudden climax caught her by surprise, the contractions beginning in her core and spreading outward like waves on a beach.

She needed it to stop for a moment so she could get her breath, but she never wanted the sensations to end. Her body mastered her mind. She couldn't help the long moan that slipped from her lips or the shiver that shook her frame. Her knees clamped against his hips as she was lost in ecstasy.

Chapter 32

It's always the same," she said weakly. "I always lose my mind around you. Is that normal?"

He patted her back with one hand, the other still below her skirts.

"Nothing about our relationship has been normal from the beginning," he said.

"Is that a bad thing?" she asked, watching him.

His eyes were closed, but a smile was curving his mouth.

"It is the very best thing," he said.

Love surged through her.

She would always remember this afternoon. Nor would she ever be able to look at this chair without blushing. At the very least, she'd smile. She couldn't help but wonder if the other furniture at Blackhall Castle had a similar history.

Moving first one leg then the other, she stood, fiddled with her skirt before adjusting the shift and buttoning her bodice.

"I'm surprised we weren't interrupted," she said.

"Our son has a great deal of tact. A trait he's probably picked up from his grandmother."

She glanced over to find him smiling at her and

for a moment her heart stopped. He was handsome and irresistibly charming. Perhaps she should make a love potion of sorts for herself. Something that would render her a little less susceptible to his appeal. No, it was an eon too late for that, wasn't it?

"I'll go and check on him," she said.

"I'll get him."

He stood and was presentable in only seconds, while it still took her a few minutes to adjust her clothing.

She finally entered the bedroom to find the cradle empty and Alex leaving the dressing room by the door to the corridor.

"Alex?"

He wasn't holding Robbie.

"Alex? Where is Robbie?"

"With my mother, I think."

They exchanged a glance. Did he share her sudden embarrassment? Had Louise come to get the baby and peeked into the sitting room? Dear God, she'd never be able to face the woman again.

Louise was sitting in the family parlor, reading. Every time she saw her mother-in-law, Lorna thought she appeared much younger than her age.

Louise glanced up at their entrance and put aside her book.

"Is Robbie with you?" Alex asked before Lorna could speak.

"Why, no."

"Nan," Lorna said, turning and racing from the room. Nan might have come to get the baby and not wanted to disturb them.

When she entered the room, Peter was sitting with

Nan, on the edge of her bed, his bright blond hair once more falling down over his brow.

"Did you take Robbie?" she asked Nan, panic a growing bubble in her chest.

Her eyes widened. "No, I wouldn't, Lorna. Not without talking to you."

When Alex entered the room, Lorna turned to look at him.

"Nan didn't take him. Your mother didn't. Who did?"

"Mary." They said the name at the same time.

Alex left the room. She followed him, racing to catch up.

A FEW MINUTES later they were in Mary's suite, a lovely set of rooms decorated in peach and a soft blue. When she thought of Mary, it was in harsh reds, blacks, or greens so glaring they made you squint.

Mary wasn't in her room, but her maid Barbara was, bent over one of five trunks scattered through the room.

"Where is she?" Alex asked.

The woman straightened.

"I don't know, Your Grace," she said, her tone civil but her sideways glance at Lorna leaving no doubt that what she was thinking wasn't nearly as pleasant.

Barbara was a brownish gray. Her hair was gray; her skin had a gray tint. Even her eyes were a grayish hazel.

Lorna had avoided Barbara when she was on staff because of the woman's sly and vicious tongue. The maid was more than willing to share tales, especially if they ridiculed others.

She'd always thought the woman cunning, but evidently that cunning didn't translate to intelligence. Anyone with a scintilla of sense would know she was in danger at the moment.

Alex's eyes were as cold as a frozen pond. His lips were thinned, as if they'd never once smiled. He was a statue. The muscle in his cheek didn't flex as it often did when he was annoyed. He didn't blink. He merely stood there watching Barbara, his attention directed solely on her.

Lorna would have been terrified in Barbara's place.

Was the woman truly that foolish? Did she think Mary paid her salary? Did Barbara believe she was exempt from being fired on the spot?

"Where is she?" he asked.

"I don't know," Barbara said, then added, "Your Grace."

"Is she still at Blackhall?"

Dear God, what if she wasn't? What if she'd left the castle, taking Robbie with her? Lorna couldn't breathe for the thought.

"You told her to leave. Maybe she's saying her good-byes." This time Barbara didn't bother trying to pretend any respect.

Alex folded his arms, his gaze still on her.

"Get out," he said, his voice calm. The expression in his eyes would have given Lorna pause, but the foolish maid didn't see her peril.

"I have to pack her trunks."

"Get out," he repeated softly, in a tone that made Lorna's skin pebble.

Barbara finally curtsied in a way that managed to convey contempt more than respect and left the room.

"What did Mary say when you met with her?"

Lorna asked. "Did she agree to leave? Was she angry?"

"She didn't have a choice," Alex said, going to the fireplace and jerking on the bellpull.

"What are we going to do?"

"Find her," he said.

She walked to him, hoping that he'd do exactly as he did, extend his arms around her.

He tilted his head, lay his cheek against her hair. For long moments they just stood there, holding each other.

"I'm so scared," she said. "What if she hurts Robbie?"

"We'll find him," he said. "Maybe she doesn't have him."

"She has him." The sick feeling in her stomach told her that Robbie was in danger.

When a maid appeared in the open doorway, Alex spoke to her.

"Ask Mrs. McDermott to call on us here," he said.

She was gone in a flurry of skirts.

"Where is she?" Lorna asked.

"That's what we're going to find out," he said.

Could someone else have Robbie? Were they wrong in thinking Mary had taken him?

When Mrs. McDermott arrived, Alex addressed the housekeeper.

"I want every member of the staff to stop what they're doing and search for Mary," he said.

Lorna pulled away, beginning to pace the width of the room. "I need to go search as well, Alex. I can't just wait here."

"I'll have the carriage readied in case she's left Blackhall."

Mrs. McDermott nodded, and left to carry out Alex's orders.

Lorna glanced around the room. "Would she have left with all her trunks here?"

"I don't know," he said. "She might have asked Barbara to follow her."

If that were the case, it was obvious Barbara wasn't going to say.

"Where would she go? Where would she take Robbie?"

"Your Grace."

Lorna turned to see Mrs. McDermott standing there, a look of worry on the older woman's face.

"Matthews says she's left, sir. She's taken a carriage and left Blackhall."

"Was Robbie with her?" Alex asked.

"Yes, Your Grace."

Lorna had anticipated the question and answer, but hearing it aloud was different from imagining it. A fist clamped around her heart and lungs.

The housekeeper stepped aside to reveal the valet standing there.

She couldn't breathe. She was going to faint. Now was not the time to indulge in hysteria. She couldn't talk. All she could do was concentrate on the air around her as if she stood in a bubble. *Take one breath, make it last. Take another. Swallow. Breathe. Hold yourself together.*

Matthews had hated her from the beginning. He'd never thought her good enough to be Alex's wife. Not because of who she was but because of what she'd done. What work she'd performed, as if work alone labeled a person.

Stepping away from Alex, she made her way to stand in front of Matthews.

"Did you help her take Robbie?"

"Of course not," he said, looking at Alex rather than her.

She grabbed his lapels and, with a strength she didn't know she possessed, jerked him close to her. Speaking calmly and enunciating clearly, she asked, "Did you help her take Robbie?"

Maybe it was madness he saw in her eyes, something that made him swallow before answering her. This time his attention was all on her, not on Alex, who was now standing beside her.

"No, Your Grace, I didn't. Nor did I know she would do something like this."

She stared into his eyes as if she could read the truth of his comment there. A moment later she released him and moved closer to Alex.

"Tell us what you do know," Alex said.

His arms were now around her. He was speaking, but his words didn't make any sense. She patted his upper arms. She nodded, but beyond that she couldn't communicate.

Her heart was bleeding inside and it felt like she was going to die from this pain.

"She's gone to Inverness. She was meeting someone."

"Tell me where."

"Innes Street," the valet said. "East of the River Ness, near the Shore Street area. That's all I know. I've no knowledge of the exact address, Your Grace."

Matthews glanced at her. For the first time, there was no disdain in his expression.

"I would have stopped her if I'd known she was going to take Robbie, Your Grace."

"Then I'm off to Inverness," Alex said, moving to the door.

"Not without me," she said.

They exchanged a look. She didn't know what he saw on her face, but Alex finally nodded.

Chapter 33

$\mathcal{T}$o Lorna's surprise, it was raining when they left Blackhall and entered the carriage. She hadn't heard the storm. Nor was she aware of the passage of time. The afternoon had advanced into evening without her knowledge of it.

Alex sat beside her and held her hand. She felt as if she were spinning out of control. He was an anchor, the only steadfast thing in a frightening world.

No matter how fast the horses went, it wasn't fast enough. She wanted Alex to give instructions to the driver to drive faster but knew it was foolhardy on this stormy night.

Alex was stoic, a man turned to marble. Even the air stilled around him, as if impressed by his statuelike form. He didn't speak, but neither did she.

When she began to tremble, it wasn't from the chilled night.

He dropped her hand and reached around her with one arm, pulling her closer. She let him, burying her face against his jacket, feeling his heat and wondering if she would ever warm.

Dear God, what would she do if Mary had harmed her son? How could she live through that?

Her breasts hurt, as if to accentuate the time away

from her child. A way of nature reminding her that her infant needed to be fed.

Where was Robbie?

"She talked about baby farmers before," Alex suddenly said.

She pulled back to look at him. Each movement seemed coated in pain, as if nature were preparing her for the worst of agonies, the loss of her child.

"She hinted that you might do such a thing."

"I never would have," she said. She would have starved before she gave up Robbie.

"I know. I knew it back then."

She lay her head against the seat, staring up at the ceiling of the carriage.

Terror slid down her throat to coil in her stomach.

"Save him," she said. It was the only thing she could think of to say, the only request or command that made any sense. She didn't doubt that Alex could rescue their child.

He pulled her hand over, placed a kiss on her knuckles, then rested it on his chest.

"I'm sorry for all the pain I've caused you, Lorna. I'm sorry for all the terrible things I've said. I'm sorry for the cruelty of others, some of them either in my employ or related to me. I should have spared you all that."

"I will admit that while you're godlike in many ways, Alex, you aren't God."

"Godlike?"

For the first time since they'd realized Robbie was missing, she felt amusement.

"We'll discuss your godlike tendencies at another time," she said.

Abruptly, the carriage pulled over to the side of the road.

"Have we caught up with them?" she asked.

Before Alex could answer, the door opened and Charles stood there in the rain.

"Sir, I can see Jeremy ahead. I know a shortcut, a way to make it to Inverness before him, but the road is bad and the journey won't be pleasant."

"Do what you have to do, Charles," he said. "Just get us there."

"Aye, Your Grace," the driver said, shutting the door with a snap.

Their horses were transformed into cousins of Pegasus, their hooves barely touching the road as they flew. The wheels were a different matter, rattling with every rut and rock. She prayed they wouldn't lose a wheel. Nothing must stop them from reaching Mary.

The carriage springs were no match for the terrain, and if she hadn't been holding onto Alex and the strap above the window, she would have been tossed to the ceiling or the floor.

Fear kept her silent, but the thunder overhead would have made it impossible to talk even if she had something to say. The storm was following them from Blackhall, the lightning flashing every few minutes as they hurtled through the darkness.

Was Robbie frightened? Had Mary brought another servant with her to hold him? Was she being gentle with him? Had she thought to bring an extra blanket? The night chill, along with the storm, worried her. Mary wouldn't care about Robbie's health, not when she had terrible plans for him.

Would the authorities be called? Would Mary be arrested? Or, because Mary's father was an earl and her brother-in-law a duke, would she be spared any punishment for her acts?

She'd never hated another human being. Some people annoyed her. A few had hurt her or left her confused about what she'd done to incur their anger. But hate was a black blob with gray and silver thorns she'd tried to avoid. But now she allowed herself to hate Mary Taylor.

The storm mocked them, the thunder an angry beast jealous that something else claimed their attention.

How would she survive if something happened to Robbie?

She had to be hopeful. She had to have faith. Somehow, they would save Robbie. Together, the two of them would save their child.

Terror was an ugly, sickly green color. Her stomach was rolling and she tasted something sour on the back of her tongue. She thought she might be sick any moment now. Her forehead was clammy and her feet felt like blocks of ice. Her fingertips were tingling. Panic kept her breathing shallow.

The jostling, jarring ride went on endlessly as they shot ahead of the storm. The thunder followed them at a distance, the faint growling sound almost petulant. Without the lightning, the darkness was complete.

She didn't know how much time had passed before the carriage suddenly veered to the left so sharply she worried they might overturn.

Please God, let them reach Robbie. Please let him be okay.

Out the window, she saw the watery glare of a carriage lantern. They drew abreast of the other vehicle as Jeremy slowed. To her surprise, Charles pulled in front of the other carriage at an angle.

"Stay here," Alec said. Before she could question or protest, he was out of the carriage and running toward the other vehicle.

Lightning suddenly hit the ground nearby, startling the horses. The storm had found them again, plucking them out of the darkness and illuminating the scene.

Alex and Charles had rushed the carriage and opened the door. By the light of the lamp, she saw Mary huddled in the corner, holding Robbie. She was screaming at them, but Lorna couldn't make out what she was saying.

Instead, she heard Robbie's crying, even over the rain.

Her nails dug into the leather window frame. Alex might want her to remain here, but she couldn't. Seconds later she was out of the carriage, running toward Alex and her son.

The storm emptied the clouds above them, drenching her before she reached the other carriage.

Alex was now inside. Robbie was screaming, his face red with the effort. Mary turned away, blocking Alex's efforts to take his son. She kicked out with her feet, but he didn't hesitate, reaching out and pulling Robbie from her arms.

At that moment Mary saw her standing at the door.

"Why her?" she shouted. "Why not me? Why a maid, Alex? A maid? My family's the equal of yours, but you have to go and bed a maid. Why her?"

"Because I love her," he said, turning and handing Robbie to Lorna.

She draped her shawl over Robbie so he'd be spared the worst of the rain as she slowly made her way back to their carriage.

If Alex spoke further to Mary, she didn't hear what he said. At the door, she glanced back to see Alex standing with Charles and Jeremy. The other carriage door was closed and Mary inside.

Once she and Robbie were in their carriage, Lorna dried her son with a corner of her shawl, crooning to him as he calmed.

Tears streamed down her face, but anyone would have been hard-pressed to distinguish her weeping from the rain. Her hair was sodden and her garments dripped.

When Alex joined her, he was drenched as well. Sitting beside her, he gazed down at Robbie. He placed his hand over the baby's small body, a benediction of touch.

"When we get home, you're having one of my teas," she said, taking in his appearance. "You will not get sick. I refuse to allow it."

His gaze flew to hers. "Now who is godlike?"

Reaching out, he brushed away her tears with his fingers.

"Why are you crying?" he asked.

She shook her head, finding it impossible to answer that question. Relief? Joy that Robbie was safe? Gratitude?

"What is going to happen to her?" she asked.

"I told Jeremy to bring her back to Blackhall. I'll summon the authorities there."

She nodded.

"I hate her," she said. "I don't want to hate anyone, but it might take a while not to hate her."

"Justice might go a long way to banishing your hatred."

"Will she get it?"

"Yes," he said.

He wrapped his arm around her and pulled her to him.

"Did you mean what you said?" she asked.

He didn't pretend to misunderstand. Instead, he looked down at her, his gaze intent.

"Yes, I did."

"You love me?"

His smile was crooked and charming.

"Yes, I do. I've fought it for weeks, if not months. Maybe a year."

"Is it something you have to fight against?" she asked.

"Oh, yes, it was. I didn't stand a chance," he said. "I was lost from the very beginning. I should have just stopped fighting immediately."

She tilted her head and studied him.

"I haven't the slightest idea if I should be offended or overwhelmed," she said.

"I felt the same," he said, "when you told me I was a prig. Shall I make it better?"

He turned to her, facing her directly.

"I love you, Lorna Gordon Russell, Duchess of Kinross." He smiled. "There, is that better?"

"Infinitely," she said.

After a silent moment passed, she smiled brightly. "You're waiting for me to say it, aren't you?"

He only raised one eyebrow at her, looking ducal and adorable.

"I love you, Your Grace," she said softly.

He leaned forward and kissed her, only for their son to take that moment to fuss at both of them, fists flailing.

Epilogue

What do you think, Your Grace?"

Peter was studying the new door he'd just installed between the sitting room and the adjacent guest room. For now it was going to be an impromptu nursery.

Lorna wasn't comfortable with Robbie sleeping in the rooms allotted for the children of Blackhall on the third floor. One day it would be time to move him, but not now.

"I think it's beautiful," her mother-in-law said. "I like the carving you've done around the edge of the door. They're herbs, aren't they?"

He nodded, his cheeks turning a little pink.

"I think it's lovely," Lorna said.

"How's the work going on the new apothecary?" Louise asked.

Alex decided that a small building on the grounds would be a better place for all her herbs and ingredients than the cottage or a room in the castle. The building had been constructed in the last few months. Peter and Mr. Stanton were completing the interior work of cabinets and worktables. There was even a small area for Robbie to play within sight of her mixing bench.

"It should be finished in a week or so, Your Grace," Peter said. "All I've to do now is finish the chairs for the mixing table."

Matthews entered the room with Robbie in his arms.

"What do you think, Matthews?" Lorna asked.

Of all the changes in the last six months, Matthews was perhaps the most surprising. He'd evolved from a gossipy, surly individual to her greatest defender. He credited her with getting his position back. She'd reasoned that everyone deserved a second chance, and besides, he'd helped find Robbie, so she'd talked to Alex about reconsidering his employment. Consequently, Matthews never failed to do or say something nice to her each day.

Even more astounding was that Robbie seemed to have developed an affection for the man. When Matthews passed the cradle or the blanket on which her son was crawling, Robbie would throw his arms up in the air so Matthews could pick him up. When he did, Robbie crowed excitedly, his dimples deepening as he gave Matthews's cheek openmouthed kisses.

"It's very attractive, Your Grace," he said, handing Robbie off to her.

Her son babbled to them in a language only he understood.

She glanced at Robbie's hands and smiled. Traces of soot remained on his fingertips. No matter how diligently Alex washed their son's hands, she could always tell when he'd taken Robbie's fingerprints.

"He's done it again, hasn't he, Matthews?"

The valet smiled. "Yes, Your Grace. He said it's been a month since he'd taken them last."

Alex was studying Robbie's fingerprints as their son

aged, trying to determine if a person's prints altered with growth.

"A study that I intend to submit to the society," he said.

She'd just shaken her head.

He'd received a judgment from the society that Simons's discovery was still valid, despite Alex's assertion that his own research had been mounted a good two years before the other man. When she questioned why he wasn't more upset, he grabbed her and kissed her.

Long moments later, when she could breathe again, he said, "A certain someone said that sometimes different people have the same ideas at an identical time. I'm willing to concede that this might be the case."

"I think they're wrong," she said, irritated on his behalf.

He only laughed and kissed her again.

Life at Blackhall had always been pleasant for her, but now it was more. Joy woke her in the morning and perched on her shoulders at night. She was passionate about her husband, her son, and the well-being of those she'd come to love. She knew she might never be wholly accepted by the society in which people like Mary traveled, but Mary was currently in prison for kidnapping.

As long as Alex approved of her, she was happy.

She was no longer seeing what she wanted to see. Instead, she was living the life she saw.

ALEX STOOD IN the doorway for a moment, taking in the scene. In this room was his greatest happiness because all the people he loved were here.

He wasn't living in the gloaming anymore, but was

standing in the sunlight, the brightness warming him from the inside out.

"You'll rid the place of that sawdust, Peter? My wife and my son aren't to breathe that," he added, then glanced at Lorna.

"Give the man a chance, Alex," she said, smiling back at him.

He came to her side and bent his head to kiss her, a sweet, reassuring kiss, one that promised and hinted at more. She pulled back, smiling, her free hand cupping his cheek.

His arm went around her shoulders as he gently drew both his wife and his son to him.

Robbie grabbed his ear and pulled, summoning his laughter.

His mother smiled at the three of them, triumph lighting her eyes. He would allow her the victory, since he was the one to reap the rewards.

Author's Note

$\mathcal{I}$'ve borrowed the name of Blackhall Castle from history. Unfortunately, nothing remains of the castle originally held by Clan Russell.

Although I have used some actual place names in the book, they're not meant to portray any actual scene or location. They exist solely in my imagination.

The Scottish Marriage Act of 1567 prohibited a man from marrying a deceased wife's sister. Those connected by marriage were considered relatives, and marriage between them was taboo. In 1907 the Deceased Wife's Sister Marriage Act was passed by the UK Parliament, allowing these marriages.

Unwed Mothers

Unwed mothers were considered an affront to common decency. An unwed mother wasn't eligible for any type of aid that might have made life bearable—or even possible—because she was considered a "loose woman." She was even prevented from entering the poorhouse because she had to be separated from the decent women of the parish and the community.

The majority of women who found themselves pregnant and unwed were forced to move away from home, pretend to be widowed, and give birth alone. The future for them—and their children—wasn't bright.

Baby Farmers

The problem of infanticide in the Victorian era was almost pandemic. The situation was made worse by legislation designed to deter illegitimacy (the Poor Law Amendment Act of 1834). Releasing fathers from all financial responsibility condemned an unwed mother to hideous choices. She could starve, become a prostitute, or hire the services of a baby farmer to care for her infant so that she could find work.

Baby farmers ostensibly worked as foster mothers or a quasi adoption agency asking for a per week fee or a lump sum to care for a child. Unfortunately, an infant's future was rarely in doubt. He would die either by starvation (feeding laudanum was popular to keep the child quiet) or by murder. (That's not to say that unwed mothers were the only ones to take advantage of baby farmers: certain families who would have been embarrassed by an inconvenient birth also used the services of a baby farmer to get rid of an unwanted infant.)

Baby farmers were found throughout the world, including the United States and Australia.

Monkwood mimics the effects of another Scottish herb. It's not my intention to provide information on how to poison people, so monkwood is a fictitious name.

The Scottish Scientific Society doesn't exist, except in my imagination.

The club Thomas belonged to, Beggar's Blessings,

was loosely based on Beggar's Benison, a club founded in Fife in 1732. However, Beggar's Benison only existed until 1836.

Scottish Phrases

At the knag and the widdie—at loggerheads.

Trout in the well—being pregnant out of wedlock.

Tune one's pipes—to set to wailing and moaning (like the sound of bagpipes warming up).

Worricow or *wirrikow*—a malevolent sprite or demon, the devil himself, or a scary, horrid-looking person.

Cludfawer—an illegitimate child.

Don't miss the next breathtaking
romance from
New York Times bestselling
author Karen Ranney!

The English Duke

Coming April 2017

SIZZLING ROMANCE FROM
USA TODAY BESTSELLING AUTHOR
KAREN
RANNEY

The Devil of Clan Sinclair

978-0-06-224244-0

Widowed and penniless unless she produces an heir, Virginia Traylor, Countess of Barrett, embarks on a fateful journey that brings her to the doorstep of the only man she's ever loved. Macrath Sinclair, known as The Devil, was once rejected by Virginia. He knows he should turn her away, but she needs him, and now he wants her more than ever.

The Witch of Clan Sinclair

978-0-06-224246-4

Logan Harrison, the Lord Provost of Edinburgh, needs a conventional and diplomatic wife to help further his political ambitions. He most certainly does not need Mairi Sinclair, the fiery, passionate, fiercely beautiful woman who tries to thwart him at every turn. But if she's so wrong for him, why can't the bewitched lord stop kissing her?

The Virgin of Clan Sinclair

978-0-06-224249-5

Beneath Ellice Traylor's innocent exterior beats a passionate heart, and she has been pouring all of her frustrated virginal fantasies into a scandalous manuscript. When a compromising position forces her to wed the Earl of Gadsden, he discovers Ellie's secret book and can't stop thinking about the fantasies the disarming virgin can dream up.